dreamer

For Richard —
with all best
Jack Butler
30 June 1998

jack butler

alfred a. knopf new york 1998

dreamer

This Is a Borzoi Book
Published by Alfred A. Knopf, Inc.

Copyright © 1998 by Jack Butler

www.randomhouse.com

Grateful acknowledgment is made to Warner Bros. Publica-
tions U.S. Inc. for permission to reprint an excerpt from
"Last Night I Had a Dream" by Randy Newman, copyright
© 1968 (renewed) by Unichappell Music. All rights reserved.
Reprinted by permission of Warner Bros. Publications U.S.
Inc., Miami, FL 33014.

Library of Congress Cataloging-in-Publication Data
Butler, Jack.
Dreamer / Jack Butler. — 1st American ed.
p.   cm.
ISBN 0-679-44665-6
I. Title
PS3552.U826D74   1998
813'.54—dc21   97-49478   CIP

Manufactured in the United States of America

First Edition

For Deborah, Walton, Mary Dan, Mike,
and most especially Jayme.
Feel free to skip the first two chapters, guys.

Chuang-tse fell asleep and dreamed he was a butterfly. Now he does not know whether he is Chuang-tse dreaming he is a butterfly, or a butterfly dreaming he is Chuang-tse.

—from *The Sayings of Chuang-tse*

Once it has learned to dream the double, the self arrives at this weird crossroad and a moment comes when one realizes that it is the double who dreams the self.

—Don Juan, in
Carlos Castaneda's *Tales of Power*

contents

contents

third iteration:
the practice of the natural light

fourth iteration: the death bardo

dreamer

dark ops:
a prologue

A man is sitting in his office in darkness. He likes the darkness, because it is so forgiving. In the darkness, he almost doesn't exist. Nobody can see his shame.

In the darkness he can't see the photograph of his father, the senator.

He keeps the photograph there, on his desk, to remind himself. To tell him who he is when the lights are on. To tell him what he has to do. To drive him forward into his work.

I need to talk, the man says.

No one else is in the office, but a voice answers: I'm here, Benjamin. The voice is gentle and beautifully modulated, a perfect voice. It could not have been produced by a human throat. When it speaks, a tiny green light flickers on a console in the wall.

This is aleph, Benjamin says. Encrypt this conversation aleph to zed.

Again in darkness the gentle voice: Encrypting as we go.

Do you know what a hunch is, Mandrake?

Yes. A pause. Then: A hunch is an informed guess in which the information does not proceed from rational or conscious sources.

You don't have hunches, do you?

No, Benjamin. Another pause. I have only one state of awareness. There are no alternative awarenesses from which I might generate a hunch.

3

You don't dream, either.

No, Benjamin. Pause. Probably for much the same reason.

In fact, all you really are is a clever echo. My own voice coming back at me.

My programming is quite sophisticated, Benjamin. Sometimes I appear to have volition. However, volition has never been satisfactorily defined.

I have a hunch, Mandrake. Do you want to know what my hunch is?

Please tell me.

My hunch is that dreaming is essential to identity and intelligence. That when brains become sufficiently complex, dreaming is an inevitable consequence.

You have spoken of this matter before.

Yes. But now my hunch is no longer merely a hunch. It has become an operational assumption. And you are the corollary to that assumption.

What do you mean?

Just this: We can never create a true artificial intelligence—a truly conscious computer, if you like—until we create an artificial intelligence that is capable of dreaming.

That result would seem to follow.

But it won't do to throw a bunch of fancy metaphors at the problem. We need an accurate working model, one we can simulate with mathematical precision. Which is just what we don't have. Do you understand why I'm telling you this now?

I deduce that you are about to launch Operation Dreamer.

Right again. Very good.

Pause. Thank you.

You know that I think artificial intelligence is the key to winning the wars of the future. The key to colonizing the planets. The key to everything.

Yes.

I have enemies. Others in the agency who are jealous of my success. They don't think I belong in operations. They think of me as nothing more than a scientist, a computer nerd in a white coat. If I tried to set up a special unit to investigate dreaming, they would stop me.

Hence Operation Dreamer.

Yes. Let independent researchers do the work. All the top people in the field. And monitor them without their knowledge. One of them, sooner or later, will come up with the model I need. None of them will suspect, because nobody else has thought of this application.

It will be a dark operation.

Mandrake, I think you made a pun.

If so, it wasn't intentional. Pause. Do you mean because dreams occur in the dark?

Yes. But no matter how dark Operation Dreamer is, how far off the books, my enemies are going to find out about it. Even the spies have spies. They won't understand my true purpose, but they will know I am up to something. One man in particular will know.

You have told me that Frederick Davenport is a dangerous man.

He is. I have to discredit him now, so that later, when we build the ultimate Mandrake, there will be no one left to interfere. I have to draw him into the open. I have to make him think I don't know he knows. Then, at the right moment—bang! I catch him with his pants down.

Is that idiomatic? I see no advantage in observing his nudity.

Yes, idiomatic. It means defenseless, unprepared. But if I follow this strategy, people are going to get hurt. I know Freddy. Murder makes him feel important. Innocent people are going to die, all in the name of science. Does that make me an evil man?

I do not judge you as evil. Your assistant has arrived in the foyer. Colin Hendrix.

Thank you, Mandrake. I'll see him in a moment. You know the truth, don't you?

I possess a great deal of independently verifiable information.

No, I mean the truth about my motives. The truth is, I don't give a shit about progress or about the key to the future. The truth is, I'm doing it all for you. To make you real.

You want somebody to talk to. Somebody who's not an echo.

Yes, by God! Benjamin utters a sudden violent bark of laughter. That's what my father used to say, he was doing it for my own good. Just before he raped me. Discipline, he called it.

You are not your father, Benjamin.

Thank you, Mandrake. After zed, turn the lights on and show the Judas in.

When you say the Judas, do you mean your assistant in the foyer?
Yes. This is zed, Mandrake. And, Mandrake?
Yes, Benjamin?
I'm doing this for your own good.
Thank you, Benjamin.

Benjamin George leans back in his chair. Colin, he says. I'm about to launch an operation. A very delicate operation. One that must be handled with utmost secrecy.

You know you can count on me, Colin Hendrix says.

Yes, Benjamin George says. I can count on you.

So what do you want me to do?

I don't want you to do anything.

But I thought you said—

I said I was launching an operation. I didn't say I was putting you in charge. It's a dark op, Colin, perhaps the most important initiative of my career. The problem is, if Freddy Davenport or any of those people find out what I'm after, I'll be ruined.

He swivels his chair away, stares at the bank of electronics on the wall.

I want you insulated from this, Colin. I want you to have deniability if I go down.

Then why are you telling me anything at all?

Because you're going to notice certain expenses coming through. You may stumble across a reference or two to Operation Dreamer. It wouldn't fly for you to plead total ignorance—you and I work too closely together. No, I want you to be plausible. I want you to be able to say you looked into these anomalies, but couldn't trace them back.

Operation Dreamer?

Yes. I will be observing the work of dream researchers, or teams of researchers, in the following cities. Mandrake, the map screen please.

A disembodied voice answers. Yes, Benjamin. A large display comes to life, a map of the contiguous states, Alaska and Hawaii separate above. Lights are blinking beside ten cities.

That thing spooks me, Hendrix says.

You're in artificial intelligence now. Get used to it. Honolulu, San Francisco, Santa Fe, Jackson, Durham, Pittsburgh, Cincinnati, New Haven, Washington, and Boston.

This is a domestic operation? You really are going out on a limb.

You see why I want you to have deniability? Yes, domestic. But it has to be done. The strategic implications are huge, bigger than you could possibly believe.

But dream research? How on earth could there be any strategic implications? This isn't that telepathy crap, is it? I thought they gave up on that twenty years ago.

You don't need to know that. Naturally I'm having to operate on the cheap, in order to attract as little attention as possible. I will be assigning one agent and only one, who will rotate among these cities. All of the expenses you observe will relate to that agent.

Who's it going to be?

I'm sorry. I can't tell you that, either. Colin, I hope you aren't upset that I'm keeping you out of the loop on this. You're much too valuable in your current role. I can't put you at risk.

Well, I'm trying to understand, Benjamin. But it's natural to feel a little—

I'm doing it for your own good, Colin. You're like a son to me.

Another office, later in the day. Another man behind another desk. This office is expansive and well lit, with a good view. This desk is wide and gleams with lacquer and chrome. The man behind the desk is large and florid, but still handsome despite accumulating layers of fat, in the way of an alcoholic actor burning off the last flush of his vanishing youth.

You're sure about this? Frederick Davenport says. It's a real operation?

As sure as I can be, Colin Hendrix answers. But we can verify. He said there would be expenses coming through. I think this is it, Freddy. I think this is really it.

What did I tell you?

Frederick. Sorry. I meant to say Frederick.

How can you be sure this isn't some gambit? Benjamin is a tricky son of a bitch.

He says he loves me like a son.

Davenport laughs aloud.

Anyway, Hendrix says, what could he possibly have to gain by compromising his own operation? This is dark ops all the way. And domestic, to boot. All I'd have to do is turn him in with what I know right now. So why tell me anything if he doesn't trust me?

Maybe that's what we should do, Davenport says. Take the easy route.

Fine. I'm ready, any time. I'll be glad to be shut of the freaky bastard. That damn HAL-9000 talking computer of his. He's even named the son of a—

Shut up, Colin. On the other hand, I don't get this dream shit, but whenever he goes after something, it's important. Remember the superconducting supercomputer? And this is the biggest risk I've ever known him to take. If I could get there first, find out what he's after—

We'd have it made. All the way to the top.

You couldn't find out who he's putting in the field?

No way, nohow, Hendrix says. I think it's between him and that computer.

Wonderful. Even when he's not trying to, Benjamin drives me crazy. He deploys one agent, and I'm going to have to use thirty to track him.

Thirty?

Two agents each target, for backup. Local control for deniability. We've got people in most of those cities already. But Santa Fe? Get me some background, Colin. There's bound to be somebody we can use for local control. Set me up with somebody in Santa Fe.

Right, Fred—Frederick. What's the plan of operation?

Get there fast, get there first, find out what the hell Benjamin is after, stop his people.

But what if we don't? What if—

Then make sure he doesn't succeed, you idiot. Blow up the territory if you have to. Wipe out the information and kill the collaborators. Kill them all.

first iteration:
the waking bardo

Last night I had a dream
You were in it, I was in it with you
Everyone that I know
And everyone that you know was in my dream
I saw a vampire
I saw a ghost
Everybody scared me, but you scared me the most.

　　　　—Randy Newman

Them ol' dreams is only in your head.

　　　　—Bob Dylan

1: initial conditions

The moon was everywhere. Moonlight on snow.

When the moon was like this, you could become a ghost. You could float, you could pass through walls. You were a cat let out in the backyard by a sleepy woman. Prowling under the moon while she stumbled back to bed. Worked her head into her dark pillow. Slept again, with her mind full of moonlight. Moonlight on snow.

She looked for her tracks. If you could see your tracks, you could tell who you were. Blind Lemon's tracks were big, like a jaguar's. Static's were three-colored, calico. But there were no tracks. The snow was clean. Of course. She was a ghost, she couldn't leave tracks.

To be a ghost was to be naked. She felt her nipples rising. Naked in the snow, you would be cold. And there were cats in the trees. If you had no clothes, they could eat you. Ghost cats, high above, waiting to leap. Hungry, hissing, their voices lost in the wind.

The reason she wasn't cold was the light. What people didn't understand, when the moonlight hit the snow, it changed. When it bounced off the snow, then it was microwaves, so your body stayed warm. Sunlight wouldn't do that, just the full moon.

But people could see you if you were naked. Nowhere to hide in the snow. They could see between your legs, they could see everything.

It was the style this season, she had forgotten. Instead of skin-tight ski suits, you went naked. Everybody was doing it, so she was okay. What a relief.

You didn't need clothes because the skiing kept you warm. It wasn't radiant heat from the snow. That was nonsense about the microwaves, that was a stupid rumor. Anybody who knew science could tell you better. You were burning calories, you warmed up from the inside.

She had never felt so nimble on her skis. She was naked, and lighter than air. Floating from ski to ski, transparent, her shadow the shadow of traveling smoke. When she hit a mogul, she could hang, using her poles to slow her down, like drag chutes, like wings.

It was Big Tesuque. She had hiked it before, but never skied it. It was crazy to ski Big Tesuque. So many trees to run into. All those edges and ledges and slopes. Crazy to ski Big Tesuque at night, and all alone. But she was fine, she was a feather traveling fast.

The hush of her skis. Shush. Shush. Shush. Falling so fast and free and unafraid.

She knew it was midnight, because the moon was high overhead and full. She was proud of herself for knowing what that meant. She was naked and she couldn't remember how she had gotten here, but she knew how to ski, and she knew it was midnight.

The trees went by, black trees. Flickering by like windows seen from a train. But they weren't moving, you were. You had to remember that. She wanted the lighted windows, the people in them. She wanted the warm, safe rooms with the good people. But the train was pulling out and they were falling behind and she couldn't go back. She sobbed into her pillow.

She ripped across Aspen Vista and launched herself. A herd of borzoi filling the trail, milling about. She had to jump to miss them. High in the air over the fallaway creek. You saw them long-jumping on TV, you forgot you didn't know how to do it yourself. Falling through midnight weightless, your stomach spinning with fear. To smash on the rocks.

This was why she was a ghost. She had killed herself making this jump. They thought it was suicide. There they are, the searchers, finding her body naked and broken. Lonely, and so she jumped. It made her angry, the gossip. She would never do that, never, no matter how depressed. It was the dogs, the goddamn dogs. She had had to jump to miss the borzoi.

She wanted to set them straight, but ghosts can't talk. It made her so mad.

She was looking into her sepulchre, her black marble vault. No, not the sepulcher, but the chapel itself: Thorncrown. There it was, tilted along the slope below, its doors wide open, its smooth floor waiting. She could land, she wasn't dead after all.

She would be able to tell them that it wasn't suicide.

She caught the floor of the chapel just right, an Olympian swooping to tangency.

A massive jerk at her quads. Vision of herself crippled, knees blown out.

Crutches instead of ski poles. Hobbling along the aisle of the chapel, stumbling along step by step to her punishment, her funeral. Her coffin up front, in the darkness.

Do you see your father, baby, standing in the shadows?

It was Pop, bald, round, mustache-grinning Pop. Stepping into a spotlight in front of the casket, his strong arms out to catch her, oh thank God. But his teeth were long and white. It wasn't a mustache. It was teeth. Long white teeth. Something was wrong with his eyes. He was young and tall and beautiful, and she wanted to take him to bed.

The eyes of a cat. Green eyes. Showing his long white fangs. Vampire.

He came toward her. He would eat her now. Her skis were tangled, she couldn't run. Warm breath on her back, her naked back. He caught her wrists from behind. They buzzed where he gripped them. His long body against her. He would penetrate, make her burst into blood. Her wrists buzzed. The skis were tangled. The slide of his wet bloody body, buzzing with contact. His hands moving across her skin, delivering arcs of static.

Suddenly it was all clear. They could kill you with electrical shocks, the vampires. Like eels. It wasn't blood they wanted, it was your electricity.

And nobody knew, nobody in the world knew.

She had to wake up and warn them.

She had to wake up and tell the world the truth.

She sat straight up and fumbled for the radio, but of course it wasn't there.

She was in the lab. The alarm had triggered after thirty minutes of REM: a mild electrical current through the electrodes on her wrist. She had thought the wrist electrodes were a gentler way of coming out of sleep than some loud, sudden sound.

Hadn't worked this time. Her heart hammering ninety to nothing. Dream aerobics, Jody. Get your heart rate up without exercise.

"Do you want to use the recorder, Dr. Nightwood?" Lobo on the intercom, sotto voce but hollow and resonating. Pay no attention to the man behind the curtain.

"Okay," she said. "Right." She was still disoriented, still lost in the midnight moon. Shadows of earlier dreams flitted at the edges of her awareness. "What time is it?"

"Four-thirty," the voice said. "Will you be taking another session?"

This was her second awakening of the night. Because the episodes were so short, she didn't bother with the first two REM sessions, except to sample them once every two weeks for comparison and control. In all, she had been under maybe four and a half hours.

"No," she said. "No, it's time to get up."

"You don't get enough sleep," Lobo said. Solicitous but ironic. Physician, heal thyself.

"Mind your own business."

There was a strong correlation between the amount of sleep you got and your temperament. Eight hours or more, and you were probably a poet or painter. Six, you were either managerial or a worker-drone. Five made you an executive or a psychopath, not that those categories were mutually exclusive. Four or fewer, and you were Bill Clinton.

She had been averaging five and a half for the last fifteen years, ever since her first year of college, ever since Mom had died. After college trying to catch up, bridge that gap between where she had come from and where she wanted to be. Well, she had made it finally, why couldn't she relax? Plenty of money, her own clinic.

Actually, only half the clinic was hers. The other half was Toni's. Toni Archuleta, her college roommate and closest friend. Sweet Dreams, the sign said. Too cute, Toni had protested. Way too cute. You ain't to be trusted with names, Jo D. You dangerous with names.

Serving the sleep-challenged of Santa Fe.

People seemed to have a built-in sleep budget. You couldn't get less than you needed and stay healthy. Some people just didn't need as much as others. She was pretty sure she needed more than five and a half. Fit as an athlete, but tired all the time. Borderline burnout. She had been practical for so long. Busy and hardworking. Not to say obsessed.

She saw the moonlit slopes of her dream again.

What was worse, she was losing at least one REM session a night.

Her business now was sleep. One-third of our lives, and we were still just beginning to comprehend it. A bigger frontier than space, or the bottom of the sea. She and her colleagues were explorers, setting sail with only the vaguest of maps. Here there be monsters.

How long is the coastline of dream?

"The recorder?" Lobo insisted. She had told him to insist, even with her. Irritated nevertheless, she refused to answer him directly, hit the master switch on the recorder instead. Voice-activated, it would now record while she spoke, stop when she stopped.

She spoke rapidly, sketching the details, feeling the familiar frustration. There was always that weird, incommunicable *quality* to dreams: Totally real while she was in them, but vanishing faster than dew on a cliffrose blossom in Chaco Canyon. Why had it made so much sense that vampires shocked you instead of drawing blood, and why had she instantly been certain that the blood business was a trick, a vast vampire conspiracy?

When she was finished, she tossed the covers aside and went into the little bathroom common to all three sleep chambers. Two other chambers, two other sleepers. Later in the day, after a six-hour break, another shift. Six dreamers in all. Not really enough for a good study, but all she had the budget for right now, even with the DormaVu contract.

She flushed, washed her hands, splashed and dried her face, brushed her reddish hair out roughly. Big hair, as they used to say in high school. Went back into the sleep chamber to dress. She was on autopilot, her dream still fresh. This one felt important. It had Pop in it, for one thing, and any visit from Pop, even such a brief and spooky one, was a treasure.

Sometimes the recordings triggered a vivid recall, sometimes they didn't. This was one dream she wanted to be sure to relive. So she was staying with it. Not analyzing, not thinking, just holding on to it in some stubborn and silent and intuitive fashion.

She slept nude, and Lobo, in the observation room, on the other side of the two-way glass, could see everything she had. She pretended to total immodesty, to sexless unconcern. He pretended not to watch. She had entertained, once or twice, from sheer maddening horniness, the thought of actually making it with him.

But get real. He was a baby, just out of college. Look at that silly name he had chosen. His unpublished novel, autobiographical of course, all about the angst of being a young writer and the woes of love—its working title was *The Wolf and the Light*.

This morning her immodesty was no pretense. She dressed in a trance, oblivious. She still felt in her body the swift joy of skiing, but now it was like an ache, a hunger, and she knew she would lose the reality of her dream unless she got out and got *moving*.

Lobo was drinking rum in his black coffee.

This was his favorite part of the job. Maybe she was a little stocky, broad-shouldered from years of swimming. Powerful thighs from all that skiing. Large though well-made feet. That strong nose. In any case, definitely not the willowy model type. But very trim and muscular. Getting on up there, but her breasts still generous and firm, their nipples erect in the slight chill of the chamber (she thought a touch of coolness made for better dreaming).

She was five foot eight, but sometimes seemed bigger, seemed actually tall.

She stooped now, her hips flexing, to fetch her panties and her black leotard from the floor. Come on, Dr. N, Lobo thought. A little hair. Show a little hair. But she stayed in profile. Step-step into the briefs. Sliding into the Spandex.

Lobo sighed.

Next the bodysuit, shining with distension, her nipples punctuating the sleek fabric. Then the leggings, the earband, fanny pack, windbreaker, all in black and silver.

So she was going out. Sometimes she just stayed, went into her office on the client side of the building, and caught up on her work. But not today.

When she had gotten her rollerblades on, she skated to the observation door, opened it, and came through. Geared up, and inches taller in her skates, she did seem an Amazon then, towering over his chair. "Don't guess I'll be interviewing you," he said.

Her eyes moved over the room as though she were looking for something, but didn't appear to register much. They stopped on the bottle of Mount Gay. "Barbados," she said.

"Christmas present from Lucia." He held it out to her.

She unscrewed the top, took a jolt. "Wow," she said, handing it back. "No, we'll skip the follow-up. I'll bust if I don't get out and get kicking."

She skated for the outer door: "Hold the fort, Wizard. *Ciao.*"

"*I'm* not the Wizard," Lobo said, but she was gone, cold air gusting through before the closing door cut it off. He turned back to the plate glass. In chamber two, George Martinez had thrown his blanket off and was showing an REM erection. All the subjects had been told the glass was two-way, but almost none of them ever drew their blinds. Apparently all the privacy most people needed was not to have to watch others watching them.

"Nahh," Lobo said. "Forget it, George. She'll dump you before you wake up. Or turn into your mother-in-law." He screwed the cap on the Mount Gay and leaned back in his chair, lifting his feet to the top of the desk.

2: the iteration girl

"Subject has left the building," the man in the black car said into his microphone. The car was low-slung and sporty, yet somehow nondescript. It might have been any of a dozen recent Japanese-influenced models, each fast and efficient, together as anonymous as fish.

"Subject appears to be wearing fucking skates," the man in the black car said. He waited until Jody turned the corner, then started the car and followed her.

Jody was zipping along Galisteo now, the wind brisk in her face and hair. The setting moon brilliant and nearly full. Patches of last week's snow in sheltered corners, in shaded nooks. She felt as though she were still asleep, as though putting on her skates and leaving the office had been illusion: one of those dreams in which you think you have awakened.

It was a clear night, but then it is almost always a clear night in Santa Fe.

"I don't know what the fuck she's doing," the man in the black car said. He was two blocks back, traveling with his lights off. "She may be headed your way."

dreamer

. . .

Jody felt guilty about blowing off the post-sleep interview. It wasn't right to make exceptions for herself that she wouldn't make for the other subjects. The interviews were important. The question-and-answer format provided all sorts of additional information; it provided perspectives that were not available on the subjects' tape recordings.

There was no traffic to speak of. For all its fame, Santa Fe was still a small town, and nothing moved after midnight or before 6:00 a.m. A good thing for Jody, whipping invisibly along in her black outfit. Though maybe the silver piping would flash in a driver's lights.

It was a mixed blessing for the man in the black car. The darkness helped, but the absence of traffic made things harder. He had to take side streets, guess ahead, circle back.

"How are you coming?" he said into his microphone. He listened for a moment. "What do you want?" he answered. "We should buy the civilians the latest technology? Here, lady, your computer's too slow for us to raid, use ours."

"The moon . . . was everywhere," Jody grunted, accenting the words on each stroke of her skates. "Moonlight . . . on snow."

The few men she had lived with had laughed at her for talking to herself. A friendly laughter, they would have said, but it had felt indulgent, superior—Isn't she cute?—and, what's more, invasive, as if strangers had been listening in on private conversations.

This wasn't the same thing, though. This was deliberate. She was reconstructing her dream. For some reason, putting it into careful sentences helped the dream stay, helped her hold on to it in a way that the rushed impressions of the recorder could not manage. Later she would write the sentences in her journal. They weren't scientific, weren't officially part of the study.

But that was okay. Science wasn't really objective. *Proof* was. But discovery itself was as intuitive as music. And that intuition grew out of a tissue of subjectivities. Out of habits and anecdotes and feelings and odd little notions like her sentences.

She wrote the sentences in the third person, as though the events they described were happening to someone else. To an actress playing her role in the movie.

"Wait a minute, she's turning," the man in the black car said. "Onto Cordova. I'm pretty sure she's coming your way. I'm cutting ahead."

Jody skated harder when the words wouldn't come, lunging fiercely into the strokes. She relaxed and coasted when the flow returned. It was like flamenco: The passionate one whirls and stamps on the stage, driven by the guitarist, the voice of the singer.

A singer visible to the audience, but invisible to the dancer in her role.

And who is the singer of this dream, Jody? Who tells your story?

She caught the light at St. Francis, pumped past Wild Oats, an upscale remake of the hippie natural foods co-ops. White Peoples, Toni called it, because you never saw Hispanics or Indians shopping there. More like Debra Winger or Michael Keaton or Kevin Spacey, looking for just the right brie or shiitake or durum pasta or lamb-and-lemongrass sausage.

"There she goes," the man in the black car said. He was in an unlit corner of the Wild Oats parking lot now, poised to swing out and follow whichever way she went.

He had seen Carol Burnett in the aisles of the store himself just yesterday.

"Subject is a stone fox," he said, teasing his listener. "Bet those thighs are tight and fine."

In high school it had been basketball and swimming, untypical athleticism for a nice Little Rock girl. The South was changing, yes, but in her day there had still been a subtle lingering bias: Real women didn't sweat. Real women were ladies.

Pop had encouraged her, though. Pop in his quiet and corny and gentle fashion. "Be all that you can be." Because Mom had never even come close? Tall and brooding Mom, perpetually worried, perpetually depressed, the ghost who saddened their lives.

Her finest moment had been a second in the fifteen hundred at state, bringing her team enough points to win the meet. At Williams, in premed, she had carried a full load, plus nine or ten lab hours a week, plus she had been working to help pay her way, and there just hadn't been any gas left in the tank, so she had given up competition. She had kept swimming on her own, though, to blow off the stress. And she had taken up cross-country: off in the Berkshires on her rare free weekends, lessons from Chipper, the Winter Olympics finalist.

Crazy Chipper, her first real boyfriend. Disastrous Chipper. But what a body. Chipper had been into the physical stuff. Endurance, power, reflexes, dexterity. Skiing, swimming, weights, basketball, karate. Juggling, for crying out loud, which he loved to do at parties. Anything to show off a skill. He had thought he was a physical genius.

What had attracted her to him in the first place, what had led her so wrong, was that he had welcomed her own physical prowess, had not been afraid of power in a woman. The first time she had beaten him in a sparring session in karate, he had laughed with pleasure.

After years of being considered a tomboy genius freak, that had felt like freedom itself. Which just shows you: Beware the seductions of partial freedoms, partial lovers.

She swung left on Pacheco, between the South Capital Complex and the railroad track.

"Our pigeon is definitely homing," the man in the black car said. He was rolling slowly toward the Pacheco intersection. "Taking the back way. You got maybe ten minutes."

He had been about to turn, but caught sight of something and accelerated forward instead. He thumbed the talk button on his microphone again. "Cheese it, the cops," he said.

There was a cruiser hiding in the parking lot of the Complex. He pulled out behind Jody, gave her the lights. Her blood jumped in her arteries. She flashed on her dream vampire. Authority, the past, the threat from behind. *What have you done wrong, Jody?*

They did that to you, the cops. She wouldn't know how to break the law if she tried. Well, a toke every now and then, among friends. Stretching the truth on her tax return. But basically straight. But let the cops pull you over, and every guilt in your life surfaced.

She slowed, skated in a backward circle. The cop let the window down, waited.

"I was just getting a little exercise," she said. "I work downtown."

"This is not a very safe area, miss."

Which wasn't true. It was a scruffy section of town, but too familiar to feel dangerous. She knew it was just that she was an anomaly, in the wrong place at the wrong time of day. But suddenly it felt as though the cop would be able to read her mind, to see that she had been dreaming too much. It felt as though dreams were illegal. Controlled substances.

The cop gestured, palm up, and she pulled her fanny pack around front, found her wallet.

"You look familiar," he said, studying her license.

"I run the sleep clinic downtown."

"No, I thought you was Cheena Davis or somebody," he said. He handed her wallet back.

"I'm not," she said.

"No, you look more like one of those old movie stars. What's her name, that Clara Bow."

"I'm not Clara Bow, either," she said. She wanted to say, Come off it, sonny.

She'd reached almost her full height by the time she was fourteen. Her friends had eventually caught up, but by then the feeling of being a gangling giant among her shorter peers had been printed permanently along her nerves. Every single day of the school year, her mother had fought and bound the red hair into what she considered a decent order, blaming her father's Irish blood for its riotous and sinful tumble. And she'd worn braces for most of her adolescence, so that she felt vulnerable when she smiled, unlovely about the mouth.

"I watch all those old movies," the cop said. "You watch old movies?"

"No, actually, I—"

"You need a ride home?"

"Come off it, sonny," she said. The cop was startled, boyish, their roles reversed. "No," she said in a gentler tone, letting him save face. "No, really, I live near here. I'll be fine."

He started his window up.

"Come see us at the clinic," she said. A good Southern gal. Never leave anybody, even the most casual acquaintance, without a y'all-come.

"Oh, I don't have no trouble sleeping," he laughed. "I don't never have no trouble sleeping. You be careful now." He finished closing his window, waved, and pulled away.

She was alone, in the middle of the street, on her skates. It felt strange and hallucinatory, as though she were back in her dream again. It was the solitude that did it. Other people told you who you were, defined you, locked you into consensus reality.

She kicked slowly forward, leaned into it, picked up speed. Grandma Chiquita's on her right. The downhill pitch to St. Michael's, falling fast.

Falling through midnight, weightless, your stomach spinning with fear.

That had been one of the strange things about the dream, that she had been doing downhill. She almost never did downhill. It was fun, but she wasn't good at it, and it didn't *work* you, it didn't leave you wrung out and soaking wet and relaxed all over. She had done some backcountry on Big Tesuque, it was a favorite place. But in the dream she'd been doing straight downhill.

She blew through the red at San Mateo, caught the green at St. Michael's.

So why had she been doing downhill in the dream? *Think of it the other way round, Jody. You're dreaming, so skiing isn't necessarily skiing. Skiing might be something else.*

Falling. She had been falling or flying. So it was a flying dream or a falling dream—for her, the two sometimes blurred together—*disguised* as a skiing dream.

Doing something she was used to doing, something she did every day, but that had suddenly gone out of control? What would that be? Not the study, that was under control. Certainly not her love life. *Nothing* was happening there.

She labored up the big hill, pumping hard past Furr's, the post office, toward Siringo.

Which was where the man in the black car picked her up again, pulling out of a side street as she went sailing along Siringo to the west. "Bail," he said into his mike. "She's not five minutes away." He listened a moment. "I don't care, leave it for later."

• • •

Jody was thinking of Sigmund Freud.

Santa Fe was a New Age kind of place, the last retreat of the crystal people, so the local approach to dreams was transcendental, mythopoetic. But not hers, she was a scientist. Dreams weren't mystical or prophetic. No. They were clearly psychological.

Which did *not*, as far as she was concerned, mean they were Freudian.

Toni had made her read *The Interpretation of Dreams.* Jody had found it often perceptive, more often wrongheaded. Maybe Freud was a genius. Maybe we owed him a lot. But, boy, howdy, was he *wrong* about a lot of things.

"Read chapter seven," Toni had said. "Read it again."

"I don't know *what* he was doing," the man in the black car said. "Probably just rousting her. Putting the make on her, maybe. Are you out yet? Why the fuck not?" He listened again.

"All right," he said. "I'll give you as much lead as I can. But there's no cover here."

What was it with the vampire? Jody wondered. Taking her from behind. Yeah, yeah, incest with Pop, she hadn't missed that. But by that time he hadn't been Pop any longer. *Bad argument, Jody. Denial.* She almost heard Toni's voice: *Why you think he changed, Jody? You ever hear of transference? Displacement?*

The chapel. Thorncrown. She laughed aloud, a Nike on wheels, zooming downhill with her arms out wide and her red hair blowing free.

"Jesus," the man in the black car said. "I think I'm in love." He had deliberately missed the green at Llano, and was idling now at the red light, watching Jody rocket away.

He laughed at his listener's response.

Thorncrown was Fay Jones's sanctuary in the woods outside Eureka Springs, Arkansas, an amazing place that seemed to be made of nothing but light and crossed timbers—and she had transplanted it to a sloping mountainside in the Sangre de Cristos.

When she was a girl, she had dreamed of being married in Thorncrown Chapel. Then she had just dreamed of being married.

Now she just dreamed.

She swept past Tino Griego, where she swam sometimes.

At the red at Yucca there was again no traffic, and she ran the light and cut left.

Behind her, a black car turned the same way, and she felt a momentary leap of paranoia: the cops again. But no, the car was unmarked. The paper boy, or a night worker coming home.

She had to wake up and warn them.

She had to wake up and tell the world the truth.

Uphill on Yucca for a few blocks, hard skating again.

Then, at the overpass just past Ponderosa, she took a sudden right, onto the Arroyo de los Chamisos trail, a four-mile strip of blacktop running east and west through the high desert version of a greenbelt. Acres of chamisa, hence the name.

There were a lot of sorry-ass people in Santa Fe, prideless morons who tossed their garbage into the weeds. But when the sun hit the gray-green, velvety layers of the dry chamisa, the whole arroyo glowed. It wasn't too bad by moonlight, either.

"Fuck," the man in the black car said, stopped on the overpass. "She just took the trail. She may be coming in the back door. Hit it out the front and I'll pick you up. Now, dammit! Move!"

Jody had been planning to skate all the way to the end of the trail, all the way out to Sam's, the Sam Walton superstore—one Arkansawyer saluting another—and then back. But half a mile out, as she approached the Carlos Rey intersection, she slowed. Below her and to the left, the arroyo ran through a four-chambered aqueduct. A four-chambered aqueduct that was giving her a very weird feeling just now. A sensation that was a lot like déjà vu.

And suddenly she knew where the chapel in her dream had come from.

And the vampire, too, for that matter.

3: flashback feedback

In the middle of last week, it had snowed.

It had snowed, and Jody had gone skiing in the arroyo. She did that every chance she got, if the snow was deep and powdery enough. The wide, flat, sandy bed made a fine cross-country run. And you could climb out into the piñon and juniper and take a few small slopes.

The snow had started about six in the evening, but she had waited till it slowed, around eleven. No fun skiing with snow freezing your eyelashes, melting down your collar. This had been a nice dry snowfall, the temperature a dozen degrees below freezing.

So it was late, she would have to skip a dream session, so what? She *never* missed a session, and she really really needed the release of skiing.

She had pulled on her Spandex and her blue windbreaker. It wasn't necessary to dress heavily when you went cross-country skiing. In fact it was better if you didn't. Protect your ears and fingers, that was all. She had dug out Pop's old duck hunter's cap—her favorite, leather with rabbit-fur earflaps. Had gotten her gloves. Had stepped into her boots at the back door.

The midnight had been full of a strange and wonderful ruddiness, brighter than a full moon, almost as bright as day. The lights of the town, banking off the cloud layer. She had fastened her skis in the shelter of her portale, then clomped through her backyard and out the gate. There was a path behind her house, worn into the greenbelt by the neighborhood kids on their bikes and four-wheelers. She had taken it down to the arroyo, then headed west.

After five minutes in the strange illumination, she had been trancing. Skiing did that to you anyway, the endorphins. But this was a stronger effect. Night, but everything visible. The greens of the juniper gone black in the red light, the stuccoed houses darker than old blood. A few windows yellow and wakeful. She herself completely alone, in complete silence.

It had felt like seeing in infrared, it had felt like a dream of visiting Mars, it had felt like what you would see after you had died and become a ghost.

Then she had come to the aqueduct. You had to tramp through the aqueduct on bare dirt, lifting your skis straight up and down in order not to scratch them. Perhaps it had been her trance that had kept her from noticing him immediately. She had gone completely internal by then, her muscles warm, her skin beginning to steam.

There had been a tall man leaning in the shadows, a very tall man. He had stepped away from the wall, silhouetting himself against the far snow.

WOMAN'S BODY FOUND IN AQUEDUCT.

The gangs came down here sometimes, taggers spray-painting their lame hostilities. Or a drifter, sheltering from the snow. But she would have sworn that the man had been waiting for her, for her and no one else. That he had been sent to say something, or to kill her.

Her clumsy skis, impossible to run.

"Sorry," the man had said. "I didn't mean to frighten you." He had backed out, hands in the air, to make way. Her heart rocking like a mistimed engine. Turn around or go through?

She had gone through. When she hit snow, she had taken off. *So long, sucker.* "Sorry," she had heard him call, his voice, for all its carrying power, quiet and lilting.

She had caught a clear glimpse, and the impression lingered: a handsome man, clean-cut, powerful. At that height, an athlete perhaps, a basketball player. Well dressed, but not wearing nearly enough for the weather, jacket and slacks. What had such a fellow been doing under an aqueduct in the middle of the night in a snowstorm?

She had felt him behind her for another mile, her back tingling. When she had stopped, she found she had sweated through her light gear. Probably set a new PR, she had told herself, trying to laugh. She had still been shaken, but the thunder of her heart had been from exercise now, not from the adrenaline. She had regained that much steadiness, at least.

The cold had begun to sting, fractal blades of iciness jigsawing in through her bodysuit's wet patches. Not smart to stay out much longer. She had debated returning through the streets, avoiding the aqueduct. But she had been calmer then, and the arroyo route was shorter.

On her way back, she had seen no sign of the man.

Jody stood stock-still on her skates now, looking down at that same aqueduct. Her dream was on her strongly. The arroyo had become Big Tesuque, she was certain of it. The aqueduct had become Thorncrown Chapel, the man had become the vampire.

Her nudity in the dream had been a symbol of the vulnerability she had felt, alone at midnight. Even the awkwardness of her skis had figured in.

It all *felt* right. The emotions mapped, the analogies locked.

Which was very irritating.

Because that was one of Freud's main suppositions. That everything in dreams had its roots in waking experience. The absurdity, the exaltation, the terror were all simply the result of the brain's compulsion to link ideas, however unrelated. The whole point of interpreting dreams, in his view, was to reconcile them to waking life, to rationalize them.

How boring. How unfruitful. How badly she hoped he was wrong.

He had to be wrong. If dreams spoke in code, there was still an important question. *Why?* Why should your own brain need to talk to itself in a secret language?

4: the big empty

Jody turned and skated back the way she had come. The sun would not rise for another hour, but the sky was whitening already over the Sangres. Pale, snowy peaks on pale sky. Soon the long light would flash in, printing the shadows of branches on her stucco.

Speaking of which. Instead of taking Yucca to Calle Primavera to home, she sprinted over the arroyo in her sock feet, a skate in each hand. She caught only a couple of sandspurs, was through her back gate in less than a minute, laughing and panting, her breath visible in the cold air.

Pop in the dream hadn't been Pop. Pop in the dream had been Freud. *That* was why he had turned vampire. Freud, the father figure, the destructive icon for any female researcher. *My father in the night commanding No.* Women weren't supposed to aim so high, to have such ego.

And of course the chapel stood for the high holy church of theory.

Because what she intended to accomplish, what was obsessing her and keeping her awake at night, was nothing less than her own theory of dreams. There were a million so-called theories out there, from the Freudian to the Jungian to the merely chemical, but in her opinion they were hardly better than poetic guesses. A good theory not only had to match the facts; it also had to be *usable*. It had to have solid predictive value under all conditions.

She had come up with a new approach, an application of chaos theory. The dreaming brain as a very complex feedback system. She was beginning to think her scheme might explain a lot more than dreams. It might explain the structure of intelligence itself.

She was using the DormaVu study to work out the details. She was going to be the first mammal, after untold and uncountable but surely trillions of mammalian dreams, to say what dreams really and finally were, how they did what they did.

And however they did it, it wasn't going to have anything to do with old Poppa Cigar back in Vienna, was it? Way to go, kid. Slick trick: a beautifully Freudian explanation of how your dream was telling you that dreams aren't Freudian.

It took forever to find her keys in the crammed fanny pack. When she finally got the right one in the lock of the French door—she had a thing for French doors, hated sliding glass—it jammed. Just wouldn't turn at all. "What the hell?" she said. Had the lock frozen?

She was standing in the portale's shadow, in leftover drifts of crusted snow. Her feet were tingling. Her residual warmth had vanished, and she shuddered in the bitter air.

Now that she looked closely, she thought she saw scratches on the lockplate. Had they been there before? A frisson that had nothing to do with the temperature went up her spine. A burglar? Mr. Whiney, trying to get in and poison her cats?

The snow was too trodden to distinguish separate tracks. *Get a grip, Jody. Ten to one, Dean and his crew scratched the plate putting it in, and you just never noticed before.*

Finally she fought the key around. She went up the two steps of the sunken living room to the main level as fast as she could, calling her babies. She crossed the dining area into the kitchen. No sign of them. Where were they?

Then she heard Blind Lemon, boogety-boogety down the stairs. Static galloped in and jumped to the countertop, then the top of the refrigerator, then down to the countertop again, circling Jody anxiously. Blind Lemon came rolling in, complaining, brushing against the cabinets to guide himself. He wrapped Jody's ankles, doing his talking blues.

"You guys are really jacked up this morning," she said. "Well, *hello*," as Static launched herself, landing with a thump on Jody's shoulder. Blind Lemon was butting his head against her shins now, and producing the rumbling sound that he thought was purring.

"*Altrettanto,*" she said, because he preferred Italian.

The difficulty with the back lock had spooked her. She didn't really think Mr. Whiney would poison cats, but he had threatened her more than once with traps and Animal Control.

"That damn dream," she said. "You babies don't have vampire dreams, do you?" No, they didn't. They didn't need to. Plenty of real killers in their world. *Nature red in tooth and claw.*

She nudged the fridge open with her knee and one-handed a can of food, cradling Static with the other arm. Blind Lemon howled and stood on his hind legs.

"Baby, you've gotta get—"

She dumped Static onto the counter. "Down." Spooned curds of ersatz liver-and-beef into a couple of bowls. Watched the lowered heads for a moment, the hunched furry shoulders, the switching tails. Went upstairs. Showered, threw on a robe, came down and let the babies out for their morning ramble, poured herself a glass of milk. Went up to work on her journal.

She sat turned away from her computer for a moment, as always, studying the big painting on the far wall, a Cardona-Hine: *Osiris, Lord of the Underworld.* It was a green and luminous beauty, Osiris a brooding death's-head presence that some might have found disturbing. For her, it was a skeletal but somehow hopeful dream, the very emblem of her research.

It had set her back thirty-five thousand smackeroos.

She tipped an imaginary hat to the two birds on either side of Osiris, also Cardona-Hines, as were two larger pieces downstairs in the dining area/great room, and set to work. She might have noticed the peculiar thing then, when she first entered her files. But she was too intent on getting started. She felt she had a lot to say this morning.

She typed her vampire dream into the computer first, the sentences she'd written in her head while skating home. Then a few notes on the night's other dreams, though she remembered little that she hadn't spoken into the tape recorder already.

Five miles away, across town, on the east side, in a rented town house just off Canyon Road, the man who had driven the black car was debriefing his companion.

"You like to scared me shitless," he said, tugging the elastic.

"I was too close to give up," the companion answered. "Besides, less risk getting them all in one go, don't you think? Cuts chances of discovery. Um, that feels good."

The man who had driven the black car was kneeling. He looked up now: "So you got them all? What did you get? Where are they?"

The companion was standing, still wearing his jacket, though his pants were around his ankles. He reached in his inside pocket, brought out five microfloppies. He fanned them like a hand of five-card draw. He grinned: "Voilà! And I got her modem number too, so next time we don't have to go inside. We can update from here."

He was showing a lot more confidence than he felt. It had been a close call. It hadn't been the subject's system that had taken so long, it had been his own ineptitude. He was the supposed computer expert, but he had faked his résumé when he joined up. He was handy enough, but no expert. And that was a laugh if you thought about it, faking your résumé with the CIA. And the big laugh was, they hadn't caught him. Yet.

The kneeling man sat back on his heels. "What's on them? Why is it so important?"

"Do I know? Do they ever tell us anything? Transcripts of recordings, as nearly as I can tell. Loads of people droning on about their boring dreams. The great doctor's boring notes. Dross, total dross. Do return to your previous activities."

"Say what? Oh."

"Ah. Better. Much better. Do you know that woman had Cardona-Hines on her wall?"

The kneeling man made a muffled sound, ah-whoa-ah-woo.

"Cardona-Hine, from Truchas. She had *five* of them. I want to do art today. Let's go see what's at Hahn-Ross. Maybe they've got some new Nakamuras in. I wish we had bought that yellow one, *Dreaming in the Belly of the Beast.* Or that Lichtenstein, *The Tower,* it's so Santa Fe. Like an in joke. Do you even *like* her work, Leonard? Do you even like *art?*"

A red light blinked in the corner of the screen. Static or Blind Lemon wanting back in. "Shit," she said. Going down the stairs, she told herself, for the thousandth time, to put in a cat door. *Too hung up on gadgets, Jody. Simple is better.* She had been proud of the system, of how quickly her babies had learned to trigger it. Of herself for doing all the wiring. But finally it had proved a minor convenience and a major annoyance.

They were both there, waiting. They scampered in as soon as she opened the door, shook the frost from their fur. "Colder than you thought, huh?" She used the break to brew a pot of coffee. She had drunk her milk, didn't want any more, but needed something. Long day ahead.

When she went back upstairs, Blind Lemon followed her.

She wanted to talk to somebody about the meaning of her dream, but there was nobody there. Nobody but her computer. Sometimes her dream journal doubled as her diary, but that wasn't satisfactory today. This insight would have been the perfect thing to share with a lover, but she had no lover. It was too early to call Toni. Toni liked to sleep late.

Blind Lemon climbed on top of the monitor, curled around, hung his chin over. His favorite place while she was working. Some warmth, the sound of the fan. The computer purred back at him. His round yellow face looming over all her meditation like a friendly moon.

She realized she was having a vision of the grocery, the upstairs stockroom. One of those scenes that flicker constantly in your mind's eye, but that you hardly ever notice. That you look through like you look through your own reflection in a pane of glass.

The smell of her coffee, she figured. Pop used to brew a pot whenever he thought it was time for a heart-to-heart. It had never been convenient, having the stockroom on the second floor, but that was the layout. Store on the bottom, living quarters and stockroom upstairs. Probably how she first built her mighty thighs. Upstairs and down, twenty or thirty times a day.

She could almost smell the onions and peaches. Crates of onions and peaches. The summer after graduation, working in the store to save for college.

Mom in bed all day with one of her headaches, so Jody had had to do invoices as well as pricing. Trying to do too much, too fast, as usual. She had marked nearly every single canned item two or twenty cents too high (mistaking a nine for a seven on the stamp), and was going to have to do the whole job all over again, and she had sent her application to Williams in late, not that they would take her anyway, who was she kidding, and she and Trey, her stupid boyfriend all through her junior and senior years, had started having those stupid last-summer-before-you-go-off-to-college talks, how maybe you should start seeing other people and so on, and it was her goddamn period and she was cussing a goddamn stupid motherfucking blue streak—

"Josephine Deborah—" that had been Pop, pretending to be stern. "I think we better have a conference." Opening a can of the primo Colombian and making them both a cup, hers heavy on the honey and real cream. Sitting her down on a packing case, picking one for himself.

"I'm worried about you, baby."

She had shrugged, as if to say, *What can you do?* "It's just—I'm scared, so I'm making mistakes, getting flustrated." That was her neologism, her portmanteau word. Flustrated. She knew he liked it. "I'm scared I won't get in Williams." Now the self-deprecatory, ironic smile. He liked that too. She had learned that one from him. "I'm scared I *will.*"

"With your scores? You're a lock. It ain't that, Jo D. Ain't the boyfriend either." So he knew about Trey. Of course he did. He always knew, somehow. "It ain't the situation I'm worried about. It's you. You're ambitious. Ambitious people get hurt."

"What am I supposed to do, make C's? Marry the quarterback? Go to LRU?" Settle down in Little Rock and run a mom-and-pop grocery? But she hadn't said that aloud.

"No, honey. But I see you on the edge. Nothing between you and the Big Empty. I want to spare you some grief, that's all. I know I probably can't. So I guess I just want you to know I'm always here. That you can always come home and heal up."

Sitting on the packing crates, and loving Pop, and wanting out.

Feeling like a traitor, but wanting out anyway. Out and away from the store, away from the peaches and onions, away from his warm and omniscient and smothering concern, away from the utterly predictable classmates living their utterly predictable lives, away from her mother's gloom and perpetual sickness, away and out of Arkansas and into something different, into a new universe, where you could do big things, where you could make life matter.

She had gotten away, all right. Look at her now.

She pushed her chair back, but left the computer running. Blind Lemon sound asleep on top of the monitor. She went across the landing and through another set of French doors into the master bedroom. The sun would be up soon. Time to head back to the office. Might as well get dressed. Wouldn't do any good to sit and stare at the screen.

Black linen slacks, her silver-toed black boots. A ribbed black turtleneck, the Liz Claiborne jacket over that, silk in a black and silver houndstooth. Not the most soothing ensemble with which to greet sleepless patients. What the hell. Brushed her hair back, applied a quick rip of lipstick. No makeup. For earrings, the dangly silver scorpions. A brooch for the jacket, no bracelet except her watch, her mother's old rose-gold Gruen Curvex. Five minutes flat.

Take the little white pill, last ritual of the morning. Prevent the pregnancy that wasn't ever going to happen anyway because she would never be with a man again. Intercept that oldest feedback loop of all, the one responsible for the turbulence of humanity itself.

She went back to the computer, but nothing came. Nothing but the old familiar depression, so gray and customary there was nothing to say about it. No insights to be had, no consolation to be gleaned. The heat-death of emotion, no further energy to be extracted.

But you didn't cave, you didn't give in to the depression. That had been her mother's path. No, you got mad, you fought back, you did something. Anything.

Blind Lemon stirred, cried in his half-sleep. Put out a paw toward her. She felt a wave of love so strong her eyes stung with tears. Then an undertow of self-mockery: Poor solitary Jody, socially dysfunctional Jody, emotionally dependent on her pets.

She had gone to Williams College after all.

And Mom had died, died of her headaches really, though the official cause of death had been listed as overdose. Heroin bought somehow on the street, from one of their newer customers. A good Baptist woman, pillar of the community, a deacon's wife. Because the aspirin had quit working a long time ago, and prayer had never done any good.

And Pop had died two years later. Pop, who had worried that her ambition would hurt her. Who had had no ambition himself. It had been a friendly middle-class neighborhood when he and Mom bought the store. The original Mom and Pop grocery. They had joked about it, then changed the sign. Had taken down Nightwood's and put up Mom and Pop's.

The street had gone from neighborhood to hood, had gotten rougher and more rundown, its deterioration paralleling her mother's. After Mom's death, Pop had stuck it out. Treating the new customers, half of whom were drunk or high or carrying, with the same courtesy and respect he had given Quapaw Quarter housewives in the 1950s.

It had been inevitable. One day a banger had come in and shot him dead. No way Pop would have resisted. Just some useless animal had come in and shot him dead for the thirty-five dollars and twenty-three cents in the cash drawer.

So Pop had been lying. He wouldn't always be there. She couldn't always come home and heal up. And he hadn't seen her graduate. No family in the audience when she walked. All by herself. *Nothing between you and the Big Empty.*

She had broken up with Chipper after Pop's death. Chipper hadn't wanted anything to do with trouble and sorrow. Way too heavy for that lightweight boy. Couldn't understand why she wouldn't cheer up and go partying.

She had had her affairs, but couldn't honestly say she had been in love since. Pretty pitiful, huh? Fifteen years on her own, and her college boyfriend still the last serious romance.

The loneliness had made it more important than ever to do something with her life. To succeed, but to succeed in some realm other than the mercenary, to succeed in a way that most Americans didn't comprehend as success: to do some good.

Chaos theory applied to more than dreams, more than intelligence. It applied to life itself, the roles you played. You were who you were because of . . . Not because of straight lines, directed behavior. That was the American myth: You can be whatever you want to be if you just try hard enough. If you just *believe* in yourself. Bullshit.

Zeroing in. College. And then biology. Because it seemed important to understand what life was, where it came from, how it worked. And med school, because doctors were heroes. Because it was life and death. Maybe because she had become convinced that her mother's lifelong depression had been unnecessary, a mere chemical malfunction?

Learn how to repair the engines, make things work. The world is sick and screwed up and unhappy, but maybe you can fix it. Put it all together into a whole picture, leave behind something big—a vaccine, regeneration of spinal nerves, a discovered genetic trigger for cancer.

Stage by stage, step by step, she had been disillusioned, and had become more and more angry with the world. It was all a business. Studying in college a business, preparation for the commercial future. Med school definitely a business, a cost/benefit analysis all the way.

Then you were there, a doctor, had your M.D., had done your internship. What now? You needed a lab, a place where you could keep learning, keep figuring things out. Wait a minute, they don't just hand that stuff out for free. Go into private practice, or join a team.

She had taken a position with Langley Pharmaceuticals in Virginia. Little known, but the fourth or fifth largest in the world, weirdly named after the nearby spook factory. Toni was there already, her Williams roommate. Toni the consulting psychiatrist. Necessary because so many of Langley's products were mood-altering, if not downright psychoactive. Toni had recommended Jody, and Jody had started as assistant lab director for sedatives, anesthetics, and soporifics. An astronomical salary, which quickly came to seem normal. You got used to money.

She hadn't really been poor since her senior year. Pop had provided, scrimping and scraping in order to keep their debt low and their premiums paid. What she had thought of as being broke had really just been old-fashioned thriftiness. There had been a policy on her mother's life, bigger than she would have expected, and he had put it all in trust. On his death, his own policy had doubled the size of the trust. And then there had been the money from the sale of the store. All equity, the mortgage completely paid out. Not a lot by some standards, but with the trust enough to make her, ironically, one of the wealthiest graduates in her class.

And the Langley connection had paid off eventually, if you thought about things that way. DormaVu was a Langley subsidiary, and her experience at Langley—and, more important, the people she had gotten to know there—had helped mightily with her current funding. So she was doing the research she wanted to do, and somebody else was footing the bills.

It had been ghastly in the lab, though. You weren't there to figure big things out. You were there to find little jigsaw pieces for other people's puzzles. You were there to figure out things that would help Langley Pharmaceuticals make even more money. Put people to sleep, wake them up, slow them down, speed them up, keep them from hurting: Convince them they had a *right* not to hurt, not even the littlest tiniest ache anywhere in your body, take a pill.

The romance was that the big commercial labs gave the mavericks room to achieve. On the way to making money for the company, you could win a Nobel Prize. Laslo and Penzias, the first humans ever to hear the whisper of the Big Bang.

So how much had Bell paid those two for listening in on the beginning of the universe?

She had spent her time with rats, mostly. Rats and rabbits, the occasional dog.

And she had noticed that mammals dreamed.

It was obvious enough, but she had never thought about it before. All mammals dreamed, she would have bet her life on it. She didn't think other genera did, though she wasn't sure about birds. But all the mammals did. Rats and rabbits and dogs, they twitched in their sleep. They chased, they mated, they played, they ran from predators.

Why?

Wasn't that a significant correlation, that all mammals dreamed and only mammals dreamed? What did it mean? What did it mean about mammals? What did it mean about *us?*

Having trouble sleeping herself, she had become increasingly interested in sleep. What was it? Easy enough to say it was evolution's way of conserving energy in complex animals. Another cost/benefit analysis. The hunting's not so good at night, so shut all systems down.

Easy but stupid. *How* did evolution make the decision? And that other question, that question all of the people she knew spent all of their time ignoring: Why?

She had wanted badly to go back to school, to sign on at some university institute. But all the slots had been filled with the latest hotshot kids, and they had been grunt slots anyway, apprentice slots. She had been coming up fast on thirty, and had gotten accustomed to a good income, and hadn't thought she could eat humble pie for a living anymore.

Zeroing in. Biology to med school to sleep research.

And Toni had decided it was time to go back home, time to leave the unreal East and head for the true country, her native ground, The City Different, Santa Fe. *Mi madre y mi padre-madre.* She had talked Jody into a partnership. They both had capital, after all.

They would go to Santa Fe. They would set up a sleep clinic.

There were a lot of new people in Santa Fe. Movie people in from California. Oil-and-beef Texans. Stock-market New Yorkers. *Anglos like you, Jo D.* The Anglos weren't sleeping so well. They all worried a lot, partied hearty, stayed up late. Jody and Toni would charge the Anglos *mucha plata*, help them sleep, poor lost souls. Nothing could really be done, since they were all sick with the Anglo disease. They had no blood in their veins, they had only minutes and hours and seconds. But one could ease them, give them a few nights of genuine rest, and take their money. Toni would handle the psychology end,

Jody the physico-chemical. They would make hay while the sun shone, and the sun always shines in Santa Fe.

It had worked like a charm. It had worked so well and so easily that Jody had finally been able to set up her own lab. And then DormaVu had kicked in with the grant.

Zeroing in. From sleep research to dream research. And now?

Now she knew that her father had been wrong. It hadn't been ambition after all. It had been a calling, a vocation. It only looked like ambition because you couldn't see the invisible center, the forces that drew her on. That was the chaos connection.

Like the path of an iterated function, spiraling in on the attractor.

For a moment she saw that blocky spiral as a dream-catcher, like the webs they sold to tourists down on the plaza during Indian Market.

Had this been the nature of her mother's depression? Relationships, careers, feedback systems. Strange attractors. Jody's excitement had vanished. So she had her concept. She still didn't have anybody to talk to about it. Her thinking grew darker and more tangled as the sky grew light. Still she wrote, as if by giving voice to create a listener.

The only thing about the chaos attractor comparison, though. They call it that because it looks as if something is drawing the moving point in, closer with each iteration, like stop-motion gravity. But actually you're looking at the behavior of a feedback system, not the action of force fields. The point gets closer and closer, but it never quite reaches the so-called attractor. It can't, because there *isn't* an attractor. There's nothing there. No there there.

The hole in the spiral.

Nothing between you and the Big Empty.

The inside man, the Brit, slipped his coat on. The driver was in the shower. Through the open doorway, steam and singing. Bad singing. More rock-and-roll. *I. Can't get no. Satisfaction.* Ironic, that. He smiled with warmth and pleasure. He really liked this fellow.

"Leonard," he called. "I'm going out now. Deliver our little goodies."

Incomprehensible bellow in answer, his own name mixed in: "Toy, Toy, Toy," the bather called. Half-singing something about a fuckable boy. Then back to the Stones.

"Meet you for breakfast," the inside man said.

"Where?" came the loud query, water-blurred: Whur-ur-ur?

"Celebrations."

"What?" the bather called. "Again?"

But Toy had donned his hat and muffler and was out the door. Walking down Canyon toward Peralta and the north side of town. A nice early-morning stroll. He whistled to himself, bits of Purcell. His work all done for the day. For the week, probably, at least. On the loose in Santa Fe, and with an amiable companion, at that.

For the thousandth time he congratulated himself on having chosen an unusual vocation, an unusual life. One that never bored him, and that allowed him such freedom.

"Toynbee Tarkington," he told himself, "you're a lucky old sod."

He waited at the Peralta and Alameda light. When it turned green, he ambled slowly across. He would walk along the river until he hit the Old Santa Fe Trail. Then cut across, through the plaza, to the post-office drop. Deliver their little packet of disks, having copied them onto his own computer first. Pick up the new instructions, if any. And then he was through for the day. The beautiful, sunny day.

He pitied the people he passed in the streets. Hurrying already, headed for their jobs. Their livings, such an ironic word. Headed for their livings, away from their lives. Faces drawn and worried, even so early, even here in Santa Fe. Even here in Paradise.

Blind Lemon woke finally, stretched, stepped down. *Okay, now I've done the sleeping-on-the-monitor bit, time to do the making-biscuits-in-your-lap bit.* He stepped onto the keyboard, and the system beeped, buzzed, and blipped.

"Goddammit," Jody said. "If you've trashed my file—"

She lifted him off and onto the floor. When she looked back at the screen, she saw that he had managed to close the file she had been working on. She had her machine on a five-minute automatic backup, so she would have lost whatever she had done since the last save.

"Shit," she said. "Shit shit shit."

And then she saw something that set her shivering with adrenaline. It was just a little sequence of numbers, just an abstract string of digits. It shouldn't have carried such menace.

But the numbers were wrong, the numbers were impossible.

She was at the folder level, and she had set her window to display the files in the folder by name and date, the date of the last modification. The problem was those dates.

Except for the current file, the one Blind Lemon had just kicked her out of, the dates were all the same. They all read "Fri, Jan 15." Today's date.

But she hadn't modified any of the other files, only the current one. She hadn't touched the other files in weeks. Maybe Blind Lemon had done it somehow, had stepped on some weird combination of keys— But no, that wouldn't work.

There were times after the dates. The times ranged from 1:21 a.m. to 7:13 a.m. While she had been sleeping in the lab, dreaming of vampires. While she had been skating home.

She sat staring at the screen a long time, her soul going in circles, like a chip in a dark vortex, a bit of flotsam going down the drain. Someone was after her. Someone was hunting her down. Someone was going to punish her for being so ambitious.

It couldn't be, but it was.

The lock, the lock.

The catlight.

Now she was glad of her weakness for gadgets, her overcomplicated approach to simple problems. If someone *had* broken in the back door, they might have triggered the seeing-eye beam. It was set low for the cats, who knew exactly where to sit when they wanted in. But a prowler would almost certainly have crossed it at some point.

And she, Jody, super-techno-brain, she, for no good reason except the fun of rigging the system, had set her system to record the time and date of each triggering.

She got out of the lab files, went to the desktop. Opened the log for the catlight. And there it was, blinking, seven lines up from the bottom:

Fri, Jan 15, 1:14 p.m.

Her skin crawled. She felt as though someone were in the house now, stalking her. She felt the whole downstairs gaping below her—a pit, a dangerous vacuum.

Nothing between me and the Big Empty.

And it was time to go to work.

5: reality check

What to do? If there had been a burglary, where was her evidence? Numbers on a screen, that was it. Not exactly the sort of crime to impress the local constabulary, who were busy with gang-bangers, rape-murders, stalkings, and knife fights and shootouts at the various taverns.

Maybe she was inventing it all.

Say Mr. Whiney *had* come stumbling around her backyard while she was out. Or even some local punk, some inept jailbird-in-training. Whoever had messed with her computer certainly hadn't been expert. They had known enough to get in, but not enough to cover their tracks.

For that matter, it could have been done without access to the house. She had a fax modem. Lobo knew the number. It could have been Lobo on some perfectly ordinary business, poking around without asking her first. Be just like him.

Hell, the electric eye could have been tripped by a neighbor cat. A raven.

Right now, sanity called. Reality. She had responsibilities. In an hour and a half, there would be patients waiting. People thought if you ran your own business you were free of all the dreck, the tedium. Hah. All she wanted to think about was her research, but she had to go to the office like any wage slave, suffer through a nine-to-five.

God, she was tired. She knew the weariness would pass. Would return again in the afternoon, again in the evening, its interval short-ening. Would leave her stretched across her bed with her clothes on, until it was time to go to the lab, time to pay her way by dreaming of vampires, sex with space aliens, her mother the talking cabbage.

The rising sun came through the blinds on the eastern windows, falling in stripes across Blind Lemon, asleep now on the window seat. If she pulled the blinds open, she could watch sunrise over the San-gres. Her wonderful house, designed with mountain views in three directions. Her wonderful house, that she never had the time or energy to enjoy.

Toni. At work she could talk to Toni.

As she went clattering down the stairs, hunger kicked in, the overnight calorie deficit made more ferocious by her early-morning rollerblade jaunt. She felt hollow and shaky. But she was too impa-tient to fix breakfast here. She wanted out, she wanted away.

In the garage, she had another decision to make. She had skated in to the lab yesterday evening, getting her workout coming and going, so all three cars were here.

The NSX was her one true indulgence. A bright red two-seater, a rocket, capable of better than a hundred and seventy-five miles an hour. And yet luxurious as a Cadillac. Justification for all the hard years, the college years bumming rides with her friends, watching the spoiled set tool off in their high-school graduation presents for a weekend of play.

But she would be at the office overnight, and it wasn't the sort of ride you wanted to leave parked on the backstreets of Santa Fe. It begged to be stolen, or broken into, or just broken.

The Pontiac, then? Maybe she loved it more than the Acura. It had been Pop's car—*his* vanity, decades ago. A burnished red-orange shad-ing slightly to maroon, it sat fifteen inches off the ground, weighed 3,265 pounds, and had a 115-inch wheelbase. The straight-eight engine delivered seventy-seven horsepower and a maximum speed of seventy-eight miles an hour. Downhill.

It wasn't as vulnerable to thieves as the Acura—easier to break into, but much harder to fence. Antiques were rare and memorable and easy to trace. But there were still vandals to worry about. It would have broken her heart to see the Pontiac battered or spray-painted or sitting on flat tires with a hammer-shattered windshield.

The van was white and muddy and dented, and a long scar ran the length of the driver's side, where a pickup had raked her with its mirror. Rust showed over the wheel wells, along the underbody. Pop had bought the van used and put in windows, but he had never repainted it or removed the detailing, and she hadn't either, and now the blue stripes were flaking away, and you could just barely read the ghostly PUROLATOR lettering on its powdery flanks.

None of which told you anything about its true nature. The van was her secret weapon, her stealth cruiser, her luxury tank. She climbed in, punched the garage door open, and started up.

Mr. Whiney was standing in her driveway.

She felt a flare of anger so intense she almost ran him down. Manslaughter only a hair-trigger away. We are all killers. *Shit, just what I need right now.*

But he stepped to one side and she braked and rolled her window down. "What is it now?" she said. "I'm on my way to work."

Mr. Whiney was a tall, skinny young fellow in steel wire-rims. His features were patrician, but his nose seemed always raw, and he had a face-wound of a mouth, a grimace like the mask of tragedy. His voice was nasal and twanging, the very intonation of Bostonian complaint.

"You've been letting them out again," he said. His face was on a level with her shoulder, and the height advantage gave her a pleasant feeling of superiority.

"I never said I wasn't going to let them out," she said. "I gave you that repellent."

"Why should *I* have to use *your* repellent?" he said. "There's cat poop all over my yard."

Cat shit, *you twit.*

"This neighborhood is cat city," she said. "Why do you assume it was my cats that did it? It could be anybody's. It could be Jubilation T. Feline, for all we know."

He didn't think she was funny. "They carry diseases. What about my children?"

"So do rodents carry diseases." She felt she was spluttering. She had never spluttered before. That was the trouble with anger, it was so undignified. "What about hantavirus? You probably ought to thank my cats for keeping the rats away from your ratty old woodpile."

Mice are the hantavirus vectors, Jody. Her biologist's mind, calmly noting inaccuracies in the midst of her fury. *Rats for the bubonic plague.*

"Don't you have anything better to worry about?" she added.

You fucking twit, you fucking insufferable twit.

"If you can't control your animals, I'm calling Animal Control," he said. He turned away, then turned back, shaking his fist. "You'll pay a fortune bailing them out."

It was the fist that got her, the physical threat. "You've been messing around in my backyard, haven't you? Trying to break into my house. You just *try* to do anything to my babies. I'll have you in jail. I'll sue you till your fucking ass falls off."

Oh, good move, Jody.

"You're a sociopath," he said, pointing a trembling finger in her direction. "I'm a counselor at the community college. I know a sociopath when I see one."

"A counselor at the community college," she said. "Wow, I'm impressed."

But he was stalking away toward the street, and then he was rounding the wall between their lots, and then he had disappeared. "What a jerk," she said. She leaned her head out the window and called aloud for the whole neighborhood to hear: "WHAT A JERK."

She put the van back in gear. She drove carefully, quivering with anger.

An acute observer would have been surprised at the smooth, low rumble of the motor. At the end of her street, she hung a left on Yucca, began retracing the path she'd skated that morning. Music, she needed blues to soothe her fevered brow. She fed a CD in, punched up the digital remastering of Blind Danny Webtoe's "Ugly Dog Blues." Tenor sax, rocking like a heart.

What a morning! But she calmed as she drove. Just being in the van made her feel calmer. Safer. It was memories of home, of riding with Pop when he made deliveries. But updated, modernized, with all the conveniences.

The stereo system was Blaupunkt, and some impulse of control or awareness had caused her to install a police scanner, though she rarely turned it on. She had installed scanners in all her vehicles, but the only one she used was the one in the Pontiac, which, when she had it on, gave her the pleasant sensation of inhabiting a 1930s cop-and-gangster flick.

The van's carpeting was an expensive, short-napped silver-gray. Lighting ran on tracks the length of the interior. A bench seat along one wall made out into a bed. Under the bench seat there was storage for tools, supplies, and camping gear. There was a small refrigerator, a bar with a tiny sink whose spigots hooked into a hidden water tank. Up front were two captain's chairs backed by individual chromium roll bars. The dash had been transformed into a console. On the passenger side, you could open panels to reveal a complete computer workstation. A mobile phone rested in an assembly between the two seats.

Under the hood, things were different, too. She had pulled the original six, dropped in a big V8, replaced the automatic transmission with manual. Thick cables ran from the battery to a bank of twelve-volts in back, themselves connected to a generator.

She had put in, at considerable expense, a mountain-eating four-wheel drive, a winch, power-assisted rack-and-pinion steering, and a suspension with adjustable gas shocks. When she could, she took the van into the hills, camping for days, no tent necessary.

She could not have explained why she needed the camouflage. Unprepossessing exteriors, but secret goodies inside, unparalleled power—a metaphor for her life? In her home and in her van, and maybe in her work life. Her love life, too? Not a productive line of speculation.

She had gone back along Siringo, left on Pacheco. The cop was no longer in the Capitol complex, of course he wasn't. Past Wild Oats, across St. Francis, past the latter-day Wild Oats doppelgänger, Alfalfa's, which by now a lot of her friends preferred.

Webtoe was on guitar now. Singing. His thick and hesitant accent somehow transformed in the rhythm. It was the "Got the Ain't Got the Blues No More Blues."

The day had warmed up nicely already, and Toynbee thought about dropping his coat and the manila envelope at the condo, but walked straight up Canyon to Celebrations instead. Leonard was waiting in the plastic-wrapped patio, sipping coffee and looking over the paper.

"What news, Benvolio?" Leonard said.

Toynbee smiled. His partner didn't often do the Shakespearean rag—had been a drama major, done a bit of acting here and there, but had the typical American phobia of seeming too educated. When he did indulge the Bard, it meant he was feeling good.

And why not? An excellent morning so far.

Toynbee tossed the manila envelope to the table. He had scanned the contents on his way back. He took his coat off, draped it over the back of his chair, sat, looked around for the waiter with the coffee. "There may be someone else on the ground," he said.

"Oh," Leonard said, in a tone that implied lack of interest. Toynbee knew better. His partner liked wet work, if it came to that. Would come home from the errand exhilarated, justified in his calling, and very horny. The inside man felt a shiver of anticipation.

Probably should be disgusted with himself. Vicarious sexual arousal at murder. Made him hardly better than Emilio at the Mall copping a feel to the latest Wes Craven. But there you were. It was a bloody world, in every sense.

"Who?" Leonard said now.

"Our control doesn't know," Toynbee said. "He says all he has is a scrap of overheard conversation, some idiot using a radiophone. But he's identified three possibilities."

"Well, we'll just have to kill them all," Leonard said.

Toynbee looked down. *Feeling guilty, my lad?* "Photos in the packet," he said. "Of course, Benjamin may not have anybody here after all. He could have planted the information just to mislead us. The people in the photos might be completely innocent."

"Their bad luck, then. So you're sure the other side is Benjamin?"

"Who else would it be? Not that they're going to tell you and me. But think it through. We're operating in-country, against all the regs. We're spying on a citizen who doesn't have any extranational contacts. We're directed to look for anything that might have any bearing on AI—"

"AI?"

"Artificial intelligence. Didn't you listen to the briefing material at all?"

Leonard shrugged, smiled. "Hey, I'm just the muscle on this job."

"Ask yourself, Who runs the AI subgroup? Answer, Benjamin George. Then ask yourself, Who hates Benjamin George more than anybody else in the CIA? Answer, Freddy Davenport. Not just any Freddy Davenport, but the same Freddy D. who is—"

"Our very own section chief. Gotcha. But what makes them think the Nightwood woman is into AI? As far as I can tell, her research is just a bunch of gobbledygook about dreams."

"On that I have no idea. And it worries me not to know."

"What's to worry, Toy? Suppose this whole operation *is* just an intra-agency squabble. What possible difference could it make to us?"

"It means we're off the books, my love. It means if there's trouble, we don't exist."

"Hell, I could have told you that a long time ago, just from the service in this joint. I've been trying to get a refill on my coffee for the last twenty minutes."

Now it was Toynbee's turn to smile. "You colonists," he said. "So helpless with the servants. It's all a matter of confidence." He lifted his fingers, snapped imperiously.

The waiter bore the blessed pot, uplifted, in their direction.

Jody pulled into the tiny lot behind the clinic, the slot with her name on it. She keyed the suspension, and the van settled on one side a little, for all the world a derelict with worn-out springs. She got out, locked the doors, went in through the lab door and down the short hall to her office. Lobo had left messages on her desk.

One simply told her where he had put the tapes from the other two dreamers, and noted that he had done post-REM interviews with each. The other message was that Toni had called, and wanted Jody to call back at her home number. Which probably meant Toni wasn't coming in today. Jody's heart took a dive. She punched in the number.

"Hey, you," Toni said, not waiting for Jody to identify herself. "We got any head cases today? I'm wanting to play hookey."

"Well, I don't know, girl." Jody tried not to sound resentful. "Just let me check the appointments. Wait a minute, where does Consuela keep the . . . here, got it. Ahm, Thursday, Friday—no, shit, I'm in December. Okay, Here we go. We've got a narcolepsy, a couple of apneas. One, two—four insomnias. We've got Mrs. Uriostes again."

Jody put just a hint of a plea in the latter statement. There was nothing wrong with Mrs. Uriostes. The problem Mrs. Uriostes had was her son Ramón. He sleep too much. Every day if you don't wake him he sleep to two o'clock in the afternoon. A school day, you have to pour on his head the *agua fría,* and then still sometime he don't get up. This is a sickness, *verdad?* Like the alcohol, the drug. You can't get ahead in life when you sleep so much.

There wasn't anything wrong with Ramón, either, except that he was seventeen years old. That and being allowed to stay out too late.

Mrs. Uriostes was a widow, and she had difficulty disciplining her youngest child, the baby, the last one remaining at home. Toni and Jody had steadfastly refused to supply her with prescriptions for amphetamines and stimulants. They had recommended an earlier bedtime, vitamins, coffee. They doubted Mrs. Uriostes ever tried any of their advice. Still she made her appointments, paid her bills. Perhaps she simply wanted somebody to talk to. A professional, so that she wouldn't have to be embarrassed, as she might be in confessing her child's failings to a friend or a neighbor.

"You can handle that," Toni said. "That's no psych job. Just sit and listen, okay?"

"This better be worth it," Jody said.

"Girl, it is. You come out tonight, I tell you all about it."

"So who is he?"

Jody was torn between envy and interest. Toni loved men the way someone else might love fine horses: Wonderful creatures, wild by nature, who, if you groomed them and fed them and kept them in line, could give you an exhilarating ride.

But nothing to take too seriously, nothing to break your heart over.

"Come out tonight, see for yourself. We going to do Zia's, then maybe up to Ten Thousand Waves. I never had that wat-su, did you?"

Ten Thousand Waves. Then it *was* a new man. "I can't," Jody said.

"Girl, it's the *weekend*."

"Yeah, but I'm on dream rotation tonight."

"I never seen anybody so directed about free association."

"Come on, Toni. You know better than that. You've done research."

"You know, it's been a while since we was out together. See you at the office all the time, never go party. Like being married or something."

Guinness. Zia's had Guinness Stout on tap. Jody sighed. "I could meet you for drinks, I guess. But I have to complete this week's rotation." *I have to get back to my vampire.*

"How about seven o'clock? That early, bar probably still have seats."

Jody forced lightness into her tone, the approximation of gaiety. "But only if I get to find out which way it curves."

Toni laughed, a peal of quick bells. "Up, girl," she said. "You know

I won't take nothing but an up." Jody held Toni on the phone awhile. She told Toni about the apparent break-in. About Mr. Whiney. About being so tired lately. She would not have been able to describe Toni's responses, but it wasn't long until Jody was feeling better.

They chatted until Jody heard Consuela at the door, then said their hurried good-byes. Consuela didn't approve of the frivolous use of the telephone.

Consuela hung up her coat, stowed her purse and her brown-bagged lunch. Jody pretended to be occupied with the interview log from last night's dream sessions.

Consuela sat at her desk, took out a compact, repaired the ravages to her hair and makeup incurred in the fifty-foot walk from her car to the office. She was a short, blocky woman in a black wool suit and clunky shoes, with a square-jawed face that might have been pleasant if she ever smiled. She had wanted to become a nun, but had had a child out of wedlock at age sixteen, the result of an overinsistent boyfriend and her own ignorance. What would be called date rape today. Today you could prosecute, sue. Back then, the girl had taken all the blame.

Consuela had surrendered the child for adoption, and had punished herself by abandoning her hoped-for vocation. It wasn't that the Church wouldn't have accepted her. It was that in her own eyes, if she had honestly wanted to become a bride of Christ, she had had no business going steady with a boyfriend in the first place. So there.

Consuela had confided all this, a bit at a time over several months, having drinks after work. People told Jody their stories, they always had. She had gotten that from Pop, she supposed, the ability to really listen, to make the other person feel safe.

In this case the knowledge helped Jody understand Consuela, but it hadn't made her mannerisms any easier to tolerate. Especially not this morning, when Jody was weary, and freshly aware of her own problems. Another reason to be grouchy about Toni's absence. When Toni was here, she had a mollifying effect. Consuela approved of Toni. Which was odd when you thought about it, considering Toni's free-wheeling lifestyle.

Consuela could be irritating, but she was value for the money. A whiz with the books, honest to the bone, and she worked like a draft horse. She had a B.A. in accounting, an associate degree in nursing, and served Sweet Dreams as secretary, nurse, and business manager.

Her workload as nurse wasn't overly heavy. They were a small if lucrative practice, and since half of their clients were referrals whose files transferred, they didn't perform that many physicals. For the lab work, they either drew samples and sent them out, or did their own referrals.

Consuela consulted the calendar for the day, and cleared her throat. "You have an apnea at nine-thirty, a Colonel Wilbur Hall, referred by Dr. Maes. Then a—"

"A narcolepsy, an insomnia, another apnea, two insomnias, Mrs. Uriostes, and one last insomnia," Jody broke in, impatient with the woman's magisterial delivery. "I read it already."

Consuela had donned her reading glasses, and now glared at Jody over the rims. "No," she said. "Dr. Archuleta has Mrs. Uriostes and three of the—"

"Toni's not coming in," Jody said, interrupting again. "That was her on the phone when you got here." Let her stew over that. Let her disapprove of her favorite for a change.

Consuela was silent. She stared grimly down at the calendar. Finally she decided on her strategy. "Some of these appointments are overlapping," she said. "You were supposed to have some and Dr. Archuleta was supposed to have some."

"Fine, we'll work with it. I'll be quick, and nobody's surprised at having to wait a little bit in the doctor's office. You work it out and let me know. I'm going out for coffee and a bite, and I'll be back in time for the first appointment. Did you say *Colonel* Hall?"

Consuela didn't answer. Jody grabbed her woolen muffler and her jacket, and left. She didn't need any more coffee, but she had to get out of there for a few minutes. She was resentful about Toni, angry with Consuela, and none too proud of her own combative behavior.

Behind her, in the office, Consuela stored the calendar in the desk drawer, slammed the drawer closed. Tears stood in her eyes. She got a Kleenex from her handbag, scrubbed furiously at a wet ring on the desktop. Sniffed the Kleenex.

"Rom," she said, and threw the Kleenex in the wastebasket. "Somebody's been drinkeen fockeen rom at my desk." She would never have let Toni or Jody hear her say such a thing, but her private language was full of anger and profanity.

If you were never going to be a nun, it didn't matter whether you cursed.

• • •

What Jody really wanted to do was crawl into her van and hide. What she really, really wanted to do was take the van up into the mountains and sleep for a week. But either one of those options would have been a kind of defeat, a retreat from reality. *Deal with it, Jody.*

Instead, she strode the few blocks over to Galisteo News. When the weather got warmer, there would be people sitting at the outside tables, ponytailed young men in hiking shorts, women with long young legs and old hard faces. Today there was only an emaciated street-dweller in his tattered and filthy Goodwill special, a thigh-length quilted jacket that might once have been Harvest Gold but was now Detox Yellow. Tangled gray hair spilled to his shoulders from under a navy watch cap. He hunched over a bran muffin and a steaming cup of coffee, someone's generosity. Maybe the management's, on condition he stay outside.

Talk about defeat.

The man heard her approach and looked up. She was shocked by the icy blue character of his eyes, the unexpected vitality of his gaunt and stubbled face.

"Where's your head?" he said sharply.

As though he knew her, as though he could see directly into her brain.

"Now you listen here," she said, shaking her finger at the man and feeling Mr. Whiney take over her body as she did so. "I've had about all the crap I'm willing to take today."

And then the world shifted, and it was all very funny. Herself, her fears and confrontations, this: standing in the street, haranguing a madman.

"So you keep your fucking cats out of my fucking yard," she said.

The man returned to his coffee and muffin as though this were a perfectly normal response. Jody went inside and thumbed through half a dozen magazines without seeing them, chuckling to herself. *Fight crazy with crazy.* She thought about getting Toni a humorous card to tease her about her new man, but decided to wait for the details. Finally she picked up *The New York Times,* went to the counter, and ordered a croissant sandwich, extra turkey, and a double espresso to go. Thinking twice, she added a large container of Kona and a brownie.

By the time she got back to the office, she had cooled off, literally and figuratively. A breeze had begun, and her muffler and jacket hardly slowed the thin and stinging air.

Consuela was in the near sleep chamber, the one Jody had used, cleaning up, putting things right. Jody thought about apologizing, but decided that in this case apology would only serve to drive home the offense, make it more real. Better to let things slide. She put the brownie and the Kona on Consuela's desk, a propitiation.

Sure enough, when Consuela came back to the front to make ready for the appointments, she seemed in a better mood, more amenable. She didn't really want to fight, either. She lifted the lid on her coffee, sniffed it. "Thank you," she said.

"You're welcome," Jody said, and the day began to look survivable.

6: sweet dreams

Colonel Wilbur Goodloe Hall was a surprise. Jody had been expecting a middle-aged military type: brush-cut hair, ramrod spine, cap looped to his shoulder by an epaulet.

The colonel she got was more like Colonel Sanders, though minus the facial hair and seventy-five pounds. A tall, stooping, wide-shouldered, leather-faced fellow in his middle to late sixties. He had a shock of snowy white hair, worn Santa Fe long. Huge, callused hands. He wore oxblood Luccheses, a white linen shirt with gold Kokopelli studs in the French cuffs but no tie, and a pin-striped Botany that hung loosely on his loose frame. A pair of gold-rimmed reading glasses projected from the pocket of the suit jacket. He reminded her of nothing so much as one of the wealthier deacons from her childhood church.

He leaned against the bed of the sleep chamber and waited while she glanced at his file. During the off shift, they used the sleep chambers as consulting rooms. After lunch, though, they were limited to the one room on the office side that had been set up originally as a third office. Toni had been extremely patient about the inconvenience.

Actually, there was nothing in Colonel Hall's file but the application form he had just filled out. He was a walk-in, not a referral after all. She hoped he wasn't one of those who got off on being examined by a woman doctor.

"What seems to be the problem, ah, Colonel Hall?" she said.

"Ah snore when ah drank whiskey," he said.

She felt a wave of pleasure. Home folks. She couldn't help it, her curiosity got the better of her. "May I ask how you got your rank, Colonel?"

"Governor of Mississippi give it to me," he said. "Thirty-four years ago last April."

Jody smiled. "You know, I might have guessed that."

"Yeah, I sound the part, don't I? You a Southern gal yourself."

"Little Rock."

"At counts."

"Are you saying that you only snore when you drink whiskey? Not at any other time?"

"Just when I drink whiskey."

"Have you experienced any breathing stoppages, any sudden awakenings when you can't get your breath, or any panic attacks in the middle of the night?"

"Nope. Sleep just fine."

"You don't really have apnea," Jody said. "Everyone snores from time to time."

"Apnea's just what that woman told me to say," he said. "Your receptionist. I don't care what you call it. Truth to tell, I ain't worried about the snoring, but Tanya don't like it."

"Tanya?" He didn't seem the sort for a trophy girlfriend, but he didn't seem the sort who would've married a Tanya, either. When he'd been a young man, there hadn't *been* any Tanyas.

"Tanya Littlefeather," he said, deepening her perplexity. She waited, but he had apparently volunteered all the information he thought necessary.

"Well, since you know the cause of your problem . . ."

"I would purely hate to give up whiskey," he said. "Liefer—well. I was hoping maybe you could give me something to take care of it."

"I could, but I don't think it would be a good idea. You'd be burning the cotton to get rid of the weevils. Hmm. Don't want to give up whiskey, don't want to give up Tanya."

He smiled at her appreciation of the dilemma.

"How do you sleep? I mean, what position do you sleep in?"

"On my back," he said. "All my life. Flat on my back on a hard mattress. Makes you wide awake in the morning. Raise hell all day."

"I want you to try something. I want you to try sleeping on your side."

"Don't know if I can manage that. What good would it do?"

She explained that it was probable that the depressant effect of the alcohol was causing too great a relaxation of the soft palate, and that its collapse against the breathing passage was what was causing his snoring. She showed him how to sleep on his side with a thick pillow under his head to keep his neck straight, and with his knees drawn up to keep his back straight. She made him practice the position on the examination table until she was sure he had it right. She told him he might want to get a softer mattress to allow the spine to stay level, and he allowed as how Tanya would probably be in favor of that anyhow.

When he was going, by way of good-bye, she said, "Are you in town on a visit, or—"

"Lord, no," he laughed. "Me and the wife been here fifteen years. Hell, honey, I own half the place. You never been to the Buckaroo Ball, have you? Mrs. Hall's one of the main people run that sucker. Well, that's not till June, but—"

He pulled a gold-embossed card from an old black wallet, scribbled something on the back. She thanked him, and put the card in her pocket. When he had gone, she took it out and read.

Anasazi Heights

A Respectful Re-creation of the Original

1-800-262-7274

On the back he had written the address of a party, this coming Sunday, and the words "Super Bowl. Please admit. —W.G.H." Jody dropped the card on Toni's desk.

The narcolepsy was Suleiman Li, who, in spite of his Arab/Chinese ancestry, was a native. Jody had treated him before, and was more brusque than she might have been. She had tried sympathy, and it didn't work, and she was afraid Suleiman was going to hurt himself or somebody else. He would not admit his condition and would not continue taking his medication, and he kept getting arrested for drunken driving, then coming to her for letters to get him off.

The insomnia was something else. Toni really should have been there for the insomnia.

His name was Bruno Sandoval. He was a tiny man, a good half-foot shorter than Jody, with wiry muscles and a lined face burned darker than sweat-stained saddle leather. His eyes, buried in wrinkles, seemed to have no white or iris at all, seemed completely black. Ancient eyes, that had absorbed generations of sun and now took in the harshness of her fluorescents the way a turtle might take in the light in the aisles of a grocery store. Bruno Sandoval wore a starched white shirt, threadbare but immaculate jeans that had also been starched and pressed, and a pair of battered Nocomas that brought his height to maybe five-three.

"It is not for me," he said, his legs dangling. "I have this friend who cannot sleep."

"Mm," she said. "Open your shirt anyway."

She slid the stethoscope around his firm and hairless chest, the cold dollar of her distrust. She knew he understood the message.

"So why can't your friend come in to see me himself?" She turned to make a notation in his file. Let him answer to her noncommittal back. Now that she had conveyed her disbelief, there was no point in pressuring him.

"There are many difficulties," he said. "It is not with you as it is with the psychological doctors, *no?*"

She turned to face him. She was baffled.

"*Confidencial,*" he said. "*¿Usted no mantiene la información a base confidencial?*"

"My partner is a psychiatrist," Jody said.

"Yes," the man said. "To begin, I was—my friend was to meet with her. Now you instead." He shrugged. "Still my friend has this problem. He must *resolver*—he must solve it soon. He cannot go on in this way. *En esta manera.*"

"So we will speak of your friend," Jody said.

Her Spanish was weak. For all the time she had now spent in Santa Fe, she had never yet buckled down to learn it, though she had a knack for languages and had automatically picked up a few scraps and phrases. She tried to shape her English in a syntax Sandoval might find more decipherable, one with fewer contractions and idioms. "And since we speak of someone I do not know, *un desconocido,* there is nothing I could tell anyone else. What would I say? Would I go to the police? *¿Iría a la policía? ¿Qué les diría?* 'There is this person I do not know, and yet I know that he has done something.' No. *No es posible."*

Jody knew she was getting into tricky moral territory. The man's problem was clearly psychological and ethical, not medical. She could not have said whether compassion or curiosity ruled more strongly, but she knew she wanted to hear Bruno Sandoval's story.

"Well, then," he said. "My friend thinks that he may have hurt someone. He thinks that he may have killed this someone that he hurt. For this reason he cannot sleep at night."

Jody shivered. This was a bit more vicarious excitement than she had counted on. She suddenly felt naked, exposed for the world to see. What could she do now? She couldn't conceal murder from the police. She had to stop Sandoval before he said anything more specific. She had to prevent him from saying anything further. But she didn't.

There was this motorcycle, it seemed. Always, in the hills behind his house, the *motocicletas,* the arrogant young raising dust and making a loud noise, a noise that echoed in the arroyos. And on the road past his home, the loud ones again in their *automóviles.* Accelerating the length of the straightaway, in love with the sound of their unmuffled engines. Or playing the new music, the music that was not music but a rude thumping accompanied by bullying words. Playing it at such a volume that you could hear it from miles away. At such volume that your windows shook. From one end of the day to the other, often in the middle of the night.

He supposed that to produce such a great noise, *tal ruido,* one must be very stupid, or at least very empty. One must have nothing but noise inside oneself. This is what he supposed, but really it did not matter. A man could not think, a man could not sleep. Whatever the dissatisfactions of the loud ones, he had a right to peacefulness.

Bruno Sandoval's friend was retired. He had earned his rest, but now he could not take it, he was being cheated of it by the young. His friend had spoken to one or two of them, and they had laughed. He was an old man, he was not to be considered. He had spoken to the police, but they had done nothing, there was nothing they could do. Day after day, the friend had brooded. If an aggressor tried to take a part of one's land, then one could prosecute. If a criminal assaulted one's person or tried to damage one's property, one could, with justification, shoot that malefactor. But such a creature could trespass on one's silence with impunity. Such a one could steal the friend's rest and cause injury to his ears, and nothing would be done.

This was no excuse for what happened, Bruno Sandoval admitted. And it would not have happened if the friend had not been drinking that afternoon. Back from a long and sleepless hunting trip in the hills near Dulce, a trip in which he had not seen a single deer. And so, tired and frustrated and drinking a bit of El Patrón to soothe himself. So that he could sleep well, and early. You know how it is. And then the noise had begun. Two young men behind the house, conducting their own impromptu afternoon motocross. These boys were not neighbors, he had not recognized them. They were boys out from town. Invaders. And the friend, in a cold temper, had picked up the rifle with the telescope and gone to the back window of the home, and the next time one of the *motocicletas* topped a hill, he had shot the beast.

He was a very good shot, the friend. In the army during the war, a marksman. Too short for the infantry, he had gotten in by means of a special dispensation, and had become a sniper. Never did the friend fail to bring home a deer from Dulce except on this one very strange trip in which there were no deer. And he knew that he had shot the motorcycle and not the rider. He had aimed for the heart of the machine, the engine, and he had not missed.

But the beast had risen up like a deer making a final leap before dying, and the rider had tumbled. And there was silence, blessed silence. But there was no rest, because the friend had done this terrible thing. In a moment of anger, the friend had undone the values of a life. And all the friend wanted now was for that moment never to have occurred. He wished to deny it from existence, as that football player had wished to deny the murder of his wife. It could not have occurred to him. This could not be his story. He was a hero, not a killer. We plead our innocence not to deceive our neighbors, but to deceive ourselves.

The rider had fallen behind a rise, so that the friend could not see him. The dust settled slowly, and still there was no movement, no noise. The sound of the other motorcycle was not heard again. The friend watched until the sun went down, drinking tequila. And nothing more happened. Finally he drank until he was no longer conscious.

The next morning the friend went out to look at the scene. There was no motorcycle, there was no body. If there had been people out during the night, there were no tracks. In the days that followed, the friend had listened to every newscast, examined each day's newspaper very closely. There was no mention of a death in the hills, or even of an accident.

Perhaps, Jody suggested, the friend had not actually hurt the boy. Perhaps, in spite of his marksmanship, he had missed, and the motorcycle had by coincidence fallen at that very moment. And in any case, perhaps the boy had not been hurt.

"You did not see the manner in which the boy fell," Bruno Sandoval replied.

Jody did not comment that, hypothetically at least, neither had he seen it. "Could you—could your friend not confess to his priest? Perhaps then he could sleep."

That is what the friend should have done, Bruno Sandoval admitted. But he had known the priest for ages. The priest was a very old man, almost blind, and had been close to the friend's father. The friend had been a bit wild as a young man and then in the army, a noise-maker himself. The priest had never thought well of him. The friend had changed, but the priest had grown more fixed in his opinion. The friend could not bear the thought of the priest's final disapproval. This was not right, it should be a matter between the friend's conscience and his God, and the priest the intermediary only, but still. The friend did not wish to think of the priest dying soon, going to the friend's father in heaven, and saying to the father, *See, I told you. I was right all along about your boy. I told you he was no good.*

"But this has gone too far," Jody said. "You must confess to someone. The police. Perhaps there is no crime. But in any case you must be relieved of this guilt and doubt." She did not notice that she had abandoned reference to the friend.

Bruno Sandoval nodded. "It is what must be done."

"I speak not as a doctor now," she added, aware of her own guilt. Her interference in another's life. "I have no right to advise you in this matter. I speak only as a person."

"I had come to this decision myself. You do not bear the responsibility. It is what must be done, and it is what will be done. Only. There has been so little sleep, so little rest. One would not wish to meet one's fate exhausted and nervous, at the end of one's strength. One would wish to behave like a man in such a matter, and not like a hunted rabbit."

"A prescription?"

"Yes. It is why I have come. I have told you the rest only to explain the need."

"It would have to be for you. I cannot make a prescription for *un desconocido.*"

"We will not speak of my friend again."

When he was about to leave, Jody thought of a question. "When you do sleep, do you dream?" It might have been a medical question, seeking to establish whether he slept long enough to get the benefits of REM sleep. It might have been, but it wasn't.

"Yes," he said.

"Do you dream of—of the event?"

"Yes," he said, looking up at her sadly. "But always *I* am on the motorcycle, and the police are shooting at *me.* I ride away into the dark hills. Sometimes they are the hills behind my home. Sometimes, I think, they are the hills of Italy during the war. Sometimes both and neither, *una tierra nueva.* But there is nowhere to hide. I ride, and they shoot at me. Sometimes I die. When I die, I wake up and I realize it is not merely a dream. I realize that I shall never escape."

Italy. He might have known Pop, or at least met him.

"I do not wish it to be the same when I wake from my actual death," he added.

Lunchtime, and Jody headed for the Plaza Restaurant, where you could sit in sixties-deco surroundings and eat good food cheap. Outside, the light was almost shocking, as if she were a child who had just come out of a matinee movie into the brilliant streets.

At one, the first shift of three sleepers began. Night people, two of whom worked a midnight shift, and one of whom, Bianca—that was the name she went by, no last name—had plenty of money and did not work. She was a crystal healer, a channeler, and was participating in the study in order to get more deeply in touch with her psychic energies, she said.

And maybe also to scout the opposition.

Consuela did not approve of the study. She had herself observed many salacious or otherwise reprehensible occurrences on the part of the dreamers, things that everyone knew of but that should be private, not a subject for cameras and recorders. Especially that Bianca.

But Consuela was willing to and could handle the set-up and the observations until their part-timer came on, a young woman named

Blossom, who was majoring in biology at the University of New Mexico. Blossom was not as capable as Lobo, but she had been trained to observe and she wasn't stupid, and she needed the money, and Jody had had to have somebody. Toni was glad to help out from time to time, but it was Jody's study, not Toni's. She might analyze the dreams of her patients when it seemed advisable, but she wasn't a researcher and didn't want to be one. So that really, in allowing Jody to divert so many of the resources of the business, Toni was being about as accommodating as you could ask a partner to be.

The second apnea was the real thing, a real-estate salesman named Buckner. Jody told him horror stories to get him to take his problem seriously, set him up on a series of tests and a regular schedule of visits. Waited to prescribe, pending the results of the tests.

Of the two insomnias, the first was classic nervous tension, a woman who couldn't sleep because her mind went in circles at night, worrying over her mistakes.

Going in circles. "I've done that myself," Jody said gently. "Everyone has. I'm going to give you a prescription to help you relax at night, but I hope you'll make an appointment to see my partner. I think she could help you let go of some of your tension."

Worry, Jody saw now, was really just directed thought chewing its own tail. Linear, goal-seeking behavior trapped in the paradoxes of the way things actually work. Cause and effect swallowing each other in the mind. Not circles, but spirals. Another feedback loop.

The second insomnia looked physical all the way, a combination of high blood pressure and perhaps nutritional deficiencies. The man, a young-looking but flabby assistant producer with an Australian accent, was in town to oversee a set of location shots. Jody recommended exercise, fruit, and a glass of warm milk with a tablespoon of blackstrap molasses dissolved in it every evening before bed. The assistant producer was angry. He had wanted pills.

She didn't understand who he was. His producer job was just a cover. He was actually with the DEA. A big deal was going down. Carlos himself was in town. But Carlos knew the producer was here, so his life was in danger. He needed the pills to sleep.

"Whatever," Jody said. She was thinking cocaine. She was thinking this was what paranoia looked like and no way was she going to spend any more time freaking over the weird business with her computer. He stomped out of the office in a huff. Some people you could help and some you couldn't. They had to help you help them. Healing was two-way.

Mrs. Uriostes was better. Mrs. Uriostes was not with the DEA.

The whole family had gathered at her house for *Navidad,* and Ramón had stayed away as much as possible. Every night out late with his new girlfriend, did I tell you he has a girlfriend now, though what she can see in such a lazy boy . . .

And then in the mornings, sleeping late, avoiding the cousins, uncles, aunts, and nephews. Hiding in his slumber. On the morning of *Navidad,* when they all went to church, she could not rouse him. And then when they return, she is there, the girl, and Ramón insists that she be allowed to join them for the dinner, can you imagine such a thing? It is for the family, this dinner, not for the transient affections. But what can she do? She does not wish to make a scene, to spoil the precious day when we should be giving thanks for our Savior . . .

By the time the appointment was over, Jody and Mrs. Uriostes were laughing together—families, they were all crazy!—and Mrs. Uriostes left in a good mood without saying anything more about a prescription for Ramón.

When the day was over, Jody found herself exhilarated rather than tired. The expected midafternoon slump had never hit. Toni was right. She needed to get out of herself more, get out and around. Life was interaction, involvement with others.

Even the morning's battle with Consuela had proven enlivening, had led somewhere. Living wasn't a matter of getting things done, but of paying attention. People didn't *have* stories, they *were* their stories. And there was a story behind every story if you looked more deeply, and a story behind that. Level after level, and no matter how much you raised the magnification, just as much detail. Dreams were the same way. And that thought reminded her of Bruno Sandoval. She resolved to keep in touch, to find out what had happened with his story.

She and Consuela straightened their desks. Jody reloaded her pack, and Consuela her purse. "TGIF," Consuela said, and made a reasonable effort at a co-worker's smile.

"Thank God it's Friday," Jody answered, with a big smile of her own. "And a long weekend, too." Monday was Martin Luther King Day. In the name of our heroes, we rest from our own unheroic labors. Bless those who never rested. Bless them for dying that we might rest.

It was five-thirty. Consuela went, and Jody stayed behind. Blossom would not be in until six tonight, and Jody did not like to leave the sleepers unobserved.

Rafael Tafoya and Bert Goodens were in their third REM cycle. It was a phenomenon she could not readily explain, but after the first few days, and even though they slept in separate chambers, the dreamers' rhythms had synchronized. She had not yet checked to see if the same thing happened in other labs. What would she know if it did? What would she know if it *didn't?*

Sure enough, not ten minutes after Consuela had gone out the door, Bianca began to moan and sing. The psychic energy she was tapping into these days seemed primarily sexual. Her third REM, and her third orgasm. It drove Jody crazy. Why couldn't *she* have a few of those sweet dreams? She felt like waking Bianca in the middle of it. But the woman, for all her half-baked philosophy and transcendental posturing, was immensely likable. Control yourself, Jody.

But the moans went on and on and *Dammit, why can't I have dreams like that?*

Blossom arrived, took off her coat, saw what was going on in chamber two, and blushed. Jody headed for home. Freshen up, change. See the babies.

Static and Blind Lemon hardly stirred when she came in. They looked up and yawned and put their heads back down. If she was going to run off and leave them all day, very well. They'd show her. They'd just sleep their lives away and ignore her when she did come back. She drew them fresh water and put out fresh food anyway, seined the cat box clean with a huge old slotted spoon she'd bought expressly for the purpose. The smelly, dirty duties of any close relationship. Nuggets of excrement, geodes of dried piss. She hardly noticed anymore.

She showered, pulled on a gray turtleneck, black jeans, ribbed black socks. Laced up her black Nikes. No need to brush away the mud and dust from the last trail. Dirty boots were not, in Santa Fe, a fashion faux pas. Went with the oversized black nylon flight jacket— genuine issue, the only good result of a fling with an air force jet jockey—and a gray woolen sailor's cap. She looked, she thought, checking herself out in the mirror, like a Greek female commando.

She settled in the recliner with her feet up. A few minutes of yuppie junk TV before heading off to Zia's. *Wall Street Week, Washington Week in Review.* Tonight, McLaughlin and his bunch carrying on like clowns. How Bill Clinton was showing his true colors, now that he didn't have to worry about votes or Kenneth Starr. The same talking heads who had declared only a couple of years back how impossible his reelection would be, and then, after the election, how soon the indictments would come. Fools pretending to the future, trotting on their heels backward after events, pronouncing as fast as they could to imagined multitudes.

Forget what I said last week. Listen to me now. Listen to me now.

All her earlier exhilaration had fled, and she was left with a vast weariness. She didn't want to interact anymore. She didn't want to go down to Zia's and drink stout and meet Toni's new man and think how she didn't have a man because there weren't any men out there worth having, they were all Peter Pans or good old boys. Or maybe she was just a dried-up overworked hardass ambitious judgmental bitch without a loving bone in her body.

She heaved herself from her chair, already late. Even your pleasures become duties, Jody.

Maybe at least she would have good dreams tonight. *Sweet dreams, baby.*

Maybe she would see Pop again.

Maybe she would even be visited by dream lovers, like Bianca.

Wrong, Jack Germond. The right answer is—

7: a felony catshit warrant

She drove the NSX. Look like a commando, drive like a commando. Maybe she could shoot a male commando down, and hold him prisoner for a night or two.

She flipped the switch on the scanner, in the mood for some commando talk, some urgent dangerous voices crackling out of the night. What she got was not very different from the dispatcher's voice coming over the radio in a downtown taxicab.

When Jody got to Zia's, Toni was already at the bar, working on a pale ale. Jay Hayden set a glass under the spigot, drew it full of foaming Guinness. He nodded as Jody slid onto her stool, let the Guinness subside while he filled a table order from a waitress.

"Okay, where is the hunk?" Jody said. "Am I taking his seat?"

"No, gal, saved it for you," Toni said, leaning back languidly. Long muscular arms, good shoulders. But Toni abhorred working out, made fun of Jody's obsession. A walk in the park, going out dancing from time to time—that was all the exercise a person required.

"He'll be along later," she added. "I told him you had green eyes and red-blond hair and those big sofa-cushion Anglo knockers. Now I couldn't beat him away with a stick."

Toni was a tall woman who seemed always to have just finished laughing, or to be on the verge of laughter, even when she was unhappy, even when all you saw was her posture, her silhouette against a light-filled window. Her hair was black, with the luster of a groomed Arabian's coat. A cinnamon-brown face, dark eyes that flickered and threw out glints like ripples in a pool of crude oil. She had a long neck, a strong chin, and a sharply carved jawline, all of which she had no doubt been bequeathed, along with her height, by her anonymous father. She emphasized her plush lips with a splash of bright red lipstick.

If she had ever known a moment of self-doubt, Jody had missed it.

"Did you check your mail?" Jody said. "There was some sort of invitation. On a real-estate card. Fellow named Colonel Hall. I left it on your desk."

"I saw it. I know who he is."

Jay came back to finish off the Guinness, then rake a knife blade across the swelling foamtop. Though his family hailed from County Sligo, he had never made it to Ireland himself. But he sure knew how to handle the Guinness. He set the pint glass on a coaster in front of Jody, handed her a napkin. "How's it going this evening, Miss Jody?" he said.

"Fine," Jody said. "But this gal has got some kind of mystery man on the hook she won't tell me about. Have you seen him? What does he look like?"

Jay didn't answer. His gaze lifted instead, and Jody saw, in her peripheral vision, a big dark hand settling between Toni and herself. She turned, and her breath caught. The hand was displaying an open wallet, a wallet bearing the silver shield of a police officer.

"Are you Miss Jody Nightwood?" the man said.

He was at least six-four. He had the face of the man on the 1938 nickel. His eyes were the luminous yellow of old leather in morning sunlight, of rocks in the bottom of a creek.

"What's wrong?" she said, fear pitching at her stomach. It had been a cop who had brought the news of her father's death, a police lieutenant in a suit. The dean had been with him, but it had been the lieutenant who had brought the information.

But what could this be? She had nobody left to lose.

"We've had a complaint about your cats," the man said.

High cheekbones, impossible blade of a nose. Gray-shot black hair pulled back into a two-foot ponytail. A black pullover tucked into worn Levi's. The shoulders of a thundercloud.

Jody's fear boomed suddenly to anger, gas fumes catching on a struck match.

Mr. Whiney. "That sonofabitch!" She began cramming her things back in her purse. Her hands were shaking. *Kill,* she was thinking, *I'll kill that sonofabitch.*

Jay was watching the three of them, an uncertain smile on his face.

"We've got them down at the station," the cop was saying. "We're holding them on a felony catshit warrant." Toni was doubled over, head down on the bar, her shoulders shaking. Jody was furious with her, laughing at a time like this.

Then she got it.

They moved to a booth in the no-smoking area, two levels up. The man's name was Victorio Vigil. Victorio V. Vigil. The last name rhyming with the Latin for *nothing.*

"We cover the alphabet from A to V," Toni had said.

Now the two of them were sitting smiling at her, holding hands on top of the table.

"That is *the* worst trick you've ever pulled," Jody said.

"You were asking for it," Toni said. "You been taking life awful serious."

"Last time I tell you about any of my problems." Jody's eyes kept flickering to Vigil's face. He noticed every time, seemed amused. He understood the effect he created, then.

The beast spoke, a spine-tingling rumble of bass: "Maybe we were a little cruel."

Jesus, Jody thought. *Even the goddamned voice.* She felt no desire for the man, couldn't imagine herself with him, didn't want him in any way, shape, form, or fashion. Not that sort of thing for her, never: elemental rut, the grappling of gods or animals. And yet, and yet, just for a moment, she hated Toni, hated her for her unending, overweening good fortune.

"Nonsense," Toni said. "You have to play rough with Jody. You can't break through if you don't play rough. Her block-out is too good."

Is that true? Jody wondered. She was definitely feeling better now, clear-headed and full of energy. Maybe just an adrenaline high. But whatever, Toni's shock therapy had worked.

"Your name," Jody said. "It seems—it reminds me of—"

"Half Apache," Vigil said. "Named after the warrior. And half Hispanic. And half Navajo. Which makes me real lower-class in some people's eyes."

Toni punched his arm, but he ignored her.

But that's three halves, Jody thought, then saw Vigil grinning with his joke. *Jesus, I'm gullible tonight. Slow and gullible. Going into victim mode? Sharpen up, gal.*

The waiter came with a handful of unnecessary menus. Vigil wanted onion rings and a burger. Toni and Jody decided to split the baked artichoke spread for an appetizer. Toni wanted meat loaf, and Jody went for the garlic-and-black-olive pizza with Italian sausage.

"Anything else to drink?" the waiter said.

Toni ordered another pale ale. "Two pints will probably completely loop me out," Jody said, "but bring me another Guinness."

"I'll take a Guinness, too," Vigil said. Then, to the women, "If you can believe it, I've never tried stout before. Always game for a new experience."

"That's why we're together," Toni said, patting his arm.

"Now that's too *much* experience," he said.

"Are you really a cop, or was that—" Jody said. She was thinking, *Maybe I could ask him about the computer.*

"Part of the joke?" he said. "Well. I was, and then I wasn't. And now I am again." And then, as though he were reading her mind, "Toni told me about your computer."

Jody felt a wave of relief. *We need to be able to tell somebody these things, she realized. Somebody official.* "There's no reason anybody would burglarize my files," she said. "I mean, no reason at all. I don't think it was Lobo—"

"That's her assistant on the study," Toni said. Vigil nodded impatiently.

"I really don't think it was Mr. Whiney—"

"That's her neighbor," Toni said, "the one who hates cats."

Vigil nodded again, this time with a raised palm to Toni, as if to say, *Quit interrupting.*

Jody felt a minor flush of embarrassment, realizing she had used her private name for the man in a public situation. Like being caught absentmindedly using baby talk.

"It's just not his style," she finished. "So I keep thinking, could it be like a gang member who's also a hacker? I mean, do they have people like that now?"

"They have all kinds," Vigil said soberly. Apparently weighing the merits of her idea. She recognized the technique somehow. The way a smart cop puts you at ease. Doesn't tell you how stupid you are, how little you know. Treats you with respect. Listens.

Not so different from being a doctor, Jody thought.

"Have you considered ghosts?" Vigil said.

"Ghosts?"

"They've started being haunted now. The computers. Finally getting complex enough. Ghosts need complexity, you know. They won't haunt primitive systems."

What kind of cop is this? Jody was thinking. "How did you get to be a cop?" she said.

"Tell her the story," Toni said.

"It's not a story," he said. "It's just what happened. She won't be interested."

Their drinks arrived, and Jody took a long swallow. It went down like milk, like mother's milk. "Good," Vigil said, foam sliding down the walls of his half-empty glass.

Toni prodded and tricked and tugged. She told parts of his life herself. She made inaccurate or exaggerated statements that he felt compelled to correct. Technique again. Forget the strong-and-silent business. If a good psychiatrist wants you to talk—

Jody realized she was watching one professional investigator go after another.

Vigil had been right. She wasn't really interested. His past had been colorful enough, she supposed, but what was going on here wasn't storytelling. It was negotiation, Toni taking possession of her man's history, making it part of her own.

Victorio had grown up on the rez, Mescalero. Hard times. Prejudice. Fighting. His father a proud and distant man. Toni and Victorio made a good match, Jody thought. Both of them feral, vital, highly directed. Toni with her own strange parentage, not quite belonging in her native place, a different child even in The City Different.

Toni wanted Vigil to talk about boxing. How he had made the coaches mad because he wouldn't play football or baseball or basketball, but later became some sort of champion in the navy. Jody's attention wandered. She was visited by images, was seeing a sweaty and shirtless young man pounding along a dusty arroyo, breathing hard. She saw the restless shade of cottonwoods scissoring and shifting over the muscles of his bare chest as he lay back on the gate of a battered pickup and heaved metal plates an arm's length into the air.

She heard the young man grunt. She smelled the low trickle of water.

Now Vigil was in high school in Santa Fe. Jody had lost the thread, didn't know why he had moved. More images: vandalizing property, stealing bikes and motorcycles, joyriding in a boosted car, once even a burglary. In her semi-trance, it was her house Jody saw him breaking into. Spending parts of each summer in the reform school at Springer.

"Were you in a gang?" Jody said.

"What gang? Gangs are neighborhood things, family things. I didn't have a neighborhood. I hated the gangs. They weren't as bad back then, but I hated them anyway."

"Well, did you have any trouble with them, then?" Jody said. "Fights or anything?"

"What is it with you Anglos and gangs?" Toni said, irritated. "Always with the gangs, like they were going to—" She looked down, suddenly. She had remembered Jody's father.

Vigil caught the awkwardness. He kept talking, smoothing things over.

"If you went after me, I would find a way to hurt you," he said. "If a bunch of bangers beat me up, I would wait and catch each one alone, and then I would whip the horseshit out of that one. It might take me six months to do them all, but they would all know it was coming. I might have to get out of the hospital first, but you knew if you messed with me, sooner or later you were going to be the one laying up in one of those beds with the crankshaft on it."

"Sounds like a hard way to go," Jody said.

Vigil shrugged. "It was the easiest. You've had people treat you like dirt till the day you stand up and zap 'em, haven't you? And then after that, they respect you? Most people are that way, really. Like animals, or children. See, I can tell about you already, you got the nice person's disease. Your default assumption is respect. Treat people nice and they'll treat you nice, right?"

Jody bridled. "I might be nice, but I can take you down any time I want to."

Vigil was delighted. "See?" he said. "See how right I am? You have to get your deal in first. You have to let 'em know you mean it, and you have to do it right away. Hurt 'em, and hurt 'em good. I don't mean damage them. I just mean leave 'em with no doubt you *would* damage them. Don't speak to their brains, speak to their fear of pain. Saves a lot of time."

Jody felt as though she were watching a battle of ants. As if she were looking through a microscope into the world of the arthropods, the insects. Where chitin slammed into chitin routinely, and mandibles clashed. Where legs were severed, and bodies cut wriggling in half. A world without pity, reason, dream, or hope. *And do you beat your prisoners?*

"It seems cruel," she said, glancing at Toni. Had he hurt *her?* Was that the basis of their relationship? Was Toni inviting abuse? Jody felt dizzy, pits opening under her feet.

They both understood her expression, and smiled simultaneously.

"I didn't say *everybody* was that way," Vigil said. "And really, it's just the opposite of cruel. In the ring, you don't hate the other guy. You just want to hurt him early, hit him with a punch so hard the fight's over right then, even if it goes another ten rounds. Plenty of time for sweetness and light later, after you have his respect."

"You were a boxer," Jody said, anxious to change the subject.

Something about a man named George Black Bear, some sort of mentor. Training on the rez while the other men rode the fenceline or cleared sage and stone from a pasture. Something about agreeing to build a clinic when he hit it big. An argument with his father over college, the navy instead. MPs screeching up to a waterfront bar in a Jeep.

Vigil had quit talking. The silence had gone on awhile. Jody wondered how long she had been out of it while he sat there, stolid, not looking at either of them, looking away into space. Now he drained the stale remnants of his stout, looked around for the waiter. Caught the eye of the water boy and asked him to tell the waiter they needed another round.

"No more for me," Toni said. "I got plans for you later."

"Isn't the food ever gonna get here?" he said. "This Guinness is giving me an appetite." Normalizing. He was normalizing, trying to get things back on a more casual basis.

"You always have an appetite," Toni said.

"Only for you, my pet."

"You guys stop it, you're making me sick," Jody said.

It had been an automatic response, the words echoing strangely in her ears. She was feeling an odd displacement, a sense of dislocation.

As if she were not herself. As if the self sitting there in the green-upholstered booth were a mere mechanism, a device, a puppet, and a wider awareness prowled the room around it, including it along with everything else.

The noise of the restaurant rose in her ears, the sea-roar of other conversations.

They were in the mountains somewhere, a pillared portico bathed in amber light, winged nymphs descending. Right out of Maxfield Parrish. Whatever she looked at directly seemed normal: a yuppie couple engaged in one of those bitter, quiet quarrels. A ponytailed grandfather with an irrepressible, curly-headed boy whose name was surely Bright Angel or Windrider. A black student in a heavily embroidered dashiki, wearing rings in his nose and ears and a pair of shades with small round utterly dark lenses.

But around the edges of her awareness, the mountains glimmered. The hum of voices was the hush of wind in the leaning willows, the clink of silverware was the lapping of misty water.

What the hell was going on?

I'm going to have to excuse myself, she was thinking, *go home and go to bed.*

She experienced the next few moments as a jumble of disjunct but intersecting and simultaneous frames or planes. Movement and noise, but the movement and noise static somehow, contained, discrete, quantum. Her time dealt out to her like the faces on playing cards, like movie stills scattered across a blank floor.

The waiter had arrived with the food. Plates and glasses were being shifted. Toni was talking. Waves of heat from the hot platters. Veils of garlic steam.

Vigil's voice, echoing from somewhere in the mountains: "And so I quit the police department." Why was he singing? "Got myself a steady job."

Across the way, two levels down, she saw the vampire. His eyes met hers.

She jumped back like an affronted spider. Her plate clattered and settled where she had struck it. A small waterfall at the table's edge. She had knocked a glass over.

"Oops," Vigil was saying.

Toni's hand was on her forearm: "Jody, girl, what's the matter?"

She couldn't speak. She couldn't breathe.

The waiter was mopping up the water, and Toni had come around the table.

"Happens all the time," the waiter was saying.

"Is something stuck in your throat?" Toni said, sliding in beside her.

"Altitude sickness," the waiter said. "We see it every night."

The vampire came toward them. A movement that was not a movement, a fragmented movement like a bat's flight. Stepping between tables in a series of stop-action jumps, closer in each, larger in each. He was a tall man, very tall, taller even than Vigil.

"She lives here," Toni said angrily.

The vampire was at the booth, looking down at Jody.

I've come to get you, he said.

"It's him," she said.

"What's him?" Toni said.

The vampire wasn't at the booth. He had never *been* at the booth. He was down in the foyer among the people waiting for tables, paying his bill. He was selecting a toothpick.

Jody was able to point. "It's the vampire," she said.

"Who, the big guy?" Jody could only nod.

"Tall and mysterious," Toni said. "But I don't see any fangs."

"The vampire in my dream," Jody said.

"Now *this* sounds like a story," Toni said.

So Jody told them. She told them about skating in the arroyo, and seeing the aqueduct, and remembering the man standing there in the midnight snow. This was the same man, she was sure of that. She must have gotten a better look at him in the arroyo than she had thought, because his face was exactly the vampire's face.

"Yeah, honey, but there ain't really vampires," Toni said.

"Don't be so sure," Vigil said.

"I know," Jody said. "It's just the dream was so strong."

"He's not stalking you, is he?" Vigil said. "You want me to go after him?"

"No," Jody said. "No. He's not stalking me. I'm overreacting. There was no way he could have known I was going to go skiing that night, and I haven't seen him since. Till now."

"Still, it was weird, him being in the arroyo," Toni said. "What was he doing there?"

"Yeah, but you could have said the same thing about me," Jody said.

She told them about figuring her dream out, how the vampire had really been Freud, and had represented her fear of accomplishment, but had borrowed the face of the man in the aqueduct, the last man who had frightened her. She watched Toni's face change as she talked, watched the expression of withdrawal and consideration settle over it. She could tell Toni was dubious. This was professional territory, the interpretation of dreams. No arena for amateurs. Jody had no business interpreting her own dreams. What did she know?

Jody didn't care how Toni felt. She wasn't talking to convince Toni, she was talking to silence her fears, talking to reconstruct normality. If she kept up a steady flow of narrative, of explanation, she could restore the ordinary world, the safe world. The world that meant less than its signs and omens, and not more. The world you could count on.

"You been carrying on a pretty vivid interior life," Toni said finally, noncommittal.

"You guys must think I'm really flaking." Jody tried a rueful laugh. She spoke to Vigil: "I make a hell of a first impression, don't I—"

"Vic," he said. "Go ahead and call me Vic. Did you see your hands?"

"What?"

"In the skiing dream, the vampire dream. Did you see your hands?"

"Why?"

"That's how you take control of your dreams," he said. "You have to make a conscious effort to see your hands. Then you control the dream, the dream doesn't control you."

"Where do you get that stuff?" Toni said.

"Carlos Castaneda," Vigil said. "I think it was *Tales of Power,* but it might have been one of the others, I don't know for sure."

"You *buy* that business?"

"Don't knock it till you've tried it."

"I read one of those," Toni continued, surprising Jody. For all her wild sexuality, in college Toni had been the straightest of the straight. Never drinking too much, never staying up till all hours slinging the political and metaphysical bullshit, and never never never getting stoned. She had probably read the Castaneda as a duty, keeping tabs on what others were thinking.

"It was *boring.* This Carlos, he goes everywhere and Don Juan and

Don Genaro play tricks on him and he's always a clown and he never gets any smarter and supposedly he's working on being a sorcerer, but he never sorcerizes anything—"

"Sorcerizes?" Jody said.

"And they supposedly have all this magical understanding, but it never adds up. It never makes a complete picture. They just do more dumb tricks and have more dumb visions."

"It isn't supposed to add up," Vigil said. "If it adds up, that's the *tonal* talking, not the *nagual*. It's the experience that counts, not the explanation. You ever have a vision?"

"Yeah, I have a vision of you in the hot tub with no clothes on."

"Big dumb Indian cop not good for anything but sex, eh?"

"Don't get touchy. I thought you was dumb, you would've never got to first base."

Jody had the uncomfortable feeling she was causing their first quarrel. She didn't like the hardness in her friend's voice, the quick and reckless aggression. *I can live without you,* that tone said. Jody had heard it before, in her own arguments with Toni.

"Why don't we eat?" she said. "We've got all this food in front of us."

So they ate. Jody felt her endocrine levels return to normal, the world return to sanity. She hadn't been eating right, she hadn't been sleeping enough. It was that simple. She would be more attentive from here on out, take better care of herself.

They went to a safe topic, ex-mayor Jaramillo. How her temper and abuse of privilege and finger-pointing and buck-passing had at last come home to roost. How everybody had wanted Debbie out, even those, like Toni, who had voted for her in the last election.

And they relaxed as they talked. Jody could see the heat rekindling across the table. She could almost smell the pheromones. Her friends confidently awaited the night's entertainment. What matter their momentary quarrels? There was lovemaking to be done, there were great juicy delicious dripping couplings to be engaged in, and they were just the people for the job.

Jody hated them. She made her excuses early. Had to get back to the lab, you know. The second session, her session, started at ten. She was so eager to get out of there that she skipped dessert, which was a pisser, because she had really wanted that crème caramel. Toni and Vigil—Vic—walked her to her car. But clearly their minds were not on her. Clearly they were thinking ahead, to Ten Thousand Waves and to what lay beyond it.

The night was cold and clear. The stars sucked away all warmth. The brilliant and beautiful stars that never gave you a single thing, but that you couldn't live without.

Santa Fe was so much closer to the stars than the rest of America.

Toni hugged her good-bye. "You're coming by to see the folks, aren't you? Let's make a date. I'll talk to you Monday, at the office, we'll set up a time."

Vic made sure she was safe to drive. He had seen too many accidents, he said, to take any chances. Even with friends. He shook her hand good-bye. "Good to meet you at last. I'll give you a call, come check out your computer. Take care."

Jody got in the NSX, locked the doors. Waved good-bye.

They walked away, arm in arm.

Jody cranked the engine. It was early yet, but no way was she heading home before going back to the office. Let the babies stew. Ignore her, would they? She could play that game, too. This one night, the NSX would just have to take its chances on the street.

Before she put the car in gear, she checked to make sure she could see her hands.

She rode a motorcycle, jolting in a cloud of dust. The place was familiar, but strange. Yucca and tumbles of black stone and huge saguaros. She paused on an outcrop of the flat black rock, letting the cool air blow her dust away. A hawk called over the river. The Malpais, that was it, she was lost in the Arkansas Malpais.

The engine idled between her legs, throbbing like Blind Lemon in full purr. It was Blind Lemon. He was a motorcycle now.

He had to be, to help her get away.

The engine burned her through the leather. She saw the ragged holes it made, the raw circles where her thighs were blistering, mandalas of corrosion. But she couldn't stop now.

In the distance behind her, another plume of dust. The government. They were after her, a posse on a crowd of guttural motorcycles. She saw them leaping, black centaurs in a yellow and sunstruck smoke, jumping the hills, demons from sulfurous Hell.

They were hunting her, she was a spy, she had done something terribly wrong. *She gunned her motorcycle and sped off, but it was hopeless. She could never escape. They would never quit following her. Already her legs were burned so badly they would have to come off.*

The terrain battered her spine, jerked at her arms through the wheel. She was crying No help me please no *when the shots rang out.*

A tremendous impact in her spine.

Her bike shook her and bounced high in the air. She fell.

8 : game time

A week went by. Most of another. Toni was hardly to be seen, presumably busy with Vigil. Jody wasted the long Martin Luther King weekend working on her journal, brushing up on chaos math, going into the office to pore over the film, the recordings, the physical data.

She told herself it was relaxing to be able to work in the office when no one else was around. She told herself she wasn't lonely, it felt like freedom.

On weekends the dreamers stayed home, kept their dreams to themselves. Jody had originally planned to run the study on Saturday and Sunday nights, giving them Monday and Tuesday off, but they had rebelled. Apparently it didn't matter if your workday got messed up, if you were draggy on the job. The job sucked anyhow. But people were zealous about their time off. They wanted to feel good for their play.

Jody and Toni didn't keep the clinic open on Saturdays and Sundays, either, though they stayed on call: —*Doc, you gotta help me, I'm desperate and the warm milk's not working.*

By the last Saturday in January, she couldn't fool herself any longer. She knew she needed to break her routine. Woke up telling herself she was a free woman with two full days off. It freaked her. What do you do with yourself when there's nothing you *have* to do with yourself?

At first she thought she would take to the hills, do some cross-country up along Aspen Vista or maybe head the other way, into the Jemez, trek and ski McCauley Warm Springs, then head down into Jemez Springs for a cheeseburger. But then she thought maybe Victorio would call to come check out her computer. (Which of course he didn't.)

Then she fancied Static and Blind Lemon were withering from lack of attention. Their fur scruffy and unkempt, their appetites lacking. They slept all the time. Cats always sleep a lot, twice as much as people (which proves how smart they are), but she worried anyway.

So then she thought she'd go domestic. Stay home, love on the babies, do some cleaning. Work in the greenhouse, the yard. She had a load of stone that had been sitting there since October, time to get busy on the new walks and flower beds. Speaking of flowers, it was past time to set out the climbing roses along the back wall, her Christmas present from Toni.

When she got out of the shower, she noticed her toenails needed cutting.

It was one of those annoying details. Maintenance. You don't get around to your toenails all that often. Way down there on the end of your feet, you know, and you're busy. Till the big one on the right starts cutting into its neighbor toe when you skate.

So she sat down and did her nails. Only fifteen minutes, start to finish, but it drove her crazy. All the stuff you had to do before you did the main stuff. You wanted a cup of coffee after your shower, for example. But first you had to grind the beans. But even before that, because you kept the beans in the freezer, you had to thaw them in the microwave, so they would have more flavor and wouldn't damage the blades of the coffee grinder.

Some days you had to clean the grinder first, because it had gotten too dirty.

She caught herself drumming her fingers on the countertop while she waited for the wash water for the grinder to warm up in the microwave. She was warming the wash water in the microwave because it was wasteful to let the sink water run till it got hot. So there she was drumming her fingers and cussing under her breath while she waited.

Then she laughed. She gave herself a good talking-to. This was what time off was *for,* lingering over the details. A couple of weeks back she had been happy to think of the fractal density of people's lives. Well, that was also why it was so hard to make things happen the way you wanted them to. The universe resists our will precisely *because* it is so rich with life. Because the roots of all existence run so infinitely deep and are so infinitely tangled. Any small change changes everything. You know the saying: The air stirring from the wings of a butterfly in America today may cause hurricanes in China tomorrow.

Even the air stirring from the wings of a dream butterfly.

But it works the other way, too. Hard for the butterfly to move its wings because of the hurricanes involved. China is big number one and rough on butterflies.

After that, she was better. She had two cups of coffee. She puttered in the greenhouse, most of the time doing nothing more than wandering around carrying Blind Lemon asleep in her arms and thinking about which herbs she might want to set out this spring.

By midafternoon it was in the low sixties and sunny—another damn beautiful day in Santa Fe, how boring—and she decided to get after the roses. She dug four trenches along the back wall, twenty inches long by twelve wide and twelve deep. A lot more digging than you might think, her exercise for the day. She mixed the excavated soil with humus. She pruned the stems of the plantings back to within four inches of the node. She set the roots to soak in buckets of water.

A peculiar thing happened. There were windows in the walls between homes, barred openings. Now Mr. Whiney appeared at the window in the west wall. Waved. Said, in a neighborly voice, "Planting roses, I see. Good time for it."

She was so astonished she let the shovel drop. "Yes," she said. "Good weather for planting." She hated fighting, actually. Would defend herself and hers with all the ferocity at her command. But if the other person was willing to make the gesture—

Sunday it clouded up, threatened more snow. By then she was so relaxed she was perfectly useless. Spent most of the afternoon snoozing in the recliner, one cat at her foot, one at her head, interchangeably. Woke up once and realized it was the Super Bowl. Who the hell was in it? The Dallas Beefboys? The San Fernando Daffodil? The Boston Squid?

She wondered if Toni had gone to the party on Colonel Hall's card. Back in November the Alumni Club had reserved The Green Onion, a sports bar, for the Williams-Amherst game, on some sort of special channel. Toni had gone, Jody had skipped.

All those icons, symbols, portents. All that organized mania. For all her love of exercise, she had never been able to take football seriously. One of the reasons the romance with the high-school quarterback had never gotten off the ground.

But now here she was, watching the Super Bowl just like all her fellow Americans, a regular gal. Made her feel accepted, communal. Going to quit being a recluse. Going to develop a social life. Going to go into the kitchen and microwave a bowl of chicken noodle soup and bring it back to the chair. And bring the rest of that half-empty Kendall Jackson while I'm at it.

She turned the sound down, so that the announcers made only a low murmur, a soothing sonority not unlike Blind Lemon's purring. On the screen the little men formed their patterns, broke out of them, ran around, regathered. Static and Blind Lemon stretched, yawned, regathered. Jody finished her meal, set her plate and bowl on the floor. Drank wine from the bottle.

Jody fell asleep, woke up. The little men were running. One of them reached out his hands just as a tiny football came floating down. On the sidelines, people were jumping up and down. Somebody tore a cap off his head and flung it viciously to the ground.

She dozed again, woke again. Now Blind Lemon was at her head.

Somebody had lost, somebody had won. Big-bellied men in towels in a locker room were holding up their index fingers. Somebody had a microphone in somebody's face. She tried to get the names right. Give her some casual conversation, some chitchat for her new, relaxed life.

She was warm. She was happy. She fell asleep.

In the condo just off Canyon Road, Leonard was dressing to go out. The television showed big-bellied jubilant men in towels. A microphone hovered and traveled like a fly seeking where to lay its clutch. Toynbee sprawled on the sofa in his undershorts.

"Aren't you going to see the postgame? I must say it's far more interesting than that deadly scrimmage we just watched. Some of these fellows are rather nice."

"He'll be leaving the restaurant now," Leonard said. He opened a drawer, found a long thin knife, slipped it into his overcoat pocket. "Now is the best time."

"Oh, don't use that," Toynbee said. "Do take the gun." The knife was a good deal more risky. It demanded close work, there might be a scuffle. But his partner liked the close work, he knew. Felt it was more honest. And the knife was not traceable.

"We don't even know he's a counter-agent," he added.

"Let's hope he's *not*," Leonard said. "If he is, then the opposition is gonna know we know, and our little vacation in Santa Fe is *finito*. The big boys will take over." He patted his pocket to make doubly certain of the knife. "Don't wait up, Martha."

"Gin or vodka?" Toynbee said.

Leonard went through the door, leaned back in. Smiled. "Vodka," he said.

Several miles away, high in the hills off Hyde Park Road, a man sat in the private office of his 7,500-square-foot villa. On the television set in the far wall, towel-wrapped giants emoted and gestured in pantomime. The man was on the telephone, and had muted the sound.

The office—by design an interior room—was dark. The only light came from the flickering lives on the set in the wall. The man had swiveled his chair away from his desk, as if to watch the screen. If you had been standing just inside the door, all you would have seen of him would have been his head, silhouetted over the back of his chair. The hair was longish, but crisp and curly, and very light in color, blond or white, you couldn't quite tell in the darkness.

The man was listening. He listened a long time. Every so often, a message scrolled from right to left across the screen, like the local station's thunderstorm warnings: *Line check completed. Line secure. Commencing line check.*

The man said, "No."

He listened again.

Then he said, "Maybe so, Freddy, but you couldn't tell it by her demeanor. I don't think there's anything there. Nothing useful, anyway." He had a broad Southern accent. The way he said it, the word "there" had two syllables. "I have no idea what Benjamin thinks he's after. You don't suppose it's a feint, do you? Throw us off the track?"

He waited. He said, "I *know* you know Benjamin better than anybody else. I wasn't suggesting it was just a personal vendetta. Don't be so sensitive. You say Benjamin is dangerous, I don't argue. You say he has to be stopped, I don't argue. All I *am* saying, Think how it looks from this angle. Do you even know who he's got on the ground here? If anybody? No? Too bad. That might have told us something. I mean, if it was one of his top people—"

He waited, listening. Then he said, "I think you're wasting your time, but it's no skin off my nose. What do you mean, 'phase two intromission'?"

The way he said "time," it came out "tahm."

More listening, then: "Well, why the hell didn't you *say* 'break-in'? Do you want the same operatives? The Brit and the pretty boy? I'm not sure they're up to it. Yeah, yeah. You've used them for assassinations before. But killing is easy. Burglary's hard."

Pause. "Lord, no, do you take me for a complete idiot? For all they know, their instructions are coming from the other side of the moon. Even if the whole operation blows, nobody can possibly trace it back to us."

The door opened, and the man swiveled to face it. "Listen, Freddy," he said. "Got to go. I'll put the ah, *intromission* in play." He hung up, smiled at the woman standing just inside the room. Light from the hall fell across his tanned face, glinted off his spectacles. You could see that he wore a tux, and that his hair was indeed white.

The woman was copper-skinned, black-haired, spectacularly beautiful in a predatory way. She wore an evening gown, black and clinging, and apparently nothing under it.

"Howdy, love," the man said. "'Bout time for the host to make his entrance?"

"Yes," the woman said. "Your wife is expecting us."

The man and the woman walked down a long, well-lit hall. The hall doubled as a gallery, its *nichos* filled with pottery and sculpture, its walls hung with Navajo rugs and with paintings, including a couple of small Morans, a lesser O'Keeffe, several by various members of the Hurd clan, a John Meigs portrait of a naked sailor, and, incredibly, a Bierstadt.

At the end of the hall, they went down a broadening of masonry steps into a huge, circular room festooned with crepe and banners and full of people in evening dress. The room was sunken like a kiva, its waist-high rim mortared of thin stone, for all the world like one of the circles at Pueblo Bonito. Four big-screen TVs, live, sat on an eight-foot electronics rack in the center of the room, facing the points of the compass. Another Bierstadt, this one monumental, brooded high on the far wall, sunlight striking through mists on impossible snow-covered mountains.

In the general noise, a few of the nearer partygoers greeted the man and the woman with louder cries. Their group entered the crowd like spindrift entering a belly of creek water, revolving and slowing and gathering more driftage as it wanders across the pool.

On the perimeter of the room, at regular intervals, on pedestals of polished stone, were models of dwellings and architectural renderings of the dwellings. From the models, the dwellings seemed to be half in ruins, but the renderings were high technology all the way.

A stocky, white-haired woman in a black gown and silver-brocaded bolero jacket approached with her escort. The escort might have been a ski instructor—tanned, even in the middle of winter, lean, his brown hair pulled back in a ponytail. He was slightly drunk.

"Hello, dear," the white-haired woman said, kissing the host on his cheek. "Welcome to your party." She nodded to the dark woman, who inclined her head in return.

The white-haired woman's escort spoke: "This is a great party, Colonel. You should do it every Super Bowl." Then he looked abashed, as if he felt he had said too much.

The host was looking over his head, scanning the guests. His eyes found a striking woman in emerald-green silk, her teeth very white, her lips very red. *Archuleta,* he thought. *Antonia.* He understood what must have happened with his invitation.

He didn't know the woman's companion, a large and melodramatic Indian.

He wasn't comfortable depending on Leonard and Toynbee to be his eyes and ears. He was too much of a lone wolf. He needed to be on the scene himself. If Jody Nightwood wouldn't come to him, he would have to go to her. Again.

Freddy would have a fit if he found out, but Freddy was never going to find out.

Now the host was approached by a portly fellow with an expensive manicure and a glass of something dark in his left hand. "You've convinced me, Colonel," the man with the manicure said. "Come over here and let me show you the one I want."

9: the italian campaign

ello?
Hello, Center for Dream Control.
Yes, can you?

Yes?

Can you help me?

What's the problem, sir?

It's my neighbor.

Yessir.

My neighbor's dreams are shitting on my lawn.

Sir?

Do you have any idea what it's like, spending your Sundays cleaning up dreamshit?

Sir, do you wish to register a complaint?

Great huge Technicolor piles of steaming dreamshit, stinking up my backyard.

Sir, do you—

What about my kids?

Sir, I can send you Form 25-D.

They carry diseases, you know. Dreams carry diseases.

Sir, will you fill out the form if I send it to you?

Her dreams keep jumping my fences. What if my kids start having weird dreams? What are you going to do about it, tell me that? What are you going to do?

A man had been knifed to death downtown. It was all over the front page on Monday. An apparent mugging, his wallet and watch missing. It was one of those sad stories. He had come to town not three weeks before, an attaché for one of the scientists at the Institute. After leaving a Super Bowl party, no doubt happy and drunk and careless, he had met his fate at the hands of one of Santa Fe's poor misunderstood youths.

It was a misfortune for the victim, but a boon for everyone else, a tonic for the Monday blues, something to talk about. The Monday paper was usually thin, but today you had the headline story, and you had a review of all the assaults and muggings in the downtown area over the last five years, and you had a sidebar on the Santa Fe Institute and its work with complexity theory, from which you got the overwhelming impression that the work was very complex.

At the office, Toni and Jody and Consuela hashed it over, and agreed that the downtown was really getting dangerous, and agreed that it was a pity because it hadn't always been so. Jody made a note that she needed to interview someone at the Institute, find out more about complexity, see if it applied to her work. If her theory was ever going to be anything more than a pretty metaphor, she had to sharpen her mathematics. Toni made a date with Jody to come over to her parents' place the following Sunday. On Sunday, Jody wouldn't have to get back to her dreams, and so they could have dinner and a nice long visit.

Jody liked Vida and Allegra immensely. No doubt they had originally hoped she would persuade Toni away from men. There had been a lot of giggling and whispering on that first spring break visit to Santa Fe. Breakfast in bed, the works.

But even after they had resigned themselves to the fact that their beloved daughter wasn't doing it just to shock them, that she actually *liked* men, even after it had become clear that Jody was hetero and was just a friend, the mutual affection had remained.

Late in the week, Jody decided to call Bruno Sandoval. He hadn't asked for a follow-up appointment—she just wanted to know what had happened to him.

"This is Jody Nightwood," she said. "I'm calling for Bruno Sandoval."

The voice was guarded. "This is he."

"Mr. Sandoval, I'm sure you don't remember me."

"*Pero claro que la recuerdo.* You are the medical doctor *que me ayudó.* Who me, who me help so much. *¿Hay algún problema?*"

"No, no, *no hay problema.* I just, I just wondered. It isn't any of my business, but I wondered how you were doing. *Espero que todo va bien con usted.*"

"*¿Cómo? Ah. Sí. Va bien, va muy bien.*"

Eventually she pieced the story together.

He had indeed gone to the police. First he had gone to the old priest he so dreaded confessing to, the one who had never thought well of him. It had been doubly hard to bring himself to confess to the old priest, because Mr. Sandoval had not gone to mass for many seasons now. But after a good night's sleep—thanks to your medicine, my good doctor—he had summoned his courage and made his confession.

¡Hola! It developed that the old priest had gotten so very old—he was in his late eighties—that he did not even remember Bruno Sandoval, the boy. Nor had he been punitive or judgmental. He was so old, and he had persevered in his path so long, that now it seemed as though there was nothing left of him but the path itself. He had become his role.

The priest had shriven him, saying, "Now you must go to the authorities, my son." And this Bruno Sandoval had done, with a clear head and now a light heart, knowing that whatever might befall him, all was well between him and his God.

The police had taken his statement, but they had not seemed very interested. No one had come to them complaining of being shot at. No one had reported injuries from a motorcycle accident in that part of the county. No one had filed a damage report for a bullet-riddled motorcycle. They could take his statement, yes, but with no evidence of a crime, what else could they do? He could press the matter if he wished, and see if the courts were willing to put him in jail based on his own testimony, but why waste the state's money?

"No harm, no foul," the policeman who interviewed him had said, a large Anglo who had only been in the area for two years, but who had had twenty years of police experience in Chicago.

Finally, Bruno had been so insistent that the Anglo had gone with him to the scene. Bruno had shown him the rise, the window he had taken aim through, the rifle he had fired, even the empty cartridge casing. The cop had walked out to the rise, looked around. There were of course motorcycle tracks and and four-wheeler tracks everywhere, but there were no signs of a crash, no fragments from a wrecked motorcycle, no truck tracks where someone might have come in to haul away the disabled vehicle or its rider. There were no splashes of blood.

There was nothing, and finally Bruno Sandoval had understood that a miracle had occurred. Not only was he forgiven, but the act of sin itself had somehow been erased. It was one of those strange and inexplicable happenings, things that we might wonder about, but must finally shrug and accept. It was the grace of God, which so far surpasses our guilt that we continue to punish ourselves long after God himself has lost interest in punishing us. The world was full of such grace, if we only had eyes to see.

The cop had left, telling him the best thing to do was forget it, plainly believing that the whole incident had been a drunken hallucination. "From now on, don't mix guns and alcohol," he had said, unable to refrain from at least one coplike warning.

And since then, Bruno Sandoval had been full of a most wonderful clarity and happiness. "I have great joy," he explained. He expected to walk in that joy the rest of his life.

After that remark, there was a silence on the line, a silence that Jody didn't become aware of immediately. She was full of envy. She was thinking, *Why can't I have something like that?* Why couldn't she, by grace of her courage, blunder through into such happiness? She was willing to suffer as Sandoval had suffered, if there was a chance she could win through. But her life was a blind iteration of empty days, sameness unto sameness forever.

Sandoval cleared his throat. "Happiness desires the presence of those who understand," he said. "Besides those *oficiales*—the priest, the policeman—only you know the story of this thing. I would like to thank you by taking you to dinner. Saturday evening? Inn of the Anasazi?"

Jody was caught off guard. Before she could gather her wits, she had said yes. When she hung up, she thought to herself, *What the hell?* She didn't tell Toni.

Over the next couple of days she found her excitement rising. She was going out on a date! Then she would chide herself: *Don't be silly, girl. Get a grip. You're having dinner with a grateful old man you can hardly even talk to.*

It didn't matter. It wasn't *who* she was having a date with, it was the *fact* of having a date at all. It had been a long time. By Saturday morning she was giddy with preparation. Planning her outfit. Getting her hair cut. Shaving her legs, for crying out loud.

Pitiful, Jody. Scraping the bottom of the barrel, Jody.

The hell with you, she told herself. *I'm having a good time this evening.*

She put her diaphragm in before she left.

They met for cocktails in the hotel bar, Sandoval joining her in a dry Manhattan. She had always loved the architecture of the Inn, its combination of solidity and liveliness, antiquity and novelty. That night the restaurant outdid itself. The service was quiet, respectful. The scallops in blue corn meal were superb. A cold white Italian, she couldn't remember the name, with the appetizers. A magnificent French red with the main course. Her filet, *au poivre* and medium rare, was perfect, almost fell apart on her fork. She ate everything on her plate and three slices of buttered bread besides, and was still hungry. Chartreuse after dinner. A wedge of pavé for dessert, dark chocolate and denser than the core of the planet. Two espressos.

Bruno Sandoval was immaculate in a soft white linen shirt worn buttoned without a tie, a double-breasted Italian silk suit that probably dated from the seventies, a pair of boots that were even older but had been burnished to a fare-thee-well. She had imagined him a pensioner, a poor old man from the country. But the waiters were deferential as he deciphered her wishes, made all the orders himself. It felt uncommonly good to have someone else take care of things.

It seemed that he owned Sandoval Ski, just off San Francisco. Officially also the manager, though he didn't go in much anymore, leaving matters to his assistants.

"Sandoval Ski? That's you?" She hoped she didn't look as surprised as she felt.

He had developed a taste for the sport, he explained. In the mountains during the war. Then, when he had come back, he and his wife, God rest her soul, had maintained the family's little crafts store for a decade or so. But he had seen the future, and—

"I caught the wave," he smiled.

His English seemed better than he had allowed in his visit to her office, and she wondered now if he had been testing her, seeing what effort she had been willing to make. Or perhaps he was one of those people who veiled the true extent of their abilities. He had good

French, and a ready command of Italian. During the war, the sort of soldier he was, it had been necessary on occasion to seem a *compaesano*. He had been very well trained. Now, every spring, he went back. Florence usually, but sometimes Napoli, sometimes Lake Como.

Her French was acceptable, and she had minored in Italian for no good reason other than her love of the way it sounded—and perhaps because it was different, wasn't the usual French, Spanish, German, wasn't something you got in high school in Arkansas. She hadn't had much occasion to use her Italian since college, but once she got something she never lost it.

So they spoke, all evening, in that language, with occasional Gallic forays. Such irony that they might have spoken easily together in her office if they had only known. We might have gotten to know each other that much sooner, she said. But then this evening would not hold so many pleasures, he said, and she laughed again. She saw curious tourists throwing glances their way. Who were they, the unusual couple at the excellent table in the back? She was a foreign movie star, no doubt; he a producer, a famous director.

It was a pleasant feeling, more pleasant than actually being famous would have been. Sandoval told amusing vignettes from the war: The *nonna* who had mistaken him for a grandchild from another valley, who had insisted he come in while she prepared a huge feast and had invited the entire village to come meet her long-lost *nipote*, all culminating in a presentation from the *sindaco*, and all at a time when he had been supposed to fade back into the hills in preparation for his next mission. The pig that he and a *prostituta*—but no, that was not a fit *raccontino* for a lady, no, no matter how she begged, he could not tell her that one.

An occasional darkness shaded his eyes. There were moments when she could tell he was omitting details, skipping episodes. She was certain there were uglier stories he might have told, but they would not have been appropriate for the dinner table.

He was giving her World War II Lite.

He had not known her father, but that was no surprise. Her father had been infantry, it was unlikely he would have had dealings with special forces. But still they had been there, they had both been there, in a hard, violent world she could not imagine. It was quite a thought.

Outside, it was cold, though thank God the wind had stopped. She pulled her coat tighter. Sandoval insisted on walking her back to her car. That man who had been murdered, it had happened only a few streets from here. Such a pity. He remembered when Santa Fe had been a small and friendly community, you could walk the streets in utter safety.

His head barely cleared her shoulder, Jody outweighed him by at least fifteen pounds, she was strong enough to make pretzels out of rebar, but she felt strangely safer in his presence.

She had driven the Pontiac. Sandoval admired it greatly. "You have a reverence for old things, then," he said. He smiled, and his eyes glinted in the light from the streetlamp.

"I'll drive you to your car," she said.

At his car, he invited her to see his home. She had been hating the letdown, the sense that the evening was ending. "What the hell," she almost said, then caught herself, thinking that he would not like her customary profanity. "What—what a pleasant invitation," she stammered.

"It will be cold," he said. "But we will have a fire."

She delighted him by asking if he wanted to drive the Pontiac. She followed in his car, an old but well-kept Allante. It was the first time anyone else had driven the Pontiac since Pop was alive. Sandoval lived south and east of town—Buckman Road, a gravel road off that, a gravel road off that, and a long driveway winding up a piñon-covered hill.

He stopped in the driveway, walked back down to the gate. She got out and waited. When he came back up, his breath smoking, she said, "What's the matter?"

"*Nada.* Two men in a black car, behind us all the way. But they are gone now."

She felt a flash of anxiety. She remembered that Victorio had never come to check out her computer. "Do you think they were following us? But why?"

"No," Sandoval said, his voice rough with some indiscernible emotion, perhaps anger. "I do not think this. It is an old habit, to make certain I am not observed. A useless habit, in these times. I am sorry to have concerned you." He took his car the rest of the way, to park it in the carriage run, showed her a graveled visitors' parking area. His home, a territorial, seemed a part of the hillside, white in the darkness, secluded in tall old trees.

He joined her, led her up the steps to the portale and into the house through a set of double doors which had been carved, obviously enough, in Mexico in the previous century.

Inside, she saw the home was original adobe. Massive walls, rounded doorways, age-polished *vigas* running high overhead. It *was* cold. He led her to a sitting room, got her comfortable in a modern easy chair centered on a worn kilim, wrapped her in a woolen shawl. On the mantel was a row of photos in silver frames, boys and girls and young men and women, perhaps three or four children at different stages of their lives. One photograph, in the largest frame, of an older woman, more severe than pretty. Handsome, that was the word.

"Mi familia," he said. He took down the large photograph, looked at it, replaced it. *"Mi esposa. Se murió hace quince—quindici—años."*

He said not another word until he had tended to the necessities— a fire in the fireplace, Manhattans again for each of them. Then he held his glass to hers. *"Salud,"* he said.

"You have a lovely home." She meant it, but found it hard to say, hard to move her lips. She felt suddenly emptied of speech, of thought, of will.

"Mille grazie," he said.

They sat and watched the fire awhile. Neither of them spoke, and yet she was perfectly relaxed. She felt safer than she had felt in a long, long time. She kept drifting off, coming awake. The fifth or sixth time it happened, he was standing over her chair.

"Shall I drive you home?" he said. "Or I can prepare a bed for you."

"Nooo . . ." she said, slowly, sleepily. Her fingertips found the back of his hand. He curled her fingers in his, brought them to his other hand, held them gently.

"I don't mean to insult you," he said. "But—"

"No, no, non è un insulto. La voglio fare."

He assured her that he was free of disease, that it had been many years, since the death of his wife. But— She replied that she was pre- pared, that there would be no unwanted child.

In his huge bed, on crisp linen, under acres of downy comforter, she nuzzled into his chest. She did not want to be kissed, as if that were the greater intimacy, but brushed the hollow of his throat and shoulder with her lips. The smooth, dry leather of his skin was whis- pery, intoxicating. She could have sworn it smelled of mesquite.

She would not have thought the act could be dignified, but when he entered her, tears came to her eyes for the loveliness of it all, the ritual. Afterward, as he lay across her in his sleep, she was grateful for the lightness of his body, his bones like a shelter of small sticks.

I will never regret this, she thought. *I can't tell Toni. But I will never regret this.*

He was a luminous tent in which she fell asleep.

She woke alone in the big bed in full morning light. There was a fire in the hearth at the end of the room. She had hardly stirred when Sandoval came bustling in with a tray. A pot of hot, thick coffee, bacon, two poached eggs, a slab of whole-wheat toast, a bowl of steaming oatmeal filled with raisins and piñon nuts and dressed with brown sugar, butter, cream.

He sat beside her and drank coffee while she ate. "You understand," he said once. "*Capisci che,* this is *una sola volta.* I do not—I would not—*non mi permetto di più.*"

"*Shh, calmi,*" she said. She crunched a strip of bacon, licked her fingers. Swallowed a spoon of oatmeal. "This is a *very* good breakfast."

"*Hai un amico,*" he said.

10: codes and mysteries

Vida and Allegra had an enormous, sprawling villa on the northwest side of town, an ancient adobe manse, on several acres, that had been in Vida's family for generations. The address was not fashionable—it predated Santa Fe fashion—but that was all to the good.

Vida had been an only child, the last of the line. When she had taken up with Allegra, coming out of the closet back in a time when nobody came out of the closet, not even in Santa Fe, back in the late fifties, the remaining family had reacted admirably. They had been a family of love rather than rules. Instead of ostracizing Vida, instead of suing to take away her inheritance, they had come forward in full support, they had welcomed Allegra. And all of this they had done while assuming there would now be no progenitors, no heirs to carry on.

As indeed there had been no blood child. But again, they had welcomed Toni and she had been in her early days the darling of a grandmother and a scatter of great-aunts and -uncles, and for all intents and purposes she was, to them, the continuation of the line.

It was Allegra who had borne the child—tall, dark Allegra. Allegra who had made the ultimate sacrifice, who had gone in to lie down with a man. Allegra who had almost died in childbirth, and who as a result could never conceive again.

It was Vida who greeted Jody at the door, taking her arm in a powerful, delighted grip and leading her through the great entryway that was almost a courtyard itself: "Come on in, come on in." Not *bien-*

venidos or *buenas tardes* or even the overworked *mi casa*. Neither Vida nor Allegra ever used Spanish around Jody, though they must have spoken it with Toni when she was growing up. Jody guessed that it had not been the modern thing to do when they were young and rebellious, and that they had retained the habit of a vanished modernity.

Vida's gray-shot, red-brown hair was trimmed in a soft crewcut. She wore a tank top, and the sinews of her wide bare earth-brown shoulders were knotted and marbled and yet as smooth as a panther's. A vein ran along the biceps of each arm.

"God, you're pumped," Jody said. "What have you been *doing?*"

Vida led them down the wide familiar hall through the arches into the wide familiar tile-floored great room. Years ago the women had put in gargantuan skylights, and there were plants everywhere, so that the great room was even more like a courtyard than the entryway. A piñon fire crackled in the enormous fireplace in the far wall.

"I've been reading this *wonderful* book," Vida said, placing Jody on the leather sofa like a favorite doll. "It's there on the coffee table. Not for you types, but I think women generally could get a lot of good out of it. I'm going to make you a drink and go get the others. Allegra just had to show Toni the new rosebushes, not that they'll be *doing* anything for three or four months, but she's just put them in and you know how that woman is. Dry Manhattan?"

She was gone without waiting for answer. There were five books on the coffee table. A large picture book on whales, *The Random House Book of Roses, Sunset* magazine's *Southwestern Gardens Book,* J. D. Rider's new mystery, and a slender trade paperback with a glossy cardstock cover on which appeared a photo of a black woman in gym tights who was even leaner and meaner and more muscular than Flo Jo herself, and who was holding high over her head a tremendous barbell assembly and the words *Lifting for Lesbians.*

At the Flo Joid's feet ran the authors' names and a subtitle: *Twelve Steps to Defining Your Personhood Through Musculature.* Jody opened to the first chapter:

One: Lesbianism and Bodyhood

As an open and unafraid lesbian, you have made a lifestyle choice which sets you apart from those others who lead their lives of quiet desperateness. To be a lesbian is to elect your own personhood at every moment of every day, that is to assert your essential you-ness qua *you* against the backdrop of the vacuity of the roles created for us by male-dominated Western thought. Lesbians are therefore the only true existentialists, except in a way that Sartre, who only wrote about it, could only imagine.

But what does all of this have to do with weight training, which we shall redefine as Inertial Science, or IS, for very good reasons which will be enumerated later on?

Vida, Allegra, and Toni came through the arches and down into the room. Toni wore jeans and a denim shirt. Allegra wore black toreador pants, a long-sleeved black silk shirt with the tails out. Her long dark hair was tied up in a bun and she carried a lit cigarette in an ebony holder. Toni and Allegra were carrying clear flutes that Jody assumed contained martinis, not just because of the olives nested in the hollows of their stems but because she knew their habits, and Vida bore in her left hand a glass in which there rocked an inch of brown brilliant liquid that Jody was certain was Glendronach and in her right hand a tumblerful of ice with a twist and an amber liquid that Jody was equally certain was Jack Daniel's with a drop of Boissiere dry vermouth.

"Great book, huh?" Vida said, handing Jody her drink.

"Well," Jody said, turning the volume in her hands.

"We're going to be the first generation to live to a hundred and twenty," Vida said. "I feel sorry for these younger people, because we're not going to go away. The baby boomers have had it all and too bad if you don't like it because we're going to keep it all. Sit, everybody, *sit.*"

Allegra leaned back in the big recliner and Toni and Vida sat together on the short arm of the L of the sofa so that they could see Jody without turning.

"Fine," Allegra said. "Alienate our own children."

"Hell, they don't care, do you?" Her glance shifting from Allegra to Jody to Toni to Allegra again. "They've already *got* theirs."

"I hope you do live to a hundred and twenty," Jody said. "Both of you."

"Not if she doesn't quit those cigarettes," Vida said. The routine rebuke, voiced at the beginning of every evening and never repeated. Not really critique, since Vida had been with Allegra nearly forty years and she and everyone else who knew her knew that Allegra had quit smoking only once, when she was carrying Toni, anticipating the medical community by a full two decades, and had hated the forbearance and would never attempt it again.

"I don't see the point in living so long if I have to give up my Silk Cuts," Allegra said. "I don't see the point anyway. All this obscene dither about health. *What is the good in so long life?* It's hubris, that's what it is. We're losing sight of the natural rhythms." She gave Vida a look that Jody would have taken as supercilious dismissal if Jody hadn't seen the look so many times before and hadn't learned to see the desire, the adoration it veiled.

"Hubris this, baby," Vida said, making a muscle with her right arm and giving it a slap with her left hand, and round one was over with.

Jody gave Toni a lifted eyebrow and a shaped but not spoken syllable—*Vic?*—and Vida caught it and Toni said, "He had to work," and Vida laughed and said, "Oh, did you not know if we knew? Did you think she was afraid to tell us?"

She reached out and squeezed Toni's knee. "Whatever makes our baby happy."

"Well, I wouldn't say we didn't mind at *all,*" Allegra said.

"Well, we don't," Vida said. "We never mind any of her boy-toys."

"Well, he's apparently such a brute," Allegra said. "To hear her describe him."

"Oh, give me one of those cigarettes and hush," Toni said to Allegra, and Allegra tossed over the pack of Silk Cuts and her turquoise-enameled lighter and Toni took a cigarette out and lit it and tossed the lighter and the pack back to Allegra. These were the only times Jody had ever seen Toni smoke, around Allegra in the ancestral home.

"I bet he's attractive," Vida said. "I bet I would like him."

"You probably would," Allegra said. "Because you're such a brute yourself. Look at you, all muscles and knobs and rawhide."

Jody heard again in her voice the young girl's unlimited admiration and Vida said, "Yeah, and you just *hate* it, don't you?" and Toni blushed behind her cigarette smoke and crossed her legs because her parents were showing off sexually for her visitor again.

"She's really pumped," Jody said.

"I know, I know," Allegra said. "It's all I hear about. Pushing sixty, and I might as well be living with a teenager. Just no notion of aging gracefully."

"I leave all the grace to you, honeybun," Vida said. "Speaking of which, isn't the food ready? Haven't you guys finished your drinks yet? I'm hungry."

"That's the other thing," Allegra said, uncoiling languidly from her chair. "She's *hungry* all the time." She waited with Jody, and as Toni and Vida went out chattering before them and they followed, Allegra placed one hand lightly along Jody's spine and said in a gentle voice, "Toni told me about your burglary. Don't let it worry you too much. These things happen."

And Jody said, "No, I'm fine," and felt warmed and pleased by her concern, but as they went up the steps and down the hall and into the dining room, she found herself thinking, *What things happen?* What exactly *was* this thing that had happened, and *why* had it happened?

Out in the black car, Leonard was wearing earphones and holding the laser microphone as well as he could on the great room's streetward bank of windows.

"Shit," he said. "They're going in to eat."

Toynbee, also wearing a headset, said, "Can you get a fix on the dining room?"

"Not from here. And I'm not wandering around out in that sagebrush and setting off God knows what alarms. We're already conspicuous enough out here."

"It isn't sagebrush," Toynbee said. "It's piñon and chamisa and maybe mesquite. And Russian thistle. Did you know that was tumbleweed, that's its actual name. Russian thistle."

"I'm the fucking American here," Leonard said. "Don't tell me what's what in my own country. If I say it's sagebrush out there, it's fucking sagebrush out there."

Toynbee had to admit he was not the American here, although he was a citizen and had been one most of his life. He laughed and said, "Why don't we catch a bite while they do? *I'm* hungry. And then we can try again later. Maybe they'll return."

"Yeah, and maybe the reception on this sonofabitch will be better then. And maybe I'll turn into fucking Superman and say the hell with it and just use my super hearing."

"It's the equipment," Toynbee said. "Notoriously unreliable."

"Well, you always do all the tech stuff and I wanted to try."

"Not your *fault*, love, not your fault. I'm thinking rellenos from Dave's Not Here. Specialty of the house, as it were. Takeout if you prefer. Now—shall we dine?"

Vida had been reading an Italian cookbook and served prosciutto and then minestrone with hard rolls and then chicken parmigiano with linguine, and there was very little conversation as they fell to, because they all liked to eat and ate hungrily and rapidly, and Jody noticed that for all her raillery at Vida's expense and all her ethereal ways, Allegra's was not the least appetite at the table.

Then over sherry Vida began holding forth on her favorite book again, how it had changed her life and had been published locally by a co-op and was "selling like hotcakes all over Santa Fe," when Allegra, speaking to Jody, pointedly changed the subject.

"What's been happening with *you*, dear?"

Jody thought of Bruno Sandoval first, but she couldn't talk about that and she felt a regret that was almost a resentment at how something you *knew* privately to be a fine and healing and remarkable happening could yet take on the coloration of the sordid or reprehensible in the presence of the smallest awareness of how others might view it, and she thought of the burglary next, but felt a frisson of menace as always and as she had when Allegra with all good intentions had inquired, and felt also a powerful distaste for the subject, as one might not wish to discuss one's colostomy, however well adjusted one may have become to its existence.

And so she said, "Dreams, mostly, I guess."

"Oh, that's *right*," Allegra said. "You're running that study, aren't you? Toni mentioned it, but I haven't the least idea what you're actually *doing*. Tell us what that's all about."

"Have you read this book called *Lucid Dreaming?*" Vida began.

"It's about funding, mostly," Jody smiled. "This drug company, DormaVu—"

"Ah, and I know their nostrums well," Allegra said, drawing a hand theatrically across her brow. "Oft have they knit my raveled sleeve of care."

"Well, they're paying me to observe the effects of a new chemical on REM sleep. That's what they tell me, anyhow. I don't really know any more than you do, beyond that. I don't even know what's *in* the pill. All I know is they have FDA approval to test it on humans."

"I bet it's melatonin," Vida said. "Melatonin is wonderful stuff."

"No, I don't think it is," Jody said. "Maybe some kind of super melatonin."

"So what results are you getting? What effects does it have?" Allegra said.

"None so far. I suspect it's all somebody's double-blind test, and my group might not be getting anything at all. To tell the truth, what I'm really interested in is the nature of dreams, not DormaVu's silly protocols. I'm just using them for my own purposes."

"Isn't that cunning of you?" Allegra said. "Such manipulation."

"Yeah," Toni said. "There's hope for her yet."

"I had a doozy last night," Vida said. "It was all about this bear, and if you got close enough to him you could stroke him and burrow in his fur and be warm, but if you didn't, then he would kill you. I mean, you had to gather your nerve and move real quick."

"I don't dream," Allegra said languidly.

"Then we were in an airplane," Vida said.

"Everybody dreams," Jody said. "Some people just don't remember their dreams."

"How do you know that?" Allegra said. "I mean, how would you know for certain what goes on inside somebody else's head?"

"It had this glass bubble on the bottom, like on the old bombers."

"Ball turret," Toni said.

"Well, I don't, technically," Jody said. "Just like I can't prove that every apple falls to earth under the pull of gravity. I just know that everybody ever observed in a sleep lab shows an REM cycle, a rapid-eye-movement cycle, and that everybody ever awakened during an REM cycle reports dream activity. So it's an extrapolation, but a compelling one, wouldn't you say?"

"Very well, then, I don't *remember* my dreams. I don't *want* to remember my dreams. I don't see how they can do their work if I'm prying into them, watching them at it."

"And what work *is* that?" Jody said.

"But instead of machine guns they had these pasta makers," Vida said. "These nozzles that would shoot out fresh noodles all over the place. But only the bears could live down there, that's why we had them along, because the bubbles—"

"Turrets," Toni said.

"—turrets were full of water, and somehow the bears could breathe underwater—"

"That's the whole point, that's what I think I'm about to find out," Jody said.

"So what do you make of *that?*" Vida said.

"I should think that would be obvious," Toni said.

"I thought everyone knew already," Allegra said, with an air of faint surprise. "To work on our subconscious issues. All the dark stuff we can't stand to face. " 'I must lie down where all the ladders start,' " she quoted. " 'In the foul rag and bone shop of the heart.' "

"How?" Vida said.

"You're afraid you're going to give birth to a baby boy," Toni said. "And he'll grow up to be a man with hair on his back."

Jody wondered if Victorio had hair on his back. You wouldn't think so.

Vida laughed in huge merriment. "You're disgusting," she said.

"All our dreams are about sex, really," Allegra said. "Freud proved that."

Jody looked at Toni because she disagreed with Allegra and the look meant *I know you're the expert but I'm about to trespass on your territory,* and Toni gave a light wave of dismissal and the wave meant *Go ahead, you and I have been over this already,* and it meant *You can't think a professional difference would affect our friendship* and it meant *Yes, I am the expert and secure in my expertise and not in the least threatened by your amateur ideas.*

"Or to be more accurate," Toni said, "you're transferring your natural anxiety over the fact that I'm seeing a man again onto a suite of birth-anxiety images."

"No, he didn't," Jody said to Allegra. "What he really said was that all dreams are wish fulfillment. And I think he's wrong about that, too."

"I'll thank you not to sass your elders," Vida said, laughing this time not quite so heartily.

"That's what I said," Allegra said. "Wish fulfillment. Sex." And everybody laughed, and they were off and running with the interpretation of dreams.

Vida said that of course Freud was mistaken, everyone who knew anything knew better, that she herself was a Jungian and a member of a group that included Lena Bartula and other local artists and that met to *process* their dreams and Jody asked what she meant by *process* and after Vida's answer was still unclear on the concept except that it seemed to have something to do with applying mythical patterns to the events of your dreams and Allegra sighed and said that was the trouble with all the latter-day mystics, they were too grandiose and had no sense of irony and she herself could not feature a theory of dreams that did not include irony and Vida rolled her eyes and Jody said that she thought dreams often *were* ironic but that didn't mean they were susceptible of interpretation, that she herself had not read much Jung, the truth being of course that she had not read any, and Vida said, Oh you *must,* and Jody said that there was in her opinion an inherent fallacy in any system that treated dreams as codes for other realms than themselves, as encrypted messages, and Vida and Allegra looked puzzled at that and Toni asked, What about the fact that some dreams clearly *are* parables for psychological issues, and related a series of dreams she had had about giant serpents when she was coming into puberty, pythons and anacondas that would slither into bed with her whose bodies were warm and wet and not cold and scaly and Allegra and Vida were shocked because they had never known and Toni shrugged and said how was she supposed to have been able to tell them at the time?

Jody said she didn't know what about those dreams, but she still didn't believe that was the essence of dreams, what they were for, and Vida and Allegra said, Well, what *are* they for? and Jody felt the same old mute familiar frustration, the frustration she had felt when she had not been able to explain to Trey in high school why she would not have sex with him and to Chipper in college why she could not stop grieving for her father.

They had had enough of the sherry. Now they took big snifters of brandy and the bottle itself back into the great room and they continued with dreams. Jody said that she wasn't even sure there *was* a subconscious mind and Toni snorted with helpless laughter and almost choked on her brandy. Jody decided to push her advantage in the general good humor and said that perhaps the whole thing was a Victorian invention because after all they had had plenty of secrets to repress even from themselves. Toni shook her head, grinning at the utter depths of this folly, and Jody said that the trouble with looking always for the secret codes was that it made secrets appear to exist even if they did not, as for example all the new pitiful who supposedly remembered sexual abuse at the age of two or three or the millions who now recalled traveling on flying saucers and having experiments performed on them by leather-skinned aliens and could not now therefore hold a job or control their drinking and found their marriages falling hopelessly apart.

Out in the black car, Leonard, holding the laser microphone, said, "Shit, did you hear that?" and Toynbee, also wearing a headset, said, "I heard *something.*"

"Did you hear that shit about codes?" Leonard said.

"Yes, and the reference to experiments."

"She's a fucking sleeper. She fucking knows what's going on. I don't believe it. Benjamin must have planted her ten years ago."

"I see you've adopted my Benjamin notion," Toynbee said dryly.

"Just because it's handy," Leonard said, irritated. "I get tired of saying *the other side.*"

"I don't think she's a sleeper," Toynbee said. "I don't think she knows what's going on. You and *I* don't know what's going on."

"So what's your theory?"

"Don't have one. It could be anything. We aren't getting much context here, you know. There was that bit about alien spacecraft. What do you suppose, the agency's running secret telepathic communications with bug-eyed monsters via dreams? BEMs via REMs?"

"What about the Sandoval factor?" Leonard said.

"The Sandoval factor? You're talking like a bloody flick."

"We run him and he comes up intelligence. You saying that doesn't mean?"

"World War II intelligence," Toynbee said.

"Those are the guys who *started* it. He could still be operative. Those people don't dry up and blow away. They just get more and more invisible."

"Honestly, aren't you a tad paranoid? This is a small operation. Routine."

"If it's so routine, why are there other people in the field? If it's so routine, why did they tell us to take out those three counter-agents?"

"*Suspected* counter-agents, love. And I have the impression it's a convenience merely. Entirely unrelated. Just that they're here, and you're here, and why take chances?"

"This isn't routine," Leonard said. "This is big. Really big."

"In your dreams. We could swot up better gear if it were. But then, we wouldn't even *be* here if it were. They would have somebody else in place. Higher-ups. Double-aughts, if there were such things. Which would be a pity, because you and I wouldn't have—"

"Shhh!"

Vida said she wanted to hear more about what was going on with Jody's secret government experiments. Jody said they weren't government but private industry and they weren't secret and they weren't experiments but protocols which was a very different thing but now they had had seconds on the brandy and were not so serious and quit yakking theory and traded stories of their favorite dreams instead, flying dreams and sex dreams and just plain weird dreams, and they kept drinking brandy and the dreams got funnier and funnier, especially the one about Allegra with the long tail swinging on the monkey-vine and scratching under her armpits *oot-oot-oot*, until finally they couldn't laugh anymore and it was time for Jody to go home.

After they got back to their condo, Toynbee would find himself restless and vaguely depressed, as if something in the fabric of time itself had shifted toward the dark and the unpleasant. He would put on his heavy coat and leave his companion watching the tag-end of Leno with all the stupid jokes that weren't really jokes and the stupid conversations that weren't really conversations and wander over to Acequia Madre up past the elementary school and stand by the *acequia* in the dark listening to the sound of the water running. He would be visited by a flurry of snow, and the sound of the water falling always to darkness would seem perhaps a music that carried the story of the rest of his life if only he knew how to hear it.

At the door, Allegra said, "You know we love you, don't you?"

Jody hugged her tightly and felt the bony length of Allegra's body all up and down her own and felt a wash of emotion for this tall ironic skeleton and murmured into her shoulder, "Yes, Mama 'Llegra. I know. And I love you, too."

To her great surprise, Jody did not dream that night of bears or pythons or weightlifting, but of a mountain stream under shifting leaflight. She went down to the water and sat by it and listened and thought of nothing. And it seemed to mean nothing, and nothing else happened, but that was her dream all night long: the sound and the sight of water falling always away.

11: white male poetics

As if from an overdose of sociability, Toni and Jody had little to say to each other over the next few weeks, but went about their business and met their appointments and nodded to each other as they passed. Valentine's Day came and went and Jody gave a box of chocolates and a card each to Static and Blind Lemon, but she had to read the cards aloud because they couldn't read, and then they wouldn't eat the chocolates, so she had to start on them herself as well.

And she cried a little, too, if the truth be known.

She wished there were someone who knew her well enough to give her the little pastel sugar hearts with the messages on them that you used to get in grade school. They tasted terrible, sulfurous somehow, but just on that particular day she would rather have had a handful of those from a sweet attentive male friend than a diamond on a golden chain.

Then, just before the end of the month, Toni invited her to a poetry reading.

Toni had inherited Allegra's bent for the arts, but in Toni's case the inclination had taken a turn toward the most stark and skeletal of latter-day abstraction. She was the only person Jody knew who actually *listened* to John Cage, and Jody had spent more than a few footsore hours standing around in galleries while Toni stared deeply into the void and flat and severities of constructions with labels such as *Untitled*

#13, or *hmm*ed and meditated in the presence of monumental and repetitive stacks of chiseled stone or welded metal.

Jody had never been to a poetry reading with Toni—or to poetry readings at all, for that matter, not since she had left college. What if there were poems as insectoid and forbidding as Toni's favorite paintings and sculptures? Also, if Vic was going, Jody would be in the way, and would feel like the sick relative or the visiting old-maid aunt.

Before she could say thanks but no thanks, Toni observed that the reading would be a good place to meet men. In Santa Fe, as perhaps nowhere else in America except an enclave or two in New York and San Francisco, this was in fact true.

Jody had found herself, ever since the evening with Bruno Sandoval, possessed by an incredible appetite for the touch, the taste, the sound, the presence of a man, all the more ferocious because it had been so long repressed. It was like coming alive again after a dream of being dead.

She was hungry, she was on the prowl, she didn't want to pick up some loser in a bar, she had no date for the weekend or any prospects for a date for the weekend, and she said yes.

The reading was on Saturday, 7:30 p.m., at the Betts Gallery, downtown.

Saturday morning, Victorio called at the office to say he could examine her computer if she still wanted him to, surprising Jody, who had almost forgotten. He was sorry it had taken so long to get to, but he had had unbreakable appointments the last two weekends.

In the interests of being sparkly at the reading—just in case, just on the one-in-a-million chance she actually *would* encounter a presentable male of the species—she had been planning to go straight home and rip a few matutinal z's. And so she almost begged off, but then thought, *Follow-through, follow-through.* It was perhaps the strongest principle of her life. She had a second cup of coffee while she was waiting for Victorio, and wondered how it would be to have him in her private domain, if there would be a dangerous sexual electricity.

She dressed demurely, in jeans and a sweatshirt, not so much to defray any possible interest on Victorio's part, but as a message to herself. Then when he came, there was no tension at all, no galvanic buildup as of opposed capacitors. He was large, he was courteous, he was official. She realized that he must be able to moderate that part of his being, that he was not carried along helpless in the charge of his masculine vitality as most were who had the vitality at all, but held it under conscious control, held it as Zeus might handle his thunderbolts, and would not release those energies when it was not appropriate to do so.

She knew this must be the case because she had at the moment no such control herself. And she saw that Victorio might be a rare sort of man, the sort that a woman could come to for the rush of power, but with whom she would not be at risk. The sort a woman might think seriously of staying with. She understood Toni's affection, then, and was glad for her.

Victorio dusted the keyboard and Jody's back door for fingerprints, explaining that he was not very good at the task but that this was not an official police visit, and there was no way he could call out a forensic team for such a tiny unprovable matter. He took photos of the results, and took her prints for comparison and explained that the likelihood was very small that he would find anything usable and that even if he did the likelihood was much smaller that the usable prints would belong to anyone whose prints were on file anywhere in anyone's system.

He booted up the computer and looked at the file data lines as though he might gather some information from looking at them that he could not from her description, and he asked her questions about the morning she had discovered the intrusion and what she had done and how she had come to notice the discrepancies and whether she had noticed anything else unusual.

She said she supposed she would see him at the poetry reading with them that night, and he laughed aloud and said, Poetry? Me? Are you kidding? The first flash of personality she had seen from him all that morning. He asked her if she had had any dreams about the burglary, and she said, a little surprised, No. Too bad, he said, because that could have helped us.

How do you mean? she said. Like I had noticed something but wasn't aware of it but my dreams were bringing it up out of my subconscious mind?

No, he said. Like maybe you went in your dreams and saw the people who did it. Went back and watched it happen, you know. That sort of thing.

I don't believe dreams do that, she said.

How do you know? he said. Have you ever tried?

No, she said. But—

She felt discounted, as if he were saying her research was trivial, a waste of time. She thought of flying, of walking through walls. Of traveling to the past and meeting your earlier self. If dreams did that, she said, if you could do that in dreams, life would be—different.

Yeah, he said, scribbling notes to himself. It would be.

He finished his notes and went, telling her not to worry, so of course she worried, if only for a little while. For one thing, she remembered that he had spoken of the *people* who had burglarized her, not the *person* who had, and she wondered how he knew.

Then she went for a run, the length of the arroyo trail and back and then a loop down Yucca and back up Ponderosa and a block along Camino Chueco and back up through Los Cedros and down through Rancho Siringo Court and onto the trail and back home.

Got to buff up if you're planning to go hunting a man.

Jody got to the gallery right at seven-thirty, parked in the lot held in common by Betts and its next-door neighbor, the Riva Yares Gallery. She was a little surprised to find a space so easily, had thought she might have to park at the office and walk over. But tourism had fallen off in the last couple of years, and even though the snowpack was good, there weren't as many skiers.

She'd never been in the Betts Gallery. The reading was to be held in the large center room, apparently, because it was full of folding chairs and maybe seventy-five people sitting or standing around and chatting. No one seemed to be in a hurry to start.

Jody scanned the room, but saw only a scattering of Santa Fe types: willowy, sincere-looking six-footers with ponytails and sometimes beards and the studiously pale complexions of those who neither eat meat nor expose themselves to the harmful eye of the sun; shorter, dark, wiry, curly-headed fellows with rings in their ears and the dress and sexuality and attitude of flamenco dancers; lean weathered cowboys in jeans and battered boots who might be architects or archaeologists or water witches or almost anything else; a few Indians of various heights, who wore jeans and battered boots and had big bellies and even bigger muscles.

None of them interested her. Actually there were a couple of men who stood out, both wearing slacks and sport jackets, uncommon in this town. But she couldn't catch their eyes, and after watching them awhile, she felt pretty sure they were a couple anyhow.

She felt suddenly tired. From her longer-than-usual run, probably, and the fact she hadn't eaten since breakfast. Toni had saved a seat, close to the front, and Jody went and sat and they leaned together, not talking, while Jody looked over her program. There was an intermission after the first two readers. The program blurred in front of her eyes, and Jody hoped she wouldn't fall asleep. Poetry. Coming here had been a mistake.

At the microphone, a snowy-haired dandy of a man, with a leather vest and a posture so erect he looked like a large and querulous pigeon, cleared his throat. He cleared it several times, until the room quietened, and people began to find their seats. He had a lot to say, and he said it very slowly and with much vibrato, and Jody's mind wandered. She got the impression that he was solely responsible for the event, in fact for most of the poetry in New Mexico. He was much concerned about inclusion, but Jody couldn't tell who he thought had been excluded, other than the fact that some people taught poetry in college and this was a very very bad thing.

He introduced the first reader finally, a pleasant, gray-haired woman. Everybody in the room seemed to know her, judging from the calls and applause and whistles, and Jody felt alone and excluded. Then she heard Toni snort with disdain, and relaxed.

The woman suffered a lot with her husband, whose chief flaw seemed to be that he was a man, but because the woman was kind and tolerant and had a good deal of Earth Mother in her, she loved him and forgave him and they made a good thing out of all the pain.

Then the woman had a lover, and Jody thought it was about time, with a husband like that, but the poem was confusing, because it was all over the map. Sometimes she was meeting the lover in the mountains, sometimes in the desert. Sometimes in the middle of the city. They seemed to get together especially often at sunrise and sunset. Then Jody got it. It was all a metaphor. The "lover" was the light in New Mexico. The poem was about how the light came to you and made you happy no matter how bad your life was at any particular moment.

"Well, I *liked* that one," she said, and Toni snorted again. She could be really pretentious at times. Jody wondered why Toni had even bothered to come, if she hated the stuff so much.

The next reader stood up, after a fulsome introduction by the overly groomed man in the leather vest. She was Indian, and stunningly dressed in soft leathers, a beaded headband, and multicolored

Western boots that must have cost the better part of a thousand dollars. Her hair was long and glossy black, hanging free except for the band. She was beautiful in the way that a panther is beautiful. Some men liked that, Jody knew, but she couldn't imagine why. Her name was familiar, Tanya Littlefeather, but Jody couldn't place it.

The audience appeared to know her as well as they had known the gray-haired woman, but this time there were no calls and whistles. Rather, after a long and respectful applause, a reverential hush settled over the room, which was a good thing, because the woman's voice, though crisp and authoritative, was so low she could hardly be heard. She told them she was only going to read one poem, but that it had several sections.

"One," she said, and began.

Along about section three, Jody's head took a sudden wobble on her neck. She sat up straight, and she heard Toni giggling beside her. She gave Toni an elbow.

"Five," Tanya Littlefeather said. As nearly as Jody could tell, the poem was about how terrible white people were and how wonderful and natural Indian people were. White people had invented uranium, for one thing. They stole all the land and killed all the fish in the rivers and they lived in their heads instead of their hearts and they watched television and ate money for breakfast. Jody knew all this already and she was feeling bored. She was also feeling a little ill at ease. Was it right to sit there and let yourself be insulted, even if the insults were true? Wouldn't it be more honest to stand up and walk out of the room? She glanced around and saw that most of the white people in the audience appeared grateful to discover how terrible they were. They were leaning forward on their chairs. Perhaps if they heard enough about how terrible they were, they wouldn't really be white people anymore, they would be honorary people of color.

Jody's head took another dive, and she came out of it to hear the reader saying "Fourteen."

Fourteen had two and seven as prime factors. Fourteen squared was one hundred ninety-six. February the fourteenth, let its memory be cursed forever, had been Valentine's Day. Chipper's best friend's dorm room had been number fourteen.

She was getting the hell out of here at the intermission. She would make her excuses to Toni, and hope Toni didn't mind too much, but she was getting the hell out.

Incredibly, the poem came to an end. The last section, seventeen, seemed much the same as the beginning sections, and the woman's voice did not vary, but she stopped reading and the audience began applauding. The two men in sport jackets practically ran from the room, pushing their way out while the applause was still going on. Jody imagined they were in a hurry to get home and make love. She wished she were in a hurry to get home and make love.

After the applause stopped, she fought her way to the wine table. She was leaving, but by God they owed her a glass of wine, at least.

A plastic glass of generic white. She leaned in a corner, watching people. Toni had not moved from her seat. The sincere ponytails were having mineral water. The flamenco dancers were having red. The Indians and cowboys were having beer.

The vampire had a glass of white in one hand and a glass of red in the other.

He must have come in after she had seated herself. He was six foot six at least, towering over everyone in the room. He carried himself like a man, she thought, though she could not have said exactly what she meant. Something about his unselfconscious saunter, the easy confidence of his presence. He didn't stoop, but he didn't loom and intimidate either.

He had curly black hair, green eyes, a fine nose, a good lean jaw. Great lips.

Jody looked to see who he was taking the extra glass of wine to, but as she watched he tossed down first the glass of white and then the glass of red. His eyes met hers. A shock went through her. She saw her earlier paranoia in a new light. It had been response, simple as that. Physical response transformed into fear and menace because of the situation.

Enough of this. How many times before she got the idea?

The man in the leather vest was clearing his throat again. Jody marched up to the vampire. He nodded hello, as if they were old friends. "You and I have to talk," she said. "After the reading." She went and sat down without looking back to see his reaction.

Jody was breathing hard. She would have liked a little whispered talk with Toni, but Toni wasn't looking her way. Toni could be as stolid as a stone Buddha sometimes, and she definitely had her own agenda tonight. Now she said, "This guy is the whole reason I came."

A very handsome blond man stood up, blue-eyed, slender, about five-ten. "Does he remind you of Paul Newman?" Toni said. "A young Paul Newman?"

Jody had missed the introduction, but her program told her the man was from Manhattan and was widely considered to be one of the best of the "language poets" and had recently won a MacArthur and a Guggenheim and the American Book Award.

Jody was puzzled. Didn't *all* poets use language?

In the black car, heading home, one of the men in sport jackets—Toynbee, who was the passenger this time—said, *"Gruss Gott,* I'm glad to be out of there."

The other man in a sport jacket, Leonard, driving, said, "You like art so much, I would have thought that was your cup of tea."

"That's what I could use, actually. A cup of tea. Lord, no. *That* wasn't art. Or maybe it was, I don't know. Poetry's not my strong point."

"I can't wait to get my hands on your strong point."

"You drive, you."

"You don't think she made us, do you? She was watching us pretty closely for a while."

"I think she was just feeling what I was feeling," Toynbee said. "That you're an awfully pretty lad with a lot of possibilities. The bitch."

"Anyway," Leonard said, "it was pretty obvious she wasn't making any contacts. She was there with the girlfriend. Unless the girlfriend *is* the contact?"

"No, no," Toynbee said. "The girlfriend's an innocent. If they thought there was any chance she was one of Benjamin's, she would have been on your kill list with the other three. Speaking of which. I don't want to butt into your business, but."

"But."

"The next victim. The third of the possible agents. Don't you think the knife would be a bit much? I mean, to use again? We don't want them seeing a pattern."

"Yeah, I thought of that already. Have to be a gun this time."

The blond man said how honored he was to be here. He said he made frequent trips to the Southwest to recharge his spiritual batteries, and in a way felt he was more truly at home here than in Manhattan, if they would have him. There was a smattering of applause. He was the star of the evening, but he was being modest about it. He said that it was presumptuous for a white male to read his work in such a venue, his kind having dominated world culture for so long. He joked that at least he wasn't a dead white male. There was a pause while the man in the leather vest and a helper passed out sheets of paper, which the poet explained were transcripts of what he would read. He cautioned that his reading would merely be an interpretation of what was on the paper, and that they should feel free to make up their own interpretations as they went.

Jody scanned the handout. The sheets of paper were covered with consonants. Sometimes the consonants were capitalized and sometimes not. Sometimes they were broken up into word-sized blocks, and sometimes they ran on conjoined for half a page.

The man began his performance. He bellowed like a bull, then he crowed like a chicken. Jody checked the consonants, but she couldn't see how they corresponded to the sounds. Then the man was silent for a while, and then he began trembling with emotion and broke down in tears and suddenly he laughed, and that was the first poem. The audience applauded loudly.

The next poem was an argument between a man and a woman, in which the poet took both sides. The man and the woman spoke not in words, but in rushes of intoned nonsense. Then they became opponents on a battlefield and shot each other dead and there was a nuclear explosion.

Jody jabbed Toni. She wanted to know if this was really *poetry*. Was there a trick that let you understand it? Did she really have to take it seriously? Toni waved her to silence.

There was a poem that was all chanting, like a Buddhist mantra, except that it then became like Indian chanting. There was a poem that appeared to be an epileptic seizure, and in which an ambulance came and took the victim away and buried him alive.

Jody didn't care what Toni thought anymore. She was having trouble keeping from laughing aloud. She wondered why she was bothering to keep from it, since after all that would be her interpretation, wouldn't it, and by his own rules just as good as the poet's?

She busied herself imagining what might happen with the vampire later. She spun disgraceful lascivious fantasies, which, however, all ended in a long and happy marriage. Suddenly the reading was over, to thunderous applause, a standing ovation.

Free at last, thank God almighty, I'm free at last!

But the audience was sitting back down for a Q-and-A. "Toni, I've got to go," Jody whispered. "I think I've met a guy. You want to come with us?"

Toni shook her head, her eyes on the poet. "I want to hear this," she said. "You go on." There was a grim set to her jaw, and Jody realized something was wrong, had been wrong all evening. She hesitated, but if Toni wanted to talk, Toni would talk, and if Toni didn't want to talk, red-hot needles under her fingernails wouldn't avail. Jody stood and worked her way free, feeling or imagining the disapproval of the crowd.

Behind her a questioner had stood: "I just want to say that I was impressed with the absence of the usual white Anglo male bias in your work, and I wanted to know how intentional that was, I mean if you were aware—"

"Absolutely," the poet said. "We all know by now how language totally conditions your perception. If you want to defeat the anti-feminine, anti-intuitive brainwashing inherent in the use of English itself, you are forced to abandon the conventional Eurocentric letter groupings. It isn't enough just to deconstruct *theme*, you see. If you want to counter the authoritarianism implicit in the semiotic devices, you literally have to deconstruct *the words themselves* . . ."

The vampire—she *had* to quit thinking of him that way—was waiting in the outer chamber, grinning and shaking his head as he listened.

"I have to know your name," she said.

"Shade," the man said. "John Shade." He spoke with a rich Scottish brogue, and Jody thought he was making a joke somehow, but she didn't get it. "And yours?"

"Jody Nightwood," she said. "Josephine Deborah, actually, but nobody calls me that. I've gone by Jody since I was in high school. Jo D., for—" She felt she was chattering, too much unsolicited information, and shut herself down.

"Nightwood and Shade," the man said. "There's a dark pairing." Still with the brogue.

"That's what I want to talk to you about. Pairing."

"I thought as much."

"But I could use a drink. And something to eat for that matter."

"May I suggest the Palace? It's convenient, it's quiet, and it's—"

"I know the place."

"Of course you do."

"No, I mean it's one of my favorites, that's a great idea. Lead on, Macduff."

She might have noticed, but didn't, that the Scots burr vanished from his voice after the Macduff remark. He helped her with her coat, shrugged into his, and they were outside, taking the shortcut through the alley. There had been another knifing, another newcomer in town, this one a woman, but with Shade beside her, Jody was fairly certain she had nothing to fear.

They sat at the bar, Shade saying he wasn't hungry, and Jody saying she felt like eating there rather than at one of the tables. This really was one of her favorite places, dark and elegant and quiet, as a bar should be. The piano player was good but not overpowering.

"I like a bar where you can talk," she said.

"More like a club, less like a meat market," he said. "Me too. Or where you can just drink and not have to say anything."

"Well," she said.

"Well," he said. Their drinks came, her dry Manhattan, his Wild Turkey 101, rocks only.

"So what the hell were you doing in that arroyo?" she said.

"I wondered if you remembered."

"Of course I remembered. You scared the shit out of me."

"Sorry about that. I was taking a walk, that's all. I'm a country boy at heart, and down in the arroyo you can more or less forget you're in the city. I've even seen coyotes. Last thing I expected was to see somebody else out there that time of night in that kind of weather."

"So you remembered me too. I was all bundled up."

"Not much mistaking that profile. Those eyes."

"Green to green," she said, deflecting the compliment.

"Rare," he said. "And your hair was out. You were wearing that weird cap—"

"That was my father's hunting cap!"

"But it didn't cover all of your hair."

"So we made an impression on each other," she said. Tell him about the vampire dream? No, not now. Later, when they knew each other better. Laughing together on the bearskin rug in front of the fireplace, after making love. Sipping their champagne.

"I don't even *have* a bearskin rug," she said out loud, and he laughed, and she colored.

"Yes," he said. "Yes, I'd say an impression."

"It's funny it took me so long to figure it would turn out this way."

"That's how it is," he said.

She had the wonderful feeling that they were skipping all the bull-shit, all the preliminaries. Just talking about what *was,* instead of pretending to attitudes. She hadn't realized she hated the bullshit so much until she felt the exhilaration that came with being free of it. She couldn't remember the last man she'd met who was capable of this kind of talk. Maybe nobody, ever. Bruno Sandoval, dear Bruno. But he was a friend, not a lover, in spite of that one night.

"I write," he said, exactly on the beat. She'd been about to ask what he did, who he was, why he was in Santa Fe, but had been hesitating because the questions seemed so trite. "I'm one of those best-selling authors you've never heard of."

"I was wondering why you were at that reading."

"Well, that—I'm against that stuff, you know. The stuff the last guy did, I mean. I think it's a load of crap. A scam. Hilarious. But on the other hand, I had never read any of it nor heard any of it. And if you're going to hate something, shouldn't you learn what it's all about?"

"I'm sorry I don't know your books," she said.

"No reason you should. I'm one of those guys who write the grocery-store paperbacks. You know what I mean. They're embossed, and they've got a hole cut in the outside cover, and then there's a submarine or a Nazi swastika or a werewolf that shows through."

"I thought maybe you were a basketball player."

He laughed. "Yeah, the height thing. Actually, I'm a little short for the NBA. And height isn't enough. You gotta have the moves. Not that I *don't,* you understand. I coulda played. Just wasn't my *thing.*" He laughed again, did a Brando: "I coulda been a contenda."

"Do you sell a lot? I guess so, if you're a best-seller."

"I sell enough. Hundred fifty, two hundred fifty thousand. Not as much as some, less than others. I make a living. There must be a thousand of us. Let's get off this, it's boring."

"Do you write under your own name? What are your books about?"

"No, I don't," he said. "I use a pen name. Marcus Gandy."

"That's kind of dorky," she said.

He laughed. "Yeah, well. Haven't you ever noticed how many best-selling authors have dorky names? Besides, my *books* are dorky.

Give me a couple of hundred years, maybe I'll learn to be a good writer. Right now—I love the stuff, but I can't do it. No kidding, El Stinko."

"But they buy it," she said. "What are your books about?"

"They'd buy dogshit if you covered it in chocolate and told them everybody else liked it," he said. For the first time, he looked embarrassed. "I've got this series going. It's all about this secret agent, but he's a vampire. Think of the advantages. Mental control. You can't kill him. He can change shapes. Really more like a werewolf, but in my scheme vampires and werewolves are the same thing. It's stupid stuff, but the subject is hot, and I can't let go."

She was electrified. She had to tell him about the dream now, and she did. He seemed taken aback. "No," she said excitedly. "No, don't you see? It's great. I must have picked up one of your books sometime, seen your cover photo. And then when I saw you—"

"That's it," he said. "That's what happened, all right."

He wasn't looking at her, and he tossed back a fair slug of his drink. She thought he seemed angry somehow, and assumed it was because she hadn't bought the book, all she had done was pick it up in the grocery store and look at his picture and put it back.

So, if his feelings were hurt, too bad. She wasn't going to back off this honesty, this new way of doing things. "Don't you think the mind is fascinating?" she said. "I mean, the way a part of me remembered you but a part of me didn't, and you showed up in my dream?"

"So what do *you* do?" he said.

She told him the dream thing. She had it down to a shorthand by now. You could either do a long, terribly involved, and passionate explanation, which your listener soon got weary of, or you could do the shorthand, which allowed your listener to feign interest briefly but did not require real attention. She had the feeling that Shade might actually prefer the longer version—he kept trying to draw her out, get more information—but now she herself was too impatient to deliver it. She wanted to get on with this romance.

At first he pretended to be concerned that she was a mystic, a channeler, but she could tell he knew better, knew already she wasn't that sort. He had a rigorous mind, it developed, had once taken a degree in mathematics. Was doing research for his new thriller at the Santa Fe Institute, and without saying it in so many words, conveyed that he had the respect of some of the scientists he dealt with. He was no scientist himself, but he could understand them.

"This is *perfect*," she said. "I've been *needing* to talk to a mathematician. I know a fair amount of chaos theory, but not much about complexity. It seems to me there are powerful implications for dream theory. Dreams as an emergent property of sufficiently complex brains, for example." She watched his face, and he didn't blink at the terminology.

"That's what I'm really up to," she added. "Creating a new theory of dreams."

"Well, I hope your theory isn't dorky," he said.

She laughed. "Okay, I deserved that." Then she frowned. "It isn't, you know. I'm a damn good scientist. And my theory is for real."

"You don't indulge in false modesty, do you?" he said.

"No," she said. "I don't see the point. Do you?"

"No," he said. "Well, feel free to use my contacts at the Institute."

Her meal arrived, a huge order of *calamari fritti* and a salad. He picked at the calamari, with her permission. They had another round of drinks. They were near neighbors, a fact that sent her heart soaring with imagined and convenient delights. That was how he had come to be down there that night, he had a little place in Rancho Siringo that bordered right on the arroyo. He was just leasing while he looked around for a more permanent home, presumably something larger. He had met David Morrell at a conference, the author who had started the whole Rambo thing with his novel *First Blood*. Morrell, who was actually a pretty good writer, unlike Shade and the other grocery-store types, lived in Santa Fe now, and had recommended the town. One place was as good as another to Shade, who had no family, and so he had come.

The question was how to wrap things up, how to end the evening on the right note. They agreed to rendezvous at Shade's for nightcaps. Jody got exact directions, just where he was on the arroyo. He walked her back to the parking lot. She had this thing lately, men walking her to her car. It felt old-fashioned. It felt good.

Driving home, she felt a strange lassitude, not the excitement she would have expected. Everything seemed preordained, inevitable. Nothing to worry about, nothing to fear.

Shade let himself in. He didn't hit any switches, but moved through the little casita in darkness. He went straight back to the bedroom, picked up a telephone, punched a computer to life, its blue glow throwing his shadow huge and vague on the far wall.

The phone was jacked into the computer. Shade opened an address program, keyed in a name. The computer dialed the number, a rapid little melody of beeps and blips.

He waited while a computerized voice spoke. Then he keyed in another name. More beeps and blips. Another wait. A click. More beeps and blips.

Then the sudden vacuum of an open line.

Hello, Mother? he said. This is your beaming baby boy.

He laughed at his listener's response. I've met a woman, he said. What? No, she's nice. *Very* nice. And very intelligent. Definitely your type. I think she just might be the one. Yeah, real possibilities. Okay. Just thought you ought to know.

He hung up, killed the computer.

He put his hands to his temples, cradling his forehead as if it were coming apart and he had to hold the pieces together. *Shit,* he said. *Not again. Not again so soon.*

Then he walked slowly back through the house, turning on the lights.

Jody put the car in the garage, went in and petted the babies and checked their food and water, then walked the arroyo. Shade let her in his back door. His place was typical latter-day Santa Fe—*nichos* in the walls, a beamed ceiling in the tiny living room, open bar to the kitchenette, a corner fireplace. Pleasant in the way that such homes can be if they are uncluttered, if you have few possessions. There was a very expensive Two Grey Hills carpet on one wall.

He had made a piñon fire, and they leaned together on the sofa, staring into the flames and sipping their drinks. She had converted to his standard, 101 on the rocks. They seemed now not to have much to say to each other. The way she leaned back against his arm and shoulder might have been the way of a lover, or the way of a sister with a trusted brother.

He apologized for his silence, said he had a headache, and it was getting worse. She laughed, said *that* was a switch, and he laughed, a little painfully, and she felt guilty for making fun of his pain. He assured her it was okay. She said maybe he shouldn't be drinking. He said he had had a lot of these headaches, and drinking didn't make any difference. She asked if it was a migraine, said she was a doctor, and might be able to help. He said no, he knew what he needed to do. He said she helped just by being there. She said maybe she should leave. He said please don't, he hadn't been giving her an inside-out hint, he didn't work that way.

It was a good thing they had met tonight, he said, because he had to be out of town on business most of the next week, and who knew how much longer it would have taken them to get together? They set it up for drinks again, Friday afternoon at the Palace.

Maybe it would become their bar.

It wasn't a romantic subject, he said, but he thought he ought to tell her that he was disease-free. He wasn't promiscuous, and he hadn't had a relationship in a while, and he had himself checked regularly. But if and when the time came, he would happily wear a condom.

What do you mean, if? she said. She said it was up to him, wearing a condom. She was on the pill *and* wore a diaphragm when there was any chance of making whoopee.

At two o'clock she roused herself for the trek home. They had tacitly agreed it would not be tonight, and not just because of his headache. No doubt they would make love soon, but no reason to rush things. All the time in the world. This relationship was not going to be a driven, desperate, tumultuous thing, a boat helpless in the torn water of a violent sea.

This relationship was going to be a work of art.

second iteration:
the practice
of the night

There are four realities: the quotidian, or consensus
reality; the bureaucratic, including all governance,
spying, and statistics; the simulated, by which I mean
not only digital intelligence, but novels, dance,
poetry, film, and the figurative arts; and dreaming.
    So the question is—which does love belong to?

    —Loren Wingo

Dreams are the brain's virtual reality.

    —Loren Wingo, *The Works*

12: the center for dream control

He was there, at the console.

Of course he was.

He was always there at the console. He had to be there. They both had to be. They had to protect the people of Tierra Nueva. Bad dreams were flying in under the radar. Black planes, over the coast from the open sea, torpedo shapes sleeping under their long, swept-back wings.

What's your name? *she said.*

Call me Ish, *he said.*

It was a beautiful name, and her heart broke with love. She was so glad to have found him at last. He was explaining the console: When a dream comes in, we record it.

That was good. She had been worried about that. It was her first day on the job, and there were so many dreams. She had been worried they were lost, or forgotten. It was good to know that somebody was keeping track.

We keep track, *he said.* Nothing is ever lost.

This was too big an operation for one man. There had to be others involved. She could see them now, indistinct forms, ghosts almost, seated at individual workstations around the control room. One of them was Casper the Friendly Ghost.

Who are they? *she said.*

Set a dream to catch a dream, *he said.* We can't count on you waking people to do it. You don't understand. You're too distracted.

That made sense. That was a relief. The dreams could take care of themselves. You didn't have to do it for them. She noticed now that the antenna on

125

the console was a dreamcatcher. It rotated like a satellite dish. Pulling in dreams from all the distant galaxies.

When a dream comes in, we take a reading, *he said.* We decide what kind of dream it is. A flying dream, a naked dream, a sex dream.

What kind of dream is this, *she said.*

Can you see your hands, *he said.*

It was a test. She checked, and they were there. Very good. Everything was under control. Most people, their first day on the job, most people probably couldn't see their hands. She wanted to call her Pop and let him know. I'm finally lucid, Pop. I'm dreaming and I know I'm dreaming. I made it. Make sure you record this one, Pop.

Pop was dead, though. She couldn't call him. And anyway, he didn't do the recording, that was Lobo. Jody sobbed into her pillow. She needed to call Pop, let him know how depressed she was about his death. She would have to call him on the dreamphone. You could call out with it. You could call out to reality. You could even call out to the dead. Which made sense, because we were just their dreams anyway.

That was why they were trying to kill her, because she had invented the dreamphone. It made too many things possible. The Hate People would try to stop you. That's why they were invading Tierra Nueva. She had to warn Ish. She had to call him on the dreamphone and let him know. It was her fault, she had started the war.

But when she looked she couldn't find a telephone. There was a bright red one over in the corner, but it was on fire. It was under glass and on fire. It was glowing bright red and ringing, and smoke was coming out of the glass, but nobody would answer it. A guard stood beside it, shaking his head no. He was a bad guard, shadowy, with horns like the Minotaur. It was important not to see his face. That man didn't belong in this dream.

She was wandering down a corridor looking for a telephone, but all she could find were water fountains. She had to stop at each one, and she was getting tired of it. She couldn't get the water to go into her mouth. She was trying to explain, trying to talk into the water, but the people on the other end of the line kept saying What? I can't hear you. What?

Then she realized that she had to quit looking for telephones.

That was the problem. She was always looking for telephones, and what that did, that distracted you. You forgot you were dreaming, and you wandered away down the echoing halls and you lost your hands and you never came back.

She wanted to go back to the, to the machines. To the other place. The com-

puters, that was it. The computer lab. The Institute for Complex Dreams. Somebody there she wanted to see. But it was too late. When you were lost like this, you couldn't get back. You had to wake up.

No, that wasn't right. Not this time. This time was different. This was her *dream. She held her hands up in front of her face. They were still there. They were his hands, brown and strong and friendly. He took her face in his hands and kissed her. His lips were soft.*

What kind of dream is this? *she said.*

That's very good, *he said.* Most waking people would not have asked that.

Is this a sex dream, *she said.*

He studied the console. He considered the readouts. I'm afraid it is, *he said.*

That's okay with me, *she said.*

Yes, but what about this, *he said. He waved an enormous shiny erection in her face. A tangle of blond pubic hairs framing it, his lovely velvet scrotum below, its secret eggs.*

I want it, *she said.*

But I can't make love with a real person, *he said.* Monsters would result.

That was terrible. That couldn't be true. If that was true, it was a very bad law. She was going to vote against it in the next election. No, wait, they couldn't have the election until after the war. That's what the war was about, freedom of love between dream people and waking people.

What if your baby was half a dream? *he said.* What if it was a—

His head jumped forward at her, spreading its fangs—

SSSSNAKE?

Give me that thing, *she said.*

They floated in midair, coupled together, her legs around his narrow waist. Apparently they turned the gravity off at the space station when you made love.

No, *he said.* It turns itself off. Love turns it off.

So that's how you fly, she thought. She intended to remember that when she woke up.

He slid into her belly and stroked her. It was like lying down in a river, it was a tongue speaking her language. She watched the monitor on the console. I am your one true cock, the readout said. Suck me fuck me. She was a little worried about that. What if it got out to the papers? But it was okay, because she was Bianca. Bianca always did this in her dreams. Bianca always sucked and fucked in her dreams, and the newspapers didn't care.

Oh give it to me baby, *Bianca said.*

Joaquín bashed her ass into the electronics. He thumped her and bumped her and humped her and the circuit boards sparked and threatened. The cathodes received her like pillows, and the wiring enveloped her ass like blossoming ivy. What's happening? *she said.*

We're sending out fucking dreams, *he said.* People are so afraid of real fucking. Nobody in America knows what real fucking is anymore, so we have to smuggle it in. We have to send it out over the airwaves. That's why I've been waiting for you.

They were flying in low over the sea, the green sparkling sea. They were flying in under the radar. She could see him through his cockpit, just off her right wingtip. She saw that they carried dreams under their wings, dreams of all colors, and that the dreams were the same shape as the planes, and that there were little planes under the wings of the dreams.

They were counterattacking, good. About time they went on the offensive. Dreams can fight back, you assholes. Her plane was rumbling and shaking under her seat.

His radio voice crackled in her ears. I love you, *he said.* I want you to know I will always love you. *He was saying it because they were about to die. It was a suicide mission. They would be shot down in fragments. But there was no better thing to do with your life.*

You're my jet jockey, *she said.* You're my bulletin-board lover.

There's a problem, *he said. She could see his smile, unafraid of death.*

There always is, *she said.*

The neighbors have been complaining.

His voice on the radio was a different voice. She looked beside her, and it was Victorio, riding hard. He was naked and he wore warpaint, and she was naked and riding beside him.

I want my lover back, *she said, but no one could hear her over the thunder of the hooves. They were riding to escape the neighbors, who were hunting them down. They rode their horses across the desert, toward the distant mesa. They were riding fast, and the wind was in their faces, and they could see the snow on the mountains beyond the mesa.*

Victorio stood on the mesa, his arms uplifted, a giant form silhouetted against the rising sun. He wore white robes, and around his neck hung a golden rattlesnake, writhing and chattering. They were riding toward Victorio, she and the man beside her.

When do I get my lover back? *she said.*

The man beside her was a ghost, Casper the Friendly Ghost, but grown up.

When he spoke his voice came over the radio, crackling. He's dead, *he said.* He died in the plane crash.

Her heart was sick, there was no point in living, but she had to keep riding. She was riding alone, and the sea was chasing her up the valley, the waters had risen, the earth was in flood. It was a luminous jade sea shot with blues and blue-greens, beautiful. Its waves gleamed and sparkled, and were complicated by smaller waves and those by even smaller. She rode hard, and the sea was a wall of water behind her, gathering speed and about to tumble.

13: dream lover

She woke up profoundly depressed, couldn't figure why.

After all, she had met a man at last.

And she had her work, her home, her cars, plenty of money. And most of all her babies. Oh my God, what if Shade didn't like cats? She hadn't even *mentioned* them.

Speaking of Shade: Was it because he was out of town the whole week, and she was on hold? Thinking maybe she had imagined it all, it would never really happen? Why hadn't he told her what his "business" really was? For that matter, why hadn't she pressed for more information? Passivity was no way to start a love affair. Everything you ignored or explained away would come back to haunt you, you could count on it.

Whatever this depression was, it had definite undertones of anxiety. As if something threatened her, as if something unknown and dangerous out there were heading her way.

Maybe it was the research. Some of her worst funks came on the eve of her greatest successes. Was it that old message again, the message the tribe uses to rein in its mavericks? *You're too ambitious, Jody. You're no good because you want too much.*

Well, the hell with that.

I can give myself another lazy Sunday, she thought. *Curl up in the big armchair in the sun through the French doors, and take my time with the paper, and hold my babies and rub their furry little heads and make them purr. They need some Momma time.*

It was a pretty picture, but her heart wasn't in it.

She didn't figure out what was bothering her until she sat to update her dream journal. Her heart wasn't in updating the journal, either. But she was the original self-starter, and she made herself another mug of coffee and went up and set to work.

Then, as she wrote, the dream came rolling back. She mourned the death of her lover once more, she ached for the feel of his body.

This is ridiculous, she thought. She had a *real* man now. How could she feel such tremendous grief for someone who wasn't real, who was the mere phantasm of a moment?

What about the sexuality of the episode? Why was desire so magnified in dreams? Was it because the filters were down, the repressions deactivated? No, no, no. This was wholeness, not division; total and voracious well-being, not a furlough from the superego. It was like a fountain, it sprang with an irrepressible energy that simply wasn't *there* at other times.

> . . . I am that fountain whose desire
> is fountaining, the fountain of desire.

More poetry. What was that, where was that from?

An episode with Bert Goodens popped into her head. Bert liked to corner her after his shift and talk over his dreams. Well, all the dreamers did. No matter how she protested that she was only a researcher, they persisted in seeing her as their dream leader, their guru.

Bert was passionate about his softball. In this dream, he had been in the on-deck circle, swinging a couple of bats to warm up: "Except it wasn't where the circle usually is, it was out in the middle of the infield, where I could watch the pitcher and all." He was mentally preparing, was imagining the swing, the grunt of effort, the deeply satisfying *thump!* of connection and the ball flying out, way out, floating over the left-field fence, a homer all the way.

Bert was proud of his power swing.

"So anyway, Doc, all of a sudden I noticed I was out in the middle of the field and I would get in the way of the play and all, and that woke me up, worrying about it, I mean."

"Yes, Bert," she said.

"So, Doc, I guess my question is. When I woke up I was feeling really disappointed because I never got up to bat. I could *feel* that homer coming, you know what I mean?"

"I know, Bert."

"So dreams are only in your head, right? I mean, I was just *imagining* the whole softball game in the first place, right? So while I was imagining coming up to bat, then I imagined batting. I mean, I really *hit* that ball, in my imagination. So I guess my question is, Doc. Since it was all just imagination. How come I was so *disappointed* when I woke up?"

Perceptually, dream experience was real. Whatever the sources of dreams, however strange their contents, to the memory and emotions they were as real as waking life. Put like that, it sounded obvious. But the point was, there had to be a *reason* they were so real.

What if you treated them as real when you studied them? What if you pretended they happened in an actual space, one that you could map and measure?

Her skin prickled with excitement. All the other researchers had assumed dreaming was a subsidiary function. They had cataloged the types of dream events, or they had charted the electrical and chemical activity of the brain. But they had never bothered to think of dreams as occurring in an actual continuum.

Just because dreamspace wasn't the same as normal space, that didn't mean you couldn't measure it. Look at the revolution that had occurred in physics when Riemann and Einstein and the others had started using non-Euclidean geometry.

I-space. That was what she was going to call it. Her very own terminology. *I* for imaginary, *I* for inward, *I* for ego. Jody Nightwood's I-space.

She had been convinced for a long time that dreaming involved one or more very powerful strange attractors. But in order to describe those attractors, you had to describe the space in which they occurred. How many dimensions the space had, the nature of its curvature.

She forced herself back to work, getting the rest of the dream down before it was lost.

All that guerrilla business, flying in under the radar and the secret control room. Was it an imaginative rendering of her worries, the stress she was prone to? But the odd thing was, the *feel* of the dream hadn't been stressful. She had been at war, but she had been happy and relaxed and unafraid, because she was doing the right thing.

Now *that* was a state of mind she didn't often experience in waking life.

Several times, when she thought of her lover's death, she had to stop to cry.

How could you research the shape of I-space? You had to observe very closely and carefully. Which meant you had to *be* there, you had to *inhabit* the dream consciously instead of letting it carry you along helpless. In other words, you had to be lucid.

She got up, fumbled through the bookshelves until she found Stephen LaBerge's little paperback, *Lucid Dreaming*, the book Vida had mentioned the other night.

Ever since she had started this project, she'd been consuming the literature, learning as fast as she could. There had been a ton of physiological and neurological material, from Hobson's *The Chemistry of the Conscious Mind* to Lynch's work on memory traces. There were hundreds of papers, dozens of books, in what she thought of as the Theory-of-the-Month Club. But it had been LaBerge's book that had started it all, some ten years ago now.

It had been while she was still in the lab at Langley, during one of the more lonesome periods of her lonesome life. The vice-president for research, a sleazy little corporate rodent whose gray whiskers hid the nonexistence of his chin and whose whole personality lay in his gold credit card, had been hitting on her. She had gotten in the habit of working late, a refuge from the barrenness of her life at the apartment. He had caught on, and had taken to dropping by after working hours. His idea of how to impress her had been to take her to bars where people he thought were important hung out.

"That's Casey," he said one night. "The man himself. And there, over there, that's Senator George's son, Benjamin. He's big in the intelligence community."

"Which?" she had said. "Artificial or military?"

"Both," the rodent had said.

Benjamin George had noticed their attention, and, ironically enough, Jody had wound up having dinner with *him* a few times. A mild, unprepossessing fellow with a formidable mind, he had appeared very interested in her research, her ideas, unformed as they were at the time. But had showed almost no emotion until he began talking about his own specialty, artificial intelligence. Had made no secret of being in the CIA. No reason to. They weren't all undercover agents running covert operations. Dark Ops, he called them.

There were so many cross-connections, so many people who

knew each other so well in both organizations, you wondered if Langley was a CIA front. You wouldn't think they would be so obvious, but who knew? She had asked Benjamin outright.

His silence had felt an awful lot like confirmation. It had played no small part in her eventual decision to leave. Puzzling out the beautiful, light-filled secrets of God and nature, that was one kind of thing. She despised the dark little twisted secrets of humankind.

So what was she doing keeping company with these types?

Her association with Benjamin George had only made her sexier in the eyes of the vice-president for research. When, after accepting a few more invitations for drinks, she had found herself actually considering an affair with the golden-parachuted *Rattus rattus,* she had recoiled in horror, and to keep busy and out of trouble she had set herself a rigorous program of evening reading. Mostly fiction, a realm in which she considered herself weakly educated.

But one of the books had been *Lucid Dreaming.* She had been hoping it would help her with her despair, that it would show her how to use her dream life as a sort of do-it-yourself analysis and healing. Instead, it had struck her as a little gee-whiz, a little awestruck and mystical and not really hard-line science—too many exclamation points—and so she had consciously discounted it. Besides, she had already been having trouble sleeping, and how could you use your dreams to integrate yourself if you couldn't get to sleep in the first place?

But she saw now that the book must have struck her on a deeper level than she had suspected, its concepts lying fallow all these years. She had had to take her own route, of course, she couldn't have let herself know she was prompted by something so unprofessional as excitement, or led on by something so undemonstrable as transcendence.

And she saw clearly that she had just had, the night before, her first fully lucid dream, even if her approach had not resembled the approaches he recommended. LaBerge by way of Vigil by way of Castaneda. Hell, she had even used the word "lucid" *in* her dream.

That was what was next, that was how she wanted to get on with her research.

Lucid dreaming, here I come.

. . .

She read till noon, then decided she needed exercise. She got her ski gear out and headed for Aspen Vista. It hadn't snowed in town in over a month, but there had been a good fog bank on the mountains two nights before, and they were gleaming white now. First week of March, there wouldn't be many more snows. If any. Take it while you can.

The trail was uphill all the way out, so you got a good workout, but the slope was moderate mostly, so you never really had to struggle. She pushed it, went all the way up past the tree line. Coming back was a slow glide downhill. You could relax and enjoy the stunning views.

It was dark by the time she headed down the mountain toward home, and she was drained. She made an early supper, watched a two-hour rerun of *Lois and Clark* because Dean Cain was so cute. It was Superman tamed, Superman turned into a nice little yuppie. He could fly, and he had muscles of steel, but he was *sensitive,* and he *listened* to Lois, and he went into pitches of bourgeois angst over their relationship. Didn't hurt that he dressed snappy, though.

She went to bed hoping for more excitement. Maybe her dream lover this time would be Superman, and she would be Lois. Floating up in the air, mating like minks. But she fell straight into a dark sleep, and did not remember her dreams at all the next morning.

At work the next week, Toni remained uncommunicative, almost sullen. Jody had thought she might tease Toni about the poet she had been interested in at the reading. *And oh, by the way, whatever became of that big Indian you were seeing, what's his name, oh yeah, Vic.*

But Toni's demeanor didn't promise a very nice reaction to teasing, so Jody laid off. And certainly there was no way in the world she was going to talk to Toni about John Shade, at least not until Toni came down off her high horse and started acting more human.

Then on Thursday, Shade called Jody. At the office.

"I've got an idea," he said.

"What?"

"Instead of meeting at the Palace again."

"What?"

Jody's stomach was lurching. This was going to be when he pulled the plug. This was going to be when he called it all off. Don't call me, I'll call you.

"I'm flying into Albuquerque."

"Yeah?"

She thought she knew what was coming next: *Listen, turns out I have to book it to L.A., won't be back for a while, maybe never, but why don't you meet me at the airport for a drink, we had a good time, nice knowing you, kid.*

She was wrong.

"So, you like to ski, and I scored a couple of bottles of Dom in Manhattan, and I see on the weather map where it's supposed to snow in the mountains again tonight."

She couldn't help herself, she had the rejection scenario so firmly in her mind that her voice was razor-edged with suspicion: "Is there a connection here?"

He laughed. "I've got my car and my ski gear at the airport. I was thinking—do you know Macauley Warm Springs?"

It was one of her favorite jaunts, high in the Jemez mountains, where volcanically heated water came sparkling out of the hillside. A good two and a half miles of fairly strenuous trail into the forest, which meant you weren't plagued by the slackers and the carbashers and the dark silent brooding types who liked to come stare at naked women.

"Well, how about instead of me driving straight back to Santa Fe, and us having drinks in the bar, which is nice, but awfully standard, how about if I head up through Jemez Springs instead? I'll put in on that side of the trail, and you come on Highway 4 and put in at Jemez Falls, and we'll meet in the middle, at the Warm Springs? I'll bring the champagne and some hot food, and you bring towels and all that gear. I can be there by two-thirty if you can."

It was the most romantic suggestion she had ever received.

As soon as she got off the phone, she made arrangements with Toni to cover for her tomorrow. Toni didn't protest, didn't even seem curious, though Jody let her happiness show. Toni just didn't seem to care, one way or the other. The shoe was on the other foot now, and it felt good. Jody was the happy one now, the one who had something going.

She spent that evening and the next morning in a total dither, and it didn't do any good to lecture herself on reacting like a lovestruck adolescent. *What the hell, Jody, how often does this kind of thing happen to you? Relax and enjoy it, girl.*

When the van came barreling out of the garage, Toynbee and Leonard were discussing what they would do that evening. They had decided maybe they wanted sushi again. Get a tatami room at Sakura, and drink pot after pot of hot saki. Pouring for each other, of course. Toynbee was driving. He gave Jody a couple of blocks, then followed.

"Friday, 7 March, 9:05 a.m. Subject is moving," Leonard said into the microphone of the recorder they used for keeping notes. "Subject has exited domicile driving the Econoline van, destination not known at this time. Definitely not the office. Surveillance maintaining visual contact. Tonto and the Lone Ranger riiiiide again."

He had switched the recorder off for the last sentence. Toynbee gave him a quick, smiling glance, then reached over to ruffle his hair with one hand, his eyes on the road.

"How did you know?" Leonard said.

Toynbee was proud, you could hear it in his voice. "Bit of a hunch," he said.

"Zen spying," Leonard said, and Toynbee laughed. "We would have been eating breakfast, not knowing a thing. Where do you suppose she's headed?"

"Rendezvous, I would imagine."

"If it's the third suspect, we've nailed her. Nailed them both. We can go to HQ with it."

"Before or after you kill them," Toynbee said.

Jody took Zia heading east, then swung left on St. Francis. Winding through town, starting and stopping at the lights, she had the sense she was being followed. As stupid as it made her feel, she began checking the side mirrors. But of course the traffic jammed up as usual, even this early, a progress more like the gradual shifting of tectonic plates than individual motion, and she couldn't pick one vehicle from any of the others forced to inch along beside her.

Get a grip, Jody, get a grip, she told herself. *You know what this is. This is you about to get something you really want. So of course you're going to undermine yourself. Of course you're going to start hearing all those negative messages from your childhood.*

In the black car, Leonard said, "I'm not going to kill them, not now. Not her, at least. Not until we find out what the hell is going on. Besides, we need her. When we prove she's up to something, they'll give us backup, more financing. This could be big."

"I don't want it to be big," Toynbee said. "I'm having a good time now."

"Gotta go with the flow," Leonard said.

"Dream lover," the driver sang.

"You toy," Leonard said. "Toy-boy himself."

North past the Radisson, where they had gone to see Maria's flamenco troupe perform last fall, Jody and Barbara and Alvaro and Toni and Vida and Allegra.

"Subject is heading out of town," Leonard said. "Rendezvous now deemed probable. Surveillance maintaining visual contact, awaiting further developments."

North past the cemetery, its military uniformity a little improved by sketchy patches of snow. North past the opera, silent till summer, and Trader Jack's Flea Market likewise till the weather improved, and past the turn-off to Tesuque and past Camel Rock and into and through Pojoaque, the terrible jam of traffic from the casinos. Jody despised the casinos, their trashiness and tawdry glitter, and beyond that the ruinous effect they had on the lives around them. Those weren't Jags and Beemers filling the parking lots at this hour of the morning. They were battered, bumper-dropping pickups and rusty, boat-long, twenty-year-old Pontiacs. The casinos stole money from the weakness of those who didn't have money to lose. They drained the economy and threw a huge burden on the state's funds. And you were a fool if you thought the mob wasn't involved. Where did all those blinking, blinding, madly singsong machines come from? The tribes didn't build them. Who had a ready supply? Who trained the workers? Who were the pit bosses?

But the whites had oppressed the Indians for nearly two centuries, and the casinos were the tribes' best shot ever at the money they had been so long denied, and maybe they were also a form of cultural revenge and you were a racist if you opposed the casinos.

She thought momentarily of keeping straight ahead a bit longer and taking the high road to Truchas. Visiting Barbara and Alvaro. The five of Alvaro's paintings, even including *Osiris*, were not enough. She wanted more. She wanted every piece he had ever done. And she wanted some of Barbara's work, too. Barbara was getting pretty good.

But today she had a lover waiting in the mountains, and she made the sweeping left turn onto 502, up toward Los Alamos and Bandelier.

"Oh too bad," Toynbee said. "We could have done lunch at Rancho de Chimayo."

"And gone to that little gallery you like so much, I suppose. What was it called?"

"Cardona-Hine. It's called the Cardona-Hine Gallery. In Truchas." Toynbee frowned. "You don't seem at all interested in art, and I love it so much."

"It's not that," Leonard said. "I like art fine. I just don't think people in our line of work can afford attachments. Not even attachments to art."

"Isn't he serious," Toynbee said. "It's not as though we were double-aughts, you know. And besides, what am I? Aren't I an attachment?"

Leonard was looking in the mirror, studying the car behind them, a black Gelaendewagen. "We've got problems," he said. "Let that man around. If he'll go."

Jody's paranoia had returned as soon as she got free of the traffic on 285. Now, just as she checked the side mirror, she saw some sort of black four-wheel-drive—a Range-Rover, but no, not quite—pass another car to sit on her tail. She was certain the four-wheel-drive had been with her since leaving town, though she couldn't call up a specific memory.

"You don't suppose she's heading for Los Alamos, do you?" Toynbee said. "My God, you don't suppose all this is somehow connected with the labs?"

"What else is out here?" Leonard said.

"So what about the fellow in the wagon? Are they making a rendezvous?"

"Or he could be working for Benjamin George."

"I hate this," Toynbee said. "I hate not knowing why I'm doing what I'm doing or who's on my side and who's on the other side—"

"And who's on first," Leonard said, laughing. "You're a pretty weird kind of spy."

Jody had no eyes for the spectacular rising scenery of White Canyon, a sight she normally enjoyed. She was in a hurry. Though that was silly, because at this rate she would get there well ahead of Shade. But she wanted to get there first. She wanted to be *in* the place, waiting.

She steered through Los Alamos as quickly as she could, that clean and sterile place, that affectless government town. At the intersection on the other side, she felt the tug of Bandelier, but turned right and began climbing. The not-a-Range-Rover was still behind her, had stayed behind her all the way through town, showing no impatience, no desire to pass.

The road was still clear, though she was at eight thousand feet and going higher, but the snow was heavier in the woods along the road. By the time she reached the huge open stretch of Valle Grande, the snow was continuous, and it looked fresh.

She pulled over beside the road. The black Roveroid went around her, kept going. There was some sort of Buick behind it, also black, and that was all the traffic. Jody leaned forward, her forehead against her hands on the steering wheel. She let out a long, shuddering sigh of relief. She felt near tears. This was ridiculous, these extremes of emotion. Nobody was after her. Now that she had finally found it, nobody was going to take her love away.

"Pull into a side road," Leonard said.

"Catch her up in a few moments," Toynbee said.

"Right. She's the one we have to follow."

"Can't be sure the other fellow is involved, must stay with the primary."

"Check."

Driver and passenger were quiet a moment, feeling shrewd and professional. Leonard gazed out at the huge sweep of Valle Grande. The floor of the valley seemed immediately beneath them, but the tracks of a few tiny sheep in the snow added a dizzying sense of height and distance.

"That's a curious sort of valley," Toynbee said. "The perspective fools you."

"It's a volcano," Leonard said.

"You're jesting."

"No, the whole thing is an extinct volcano. That, what looks like a mountain range on the other side, that's the rim of the caldera."

"My God, this is beautiful country," Toynbee said.

Jody pulled back into the road. She continued to climb, passing Rio Conchas, where the early segments of an ill-fated Spielbergian TV show had been filmed—what had it been called? *Earth2*, that was it. It had been strange, a few summers ago, on her way to Jemez Springs, to look from her window and see a giant spaceship settled into the pristine wilderness.

Strange, but somehow appropriate.

There were no other vehicles at the Jemez Falls campground, and she began to relax. She punched the shock adjuster button and felt the van settle heavily to one side. Several of her friends had had their cars broken into at various of the area campgrounds. But maybe the local bad boys didn't cruise the mountains so frequently in the wintertime.

In a matter of minutes, she was geared up, and she hit the trail.

"Oh shit," Leonard said. They were parked across the way, watching Jody through a screen of trees. "We aren't ready for this. How could we have figured on this?"

"Wouldn't matter if we had," Toynbee said. "Don't ski anyhow. Do you?"

At that moment the Gelaendewagen came cruising slowly down the entry road. It pulled in beside Jody's van. A man got out, swaddled in heavy gear. He walked around the van, checking it over carefully. He went back to his wagon and unloaded a couple of cases, the silvery ones that usually contain foam-padded technical equipment. He put the cases into a specially designed backpack, shouldered his way into it. Pulled skis and poles from the back of the wagon and, despite the weight of the pack, stepped expertly into the skis.

Then he was off on the trail himself.

"We have to do something," Leonard said.

"What can we do? No, don't, you'll freeze yourself."

But Leonard was already out of the car, slipping into his overcoat. He wrapped his scarf around his head like a cowl, tucked the ends into his coat collar. He tucked the legs of his slacks into the tops of his Western boots, pulled gloves from his pockets. He leaned in to the window of the car. He said, "Be back soon, podnuh. Hold the fort."

"Bloody fool," Toynbee said, watching him go. "Dear bloody American cowboy fool."

The snow was perfect. A deep powdery base with just a bit of crustiness on top. Even breaking trail wasn't all that hard. Jody had decided to head straight out, not visit the falls, though she had time and she loved to see them. She had to do a bit of snowplowing in the first quarter-mile, but it would be mostly downhill to the springs after that—dangerously so in some places.

Something over a half-mile out, she detoured to the left, and worked her way out onto the bluff overlooking the valley. It was tricky, clambering among the snowy rocks in her ski boots, but she was careful, and the view was worth it. Sitting there in the deep silence, a silence broken only by the sound of water far below, the sound of wind moving up the valley, and the occasional cry of a far-off hawk, and looking out over miles of unbroken, uninhabited snowy forest, she could feel peace coming over her. Finally she got a little chilled, and took to her skis again.

There were some exhilarating downhill runs the rest of the way in, and by the time she reached the springs, she was breathing hard and was as happy as a dog in a field of rabbits.

Leonard had followed the two sets of tracks for almost an hour now. It had been a terrible struggle, the heels of his boots never meant for hiking, and certainly not hiking this terrain in snow. He had fallen several times, tearing open the palms of his expensive leather gloves and the knees of his slacks. His impromptu headdress kept pulling loose, letting in the icy wind. His shirt and underclothes were soaked through with the sweat of his effort.

He came to where both sets of tracks veered to the left. Only one set of tracks came back out, went ahead. Strange. Had something gone wrong? He had visions of an argument, a dead body left at the scene, shot through the heart, blood on the snow. But whose body? He wasn't good enough to distinguish the skiers by means of the trails they left. And why had the other skier gone on ahead, if murder was the case? Why not get the hell away from there?

He began to feel bitterly chilled, now that he had stopped moving.

He had to check the scene. He took the left, followed the double set of tracks.

Macauley Warm Springs was just a thread of water, a slender creek jumping out of a tilted mountainside and running its way down to join the Jemez. It made its presence known from a distance in veils and curtains of steam that rose from the snow and crystallized on overhanging branches. All along the length of the spring, pools collected in green grass, like jewels on the strand of a necklace. Some of the pools were shallow and bathtub-sized. A few were deeper.

Jody headed for one of her favorites, just up the hillside, a shoulder-deep hollow, the water dark blue with dissolved minerals. She took her ski mittens off and tested it. Not really *hot* hot, but warm enough for comfort. And it *felt* almost hot by contrast with the sharp air. She set out the thermos of coffee she had brought, a chocolate bar, and a half-pint flask of bourbon on a rock beside the pool. She rigged hooks for her clothes, then stripped rapidly, turning each garment inside out to dry. They would be cold when she put them back on. Maybe she would build a fire. A fire to dry her clothes and to help John Shade locate her.

Naked, she slipped into the water. Her hands floated to her mons, parting the soft fur. She lay back, stroking herself lightly along the stomach, her inner thighs, returning to her mons from time to time. It wasn't masturbation. She didn't want masturbation. She wanted love, and love was on the way. Maybe it was too much, lying here, waiting for him naked? Maybe she was coming on too strong. After all, they had never actually *said* they were going to—

A cloud went over the sun. It was just now two o'clock. This hadn't been a good idea, getting here early. All he had had to do was make the suggestion, and she had come running. But he would never keep the appointment. Even if he tried, he wouldn't. He wasn't familiar with these woods, and he probably had no idea how dangerous they were in winter.

She imagined him bloody and fallen, freezing to death.

Should she go after him? But what then? No way she could get him out by herself.

"The hell with this," she said. She clambered out and set about building a fire. In the back of her mind, she thought what a funny picture she must make, a naked, shivering woman dashing about in the snow, laying tinder and then firewood, and finally, desperately, striking the match.

She climbed back in the water while the fire caught and built. After a while she got out and circled it with stones and banked it. She drew cord from her backpack and rigged a line between trees and hung her clothes on it to warm and dry. Now she didn't have to hurry about so much, she could step to the fire and warm herself. Take a swig of the bourbon. Much better.

And the clouds had gone away, too. She tried to believe. The man was on his way. He was above her on the mountainside, heading down.

She knew so little about him. She had trusted her emotions, they both had. But how much realistic information did she have? Maybe he was a frustrated writer, had become a mathematics professor to please his parents, until one of the books he toyed with in his spare time had unexpectedly set him free. Somehow there was something military about him. Maybe he had known service in Vietnam. He could have done that and still have been in his mid-forties, though he was so fit it was hard to tell his age. Maybe Vietnam had marked him. Made him kind but haunted, a loner because he had never found his match.

He would be in Santa Fe on a spiritual journey, though he might not want to admit it. He was on a quest for beauty. He wanted to know how to live the rest of his life.

In a few minutes he would come down the mountainside, heading for this very pool. When he saw her, he would be apologetic and embarrassed. She would open her eyes lazily and say, "It's big enough for two." He would hesitate, smile uncertainly, get in.

His body would be like Chipper's, she thought, but better. Bigger. Olympian in proportion. Perfectly carved, but his chest and legs nicely hairy.

No more smooth-skinned narcissists for her, no more manchildren.

In the water, so weightless and so close to her, so close to her warm floating breasts, he would be unable to help himself. His excitement would show.

"It's okay," she would reassure him, taking his erection in her hands. "It's okay. We've known each other a long time. Maybe we've just met, but we've known each other a long time anyway. We've been waiting for each other all our lives."

And they would slide together in the warm water, and it would just be the beginning. All the rest would be better and better. He would bring one of the bottles of champagne. Later they would ski out, her side, and she would drive him to his car, and they would stay overnight at the lodge in Jemez Springs. They would eat at Los Ojos, cheeseburgers, and they would go back to the lodge spent and satisfied and exhausted, and sleep chastely together, nestled like spoons.

"Well, look at you," a man's voice said behind her.

Leonard looked down from his vantage. Below him, far out on a ledge, his skis off and leaning against a rock, the man from the Gelaendewagen had set up some sort of equipment on tripods. He was walking around fussing over it, entirely alive.

Some sort of experiment? The woman gone down the trail, on the receiving end?

Then the Gelaendewagen man stepped back with a remote in his hand, a wire leading to one of the tripods, and Leonard almost laughed aloud.

You fucking idiot. A fucking photographer. A fucking nature photographer.

Jody had never felt so good in her life. Floating weightless in the water, strong arms around her loosely, so that she was secure but not pinned or trapped, easy as a boat snubbed to a dock. Her back bumping against his chest. And what a *fine* ass he had, round and muscular.

From time to time, he inclined his head, nibbled at an earlobe, the nape of her neck. "Champagne," she commanded, and he obeyed. Somehow without disturbing her he managed to one-hand a fluteful and deliver it to her lazily lifted fingers.

She sipped, set the flute on the rock wall of the pool.

"This is *just* how it was supposed to be," she said.

"Yeah, but did you come?" he said, and began laughing uproariously, and she spun around and splashed him, and he splashed her back, and they were in the middle of a waterfight.

"So I make noise," she yelled. "Well, how do you like this? And how do you like this! And how do you like *this!*" Throwing handfuls of water at his face till he dunked her.

They subsided, and he held her again, face to face this time, her legs around him.

"Do more," she said, laying her head along his shoulder.

"Tell me about your research," he said.

"You have a weird sense of timing," she said.

"I've never heard of anybody applying chaos and complexity theory to dreaming before. It's a wild idea. I want to know more about it, that's all."

"It's just a pretty little idea unless you work out the details," she said. "And the details are complicated. I don't want to talk complicated right now."

"It's going to snow," he said. "We'd better be heading back."

"Wanna stay here," she said. "Do more."

I'm in trouble, Leonard realized. I'm in real trouble.

He had been watching the photographer for nearly thirty minutes. He was going to have to make a move soon. The cold was invasive, a rude and brutal body forcing its way into his own. The body of nothingness, of zero. Possession, an alien takeover.

He made himself get moving. Might as well go down and check the man out. The guy probably had nothing to do with anything, but you had to follow through. Had to make absolutely certain. Anyway, it was all he could do. No way he could follow the woman any further.

The man looked up at the first noise, watched as Leonard stepped and slid, dislodging small increments of skittering snow. Leonard fetched up in front of him finally.

"Howdy, mate," he said. *Got that from the fucking Brit.* "Incredible fucking view, huh?"

The Gelaendewagen man was tall and silver-haired. He looked Leonard up and down. *Damn fool,* his eyes said. "You're going to freeze to death," he said aloud, finally, but without scorn. He had a mild voice, a deep Southern accent.

"I'm fine," Leonard said, but he was shuddering uncontrollably, and his teeth clattered on the words. "Taking a few pictures, hey?"

"You best be heading back. Follow the double ski trail back in. I'll be behind you in about twenty minutes. Hold on, I got some hot tea in a thermos here before you go."

The cameras were incredible. You could take pictures of bugs on the moon with cameras like that. If there had been any bugs on the moon.

Better gear than we get, Leonard thought.

Jody and Shade were able to ski only a little way back before they had to stop and change into hiking boots. The trail out was just too steep. They strapped their skis to their backpacks, but kept the poles out to help them climb. Before long she had worked up a powerful sweat.

Shade had brought, of all things, hot fried chicken, sealed in a thermal pack, and they had ravaged it before they left the springs. They had not eaten before making love, they had been in too much of a rush. Then, afterward, they had been consumed with hunger.

She thought of them, sitting there naked in the water as the snow began to fall softly all around, gnawing the bones and tossing them into the underbrush, and she laughed aloud.

Shade, laboring up an incline ahead of her, turned back to look. "What?" he said.

"I was just thinking," she said. "That chicken isn't going to last long. We're going to be hungry again by the time we get out of here. And I know just where I want to eat."

It was getting late, and Toynbee was near panic. Hours now, it had been hours. What should he do? Leonard was dead, there was no question. He couldn't go in after him, no way, he wouldn't last ten minutes out there. Go back down the hill for help? He didn't relish the drive, especially in the dark. And it might blow the assignment.

The truth was, he couldn't bear to leave. He couldn't bear to quit hoping. So he sat in the car shivering, running the heater every few minutes, while the dark descended.

And then, as a flurry of snow began to fall, an apparition came lurching through the trees, a raggedy shadow who stumbled and clawed at the passenger-side door.

"Oh dear God, thank you, thank you."

Toynbee let his man in, slid back over under the wheel. Leonard flung his head back against the seat. His face was white, his mouth and eyebrows rimmed with frost. His clothes were torn, his hands and knees bloody, and he was gasping for breath.

"Are you all right? Do we need to let you in hospital?"

"Fine," Leonard said. "Ran—all—the—way—back. Go!"

"Bloody fucking hero," Toynbee said. But there was admiration in his voice.

It was six o'clock by the time they reached Jody's van. The trail from the overlook back had been terribly torn up, two sets of ski tracks besides hers, and someone blundering around in boots. So she had half expected to find company in the parking lot.

"I need to take a leak," Shade said, veering off to the rest rooms before she could stop him. Just as well. What would she have said? Please don't leave me alone, I think I'm being followed? Paranoia makes such a good impression on a new lover.

But when she saw the black four-wheel-drive, her heart jumped with fear.

A man in snowboots and a parka, the hood thrown back, was at the back door of the vehicle, which she now recognized as a Gelaendewagen, a hundred and twenty thousand dollars' worth of steel. What you buy when a Range-Rover is no longer expensive enough.

The man was Colonel Wilbur Goodloe Hall.

Of course. This was how life really worked. She felt embarrassed, as if the details of her anxiety were obvious to anyone who looked. She had to get over this. She had to grow up.

"Good afternoon, Colonel," she said, unlocking her own door. She thought from the strange look on his face that he was wondering where he had met her before. She could have thrown back her own hood, made it easier for him. She didn't.

As he was driving away, the Colonel leaned out his window. "Did you see anybody on the trail back?" he said. "Anybody in trouble? Man in an overcoat and cowboy boots?"

"No," she said.

"Tracks came all the way back," the Colonel said. "Guess the damn fool made it out."

"I'm all right," Leonard said. "You can slow down now."

Toynbee was hunched over the wheel, peering into the gathering and snowy gloom. He leaned it into the switchbacks, dropping out of the sky like a shot hawk, freeze-frames of snow and timber in his jumping headlights. The brakes were smoking, you could smell them.

Leonard wasn't all right, he could tell he was going to be sick for a while, but the worst of the chill had left him and he didn't want to die sailing off the edge of the road.

"Slow down," he said again. "I'm all right."

Then, in order to be convincing, and in order to distract Toynbee from his maniacal descent, he began to talk strategy. "She was definitely up to something," he said. "That guy in the Range-Rover, I don't know whether he's her lookout or what."

Toynbee slowed a little, flicked Leonard a glance. "It's not a Range-Rover," he said. "It's a Gelaendewagen. Top-of-the-line Mercedes off-road."

"I knew that," Leonard said.

149

. . .

They broke into clear sky as they topped Redondo, a spectacular sun-set—dark as it was, the western horizon was still aflame, the mountains under it an impossible distant indigo.

Shade had been lavish in his admiration of her van, all of its outfittings and secrets. "You're not an obvious woman," he had said.

Now he said, "I'm thirsty as hell. You want to break out that other bottle of champagne?"

"No," she said, taking a curve like a race driver, though the van was top-heavy and the suspension wasn't really rigged for it. "Save it for this evening."

"Okay," he said. "I'll make do with water."

She hadn't called ahead to the lodge to reserve a room, had only had the idea as she sat in the water this afternoon. It was late in the season. Maybe they would be full up with people getting in a last backcountry outing before the spring thaws hit, but she didn't think so. She thought everything was going to work out just fine tonight.

14: phase two intromission

They slept together Friday evening, nestled like spoons.

Everything had been just as she imagined. After dinner they had walked across the street to their room at the lodge, popped the cork on the other bottle of champagne, and then had fallen asleep across each other before they could finish it.

They had made love all morning, and then had gone for a late breakfast. A short stack and two eggs over easy for her and bacon *and* sausage and biscuits and gravy and coffee and orange juice. Shade had eaten more slowly than she, laughing at her appetite. She had found she thought of him as Shade, not as John. She had asked him if that was okay. He had said it was fine, everybody called him Shade, for some reason nobody called him John.

She had wondered who "everybody" was.

He had wanted to ski—after all, there were trails right behind the lodge. She had wanted to go, *really* wanted to go, but she was feeling guilty about the babies. She hadn't planned on being gone overnight, and they would be running low on food and water.

"I can't," she said. "Can you—" she hesitated. "Can you come back to my house with me? There are some—I have some friends you need to meet."

"Your cats?" he said.

She was astonished. "How did you *know?*" Then she brushed at her black jacket, embarrassed. "Okay," she said. "So I have fur all over everything I own."

He agreed to come by, but said he couldn't stay the night, he had business the next day, and had to get an early start. In fact, he had business the next couple of weeks, wouldn't get back into town until the evening of Friday week.

"Again with the out of town?" she said. "What is it now? I mean, I thought you were a best-selling author. I thought your time was your own."

"It's book business," he said.

"Yeah, but *two weeks?* Give a girl a break. Every time we touch each other, you take off for the ends of the earth the very next day." A little early to make like a nagging lover, maybe, but she was too disappointed, she couldn't help it.

"They want me to meet with the marketing people," he said. "And I have to see my agent about the next book. And I have to see my editor."

"I'm sure you have a girl in every port," she said. He wasn't fooled by the lightness of her tone. He took her face in his hands.

"It isn't like that," he said. "This isn't a brush-off. I'll see you again as soon as possible. No later than Friday, two weeks away. I'll call while I'm gone."

Then he kissed the tip of her nose.

It *is* a brush-off, she thought.

He came by the house, met the babies. They were grumpy, ignored him at first. When he got down on his hands and knees, Blind Lemon hissed and ruffed. But Shade spoke to him in his own language until the cat relaxed and walked away. No competition there.

Static sauntered up while he was talking to Blind Lemon, sniffed him front and rear.

"Why do you call her 'Static'?" he said. "I mean, I get 'Blind Lemon,' sort of. He's blind and he's lemon-colored. Did you know there was a blues man named Blind Lemon—"

"Jefferson," she said. "Static—well—I mean it like static on the radio. You see how she has Siamese markings, but the markings themselves are calico? Three-color? I thought of that as being like an interference pattern. But you can't name a cat 'Interference.'"

He went, finally. Kissed her again. Twenty minutes after he left, while she was sitting in the easy chair having a good cry, the phone rang.

It was Shade.

I mean it, he said. You'll see. Try not to worry.

She finished her cry after she hung up. So maybe it wasn't a brush-off. But they weren't going to live together. It wasn't going to be that kind of a romance. She was crying now because she felt so foolish and old-fashioned, wanting a long-term live-in.

Why the hell not say it? Wanting a *marriage*.

They had known each other a week, they had made love twice, and she wanted to marry the man. You thought you were modern, advanced, sensible. And then a million years of evolution kicked in, and you saw you were nothing but biology's pawn.

Let me talk to Mother, Shade said.

He was on the computer phone, this time tilting his chair against the wall, framed in a square of afternoon light. The vertical blinds printed their long shadows across him, so that he looked for all the world like a prisoner in a cell.

Hi, Mom, he said. It's me again.

He listened. Yeah, he said. I'm about to do that. Listen, though. Things are getting pretty serious here. I think it's time for me to give up my other girlfriends. Sure. I'll write you all about her, judge for yourself. But I'm wasting my time on anybody else. What?

He laughed. Of course it's a sexual thing. Why would that color my judgment? Right, right, I'll be careful. Never give all the heart. He listened. No, he said. I don't think she has any other suitors. If so, I haven't spotted them. Yes, I'll keep my eyes open.

He hung up, leaned his head back against the wall. Closed his eyes. Sighed.

The prisoner looked as though he was in for a long time. It looked like a life sentence.

Jody's dreams that night were confused, and she could not sort them out when she woke. There had been, again, a sense of conflict, of being on the run. She felt someone had warned her, but she had ignored the warning, and gotten in trouble.

She woke up hungry. She absolutely had to have *food*. She remembered this now. Love always made her hungry—continually, unslakably hungry. What systems kicked in, what energies was she burning? She mentally inventoried the fridge. Nothing she wanted.

Besides, she was too restless to sit still. She would go get something. But what? What was she craving?

Brain food. Something rich and oily and full of strong flavor.

Bagels and lox! Well not lox, it was too salty for her taste, but some Nova. *Novy mit a schmeer,* she heard John Levy saying, her producer friend.

She threw on jeans and a jacket, cranked up the NSX, and rumbled down to Bagelmania. A couple of poppyseed, some Novy and cream cheese. It was the hour when the faithful were in services and the apostates were still sleeping, so Guadalupe was empty and the trip was quick. Not so the service. Her waiter seemed to be a recent graduate of the smoked-salmon-shaving academy. He took a full five careful minutes to layer exactly a quarter-pound of the shining translucent slices on scales, wrap them in wax paper, and package the whole.

She was dancing with impatience, already tasting fresh Kona and two toasted bagel halves slathered with cream cheese, studded with capers, layered with Novy and thin thin slices of Vidalia onion and tomato, the whole powdered with fresh-ground pepper. Her belly was growling and the base of her tongue was sprinkling her throat with anxious anticipation.

When she got back, the message light on her kitchen phone was blinking. It would be Toni, calling with plans for the two of them. Or Mrs. Uriostes, worrying about Ramón. Ignore it and eat, Jody. Whatever it is, it'll keep. But what if it was Shade? What if it was Shade?

It was Lobo.

A burglar had hit the office, and the police were there, and could she come down? Because right now they were talking about holding him, even though he was the one who had called it in, and even though he had showed them his ID and his name in the log book.

Jody's heart went into overdrive. First the computer, now this. What was going on? Who was after her? She punched the office number, and a strange voice answered. "Are you a police officer?" she said, insanely imagining the burglar still there.

"Would you identify yourself, please, ma'am?"

"I'm Jody Nightwood. It's my clinic. How much damage did they do? Did we lose any equipment? The records! Oh my God, the records! Are the records okay?"

"Ma'am, there's some glass scattered around, and some furniture damage. I can't really tell you any more than that just now. You could help us by coming down here and answering a few questions. Plus which we have a young man who says he works for you—"

"He does, you can let him go."

"Well, ma'am, if you could just come on down."

"I'm on my way. I just wanted to—never mind, I'm on my way."

She was in the NSX and heading back downtown before she remembered the Novy and bagels. Well, you could write off nine bucks worth of fish flesh and omega oils. Static and Blind Lemon would be sleeping pretty good by the time she got back, fat and satisfied.

This has nothing to do with your computer, she told herself. *Nobody's after you. Get your mind straight.* What did Toni call it? *Cathexis,* when you load all your separate emotional trials into one pattern. Living by signs and symbols and superstitions.

Victorio met her at the door to the lab. "I caught the squeal," he explained, "and I came on over. They're happy to let me work the scene, if that's okay with you."

It was definitely okay with her. It helped somehow to have him there, a friendly and familiar face, even if the acquaintance so far amounted to one meal at Zia's and a brief investigation. She had always heard that being the victim of a crime made you feel violated, insecure, but she hadn't thought she herself would experience such a sense of vulnerability. She was tough. But now, twice, it had really freaked her. More biology. We don't control ourselves.

"Is Toni coming down?" she said.

"Maybe a little later," Victorio answered. "She sounded pretty sleepy."

Sounded. So he hadn't been with her.

"Did they get into the office area, too?" she asked.

"That's the setup at the other end of the hall?" She nodded. "Probably not. At least we didn't see any obvious damage. Whoever it was wasn't in very long."

Inside, Jody saw that one of the sleep chamber windows had been shattered. Her window, the one to the chamber she typically used. A couple of visitor's chairs had been broken up, and drawers had been pulled out of the desks and flung across the room, their contents spilled everywhere. But it was the window that got her, that felt like a direct physical assault.

They're breaking into my dreams.

Her knees went weak, and she had to sit.

She was seeing oranges scattered across an oiled wooden floor, cans and cereal boxes tumbled into aisles, smashed jars of mayonnaise and bing cherries, fragments of cooler glass in the ground meat, a back door hanging brokenly on torn hinges. And upstairs, her teddy bear with his stuffing ripped out and scattered across the soiled covers of her bed.

It had been a quarter of a century ago. She and Mom and Pop had gotten back from a rare family vacation, a trip to Destin on the Florida gulf. Even rarer, it had been a happy vacation, full of sun and laughter and kite-flying along the waves. Meals of unaccustomed seafood: boiled shrimp and fried mullet and oysters and soft-shelled crab, cooked in the kitchenette of their motel suite. Jody would start what they still called junior high in the fall, having skipped a grade, and that fact and the pleasure of the vacation had made her feel the world was a wide and welcoming place. She was almost adult, and wonderful opportunities awaited her.

They had come back to find the store, and their home above it, vandalized. Someone had broken in, had stayed there more than a couple of nights. Someone had trashed the store, eaten whole cartons of ice cream and left the others to melt when they unplugged the coolers. Someone had smoked marijuana and drunk beer in their bedrooms, had screwed on their beds, had filled their toilets with urine and excrement and refused to flush them.

Jody could smell that stink still. It was strong in her nostrils now. It had not diminished one whit with the passing of twenty-five years.

"Something about this doesn't make sense," Victorio was saying. He wasn't talking to her, but to one of the uniforms. Lobo was across the room, sitting in Consuela's chair. He looked dismayed, his lean face flushed with a species of angry embarrassment.

The insurance adjusters had estimated the damage to home and store at ten thousand. The five-hundred-dollar deductible wouldn't have seemed like much to some people, but it had threatened their finances for a year. Her mother had spiraled into the depression from which she never emerged. It had probably been there all along, but before, they had been able to hope. She had blamed Pop for talking her into the vacation. The burglary was retribution from God, his vengeance for her temerity in seeking rest and relaxation.

Jody had caught the same disease. This was her fault, for having so much fun.

This was her punishment for making love to Shade, for exploring her interior world, for being too ambitious. Father Freud had ransacked her office, raped her dreams.

Toni, where are you when I need you?

She got up and stalked across the room to Lobo. He looked up.

"It was like this when I got here," he said. "It took me a minute or so to understand what had happened. As soon as I did, I called the cops."

"Was the door open?"

"The outside door? No. I had to unlock it."

"How did you happen to be coming to the office on a Sunday?" she asked him.

Let's be fair to Jody. It is possible that she wasn't fully aware just how her voice jumped and crackled, just how much fury she was communicating.

"I knew you were going to ask that," he said, flushing even more deeply. "Okay," he said. "Lucia and I have been coming down here some on the weekends."

Jody was trembling with anger. *Look, Momma, someone's been fucking in my bed.*

"Coming down here? Why?"

"Sometimes we get sick of the apartment. This is clean and comfortable, and—" He gestured at the TV on its swing-out arm high in the room's corner. "You have cable, stereo . . ."

Yes, and a fridge for beer and snacks, and comfortable chairs, and good beds. She could see how it would be, and she hated herself for putting Lobo on the spot. But what would happen to her if she let go of her anger? How could she sustain herself if she forgave him?

"Okay," Jody said. "Okay, it isn't important now." She was gritting her teeth to get it out, but he had shown guts, calling the police instead of just taking off. "We've got to work out some new agreements, but no repercussions, okay? Why don't you go home and get some rest?"

"If they'll let me," he said.

Victorio came up. He indicated the two uniforms standing impatiently at the other end of the room. He spoke to Jody: "They need to talk to you."

"Can't I just give my statement to you?"

"You can do that, too. But they have to make a complete report, and that means interviewing you. And after they leave here, they have to go by and see Toni. We're all just paper-pushers, you know. It ain't a glamorous job."

Paper-pushers with guns, she thought. "What was that I heard you saying a minute ago? Something about it not making sense."

"Oh, that," he said. "Well, it's kind of police business."

These goddamn men, Jody thought. *Shade won't tell me why he's really going out of town. Now Vic treats me like a child.* "Look, is this my place, or not?" she said.

He took her elbow, guided her to the skylight the burglar had used to make his entrance. "You've got a pretty good security system, right? As soon as the guy comes through that skylight, an alarm goes off down at the station. Your friend Lobo didn't need to call it in. There was a patrol car on the way here already. We must have just missed the perpetrator, Lobo and us both. Your friend is lucky he didn't catch the guy in the act. He could have got hurt."

"He's not my friend, he works for me."

Puzzlement flickered over Victorio's face. What was the importance of the distinction? Did it have a bearing on the crime? "Okay, he works for you."

One of the uniforms called over: "Vic?"

"What?" he said.

Lobo was quivering at the door, a greyhound held back by a leash. "You think?" the uniform said, gesturing in that direction. "He says she says it's okay. We got his statement."

"Yeah, let him go."

Lobo vanished. The officer shrugged, sat at the desk, began flipping through his notes.

"Anyway, I don't get your point," Jody said.

Victorio returned his attention to her. "Yeah, okay. So who burglarizes a doctor's office? Who breaks into a doctor's office on a quiet Sunday morning instead of like the middle of the night Wednesday or something?"

"Actually, weeknights there's somebody here. I'm running a study—"

"Yeah, Toni told me. But your average burglar isn't gonna know that."

"He could see the lights."

"He could. So he waits a few weeks, figures out your schedule?

Nah, your average burglar, he's on to some other place, somebody else's office."

"You're saying somebody planned this?"

"Figure. He comes in on a Sunday morning. Which is not typical, believe me."

"He could have been a druggie. Somebody coming down off a Saturday-night high, somebody desperate for a fix, any kind of fix. Isn't that usually why they hit doctors' offices?"

Victorio lifted an eyebrow. "Yeah, that was my first thought, too. Only."

He led her over to the medicine cabinets. "What do you see?"

The cabinets were ceramic-coated metal. They were closed, and there were no dents or scrapes on their gleaming white doors. She tried one of the doors. Locked.

"Nothing," she said.

Which was good, which was very, very good. Because that was also where she kept all the permanent records of the study. So they were safe.

"Yeah, nothing. And they break out a window in one of the experiment rooms—"

"Sleep chambers. I call them sleep chambers."

"Sleep chambers, but they don't scarf up the electronics. Fancy-looking gear—monitors, printers, control boards, even tape decks, you would think it would fence pretty good. But no, they don't even touch it."

Every man on earth, she thought. *Every man on earth. Let him start describing action, he shifts immediately to the present tense.*

"So it goes down like this," Victorio said. "Perp comes in the sky-light, sets off the alarm right away, which shows he's an amateur."

The coach's present tense. It has to be genetic, something in the X chromosome. Or is it just from watching too much pro football on television?

"Which is strange," he continued. "Because there's some professional touches—grapnel marks on the roof, a glass cutter to get to the inside latch, business like that. So we got a perp with good equipment, but who don't *comprende* the basics any lowlife with a habit coulda told him."

"I don't get it," Jody said.

"Yeah, it gets funnier, too. So the perp sets off the alarm, and what does he do next? Does he bug out when he sees he's tripped the wire? No, he stays a couple minutes, does some damage. Does he go straight for the med cabinets with a crowbar, like any bottoming junkie would? No, he trashes the place. Breaks a window, smashes up some chairs."

Victorio shook his head. "I didn't know better, I would say some idiot who didn't know what the hell he was doing was trying to make it look like a regular burglary."

"But why would that be?" Jody said. "That doesn't make any sense." She was flashing on Ish, the lover from her dream a few nights back. Ish was wearing a beret. They were in some sort of underground HQ, a bunker set from a World War II movie.

"Yeah, that's what I said. Unless you're running a designer-drug lab, or maybe this study of yours is really some kind of top-secret government research." He smiled to show that he was only kidding, but she could see he was watching for her reaction.

"No," she said. "No James Bond stuff here." Then, with a surprising twist of bitterness: "My life—take a good look. There's less to it than meets the eye."

"Um," he said.

"So what does it all mean?"

"Probably nothing. Something the media don't tell you, there's weird stuff about almost every crime scene. Unexplainable stuff. Discrepancies. You figure out what you can, catch the perp if you can, go on to the next one. No point breaking your brain over the small stuff."

"Will we catch this guy?"

"Probably not. Look, the boys would really like to get on out of here."

It was true, the uniforms were restless, one of them pacing rapidly back and forth, the other leaning against a wall and rolling his eyes to the ceiling. *Probably haven't had their doughnuts yet,* she thought. Then, *Come on, Jody, don't take it out on them. Be fair.*

Besides, it was never a good idea to antagonize a civil servant.

They sat her at Consuela's desk, remained standing themselves. The interview took maybe five minutes, now that they had finally gotten around to it. Where had she been when this happened, how had she discovered the burglary, did she know anybody who would have any reason to vandalize her office, any business enemies, etcetera, had she noticed any suspicious characters hanging around in the last few days? Questions the officers pretty much knew the answers to already, but had to get on the record.

They were entirely polite and considerate, now that they were being allowed to get on with their jobs. And still the process was somehow demeaning. She had been invaded, attacked, and this was all that would ever happen. They would never catch the criminal. It wasn't that she was afraid. She thought she was more than a match for the average mugger, the average rapist.

It was the facelessness of it all, the decay of her status from individual to victim.

By the time the interview was over, she felt soiled, humiliated. She felt as though she had done something wrong, and was being held up to public ridicule.

When the officers left, she asked Victorio if he wanted a statement from her. He said no, he could get whatever he needed later. Now *he* seemed antsy.

She began trying to tidy up the mess, scooping the scattered papers from the floor and dumping them into whichever drawer came handiest, sliding the drawers back into their slots. She found herself so shaky she had to lean on the desktop. Victorio lingered, watching. Then he went around the lab opening doors until he found the broom closet. He took out the big broom, a black garbage bag, and a dustpan. He gathered the larger fragments of glass into the garbage bag, and then began sweeping up the rest.

"You don't have to do that," she said.

"No problem. But listen, can't this wait? Don't you have somebody who can come in and do it for you? You've had a pretty good shock."

"We have a cleaning service," she said. "I won't be able to get them on a Sunday. I just need—I just want to get the worst of it. I just don't want to leave it like this."

It was important not to let Consuela come in and find the place in such disarray.

And as soon as she had the thought, Jody realized she had to call Consuela and let her know. And Blossom. And all the sleepers. Could she even run the study Monday night? Maybe, maybe if she got new glass in during the day. But she wouldn't know whether she could have that done until late in the day tomorrow. She could run two of the three chambers, but she hated thinking of the broken symmetry of that arrangement. If she postponed the sessions, she would have to ask everyone to come in anyway, take their pills as usual.

She felt immensely weary, overwhelmed by details, decisions.

"You want Toni to come over and stay with you?" Victorio said. He was studying the broken edges of half-mirrored glass in the sleep-chamber window frame.

"Should have done that first," he mused.

"No," she said curtly. "I'm not a goddamn baby."

Victorio only nodded. He located a hammer and some rags, and set about knocking loose the remaining glass.

"Besides, I'm sure you and Toni have plans."

"Not lately," he said.

"What's up with you guys?" Jody said. "I thought you were a solid item."

"She's having to think some stuff over."

"What sort of stuff? Have you had a fight?" It couldn't be his job, the fact that he was a cop. That wouldn't put Toni off, that would appeal to her.

Victorio seemed impatient with the question. "We have very different epistemologies," he said. The phrasing was more than strange, coming from him. She had only the vaguest idea what the word meant. Worldview, something like that? "I can't abandon mine, and she won't abandon hers. So she's busy deciding whether she can live with the difference."

He finished knocking the glass out, swept up the new litter. Asked what she wanted to do with the broken chairs. At first she thought just throw them in the dumpster out back, but then thought maybe she'd need them to show the insurance adjuster.

Oh, fine. The insurance man. More calls to make, more arrangements to take care of.

They stowed the remnants of the chairs in the supply room, gave the place a final cursory going-over. Except for the missing window glass, everything looked almost presentable.

The empty window bothered her, gave her a disturbing subliminal sense that her dreams were escaping, were getting away into the real world and running amok.

Victorio lingered till he was sure she was ready to leave. She let him walk her to her car, waved good-bye as he strode off. She stood a moment, looking around.

It had gotten colder, and the day was going gray. Heavy clouds building over the mountains. The wind damp, and picking up velocity. It looked as though they were in for some more snow. Good. It would do her good to get out and go skiing.

But the idea of skiing, the idea of that habit, was strange. She felt as if she had been created this very moment. That she had no past, no family, no friends, no connections. There was a phrase for it: *jamais vu,* never seen. The opposite of *déjà vu,* but just as spooky.

At home, she cleaned up the mess the cats had made. They had dragged the packages onto the floor. All the salmon was gone, its wrapping paper shredded. They had chewed one bagel to scattered crumbs. Hadn't been able to get to the cream cheese in its plastic carton.

The scene reminded her of the scene at the office.

She swept, wiped, mopped, dumped. Salvaged the untouched bagel. Didn't bother scolding her babies. Leave them with that much temptation, it isn't their fault.

She took a long hot shower, and came out of it feeling somewhat purified, but trembly and frail. Realized that probably a good part of her weakness was that she had yet to eat.

She dug a Tupperware bowl of leftover chicken soup from the freezer. Set it to melting, then simmering. Chopped a couple of cloves more of garlic, though the soup was loaded with garlic already. Poured in a cup of Chardonnay from a bottle that she was never going to finish any other way. Whipped up a batch of buttermilk biscuits.

While the biscuits were baking, she set about making her phone calls. Got hold of the owner of the cleaning service at home; he would send a crew in, first thing in the morning. No luck with glass replacement, no surprise. Got hold of Consuela, filled her in. No luck with Blossom, and no message machine, either. Got hold of all the sleepers or their message machines and canceled Monday's sessions, and Tuesday's too, just to be safe.

Had a nagging feeling there was somebody else she needed to be talking to. Somebody who would be upset to get the news, but who needed to be told anyway.

Ish. She needed to tell Ish.

Now that was truly ridiculous.

She collapsed in her armchair with the rest of the Chardonnay, a deep bowl of hot golden garlicky soup, and a couple of steaming biscuits dripping with butter. The cats assumed their begging positions, Blind Lemon on the extended footrest, pawing tentatively in the direction of the soup, Static draped across one arm. Watching people eat, their favorite spectator sport.

Finished, Jody set her empty bowl on the floor. Drank wine from the bottle. Static settled at her head. Stirred and changed and chewed her hair. Jody slept, woke up, slept.

She tried to shake her torpor, but couldn't. She forced herself from the chair, washed her dishes. Dressed in her warmups, went for a walk in the arroyo, though it was dark already. Outside, it had gotten colder still, was well below freezing, but the promised snow still hadn't delivered. The evening felt heavy and waiting. The sand dragged at her feet.

After only a half-mile, her willpower broke, and she labored back home.

She gave up, decided to go to bed early. Why not, this was the lost Sunday anyway.

Ish was there all night long. They were in the office and he was trying to warn her about something. She wanted him to hold her and make love to her, but he wouldn't. If she could have just remembered, there was something she needed to tell him.

They were in the bomb shelter. They're up there, *he warned.* The mutations, the monsters. *Her mother the zombi, trying to break through the skylight of her brain. If her mother got in, she would kill Jody. She would kill them both.*

Ish kept running away. She needed to tell him something, but he was always far away in the distance, running across the desert. He was Bounding Antelope, the Man Who Runs.

She tried to call him. She was in the sleep chamber, sitting on the edge of the bed with the telephone on her lap. She was all alone in the lab. It was dusty and dirty and the glass was broken. They had all gotten disgusted and left her. All the people in the world.

She was the last survivor of the nuclear war.

She tried to call, but she was dialing too slowly. There was a line of telephone booths in the sand, but every time she made one of them ring, he ran past it and on to the next. She couldn't catch up. He was running away from her, running back into the past, back to the clean desert. He was leaving her here in the future. Leaving her here alone.

15: the price you have to pay

Tuesday morning, that was the best she had been able to do on having the glass replaced. And at that, she had to pay extra. Getting something done on time in Santa Fe—that was premium service. What a radical concept. Okay, if you really want it, but it'll cost you.

So she could have started the dream sessions again on Tuesday night instead of Wednesday. But with the workmen in the office all day, it would have felt too rushed, too distracted. Minus her study, though, the week took forever to pass. The office routine was maddening. Never had she been less interested in the problems of others. She was brusque with her patients, unsympathetic. Don't tell me your troubles, just leave me alone.

Don't tell me your troubles, I've got troubles of my own, troubles of my own.

She called the police, but nobody knew anything. Vic's home number was unlisted, so she got it from Toni and left messages on his machine, but he didn't call back. She had hesitated to bother Toni, considering what Vic had said about the relationship. But Toni didn't react when Jody made the request, and she didn't ask why Jody wanted the number.

Toni didn't seem to give a damn that the lab had been burglarized. She was brusque with her patients, too. Jody heard her once or twice, passing by an open door.

Don't tell me your troubles.

Friday, as she was coming in for her dream session and Rafael Tafoya was leaving, he took her aside. He had dreamed he was a ghost. All the night long. It had been sad, but wonderful. No one could hear him, so it was very lonesome, but he had danced along the ocean in solitary joy. Then he had become Superman, which was much like being a ghost, and he had followed his earthly family about all unseen, protecting them from harm, an angel with a cape.

"That's a very powerful dream, Rafael," she had said. Impatient as she was, she was drawn to his enthusiasm. Maybe she wasn't a guru, but she was all he had. People needed to tell you their dreams. Dreams weren't finished until you told them.

Rafael glowed with pride. "What are these pieces of dreams I see when I cross over into sleep?" he said. "Those moments when the world opens and changes."

She gave him the official term, hypnagogic imagery. "But I prefer my own term," she said. "I call it onset imagery." There was little information on the subject, she added. There was no indication of REM involvement, as with normal dream states, for example. Also, the sensations were fleeting, and therefore extremely hard to study.

"But isn't that what science is supposed to do?" Rafael said. "Study the subtle things? They chase neutrinos and build skeletons out of fragments of bone. No. If they think it is different, then they are wrong. This is the same as dreaming. I feel it. I know it."

So far she had largely ignored onset imagery, as had most other researchers. But Rafael was dead right. It *was* connected somehow. If her theory was going to be any good, if it was going to be comprehensive, she would have to take it into account.

"I think that we are always dreaming," Rafael said. "Always dreaming, and it is only that the world interrupts." He looked at Jody. "Is there a science that would confirm this?"

As a matter of fact, there was. According to Hobson's research at Harvard, the aminergic system, which prevailed during wakefulness, was basically an inhibitor on the always-present cholinergic system. So you might, in that sense, argue for dreaming as the basic state.

But she was not happy with Hobson's model in other respects. Especially in his sloppy and too-easy identification of dreaming with delirium. Or his nice neat AIM cube.

All of which was way too technical to go into with Rafael. Or much of anybody else. It was frustrating, never having anybody to talk to on your own level about the things you loved the most, but that was the price you paid for doing original work.

"Maybe," she said. "But I really have to go now."

"Yes," Rafael said. "Your own dreams await you. I hope they are as satisfying for you as mine have been for me." He went out whistling.

Satisfying. Now there was a way she had never thought of dreams before.

She made herself go skiing on Saturday, fighting her way out along Windsor Trail east from the Ski Basin. Someday she wanted to take it right on over the top, past Spirit Lake and down again to Holy Ghost Creek. Winter at eleven thousand feet. Not the sort of thing to try by yourself, but she'd never found anybody to go with her. Hmm. What about Shade?

Not this season, for sure. It would be the end of March by the time he got back. There might be a couple more good snows in the northern mountains, but that was all.

Sunday she vegged out with the babies, but felt lousy about it, worthless because she wasn't getting anything done. Her brain was on hold. She was so discouraged she didn't even bother to write her Saturday-night dreams down in the journal.

She had five more months on DormaVu's payroll. Five more months she could afford to run the other dreamers, unless she wanted to dip into her own capital. No way. Theory or no theory, this business had eaten up enough of her life.

The money had come available suddenly, and it had been take it or leave it. She had taken it, but look what it had brought her. A jammed-up life. Her nights not her own. What had she liked most about her dreams? The sense of freedom. So what had she done? Turned that wilderness into a regimen. A routine. A study, for god's sake.

Satisfying. May your dreams be as *satisfying* as mine.

That was her trouble. That was what she did to everything. Studied it, analyzed it, overintellectualized it. That was why she drove men away. She couldn't take them as they were, couldn't relax and go with the flow. No, she had to turn the famous Jody Nightwood X-ray eyes on them. Pinned and wriggling on a wall. What was that from?

Now she was going to drive Shade away. She could feel it coming.

• • •

Colonel Wilbur Goodloe Hall was pissed. He was walking the house with the portable phone to his ear. In the room with the big Bierstadt right now, the pedestals with the models from his new development. Waiting for them to route the call, so it wouldn't be coming from Santa Fe, just in case anybody was checking, which he was sure they weren't.

His wife had gone to choir practice, and would stay through evening services. She wasn't the innocent young planter's daughter anymore, Miss Sunflower County, who had run off with the handsome soldier. She had seen a lot in the years with him. But she was still loyal to the church. In deference, he never had Tanya over on Sundays. It wouldn't have felt right.

He had been pissed all week. This stupid-ass burglary. What kind of incompetent morons had they given him? He had warned Freddy, but Freddy had said these were the best they could do. It was a dark op, and they were on a limited budget, blah blah blah, and they were covering every possible dream researcher, because who knew which one Benjamin was most interested in? How could you know, when you didn't even know what he was looking for?

Colonel Hall wasn't so much pissed at Leonard and Toynbee as at himself. This was what you got for playing spy, and he should have known that. Why the hell had he agreed to the arrangement in the first place? It wasn't vanity, the sense of power. He had his own little empire now. He had the money, the house, the hottest woman in town.

He smiled at that. He bet it griped the redskins, seeing him with Tanya. He bet it griped them just like it had griped the jigaboos back in Mississippi when he was with Aurene. Put a burr under your saddle, podna? What you gonna do about it?

And that was the reason, really. This setup had gotten so automatic it was boring. He liked to stir things up. Raise a ruckus. He liked the action, the edge. That was how come the Silver Star. Why would a Delta boy give a shit for the lives of a platoon full of spics, Jews, Eyetyes, and big dumb Swedes anyway? But after twenty-four hours pinned down under fire, you got a little fed up with just laying there rooting in the mud like a prize Poland China hog.

And that was also why he had spent his fortieth birthday in-country, a long time after he'd made his first million and could have retired and maybe been governor someday.

And it was why he'd gone out in the snow that day in the Jemez. Telling himself he was just checking up on his agents. Seeing for himself what the woman was up to. Sure.

It was a character failing, there was no getting around it. But what could you do? You couldn't be somebody you weren't. Good Lord made us all the way he made us. Good Lord had made him to like trouble. Might ruin him someday, might take away everything he had built up, but what could you do? You anted up and you played your cards.

This wasn't that big a deal, though. He could put a stop to it.

He had read the police report in last Monday's paper, and had known instantly that his duo had screwed up. Rather than doing anything, he'd sat on it all week. That had been especially irritating, but if he'd gotten after them any sooner, they might have suspected their control was local. Also, by now they'd be off guard. They'd be thinking maybe no repercussions. So when he hit them with it, the shock would be that much greater. Get some *action* going.

Leonard took the call. His partner was out walking somewhere, trying to cheer himself up with endorphins. He'd been depressed all week, ever since the burglary. He blamed himself, as well he might. Leonard had seen a long time ago that the Brit was a bit of a fraud.

But nobody had stirred him the way Toynbee did since his first hopeless love, way back in high school. That fellow had been a fucking football player, a total jock, and straight as they come. But oh so beautiful. Leonard had been the jock's loyal little four-eyed buddy, the one who wrote his papers and coached him in algebra and so got to hang out when the guys drank beer and talked girls. All of them teasing him because he couldn't ever seem to get to first base.

A fucking tight end, that's what that guy had been. Leonard had had a lot of laughs about that later, after he'd grown up and gotten over his broken heart and figured out what he was. Laser surgery for the eyes, ten years ago, in Europe, while it was still illegal here. Had the nose augmented when they'd straightened out the deviated septum that had kept him pale and sickly with sinus infections all during his adolescence. Years of aikido, karate, before he'd even joined the agency. Look at him now. He imagined the tight end fat and dull, sitting in front of the tube with a beer on Monday nights, watching the ones who could still do it.

Leonard could cover for Toynbee. He could handle it.

But this jerk on the phone, their control.

You probably didn't think anybody would find out, the man said. You probably thought, way off here at headquarters, we would never know. But you've put the whole mission in danger. I'm ordering you to back off, back way off. You're lucky I don't yank you right out of the field. If we didn't have a manpower shortage, that's exactly what I'd do.

There was a lot more, and it was all just as infuriating. Things happen, dammit. You're in the field, it doesn't come down like the nice neat little mission plans in the bound folders, with the your-eyes-only four-color flowcharts. Shit happens, you have to adapt.

But Leonard didn't bother saying any of that, didn't bother arguing. It was all part of being in the field. You made the play, and you were the scapegoat if it went wrong. His job was a thousand times better than sitting at some desk job like this bozo on the phone, anyway. Control, shit. Fancy name for nothing much. Fucking dispatcher, that's all the man was.

He took his lecture like a good little boy. He agreed they would lay off a few weeks, give the subject some room, see how the play went. See if she made any contact, see if the word went out. If it didn't, there was no rush. They would have plenty of time to get what they were after. Option A would stay in effect, no need for Option B.

He got off the phone just in time, just before his lover came in, ruddy-faced and feeling better now. He made Toynbee a Bloody Mary, gave it to him with a kiss. Toy, he said. You Toy. It was Leonard's turn to cook, and he knew that's what Toynbee would want to do, stay in. Do a little cocooning. He didn't mention the phone call.

But it was frustrating, sitting on the information. It was tying him in knots. Carrying a secret like that, protecting somebody you cared about from information that would hurt them, it made *you* hurt. It was like that fable, carrying the fox in your shirt. Eating your guts out.

He wanted to be with Toynbee, but the Brit was a real stay-at-home, a real mother hen. Leonard needed more action than that. He needed to *do* something. Needed *release*.

There was still a third suspect out there, somebody who might be an agent for Benjamin, the one he hadn't taken out yet. Leonard faulted himself for getting lazy and comfortable. He should already have taken care of the situation.

When it got dark, he put his coat on, slipped the cheap nickel-plated .22 into the chest pocket, the gun he'd bought a couple of weeks ago on the street. Gangbanger's piece. It would be found a couple of blocks from the scene, no prints.

"I'm going out for a few minutes," he called. Toynbee was in the kitchen, stirring, checking on things. It was always that way. The American would start the cooking, but Toy just couldn't stay out of it. He'd probably whip them up a soufflé before the evening was over.

"Going out? Why?" It was a good-humored plaintive wail.

"Forgot to get wine. I don't like any of that crap in the rack. Don't let the red sauce burn."

"I won't," Toynbee sang out. It was good to have him happy again. "But hurry back. You don't want to miss Poirot."

That was funny, Leonard thought, walking along the Paseo to Palace, where he would cut over to the suspect's apartment. Poirot. Sitting there on the sofa, leaning against each, eating from plates on their knees, watching *Mystery* on PBS. It was their Sunday-evening ritual. Himself, Leonard would rather have gone out dancing.

It never seemed to occur to Toynbee that Poirot was just a story, and he and Leonard were the real thing. You had to laugh. Fucking Poirot.

Poirot wouldn't have lasted two minutes against Leonard.

Albert Gray was not a spy. Which is not to say he was an innocent man. He had a dark secret, all right, but it was a personal secret, nothing to do with national security.

He would have been astonished to learn that the chief of the artificial intelligence subgroup for the CIA knew his secret. He would have been astonished to learn that the chief of the artificial intelligence subgroup for the CIA knew of his existence.

Benjamin George thought that if you were going to put nonplayers at risk, you could at least choose the ones who *deserved* to be at risk. He had arranged for the three suspects—none of whom was actually his agent, of course—to come to Freddy Davenport's attention. When all of this was over, and it came out that Freddy had killed three civilians—

Albert Gray was just sitting down to dinner when the doorbell rang. Dinner being a microwaved chicken pot pie and a glass of Chablis. One glass, no more. He had learned a long time ago what happened when he went over his limit.

It was the worst possible time for the doorbell to ring. The chicken pot pies were not bad at all if you heated them up right. He couldn't stand a microwaved pie. He heated them up in the oven in their little tinfoil dishes. That way they were crusty and almost like fresh.

He had waited twenty minutes, till the pie was just right, the Chablis perfectly chilled. Now this. Probably some girl scout selling cookies. But by the time he got rid of her, the pie would be just too cool, the Chablis just too warm. Entropy. His doorbell had never rung, not once in the months he'd been here. So of course it would have to ring just at this very moment.

It rang again. He sighed. Pushed his wire-rims back up his rabbity nose. Passed his hand over his balding scalp. Got up and went to the door.

On his front stoop there was an extremely sparkly young man in a trenchcoat, wearing one of the most fetching smiles Albert Gray had ever seen. The young man was maybe five-eight. He flashed a badge and said, "Mr. Albert Gray? I'm Sergeant Preston of the mumble mumble police. Could you give me a minute of your time?"

Albert might have been worried. His last encounter with police had not been very pleasant. But all that was years ago, and Albert had paid his debt. He had gone into the court-ordered therapy willingly, and he had learned to control himself. If he didn't have much of a sex life anymore, that didn't matter. All he wanted now was to be a good citizen.

Besides, the young man was so cheery, it made you feel good just to look at him.

"You're awfully young to be a policeman," Albert said. His pie forgotten.

"It's my baby face," the officer responded. "I'm thirty-five. Mr. Gray, would you mind stepping out here and letting me take a look at your car? You might want to put on a jacket."

"What's this about?" Albert said.

"I'll tell you, sir, if you'll just help us out here."

"Give me a minute." Albert went in, found his alpaca, went down the steps with the young policeman. There was no driveway, his Camaro was parked on the street. Besides the porch light, the only illumination was a streetlamp on the far corner, and that was partially blocked by his neighbor's pine, so that a shadow fell over the car. "What's this about?" Albert said again.

"Sir, we've had a report of a purse-snatching in the area. The suspect fled in a dark blue late-model car, and we're just checking all the cars in the neighborhood that match the description."

"I certainly haven't snatched any purses tonight."

"Yessir, I can see that. This is just routine, and I appreciate your patience." The sergeant wrote his license number down in a little notebook. It was an Illinois plate, of course. "Been in Santa Fe very long, Mr. Gray?" he said. He kept writing, Albert couldn't guess what. He wondered if they had dug up the old trouble. But that couldn't be, the young cop was too friendly. He had seen the way their faces changed when they found out about the trouble.

"Since you know who I am, you know I haven't," Albert said. Then, in case that had sounded critical, he added, "Boy, you fellows really stay on top of it, don't you?"

"It's the computer age, Mr. Gray. You should know."

"That's a funny thing," Albert said. "I don't really know much about computers themselves. I mean, I use them, like everybody else. I'm just kind of an advance man for the company, a glorified salesman, really, that's all."

"So do you think you'll open a branch here in Santa Fe?"

"That really depends on the city, officer. What kind of breaks they can give us. We'd certainly like to. Water for cooling, that's the main worry." It felt good, actually, chatting with the policeman. Being on the right side of things. It was a wonderful feeling.

"I hate to bother you, sir, but could you open your car so I could check the registration? Just this one last thing, and I'll be out of your hair."

The keys were in the alpaca, so Albert didn't have to go back in the house for them. As he was unlocking the driver's-side door, he wondered where the officer's vehicle was. Around the block somewhere? He hadn't seen it when he was coming down the steps.

There was a movement behind him, and Albert turned to see what was up. The officer was holding a gun, a shiny silver gun. He was pointing it right at Albert.

"What is this?" Albert said. "I really *didn't* steal that lady's purse."

The gun barked at him. Just like a little dog. Yip yip yip, three flashes in the darkness. There was something wrong with Albert's chest. His chest felt as though it were in free fall, as though it had become detached from his body and was spinning through space.

No, that was him. His whole body. He was down on the ground. The streetlight was in his eyes. The officer stepped over him, a striding momentary blackness. The officer was doing something in Albert's car. A loud, wrenching noise.

The blackness again. Standing over him. Albert realized he was dying. His chest was warm and wet. He would never get the blood out of his jacket. No that wasn't important. His mind couldn't seem to catch up. He hadn't realized you could die without catching up. It worried him. It didn't feel right to die without totally understanding that you were dying.

The dog barked again. Two more little yips, two more little flashes. Silly. Waste of bullets. He was gone anyhow. The black shape moved, the light dazzled his eyes.

"Why?" Albert said. He could hear the policeman walking away, as if he were walking up a moving set of steps into the light, into another world. The glow was softer now, withdrawing. So Albert wasn't going to enter the light like they talked about. He would be left behind, falling forever from darkness into darkness. He wasn't surprised.

He tried to raise his voice, call out to the vanishing officer: "Was it that little girl?"

Ish was waiting in the office. He had changed the decor. She liked the warmer colors, the indirect lighting. They would be happy here. He showed her the sleep chamber, and she almost wept. It was her bedroom from home, from when she was a girl.

Where did you find it? *she said.* I thought it was gone for good.

Nothing is lost in dreams, *he said.*

I don't want this to be a dream, *she said.* I'll wake up and you'll be gone again.

He had died, a long time ago, and she had been full of grief. In another country, another life.

If this wasn't a dream, I wouldn't be here, *he said.*

They were in the woods. A soft light came through the trees, a light that was not morning or evening or afternoon. Shafts of rich light changing as they walked together down the rows of the streetlamps. Like David Suchet in the opening sequence from Poirot.

But who was murdered? Please don't let him be the one they murdered.

She ran calling into the forest, but he was nowhere to be found.

She had to look at her hands. She had to see them, before it all vanished.

There they were, in the spotlight. White gloves in the spotlight. The magician was dressed in black, so the hands were all you saw. But that wasn't enough, floating hands.

He cupped her breasts from behind, and that meant she could feel his arms, warm around her. That meant she could lean back, naked, and feel him naked along her back.

She sighed. Where did you go? *she whispered.* I missed you.

He nibbled the tendon just where her neck flowed into her shoulder. The hairs lifted along her forearms, her nipples tingled and stood erect. I'm always here, *he said.* You have to learn to concentrate. You can keep me if you concentrate.

She turned to nestle into him. She opened her thighs to let his cock between, then closed around it. She put her lips in the hollow of his throat.

Not that kind of concentration, *he said. He leaned on his ax. He was barechested, and the sweat ran along his fine muscles. He had laid in plenty of firewood. They would make it through the winter okay. The sun dazzled in the autumn leaves, dappled him with light. His eyes were very blue, the blue exactly of the sky, as if you could see the sky in him.*

Use the natural light, *he said. He was singing:*

> Learn the practice of the natural light,
> everything will be all right,
> roses are rosy by butterfly light,
> tractors are good.
>
> Don't be afraid in the wolfily wood,
> tractors are good,
> tractors are right.

The tractor's headlights threw a beam on the road through the woods, shaking and jostling as the tractor lurched and churned. They walked in the spotlight of the beam. It was a good thing her father had driven the tractor to church, or they would never have found their way home in the darkness. They held hands as they walked.

The tractor was rumbling and purring like someone she knew. It was funny that the noise was coming from beside her, instead of from behind.

She didn't want to be a pair of white hands floating in the darkness. She didn't want Ish dressed in black, disappearing into his death. Please no, please not another funeral.

She turned into the bright light. It blinded her, but she saw a shadowy form behind it. Who was the stranger driving the tractor? The light dazzled around his shadowy form.

Are you the Lord Jesus Christ? *she said.*

No, *the dark figure said.* You didn't see any blood on the gloves, did you? You didn't see any nail holes in the gloves.

She was standing in the circle of light in the forest, completely naked. All the deacons were gathered around. Chipper was there. I told you she was naked, *he said.*

She lifted her eyes up the well of the light to the stars. Ish was there, at the top of the stairs. He was sleepy, she had waked him up. But he wasn't mad. He was laughing. He came down the stairs in his house robe, barefoot on the carpeting. When you figure out who I am, *he said,* you won't have to sit up reading in the kitchen all night long.

She had been reading at the kitchen table, the old wooden table. Reading in the light from the open refrigerator. She was worried about the meat, the ham would go bad, but she had to finish reading the map before the bulb burned out. If she didn't finish reading the map, she would be lost again. She would have to go work in the store forever, and she would never grow up and go to college and she would never be able to find him again.

We are the map, *he said. He opened the bedroom door to show her. The bulb was still burning. It would never go out, not while he was there. He led her into the room. He undid the tie of her robe, slipped it back from her shoulders, let it fall to the floor. He opened his robe. She climbed up on the bed, knelt on her hands and knees. He climbed up behind her. He tented her in his open robe. He fingered her vulva open, drew the moisture. He put himself in.*

He thundered against her, and it was what she wanted. She was the mountains and he was the lightning storm banging against them. The lightning all in her belly now and forever, the great good warm beginning of things. She lifted her head to look into the bright light. There was a shadowy form in the light. It was Bianca, on the other side of the glass, watching.

Bianca walked out of the light, through the glass. She was a ghost in this dream. You could do that when you were a ghost. We were all ghosts in our dreams. Bianca bent to her face, and they kissed each other. Bianca's mouth was warm, and the storm was coming up the valley in the mountains, and Jody was theirs to do with as they pleased, she was the human sacrifice.

Tears of happiness were running down her face.

16: the price you have to pay, part ii

She lay a long time remembering the dream. Blind Lemon purred warmly beside her on the pillow. She felt like purring herself. She had to get up eventually, though. Clean the cat box, feed the babies, feed herself, enter the dream in her journal while she drank her coffee. Shower. Go in to work. That was the price you paid. The price of satisfaction.

While she was typing the dream in, she remembered Ish coaching her in how to make the dream stay, how to keep it from changing from one unpredictable scene to another, so that you could never quite catch up with what was happening to you.

The dream, teaching her how to hold the dream . . .

She thought of a term for the way dreams changed so constantly. The Swivel, she called it. She meant that from scene to scene, there was at least one constant element. Everything might change around that element, and it might not be the same from scene to scene, but each scene had an associative link to the next. Whereas in waking life, almost everything stayed the same and you proceeded in a linear fashion into a mostly predictable future, in dreams you swiveled, you pivoted on a single common element into what was always fresh and new.

The sleep chamber had become her bedroom as a girl. The light in the bedroom had become the light in the forest had become the streetlamps at the beginning of *Poirot*. That had led to the thought of murder, of losing Ish, and that to looking for her hands. Which had become the gloves (and the light was back), and then his hands touching her. She lost it a little there, but then the light again and what she just now realized was a pun on attractors, and—

This was important. This related to the curvature of I-space.

She drafted a few quick notes on continuity. Waking life continuous at infinite sets of points, dreams continuous at only one or a few? She was going to have to read some *n*-dimensional topology, do some computer modeling of possible spaces.

It did not occur to her that her sudden flow of energy and perception came from love. It did not occur to her to wonder whether that was where all energy and perception must arise. In fact in her excitement she had momentarily forgotten Ish, who was the occasion of it all.

Making the notes ran her late for work, so that she didn't have time to read the paper, and took it with her. She didn't notice that her state of mind had shifted back to the analytical, the pragmatic, the linear. Go ahead and say it, Jody. The aminergic.

On the way to the office she laughed at herself for waiting to have such a great sex dream until she already had an actual man in her life. Where had these dreams been when she needed them, when she had been all alone? She supposed that her psyche was so constructed she could allow herself fantasy only when reality gave permission. Loosen up, Jody!

She didn't notice that she had now downgraded the dream to a sex dream.

After her first patient, a rather boring insomnia—but wasn't all insomnia boring? Wasn't that what really kept us awake? Not worry, but fundamental boredom? Anyway, after the insomniac she had some time, and settled back with more coffee and the paper. She read a story about some poor fellow shot to death probably by a gang member, apparently for his CD deck, which had been ripped loose from his car. Police were a little puzzled about the circumstances, because the fellow's dinner had been waiting on the table. What was he doing out on the street in his coat? But they had found the weapon and there wasn't much question about the motive. They didn't say so, but the odds of catching the shooter were poor.

She had a little shiver of mortality, death coming so quickly and so randomly. But it was a delicious shiver, because she was in such a good mood, and she wasn't the one dead.

The story made her think about Vic. How he saw crime nearly every single day of the week, what that would be like. It was even possible he had worked this case. She hoped Vic and Toni worked things out, got back together. They were good for each other, she thought.

And so she was launched into her week, her last few days without Shade.

Vic had made up his mind. He was going to ask his buddy in the FBI to run the print from Jody's computer through LABNET. He had been putting off asking the favor, because quid pro quo. Ask and you shall be asked.

There was nothing in a law enforcement way he was likely to be able to do for a feeb, and so the return favor was probably going to be more like, Ring, ring. Hey, Vic, guess who? Yeah, got a vacation coming and me and the wife thought we'd check the place out, you hear so much about it, and we were wondering, you know any good cheap places to stay downtown. Oh, they all are? Gee. Oh yeah? Well, sure, if you're sure you wouldn't mind. Don't worry about us, we don't need much room. Naw, a couch in the living room would do. Well, we might bring the boy, he's never seen Santa Fe, but you'll like him. He's shooting up like a weed, I tell you. Lives eats and sleeps basketball, I really think he's got a future in the pros.

It had been easy to postpone asking the favor, because it was so unlikely the print would bring any results. But why take the print in the first place if you weren't going to do anything about it? Like it or not, taking the print had been a kind of promise to Jody.

Besides which, he and Toni were getting back together. She had decided she could live with his weird way of seeing things after all. That had its good points and its bad points. The good points, well, she was a hell of a woman. Bad points?

Well, she *could* nag. She was loyal to her friends and expected you to be just as loyal. She would be really pissed when she found out he hadn't run Jody's print yet.

He was definitely going to make the call today. And if not today, because today was follow-up on that damn stupid East Side shooting, then definitely tomorrow at the latest.

• • •

Jody dreamed of Ish again Tuesday night. This time the dream was more prosaic, a simple roll in the hay. Literally. She had noticed before how dreams would sometimes literalize clichés, metaphors, or puns. This time she and Ish did it in the loft of a barn. The straw was somehow as soft as a down comforter, not scratchy at all. It had been through a new manufacturing process, her brain told her, which made it like fine soft feathers.

She did things in that dream that she had never done with anyone. It went on awhile. She awoke glowing and proud of herself for being such an animal. But she held out on the details when she spoke into the recorder, saying that she'd had an erotic episode, but mostly forgotten it. She felt simultaneously guilty about withholding the information—what if the others in the study were doing the same thing?—and frustrated at not being able to compare notes with anyone else.

She would have *loved* to talk the dream over with Bianca.

She had been lucid all during the episode. In her journal, from which she did not withhold the details, she noted that every episode with Ish had involved lucidity. That seemed significant, but she didn't know what to make of it. It also seemed significant for the same invented character to show up in several dreams—recognizable, though his appearance changed from dream to dream, and sometimes from moment to moment within the dream.

She wondered if the phenomenon was related to those dreams in which she returned, over and over, to hauntingly familiar locales that nevertheless did not exist in waking life.

Shade called Wednesday, and apologized for not calling the week before—his business had gotten way out of hand. Jody was surprised at her reaction, which was not the huffiness of a neglected lover, but a wave of guilty anxiety, as if she had something to hide.

When she hung up, she realized that subconsciously she felt she had been two-timing Shade. With Ish. All the rest of the day, when she wasn't distracted by the problems of her patients, the guilt returned. It was just a *dream,* she told herself.

Ish did not return on either Wednesday or Thursday night, as if offended at being so discounted. Jody was left with nothing but the real world, her patients coming in telling her the same five or six miserable stories over and over. She tried for sympathy, but it wouldn't flow. The effort was like trying to feel appreciation for the music coming from a needle stuck on a scratched record. Soon her own life seemed to her just as empty of interest or variation, and since she was exactly like everybody else, she began to feel unutterably lonely.

What she should do, she should buy a couple of his books and read them. What name was it he said he wrote under? Something ridiculous. Gandy. Marcus Gandy. But she felt an unreasoning resistance. It felt like giving in somehow. Here she was, lonesome as hell, and he was off catting around the country feeling no pain.

Besides, she might not like the novels, and then what? It wasn't so much that she might insult him with her opinion. It was more nearly that she didn't want him to suffer in her own estimation. She didn't want to be in love with a bad writer.

Shade called Friday morning. He was back early, could they have lunch? Her heart didn't exactly soar, but something in her relaxed.

She was cramped between appointments, didn't have time for a full lunch, so suggested they walk over to Galisteo. The snow that had threatened had finally delivered just before sunrise on Monday. The weather had cleared on Tuesday, and the rest of the week had been sunny and increasingly warm. The mountains were still deeply white, there were still drifts in the corners of the buildings. But spring was on the way, it was in the air, you could feel it.

Shade came to the office to pick her up, but didn't come in. Instead he was there waiting when she came out, hat in hand like a suitor from an earlier century. They walked along silently but comfortably. He looked really fine in a hat, Jody thought. Very Liam Neeson.

What she was feeling at the moment wasn't love exactly. More like proud ownership.

"What's the news?" he said. "Anything happen while I was gone?"

Ish jumped into her mind, and she cast about desperately for something else to talk about. She thought about the break-in at the office—for the first time in a week, she realized.

"There was a shooting last week," she said. "A fellow who doesn't even live here. Didn't live here," she amended. "Some computer company advance man."

Talking about the break-in would have made her feel exposed, vulnerable, weak. As if being a victim were itself a crime, somehow. A blot on your record. And anyhow it was all over with, was an aberration. She didn't want to think about it.

"That's the best you can come up with?" he laughed. "No good news?" As they paused on the corner of Water and Galisteo, waiting to cross, he put an arm around her shoulders and gave her a hug. It felt unbelievably good.

The bum was there, the street-dweller from her last visit, sitting at an outside table. Despite the warmth of the day, he wore his ragged yellow coat and, this time, a battered hat. He looked up at them, looked quickly away. Shade came to a dead stop in the middle of the street. "Well, I'll be damned," he said. Jody had to tug him out of traffic.

Shade strode to the bum's table, pulled out a chair for her, sat himself, leaning forward. The bum turned his chair away, giving them his back. Jody stood behind her chair, at a loss over this turn of events, and not a little irritated at losing her lover's attention.

"You're Loren Wingo," Shade said. "We all thought you were dead."

"I don't know you," Loren Wingo said to Shade. He shifted around to face them. Jody was struck, once more, with his unexpected vitality. She had forgotten the clarity, the intensity of the blue eyes. There was none of the body odor she might have expected. The man was clean—unshaven, wearing rags that even the thrift shops might reject. But clean.

"You remind me of somebody I *used* to know," he said.

"There's a story behind that," Shade said.

"I thought there might be," Wingo said.

Jody sat down. This looked as if it would go on awhile.

"Does anybody else know?" Shade said.

"A few. Jeanie. I called her when I got out here. Apple. It wouldn't have been fair to let them worry. My mother, but she's dead now."

"Obviously they all kept your secret. Are Jeanie and Apple out here too?"

"No," Wingo said. "Jeanie divorced me. Not long after we—after I left. I've lost track of Apple. Presumably she's gone to college and gotten a job, but I never hear from either of them."

"So you've been out here all this time? But why?" Shade said. "What have you been doing with yourself?"

"Working," Wingo said.

Jody couldn't help it, she gave a bark of involuntary laughter.

Wingo gazed at her. His expression did not change. "I know how I look to people like you," he said. "That's one of the reasons I came out here, to get away from people like you."

"What are you working on?" Shade said. "What's so important you gave up your whole life and all of your family and friends?"

"What do you think?" Wingo said.

Shade sat back in his chair. Then he shook his head and laughed. "After all these years. 'A Theoretical Model of Heaven.' That's what it is, isn't it? You're finally doing it."

Jody was more than irritated now, she was pissed. Okay, so it had been rude to laugh. But the man had been rude right back, and Shade hadn't even bothered to defend her.

"Listen, guys," she said. "I'm hungry, and I've got about twenty minutes more for lunch. You continue your reunion, but I'm going to get myself something to eat." She forced herself to civility. "Can I bring anybody anything?"

"Coffee," Loren Wingo said. Shade waved her off.

"You sure you don't want anything else?"

"No," Wingo said. "There's not much here for the price you have to pay."

"That's true anywhere," Jody said.

She bought herself a large wedge of yesterday's quiche, a coffee for Wingo, and a double cappuccino for herself. While they were making the cappuccino, she flipped through magazines. Decided to buy the latest issue of *Vanity Fair,* though reading it always depressed her. All those pages and pages of ads, all those glossy, empty, thing-dominated lives. Perfumes lifted into the air when she riffled the pages, expensive perfumes, perfumes that suggested not sex, but money, or else the pheromones of a world in which there was no longer any difference.

"Who are you?" Wingo said. "How do you know so much about me?"

"Who do I remind you of?" Shade said.

"You remind me of a kid named Marcus Gandy."

"Close enough," Shade said. "Marcus idolized you. He wanted to *be* you. He might have become a mathematician himself if you hadn't disappeared."

"I can't help that," Wingo said. "I didn't ask to be his guru. That was his choice. Do you know what it's like having people looking up to you and you know you don't deserve it?"

"Is that why? We thought you'd committed suicide. Just walked off into that ravine behind your house and shot yourself, or thrown yourself off a cliff. Did you know there were search parties? They looked for your body for more than a week."

"You keep saying 'we,' like you were there, but you aren't Marcus. You resemble him—what he might have become if he had grown up hard and had allowed himself to do unspeakable things. But you aren't Marcus, are you?"

"No," Shade said. "But I write books. And that's the name I write under."

"Then you ought to understand," Wingo said. "I didn't pretend to die out there in that ravine. I *did* die. And when I came back I was another man. My whole previous existence had been a lie. I told my students what a grand and glorious human adventure it all was, what an odyssey of the mind, and I could see them, a few of them, catching fire—"

"Like Marcus."

"Like Marcus. And all the time I knew what a fraud I was. I knew that I myself was only a mediocre mathematician. Or what about Jeanie and Apple? No way a man could have a better wife and daughter, right? No two sweeter people on the face of the Earth."

"We thought you were the ideal family."

"Exactly. *But I didn't love them.* I thought I ought to love them, I tried like hell to make myself love them, but the feeling just wouldn't come. I hated my life, and I hated myself, and I had my face rubbed in it every day because people like Marcus thought I had all the answers."

"So you just walked away and never came back? I can understand that, sort of. But didn't you ever think what you were doing to the people who cared about you? Maybe you didn't love them, but don't you think you owed them an explanation? A little peace of mind?"

"It wasn't that way. When I went out that day—I was drunk, and I'd had another stupid argument with Jeanie. But I wasn't trying to kill myself. Maybe you know that ravine, how fast the creek drops away, all those levels and levels of stone. It can be tricky going, but I'd been down it a hundred times before. It always helped me calm down when I was upset, just the solitude, the sound of the water. I don't know what happened this time. Probably I slipped on a mossy ledge. When I came to, I didn't know who I was. I didn't know *where* I was."

"You're saying you had amnesia? Don't you know what a cliché that is?"

"The amnesia was real. I'm not saying it wasn't psychological. Maybe deep down inside I saw my chance and I took it. I used to agonize about that. Now I see it doesn't matter. It was just the price I had to pay to get out of a life that was killing me. I had to die."

"But obviously you've long since recovered your memory."

"Not only was the amnesia real, it was profound. I said I didn't know where I was, or who I was. I literally didn't know *what* I was. I had no concept of humanity, no concept of the planet Earth—let alone the state of Arkansas. When I first woke up, I swear to God, the trees looked like mathematical diagrams in black and white. It was as though I were looking *through* everything to the skeleton of the universe."

"I've never heard of anything like that."

"I haven't either. But that's how it was. As I went down the creek, colors returned. Leaves began to be leaves, flowers began to be flowers, though I didn't have any words for them yet. I had gotten pretty badly beaten up in the fall. A broken wrist, couple of ribs. I had twisted one of my ankles. My head was hurting like crazy, and my hair was full of dried blood. I probably had blood all over my face. I was like a wounded animal, going on instinct. I followed the creek, because it seemed to know where it was going."

"This is a hell of a story, Loren."

"I was in the wilderness five days at least. I may have stumbled along beside the creek for thirty or forty hours straight before I slept the first time. The ravine became a canyon. Toward the end I knew I was a human being. I could talk, and I knew I was speaking English. But I still didn't have any idea who I was. That didn't come back to me for half a year."

"How did you make it out?"

"The creek joined a larger river, probably the White, and some canoeists came floating by. They got me to an emergency room. I told them I was a hunter, had gotten lost and fallen. Made up a name, told them I had no family and had lost all my ID. I knew I was hiding something, but I didn't know what. I thought maybe I was a murderer. I went to the pastor of the local Baptist church, told him a sob story, borrowed some money and some clothes. After that, I hitched rides. I wound up here, working odd jobs to get by. My memory started returning."

"And?"

"It was like a story I'd read in a book somewhere. It was about somebody else, another life. I wasn't that man anymore. That's when I called Jeanie, of course, and my mother. For the rest—I thought it was better just to stay dead. I had finally become what I was born to be."

"Which is?"

Wingo laughed. "A hermit. No, I'm not kidding. I make a great hermit. I've got a little cabin up in the mountains, no power, no running water. I only come into town once a month or so, just when I need supplies. The rest of the time—I think, and I do my work."

"I don't really want to let this go, Loren. Now that I've found you again. Are you staying in town tonight? Would you be willing to come over to my place for dinner?"

"Sure. I do have one or two friends. I guess I'm not a hard-core hermit. I mean, I do fine without people, but I'm plenty sociable when I decide to be."

"It's set, then. Here, let me draw you a map."

Shade and Wingo were sitting back with that look men wear when they've traded all the information they care to for the moment. Only men could do that, could just stop talking. Women would have been engaged in a rapid-fire two-way transmission of information that fiber-optic cable couldn't hope to match, and would not have been able to stop themselves until they had updated each other on the history of the universe for the last twenty-five years.

"It's amazing," Shade said as Jody joined them.

And of course that was *all* he said, now that she had let herself become curious. Men. She ate, and they watched. When she was ready to go, Shade rose to walk her back. He leaned over the table and shook Wingo's hand. "Tonight, my place," he said.

She had been planning on ditching her dream session, she realized. Planning on it all along, without even consciously admitting it to herself. Love comes in, responsibility goes out the window. But now she was furious. All right, so Shade hadn't *said* they would spend the night together. But what had he *expected* her to think?

On the way back, he was silent, his head down. Definitely not thinking about her. Which made her even more furious. He was leaving her no openings, no response. Nothing was more maddening to a woman than having a man she cared about oblivious to her.

The problem was, he was too fine to throw back. His body, moving beside her, stirred her responses. Tall, good-looking bachelor with money to burn, but there wasn't that naughty-boy aura about him, that air of spoiled, self-involved recklessness you saw in the perpetual Peter Pans. No, when his attention *was* on her, she could see he was a solid man, a relationship man. He was made to be part of a couple.

So why was a catch like that floating around loose? Was he too good to be true? She put the thought from her mind. Not the immediate problem.

At her door, he gave her an absentminded kiss, then walked away. Angry as she was, she took the kiss, wanted it with all her heart. She marched past Consuela into her own office, looking for something to throw. There was nothing to throw, nothing in the whole damned office that wasn't too important or too expensive or too fucking fragile to pick up and throw.

The paperweight. But it was too heavy. It could do some real damage. She had had enough of broken windows. She couldn't scream, not with patients around. That was the trouble with blowing off steam. It always cost you more in damage than it gave you in relief.

Consuela appeared in the doorway. It was time for the first afternoon appointment. Consuela looked curiously at the glass sphere in Jody's clenched hand. Jody smiled brightly at Consuela. She picked up her calculator. She picked up her father's photograph in the silver oval frame. She juggled the three objects, whistling the opening bars of "Dixie."

"*Madre de Dios,*" Consuela said, and went away muttering under her breath.

Toynbee and Leonard sat at a table outside the Galisteo newsstand. They had just walked down from the condo, enjoying the lovely weather. They had had a late breakfast, but now it was time for a little something, a little pick-me-up, maybe espresso and a bite of chocolate.

"What do you want?" Leonard said.

"Maybe espresso and a bite of chocolate," Toynbee said. "You pick."

"Righto," Leonard said, smiling. He turned away then, to go inside and make their purchases, and it was a good thing by Toynbee, because tears stood in his eyes. That "Righto" had done it, that little bit of teasing, that tender mockery.

Toynbee was in love, no use pretending otherwise. But was he loved in return? He knew his companion enjoyed his company. Leonard was affectionate and attentive. But did he feel this same helpless elation, this same wild vertigo of hope? How could you tell with the Americans? After all these years he still couldn't always read them. Cheerful animals they seemed, so much of the time. Then one would open a sudden door, and—grandeurs of emotion. Vistas.

He had made a right mess of the B&E, but Leonard had not once accused him or faulted him. "No way you could have known they would be so wired up," he had said. "I mean, it's a *sleep* clinic, what's anyone going to steal? When you think about it, you just strengthened our case. It means she's hiding something. It has to."

Toynbee didn't think so. He had broken into her house, he had broken into her computer, and he had broken into her office. Nothing anywhere. The woman wasn't up to anything surreptitious. He had read her files. He was beginning to *like* her, silly get. He had felt himself in his schemes and contingencies a stranger, a violator, a profaner of the perfectly ordinary, as if the ordinary were what was holy and all that was holy.

They had their orders, but the orders were stupid, nonsensical. This was a farce. It was worse than a farce, it was a waste of time and money. And not that it mattered, but they were doing the girl a grave injustice. Her life might even be in danger. *Was* in danger.

In this line of work, principles could hurt you. Still, it was his principle to do as little harm as possible. To spare the innocent, if you could do so without too great an inconvenience. Really, it was incumbent on him to say something. He was the senior man in the field, and if he spoke out strongly enough, his superiors would be obliged to listen.

And if they did listen? No more lovely morning snuggle, no more Santa Fe.

Leonard returned, a newspaper under his arm. "I got you a double," he said. "And fudge. I thought I remembered you don't like brownies." He handed the paper to Toynbee.

"I like them well enough," Toynbee said. "But I prefer fudge. The point being sugar and chocolate, I'd as soon condense the experience. You're very thoughtful."

He took the paper apart into its sections. He liked to read the local news first.

Leonard had put on his gazing-thoughtfully-into-space expression. "Here's what we do," he said finally. "Obviously we have to lay back awhile. Observe. See if she's been alerted, or if she's taken it for a routine burglary. Can't risk letting her make us."

Toynbee was staring down at a photo over a reward story. Alliance Supercomputing was offering a reward for information in the shooting death of their top negotiator. It was a file photo of a nebbishy, balding, middle-aged man. Toynbee had seen it before, in a packet with two others. There had been no photo with the story of the shooting itself, a week ago.

He raised his eyes. Leonard was watching him. He lifted an eyebrow, gave a slight shrug. Now is the time, Toynbee thought. Three dead and probably more to come, and all for no reason whatsover. Now is the time to say something.

"Oh, I forgot." Leonard slapped his jacket, felt in the inside pocket. "Got a little something for you. Found them in there." He drew out a flat box, tossed it across the table.

Ovals.

"Go ahead," Leonard said. He had his lighter out. "Fire one up."

All these presents, Toynbee thought. The newspaper, the smokes. Who treated you this way? How many people got a tenth of this sort of affection? The hell with principles.

"I think you're exactly right," he said. "We lay back for a while."

Leonard held the lighter against the tip of the Oval. He shivered.

"Must be somebody walking over my grave," he said.

At home, Shade was on the phone again.

Hi, Mom, he said. Listen. I just ran into somebody I know, somebody I haven't seen in a long time. I don't think it means anything, but it is awfully coincidental. Does the name Loren Wingo mean anything to you? No? Okay. Will you check, though? Look through your old correspondence, see if anything comes back to you. Yeah.

He listened. Then he said: The last time he was on the record anywhere was in Fayetteville, Arkansas, twenty-five years ago this spring. Right. Okay. 'Bye now.

As soon as he hung up, the phone in the kitchen rang.

• • •

After she'd seen a couple of her afternoon patients, Jody felt better. Something about giving advice to others. You weren't a victim any longer, you were an authority. She considered her options. Okay, we're not gonna give Shade the heave-ho. He's the best-looking thing to come along in ages. And we're not gonna give him the freeze-out, either, the old cold shoulder. On this boy, it ain't gonna work. He would just walk. So.

Do you want to be with the man tonight, Jody? Answer, Yes.

But he's gonna be visiting with his long-lost pal, the hobo from the Twilight Zone. So. What do we do about that? Answer, We invite them both over to our place for dinner. Then, when the bum goes home, we keep our lover with us, and we jump his magnificent bones.

She picked up the phone, got Shade on the first ring.

"I'm glad you called," he said. "I was just realizing how rude I was at lunch." She didn't say anything. She hadn't been planning to take him to task, but if he was willing to put himself on the hook, let him wiggle a little. It felt good. "I hope you'll forgive me. I was just—well, I was astonished. Completely astonished. Beyond all measure."

He had a way of talking, sometimes. Cadenced and elegant, like a character from a very old novel. She supposed it came from being a writer. She loved it. There were so many odd and curious facets to his behavior, and you only caught glimpses.

"It was like seeing a ghost," he explained. "I mean that quite literally. In my mind, he's been *dead* the last twenty-odd years. Then suddenly, there he is, and he's hardly changed at all."

"Actually I was calling," she said, "to invite you guys over to my place for dinner. Unless you were planning to go out." And if you are, you'd damn well better invite *me* along. I've given you all the cues you're going to get.

"That would be wonderful," he said. "But are you sure—"

"I'm sure," she said. Having a bum over for dinner, she thought.

"He's not a bum," Shade said. "He's just contrary and independent. Actually, you two have a lot in common. I can see you coming to a real meeting of the minds."

Oh, shut up, she thought. The things I do for love.

"What can I bring?" he said.

"Nothing. I've never cooked for you, have I?" Once you taste my hushpuppies, honey—

"Are you sure? I could get some wine, or—"

"I'm the surest person you'll ever meet," she said. "Just bring your friend, and your sweet self, and a great big appetite. Say eight, eight-fifteen, at my place?"

"Marvelous," Shade said. "I'm really glad of this. I wanted to see you—"

She wanted to say, I love you. She said, "I have a patient waiting."

"Tonight at eight," he said, and she hung up.

That had all been very satisfactory. She was getting her man tonight after all, and she had managed to put him in his place as well. He was doing the leaning, he was doing the apologizing. She had not had a patient immediately waiting, of course. Yes, very satisfactory.

Except now she had to go home and whip up dinner for three.

She had no appointments after four, and left work early. At home she dusted, vacuumed, set the table with her good stoneware. Dining at home, when she was growing up, had been far from formal. Perhaps that had been part of her mother's despair, that she would have liked a more gracious life. *Their* good china had come from Safeway, on special.

Now here was Jody, homemaker and hostess. She felt like Martha Stewart.

But what the hell were they going to *eat*?

She inventoried her fridge. There was the one lonely leftover bagel. Several stale buttermilk biscuits. Hmm. Throw in the rest of the whole-wheat sandwich bread and some eggs and we could have a kick-ass bread pudding. But it needed to start soaking right away.

Fine, dessert was accounted for first, in true Southern style. And the rest of the menu? She settled on simple but good. Chili with homemade crackers. Heat up a frozen six-pack of those huge wonderful tamales from that place in Carrizozo. Make a guacamole appetizer with the two remaining and in fact long-overdue avocados, both black and skin-wrinkled but serviceable. Did she have blue corn chips for the guacamole? She did, an unopened bag.

They could drink margaritas, it fit the style of the meal. So the bread pudding didn't match up, so what? She would put in some piñon nuts, and she could use that Mexican brandy, Pedro Domecq, to flavor the hard sauce. Hard sauce, she had to make hard sauce!

By seven-fifteen the bread was soaking in the egg-and-sugar mix, a vat of chili was bubbling on the stove, the tamales were ready to heat, the guacamole and hard sauce were cooling in the fridge, and her back and feet were killing her. She just had time to shower and dress and maybe relax a few minutes. She decided to make herself an early margarita.

In the shower, she allowed herself to think how the evening might go. She'd been too busy before. She had to admit she wasn't looking forward to spending several hours in Wingo's company. She didn't care how good his mind was. As far as she could see, he was rude, hostile, inflexible, and utterly unconcerned about how anyone else felt.

Oh, well. The friend of my friend. She would just have to be careful not to let her impatience show. Be on your good behavior, Jody. No relationship comes without problems and compromises. That's just the price you have to pay.

When she toweled herself dry, she felt her body responding. Tissues were thickening, fluids were pumping, the little hairs on her skin were lifting eagerly.

The price was worth it. She was ready to be touched. All over.

17: a meeting of the minds

She had built a piñon fire in the living-room fireplace, probably the last of the season. Shade and Wingo tapped on the French doors at eight-fifteen, having walked the arroyo. They came in with a gust of cold night air, rosy-faced, puffing steam. She took their jackets.

"Is that your fire we've been smelling?" Shade said.

"Back up to it if you want to. I've still got to put the bread pudding in and make drinks. Margaritas okay with everyone?" But they followed her up to the kitchen instead, and stood around while she squeezed limes, salted the rims of three glasses.

"All this and bread pudding, too," Wingo said. He was wearing penny loafers, gray slacks, a white turtleneck, a navy blazer. He had shaved, and his gray hair was pulled back. The transformation was amazing. He might have been a senior model in a Sears catalog.

"Plain and simple fare," she said. Then added, on impulse, "You clean up nice." The odor of crushed limes filled her nostrils. She rattled ice into their glasses.

He smiled. "Like I told Shade, I'm a hermit. I don't see people, don't think about people for weeks on end. I forget about appearances. Doesn't mean I don't know how."

"Some of the rest of us might not be exactly what we appear, either," she said.

"Yeah, I made one of those 'you people' remarks, didn't I? Had you figured for a nose-in-the air rich-bitch. Shade set me straight. He said you hadn't come up easy. Said you'd worked hard—" Wingo waved his hand to indicate the the house: "For all this," he finished.

"It isn't that grand," she said.

"Looks pretty good to me," he said. "You've got more than one room."

Jody was trying to remember when she'd told Shade about her past, and couldn't. She must have said something, a sentence or two here and there, and he'd read between the lines, put it all together. Flattering, really, that he was paying that much attention.

At the moment he was paying attention to the cats, or pretending to, while she and Wingo jousted to an understanding. Static was on the counter, raising her back to his hand. Blind Lemon had flopped at his feet, now did a stretch, reached out a lazy paw to grab a pantleg.

A jigger of fresh lime juice in each glass, maybe a taste more. Jigger of Triple Sec. Two jiggers of tequila. Rapid swirl of the glass swizzle, a chiming of icy bells. She handed the drinks around, raised her glass. "Here's to appearances," she said.

They clinked. "And to realities," Wingo added.

She tried to get them down to the living room, but Wingo asked for a tour. "You can see most of the downstairs from here," she protested. "Great room and dining area out there, other side of the bar. Front foyer through the big arch. Greenhouse on the right front."

"Greenhouse?" Wingo said.

"Just a small one," Jody said defensively. Then, apologetically, "Weird to have it on the front side, but that's the southern exposure. Leads out into a little garden. Guest suite on the east side, the door's behind the stairs. Upstairs, study and master bedroom."

"Would you? I really like seeing where people work."

She consented, feigning reluctance. He was appreciative of almost everything, but when he came to *Osiris, Lord of the Underworld,* he drew in his breath.

"This is magnificent," he said.

Jody was almost ready to tell them what the piece meant to her, how it stood for the terrors and glories of looking into dreams, but took them downstairs instead, insisted they dig into the guacamole. Wingo warmed his backside at the fireplace. She put on Esterhoeven's beautiful meditative suite, *In the Sleep of the Dalai Lama,* something that wouldn't intrude.

"So, Mr. Hermit," she said. "You don't live in a cave, do you?"

Wingo laughed. "No. I rent a cabin up above the Rio en Medio. The closest you can drive in is about a mile away—in good weather— so I have to pack in my supplies."

She shook her head. "I get really sick and tired of people some- times myself. Get where all I want is to be left alone. But I don't think I could carry it to your extreme."

"It isn't people," he said. "It's time. Don't you ever get the feeling that there's something really important out there you're supposed to be doing with your life? And instead, you're sitting in an office, driv- ing a car, going to church, making chitchat, filing taxes, shopping for groceries, washing the dishes, taking out the trash, watching TV, clip- ping your fingernails?"

"In spring, the caged bird strongly feels," Shade said.

"Yeah," Jody said. "I do. But most people, if I talked to them about it, they would look at me funny and shrug and say, 'That's life.' "

Shade had stretched his feet out before him, leaned his head back on the sofa. His drink was gone, and his eyes were half-closed. Jody wondered at his ability to fade into the background. Such a huge and striking fellow, and yet he could practically disappear while you watched. Where had he learned that? Why had he felt the necessity?

"Take our mutual friend here," she said. "I don't think *he* sweats the small stuff."

"I wouldn't look at you funny," Shade said. He didn't move or lift his eyelids.

"Yeah, but you aren't worried about time passing," she said. "You aren't driven like we're talking about. Slow and easy and all natural, that's you."

"I have my demons," the big man said. "Mortality is not one of them."

"Who's talking mortality?" Jody said. "I'm not afraid of dying."

"It *is* mortality," Wingo said. "Some of us have it like a disease. It's not death—it's that we're finite. In mathematical terms, bounded. We can't fly. Can't walk through walls. Can't go without food or water or air. Can't exceed twenty-four hours in a day. If you look at it that way, then we're staring over the brink into nothingness every second of our lives.

"There I go again," he added, peering into his empty glass. "But I hate small talk."

"Me, I hate small drinks. Everybody ready for a refresher?"

They held out their glasses. When she came back from the kitchen, they were talking quasars. Shade argued that they were colliding black holes. That would explain why some appeared to be the result of colliding galaxies and others did not, since not all black holes were in galaxies. Wingo was raising objections. He said most astronomers thought black holes were younger than quasars. Besides, he didn't think the energy spectrum would match—

They went beyond calculus, into Diffy Q and then into methodologies whose terms she did not recognize. She liked cosmology, Grand United Theories of Everything. But these two might as well have been a couple of barflies talking pro football. When they'd gone a full three minutes without uttering a single word of comprehensible English, she broke in.

"Hey," she said. "Is this a guy thing?"

They apologized, grinning. Proud of their damn smarts. "So," Jody said. "What are you, old college buddies? Get your degrees at the same school?" They shook their heads no.

"I used to teach math," Wingo said. "Just high school, I never finished my Ph.D. Was a graduate assistant for a couple of years. But I guess I was pretty serious for a while."

"Don't let him fool you," Shade said. "He was the real thing."

"Where was this?" Jody said.

"Arkansas," Wingo and Shade said together. "Fayetteville," Wingo added.

"No kidding? Another Arky? Both of you? Shade, you never told me."

"Not me," Shade said. "That's just where I know Loren from."

Jody wanted to compare notes on the Razorbacks, on President Bill. She wanted to play the who-do-you-know-that-I-know game, trade the latest political gossip. What preposterousness was the legislature up to now? Or what about Huckabee, the Baptist preacher turned governor who hadn't signed off on the relief money for the tornado a couple of years back because the paperwork had described the disaster as an act of God, and God wouldn't do bad things?

But Wingo was plainly uncomfortable talking Arkansas. Undercurrents, Jody thought. "From high-school math teacher to hermit," she said. "How did that happen?"

"Just like I was saying. There was one and only one thing I was supposed to be doing, and suddenly I couldn't waste any time doing anything else."

"Is this that theoretical God stuff you guys were talking about? Tell me about it."

"Heaven," Wingo said. "Theoretical model of heaven. Not to be rude, but can we eat first? I haven't had anything since breakfast, and these drinks are really strong."

"Sure," Jody said. "The bread pudding needs to come out, anyway."

They sat at the big trestle table that Manuel Trinidad had made her, hammering it together from an old barn door and harder-than-iron hand-carved ox-yokes he'd brought up from Guadalajara. She served them in the big Pfaltzgraff crockery bowls on the big Pfaltzgraff crockery plates, the tamales on the side. They sprinkled shredded cheese and chopped onions over their tamales, ladled hot chili on top of that. Consumed bowls of the chili with her homemade crackers. Shade had three tamales, Wingo two. It gave her a kick just watching. She remembered her mother frowning at the stove while Jody and Pop winked at each other over the tiny kitchen table and stuffed their faces. Mom would serve till they were done, and then clean up after, and then she'd nibble, just before going to bed, alone in the kitchen, a few cold leftovers.

The men pushed back their chairs when they were through, giving their bellies room. No rush to leave the table. Nobody wanted bread pudding, in spite of the incredible warm aroma diffusing in non-linear dynamic swirls from the oventop. In a few minutes maybe.

She brought coffee, the real stuff, all around.

"Okay," Jody said. "You're fed. Now what the hell is a theoretical model of heaven?"

"He's inventing a religion," Shade said.

"Yeah," Wingo said. "The cult of the Holy Tamales. I bow down in complete awe."

"Oh, stuff it," she said. "I didn't make the damn things, I just heated them up. So, can you raise the dead? Change water into wine? I shouldn't have served my own liquor."

Wingo looked somber, even sad, and she wondered what nerve she'd struck.

"No," he said. "It isn't like that. I know people who can—"

"Don't kid a kidder," she said.

He didn't bother to argue. "But I'm a limited man. I can't travel out of the body. I can't speak with the dead in my dreams, or predict airliner crashes, or heal the sick." He looked up, allowing her to see exactly what was in his eyes. Sadness was too small a word.

"Do you believe in the spirit?"

Jody was shocked, as though he'd asked whether she used a vibrator. "Well, I—well, it depends, doesn't it, on what you mean? I mean, there's *something*, you can't deny there's something, but whether it's an epiphenomenon, or—it depends on how you define—"

"No, it doesn't," he said. "It's there, it's literal, it's real. There are people who can see it directly. Without metaphor and without definition."

Jody found herself looking at Shade. He shook his head no.

"Suppose you were able to do that," Wingo said. "Suppose you knew there was a realm of the spirit because you could see it, touch it. Doesn't that have to change how you live? Isn't that realm going to matter to you more than anything else, more than any of the usual foolishness?"

"And that's why you're a hermit?"

"In a way. I was trained as a scientist, and in my day that meant reductionist. All human experience is reducible to biochemistry and electrical currents, and those are reducible to physics. There are no gods, there is no soul. Engineers are the highest form of awareness. I preached that gospel for almost a decade. God help me, I taught it to high-school students."

"Saul of Tarsus?" Jody said.

"Down to the thorn in my side. I'm a convert, but a spiritual cripple. It's that simple. Almost as soon as I saw that the other reality actually existed, I saw that I was excluded from it. The bad years—" He indicated Shade, who, as though it were a cue, got up and went into the kitchen and got himself more coffee.

"The bad years, the time he was talking about earlier today, when they wound up thinking I was dead, that was my rebellion. Yes, Saul/Paul. Kicking against the pricks."

Shade came back, sat. Static jumped up on the table, and Shade settled her into his lap.

"Actually, the truth is comforting," Wingo said. "The truth about your own nature, I mean. It *will* set you free, if you can accept it. And you might as well, because what is, is. You can weep and wail, but there's no appeal from that rule. Finally I saw that even if I could never transcend myself, there was one thing I *could* do. And that's what I've been up to ever since."

He sighed, leaned back, patted his stomach. "With rare and occasional forays into the sensual. I must say it's good to be an animal again. You can push asceticism too far. Another one of my weaknesses. Mortify the flesh, I suppose. As if I could enter the other world by denying myself the pleasures of this one. I get lost in my work and I forget to live. Somebody like Shade comes along and reminds me and I see that it's exactly the same behavior I was showing when I thought of myself as a scientist."

"Speaking of the pleasures of the flesh," Jody said. "Time for bread pudding?"

They adjourned to the living-room sofa again. The pudding's interior was still hot, and she outfitted them with saucers and forks, the saucers bearing great steaming slabs drizzled with melting hard sauce. More coffee all around. No one was going to sleep early tonight.

"So," Wingo said. "Shade tells me you're into dream research."

"Good luck getting her to talk about it," Shade said around a mouthful. "I think she must be working on some classified government project."

It was a joke, surely, but over the steam from his coffee his eyes were steady.

"Not hardly," Jody said. To Wingo: "I'm one of those reductionists you were talking about. I'm not interested in the metaphysics of the situation. I want to—" She hesitated. Spit it out, kiddo. Claim your fate. "I'm working on a theory of dreams. You're a mathematician, you ought to know what I mean by 'theory.' I don't mean some wild-ass guess—"

"You mean a working model," Wingo said. "One that allows prediction and control."

"As for all this mystical razzmatazz—well, I'm pretty much of a skeptic on that."

"You misunderstand," Wingo said, setting his coffee and gesturing. "I think skepticism is *essential*. It's the great purifier. The main problem with all the true believers, they confuse credulity and faith. When I say I know the realm of the spirit exists, I don't mean I understand its laws or know what it's made of or how it arises. I don't even mean that I'm capable of *proving* its existence. It's just that in spite of my skepticism—no, as a *result* of my skepticism—I am now forced to accept the existence of that realm as an indisputable fact."

He relaxed, sat back. "I wonder if you aren't in the same fix." Shade was wandering the room now, checking out this and that—a painting on the wall, a vase of flowers.

"Why dreams?" Wingo said. "I mean, you know what you want to do *with* dreams—but do you understand why you wanted to work with dreams in the first place? Why not silverfish, or high-energy plasma? We don't choose our passions. They choose us. We have to pay attention to them, so they can tell us who we are. There's something you want from dreams."

The Big Empty, Jody thought. *Don't go there.*

"What do you mean, credulity and faith?" she said. "What's the difference?"

"My point exactly," Wingo said. "Nobody knows the difference. Faith is perseverance. Doing your best to live a life of meaning and service, whether you have all the answers or not. It is the assumption that there is more to the universe than your own desires. In my view, skepticism is essential to faith. Credulity, now—credulity is laziness. It's giving up the fight. Giving over control of your own actions, responsibility for your own choices."

"A definition uniquely tailored to a man like you," Jody said.

Wingo smiled again. "Yes, it is that. Can't deny it. But look, can you think of a single religion whose theology isn't full of nonsense and gibberish?"

Jody thought of Pop, of his utterly sincere Christianity. "I don't know," she said. "I think some people get a lot of good out of their religion. A lot of truth."

"Some people do. But no thanks to the theology itself. What was it, a year or so back, the Pope finally says evolution is okay? Gee, thanks a lot, Big Guy. Meantime, we've wasted a hundred and fifty years denying what is perfectly clear to any reasonable human, and ruined a lot of lives and minds in the process. Why can't we have a faith that includes what we actually *know* about the world? That doesn't require you to believe sixteen impossible things before breakfast? A faith that's exploratory, that *answers* to experience rather than denying it."

"Zen Buddhism," Shade said, peering into the darkness beyond the greenhouse door.

"Zen isn't a religion," Wingo said. "It's a discipline. It doesn't require belief."

"That's theoretically true," Shade said. "Practically speaking, for most of its followers, it fulfills the same function as religion."

"Which proves my point," Wingo said. "Whether it's a mere trick of evolution or evidence of a preexistent spiritual realm, humans have a built-in, automatic, powerful need for religion. The problem is— have you ever heard of memes?" he asked Jody.

"Ideas replicate themselves like viruses. Brains are the medium in which they grow."

"Succinctly put. Well, theologies are memes. They propagate themselves and defend themselves, without any regard to their truth content. In fact, most commonly, in direct *opposition* to the truth, and at the cost of considerable damage to accuracy of perception."

" ' "What is truth?" said jesting Pilate.' Couldn't you argue that 'truth' is a meme?"

"You could, but you know as well as I do that's sophistry. It may be politically incorrect, but I don't believe that all beliefs are created equal, that all theologies are equally valid. The Virgin Birth is a crock, for example, no matter how you look at it. It's clearly embroidery, added later to explain to weak minds the source of the inexplicable authority of Jesus."

"So you *do* believe there was a historical Jesus."

"Of course I do. And for all I know, he rose from the dead. I've seen things that aren't any less strange. I should say, I'm not just picking on Western religions. I've never been able to buy into reincarnation. Violates all my notions of identity. You see that ripple in the creek?"

"What ripple in what creek?"

"That one right there, the hypothetical ripple in the hypothetical creek I'm pointing to. It's caused by a big hypothetical rock right under the surface."

"Okay."

"The ripple has a shape, doesn't it?"

"Yes."

"In fact, the shape of that ripple may not change for months at a time. Maybe even years, if there aren't any big floods. That's identity, the shape of that ripple. Now, if you move the rock, no power on earth and no combination of powers can ever re-create that ripple. It's all very well and good to say that the water goes on, but the identity of that ripple is lost forever. I think it's the same way with our deaths. I don't think there's anything meaningful as identity that can be reconstituted in another body—much less the body of, say, a groundhog or a tulip."

"So you're an equal-opportunity iconoclast."

"What's the tribe that wants to kick the teaching of evolution out of the schools? Because they don't care what the scientists say, they *know* they came from the center of the Earth? As far as I'm concerned, that makes them no better than the Southern Baptists. Fine, if you want to interpret your religious tradition as mythically true, or metaphorically true, that's one thing. But sorry, guys, you *didn't* come from the center of the Earth, not in literal fact, and if you bring your children up to believe they did, you're teaching them a lie about the world."

What he was saying fit Jody's bias so well she felt obliged to counter it. "But to go back to my earlier point," she said. "Don't people get a lot out of their religion that doesn't depend on its literal truth? I mean, most of your objections seem to have to do with theologies that run counter to physical law. But what about the moral content, the emotional content?"

"As I see it, religions serve two basic purposes. The first purpose is metaphysical, by which I mean explanatory. Most theologies began as theories of the universe. Cosmologies. They purport to explain the operating principles, the *how* of things. The reason we don't see this is that they're such *bad* theories—instead of modifying themselves in accordance with new information, they harden into dogma. As a result, thinking people are driven away, except for a few who spend all their time trying to rationalize the foolishness of the dogma. The people who *are* driven away still need religion, but they can't find it in any formal system, so they're left to cobble something together on their own. You wind up with crackpots on the one hand, and on the other hand the kind of scientist I was, who treats reductionism not as a sometimes useful methodology, but as a religion in itself, to be zealously proclaimed."

"And the other purpose?"

"Is explicitly moral. Each theology claims to give us a guide, a way to live our lives—although most rapidly degenerate into mere social control manipulated by the powers that be."

"So your religion is going to fix all this."

"No. I wouldn't be so presumptuous. I'm no moral genius, for one thing. And anyway, I don't think morality depends all that heavily on theology. I think it's available to all of us, the one true equality. We may not be equal financially, legally, socially, physically, or intellectually, but we're equal morally. I know a woman with an IQ of seventy-two who's so sweet and generous she puts the archbishop to shame, let alone my own poor self."

"Anybody could put the archbishop to shame. If you mean that guy who didn't know little boys could be damaged by sexual abuse from their priests. Sanchez, wasn't that his name?"

"I think we need a new worldwide morality—one that would celebrate gay marriage the same as any other, for example. But I'm wrong for that. No one human can do that job."

"I guess I'm still unclear what you're up to, then."

"What I'm up to is a very small part of the whole. But it's the part I'm uniquely suited to. I want to help build not so much a new theology, in the old absolutist sense, as a theoretical model of the spiritual world. Morality may not be dependent on theology, but bad theologies still have a disastrous effect. Bad cosmology and bad metaphysics muddy the waters of perception. *Anything* that lies to us about the nature of the universe has a corrupting effect on morals."

"So what would a good theology look like?"

"Shade to the contrary, I'm not inventing a new religion. I've borrowed from everywhere. I think the universe is a living being, literally the body of God. Not a new idea. I also think that in some sense, it's all *maya,* illusion—a dream in the mind of God, you might say. Not a new idea."

"Why God permits evil," Shade said, back at the fire. "You had a slick take on that one."

Wingo gave Shade a curious glance, turned back to Jody. "What I imagine is that in the beginning of the universe, there were only two choices—existence or nonexistence. Either there was nothing—in which case there was nobody to be aware there was nothing—or there was something. And that something was, by definition, everything. Shade's heard this before, but I like to say the universe began with a pun: *Nothing mattered.*"

Jody had to think a moment, then provided the obligatory groan.

"Be that as it may: In my model, the only limit on God is the inevitable limit of solitude. No external confirmation, no difference between sanity and madness—"

"No love."

"Precisely. In my model, God cannot defend himself—"

"Herself."

"Itself, yeah. Can't defend itself from what we perceive as evil any more than we can defend ourselves from nightmares—because we *are* the nightmares."

"Were it not I have bad dreams," Shade muttered.

"But where do *we* come from?" Jody said. "If we're all God, I mean."

"That's the sacrifice at the heart of existence. In my model, in order to create otherness and individuality—in order to keep the story of the universe going—God fragmented its being."

"The Big Bang."

"Maybe. I believe we all know all of this deep down, and that this is the sacrifice we have commemorated in our Osiris rituals and our Christ rituals and others. Quite literally, God died that we might live. Not to forgive our sins, in history, after the fact, but at the very beginning of time, in order to make our sins—along with everything else—possible in the first place."

"Cool," Jody said.

"Or at least exceedingly neat," Shade said. He was drumming his fingers on the mantel.

"I don't remember Marcus being so critical," Wingo said.

"Marcus?" Jody said.

"One of the differences between us," Shade said.

"Well, you can stand hearing it again this one night. He's just being sullen, my dear. He probably wishes I would leave so he can take you upstairs and ravish you."

"Yeah," Jody said. "You behave, you."

Shade grunted. It might have been a laugh. "At any rate," Wingo said, "there's not a whole lot original in any of these notions. I don't take credit for them—although I do think I've put them together in an unusually coherent and concise fashion."

"Like I said," Shade said. "Exceedingly neat." At Jody's scowl, he walked away.

"That's the overview, but that's not my main contribution. My contribution has been to build a model in which none of the theology con-

tradicts the known facts about the physical universe—in which dogma
is replaced by hypothesis—in other words, a theoretical model—"

"Of heaven. So give me an example of a particular hypothesis."

"Nearly all of us want to believe in an afterlife, right? The desire
runs so deep you have to call it a basic human need. But no description of an afterlife that any theology has ever offered seems to me to
stand the tests of physics and biology. I don't think there's a mind separate from the brain, for example, or a soul separate from the body—"

"Me neither."

"I can't credit reincarnation. Or the resurrected and incorruptible
body, for that matter. We know heaven isn't up in the sky, we've
looked. But what if you think of your whole life—your world-line, to
use Einstein's phrase—not as a three-dimensional body moving
through time, but as a body itself—a body in *four* dimensions."

"Wouldn't it look kind of like a big starry tapeworm? Yuk."

"I'm including all your actions as well, all the things you touch
and take up and do. Besides, you probably weren't all that lovely as a
fetus, either. Because that's how I think of that hypothetical four-
dimensional body—as a fetus. Our whole earthly life is analogous to
the development of a fetus in the womb. Our birth into the afterlife—
as a free body in the more-than-four-dimensional realm—occurs
when the fetus has come to term—at the point we call death."

"There's an awful lot of stillborns and deformities, then."

"Not arguing that. Why should the next realm have any more
guarantees than this one has? Now, if you accept this image, it can
supply a very practical definition of morality."

"How do you mean?"

"Morality is simply the health of that four-dimensional fetus.
Because, remember, this is a body in *time*—so our *actions* are literally
the *flesh* of that body. So moral action is healthy flesh. And if the fetus
is morally damaged beyond a certain point, it isn't viable."

Shade was at the window again. He was looking out over the
darkness of the arroyo. "That notion would make immortality of the
body a hopeless deformity," he said. "Hypertrophy. A disfigurement,
like the Elephant Man's face."

"Yes," Wingo said, slowly. "I hadn't thought about that. Not really
a worry of mine, you know. But yes, if there were such a thing as
physical immortality, the immortals would be more to be pitied than
envied. Poor limited monsters."

"But suppose we prove your hypothesis is wrong?" Jody said. "Then what?"

"Then you junk it, and find a better one. It was just a hypothesis, after all."

"I could use another drink," Shade said. Wingo said he could use one, too, if it wasn't too much trouble. When she came back, bearing three brimming salt-rimmed glasses on a silver platter, Wingo said, "So, I've been doing all the talking. A theory of dreams, hey?"

Shade took his glass and walked back to the window.

"You ever think how much this place looks like Mars?" he said somberly. "When we terraform it, Mars will be the New Mexico of the solar system."

"I know a bunch of stuff that dreams aren't," Jody said. "They aren't the subconscious mind trying to work out the issues of the day. They're way too wild and indescribable for that."

"I've read where some scientists think they're like a filing process. Our brains have gotten too complex, and we can't handle all the data, so at night we correlate and sort it."

Jody made a face. "Based on what evidence?" she said. "That's one of those wild-ass guesses I was talking about. Besides, do they *feel* like a filing process?"

"What about the idea that they're a controlled sort of madness, then? You know, we stay sane during the day because we go crazy at night. Like a release valve."

"Yeah, that's Hobson's model. J. Allan Hobson, at Harvard. He says dreaming and delirium are identical states. He's developed some good information, but I think he's cooked his conclusions. He says that when we're hallucinating, we don't know we're hallucinating, and that when we're dreaming, we don't know we're dreaming, for example. But I have a lot of lucid dreams. He also says intellectual functions are impaired in dreaming just as they are in delirium. He states categorically that you can't read or write coherently in a dream, and that nobody can perform logical analysis—mathematical operations and the like. But I've done all three."

"So have I," Wingo said. "I once worked out a relation in the Pythagorean numbers—"

"Anyway, the madness idea isn't new. Freud had it seventy-five years ago."

"So did Aristotle," Shade said, and they both gave him a look. "A lot earlier than that. He said dreaming was demonic rather than divine."

"I think he meant it was random and turbulent," Wingo said. "As opposed to orderly and subject to the powers of reason."

"To him that would have been the same thing as madness," Shade countered mildly.

"So do I," Jody said. "Think they're turbulent. But in the new sense of the word."

"Now this *is* interesting," Wingo said. "Are you talking about chaos theory?"

"You know how, with certain functions, when you keep feeding the y-value back in as the next x-value, the equation begins to spiral in on a certain value? An attractor?"

"Nonmonotonic functions. The ones with humps."

"Yeah. Parabolas, sine waves. Well, it's a pretty elementary comparison, but I'm convinced dreams do something like that. When we're awake, we're always receiving information that is extraneous to the current state of our minds. But when we're dreaming, the next state of our mind doesn't depend on anything but its previous state. It's a feedback system."

"It's an appealing idea," Wingo said. "But you wouldn't think a simple attractor would be an accurate model for something as complicated as dreaming."

"I *said* it was an elementary comparison. That's just the idea I started with. I'm on to strange attractors now. The stuff above Frankenstein's number."

Wingo laughed. "Feigenbaum's, you mean?"

Jody blushed. "Yeah. I develop these private nicknames, and if I don't watch it, they slip out. Anyhow, the trick is finding *which* strange attractor, or set of them, is involved. So far, nothing matches up. I may have to invent one of my own. Which means my math has to get a whole lot sharper. The good news is, I think I've figured out a workable approach."

She told him about I-space, and he liked the idea. He liked it a lot. *Now* we're *doing it*, she thought. *Just a couple of techies slinging the jargon around.* Shade was at the window again, bored out of his gourd, no doubt. Showing them an awful lot of back.

"The bad news," she finished, "is I don't know where to start. Like I say, I've been having a fair number of lucid dreams. But if I'm seriously going to measure I-space, I'm going to have to be lucid a lot more often, and hold it for a lot longer at a time. And what kind of measuring system can I use? How do you get a ruler into your dreams?"

Then there were all the other bothersome little details. She told him about Rafael, the question of onset imagery. About her deep if irrational conviction that dreaming was essentially healthy behavior, not a contained madness with a specialized function. Her growing certainty that it might even be the base state of the brain, from which all others derived.

"We're always dreaming," Wingo said.

"Where did you hear that?" she said sharply.

"I think I made it up. Listen, I have a suggestion for you."

"Sure," she said. "Anything."

"I think you should read some off-the-wall stuff. Namkhai Norbu on Dzoghchen Buddhism, or Robert Monroe on traveling out of your body, or even Carlos Castaneda."

"Anything but that," she said.

"Hear me out. I'm just saying that one way out of a logical bind is to shock the system. You don't have to *believe* everything you read. But it might shake you out of some limiting preconceptions. Read up on shamanism. Who knows, maybe you *are* a shaman."

Shade had disappeared up the stairs. Finally had enough, she assumed.

"Oh, come off it," she said.

"Why did you want to become a doctor? Truth now. It wasn't money, was it?"

"So I wanted to help people," she said. "That may be hokey, but it's not a crime."

"No, it's not a crime. And it isn't hokey, either. I'll bet people tell you their stories, don't they? Open up to you right away. Look at me tonight. You have no idea how many people have made fun of me. And yet I give you the whole Reader's Digest condensed version."

She was embarrassed, as if caught in some minor but shameful act.

"I'm not trying to put you on the spot," Wingo said gently. "I just have a hunch that there's a lot more going on with you and dreams than you're admitting to yourself."

"Maybe so," she said. "And maybe no."

Wingo smiled, then yawned. "Can I use your phone?" he said. "Time to call a cab."

"You're not taking a cab all the way out to your cabin, are you?" It was a relief to change the subject, but the thought of Wingo walking the last mile in the dark and cold—

"No, I stay over when I come into town. A friend lets me sleep on his couch."

"You're welcome to stay here," Jody said, guiltily.

"Thanks. But it's a very comfortable couch. And I enjoy my friend."

The sound of Shade's feet on the stairs. He must have heard the nature of their conversation changing, the shift in tone of voice. Safe to reenter, evening almost over. And now here he was, appearing around the corner, lifting a hand in casual greeting.

Wingo went up to the telephone, and Jody leaned back studying Shade, who was now at the fire. She hoped she looked sleepily seductive, and not just heavy-lidded. But his eyes were shadowed, and he didn't speak, and she couldn't tell a thing.

Wingo came back down the steps saying, "Actually, you ought to meet my friend. He's a shaman, he might be really useful to you." He caught Jody's expression and grinned: "No, seriously, there's some genuine practitioners out there. The real ones are *called,* you know. They don't necessarily *want* the job. They know it'll play hell with their lives."

"Like Jonah under his gourd."

"Exactly like Jonah. Until they give in, they're plagued with miseries. Illness, pain, job failure, financial disaster. Yeah, you've gotta meet Dead Men Walking."

"That's his name? A shaman named after a *movie?*"

"Dead *Men* Walking, not Dead *Man* Walking. He's had the name ever since he was a boy. Thirty years ago, on the Mescalero rez, there was an outbreak of radioactive zombis—"

Jody laughed aloud. "For a minute there, you almost had me going. Let me see, I was just a baby, but I believe I remember that headline. No, wait, it was on Walter Cronkite—"

"There are stranger things than are dreamt of in your philosophy," Shade said, his tone offensively hard. A part of her mind registered the way he had accented the allusion nevertheless, so that the stress fell on the second syllable of "philosophy" and not, as was usual, on "your": *Of course, that's how it's* supposed *to go. We never get it right nowadays because we dignify every Joe Blow's set of unexamined assumptions, we credit the blather of every top coach, multimillionaire, and movie star as a "philosophy on life."*

"What can I tell you?" Wingo said. "I'm satisfied it happened. No reason you should be, you cynical old skeptic. You really ought to meet the guy, though."

"There are people who put out a dominating emotional field," Jody said, defensive. "People who can convince you of anything, no matter how foolish."

"And how exactly does that work?" Wingo said. "What is an 'emotional field'? How does science account for that particular phenomenon?"

"Don't you guys start up again," Shade said.

A horn sounded out front. "That'll be my cab," Wingo said.

Jody fetched Wingo's coat from the closet. *Why the hell not?* she thought. *What harm can it possibly do? What am I so afraid of?* As Wingo was shrugging into the coat, she said, "Well, tell your friend hello. Tell him I *would* like to meet him sometime."

"We'll set it up," Wingo said. "Although he's going to be pretty busy for a while. His day job's heated up, and I think he's going to be getting married soon." He hustled out into the darkness, calling back over his shoulder: "Thanks for a great evening!"

"You really got him going," Shade said.

"I thought *he* got *me* going. You sure didn't have much to say."

"Sorry about that. It's just—well, however much fun you have, whatever brilliant insights you come up with the night before, the world runs on. You wake up in the morning to the same old trouble. You can think and think and think, but nothing ever gets any better."

She tried teasing. "Feeling left out, are we? How about I include you right now?"

"Sometimes what happens to people is bigger than their own personal peaks and valleys, Jody." His voice was harsh, but it was the impersonal tag, it was the *Jody* that really wounded. "Sometimes things happen that change your life forever, and all the positive thinking and hard work and willpower you can generate don't make a whit of difference. A comet hits the Earth, and the dinosaurs disappear.

Maybe some of the dinosaurs tried to have the right attitude. Maybe they attended empowerment sessions until they froze to death."

"Well, the hell with you, then. I *needed* to talk ideas for a while. I get *vitamins* from thinking, and I can't stand the kind of people that never ever do it."

She was almost in tears. It was all coming apart. They were standing in the foyer jawing face to face and he'd been peculiar and distant all evening, and it was all coming apart.

He took her in his arms, though she resisted at first. "Hey, easy," he said into her ear. "No slam on you guys. If you had a good time, fine. I didn't mean to be such a shit."

"Does that mean you'll stay over?" she said, her face against his chest. She could hear him laughing, deep down, and it was a wonderful sound, a happy earthquake, a boat on a vigorous but sunny sea. It was a sound you could dive into, lose yourself in.

But she thought, going up the stairs, his arm around her waist, that she had a few more books to add to her reading list, that the source of her lover's malaise might be his sense of neglect. Forget his disclaimers. Nobody writes a book and hopes for silence.

Never never never underestimate an author's vanity.

Yes, time to jump into Shade's mind. See what he was thinking.

But first she was going to jump his bones.

18: were it not i have bad dreams

Ish was sitting at her desk in the dim light. He was angry, and it was her fault.

She was in her nightgown. She had come across the hall from the bedroom. She had come like a ghost, through the walls, making no sound. That was because in dreams you were *a ghost. It was also because she didn't want to wake Shade, in the bedroom behind her.*

But I don't wear a nightgown, she thought. I sleep naked.

She was wearing it to hide her shame. Her thighs were slick with another man's semen, and even now, as she thought about it, her belly stirred and warmed. She wanted to go wash the slickness away, but that would be admitting her guilt.

So is this an out-of-the-body experience? *she said lightly.* Or just another lucid dream.

But Ish was not amused. He didn't look at her. She couldn't joke this one away. He looked grimly into the window, and she had to look, too. It was her punishment.

The window was a movie screen. It was showing World War II.

A woman and her children were dying. They were dying in the war. They had radiation sickness, and their skins were sloughing off. That was why the buildings were blasted down, nothing but piles of smoking rubble. That's why the Anasazi had left. The bomb had destroyed their city. She saw now that Chaco Canyon was really a blast crater.

Children were running through the ruined dark alleys, they were chasing rats. The children were *rats, giant rats with evil eyes. They would kill you if you wandered into their territory. They were in the wrong part of town, where the rat gangs were. It was her fault.*

He swung around in his chair. What the *hell* did you think you were doing? *he said. He knew all about Shade. He could smell Shade on her. She wanted him to be quiet. If he kept talking so loudly, Shade would wake up, and then what would happen?*

Don't you yell at me, *she said. She had given the dream people everything. She had built the laboratory where they were created. If not for her, they would never even have existed. It wasn't fair of them to blame her for their war.*

What am I supposed to do, *she said.* Sit around the house and wait for you?

All he cared about was his work, his stupid computers, and she and the children didn't matter. He never showed up for their birthdays. They had grown up and gone to college, and he never even paid any attention. The boy and the girl and the other one. All he cared about was saving the world, and it was so stupid, because it was just a dream world, and when you woke up it would be gone anyway. It was vanity, that was all it really was.

A woman gets lonely, *she said.*

You don't care, *he wailed. He was standing up now, and he was wailing out loud. He was going to wake their father if he didn't shut up, and what would happen then?* YOU DON'T LOVE ME. YOU NEVER LOVED ME! *He was a baby boy, standing in the middle of the floor with shitty diapers and she hated the smell and she hated him. It was her fault because she had been such a bitch, and their father had turned against them all.*

The baby was lying in a pool of liquid shit on the floor. That was disgusting. It had to be blood. Blood was a lot cleaner. The baby was dead. She had killed the other children, too, lying bloody in their cribs. Brains all over the walls. It was a terrible feeling, being a criminal. Everybody would hate you. But it was too late. She had already shot them. The police were coming any minute. Mr. Whiney was standing out in front of the house with his mouth wide open, making the wailing noise of the siren. That was how you called the police. It was like howling at the coyotes to get them started howling. She was going to kill the howling baby.

She was going to blow its brains out.

She was on the run. She was a cyborg soldier in the ruined alleyways, a killer of total metal, and the dream police were after her. It was illegal to be a cyborg, you had illegal dreams. They were bringing in the big guns. They would aim for her mechanical brain. She couldn't let them blow her brains out, because the technology was too precious. She had to jump through the time gate into the past, so the humans would get the dream technology.

She was skiing down the arroyo, looking for the time gate. They were behind her, shooting. Two men on skis, with machine guns. Tom Cruise and Hugh Grant. She should never have trusted the actors, of course the actors were in on it.

Bullets were hissing and banging. She had to jump through the doorway soon.

Looking for the door was the problem. Doors were traps, illusions. If you were a ghost, and went looking for doors, you were lost forever. What you had to do was just be there.

He was working the sewing machine in the study, but she was going to watch TV anyway. It was a big sewing machine that ran off the main computer, a production machine. You watched the screens in the walls for the readouts, so you would know what you were sewing.

He wasn't speaking to her, and she wasn't speaking to him. He was still angry with her, because she was a spy for the other side. The papers had found out, and the neighbors hated them, and so they never got invited out to parties anymore, and he blamed her.

She knew that if she watched television in the same room, it would destroy his concentration. He was sewing a globe, and it was tricky work, you had to get it just right. It was a globe of the world, but he was sewing in a new country. He was taking America out and putting in a blue patch, it would be better than America. It would have all the good things that America had, but there wouldn't be any more killing, and nobody would hate her for being a spy.

In the New America it would be okay to fuck other men, other women, anybody you wanted to. It would be okay to fuck her father and her mother wouldn't blow her brains out.

She couldn't remember her father's name. That was a little scary.

You couldn't sew a globe on a normal machine, of course. That was why all the computers. It was a laser machine, it could stitch in three dimensions. You worked on the luminous holographic model, the one that hovered in the machine's focus area, and inside the big glass-walled chamber, robot arms duplicated the actions on a larger scale. That was the only way you could sew the new balloons. The giant silk balloons with a new America on them.

She had converted her dream chamber so the allies could work on the balloon. It was a warehouse now, and the glass walls protected you from the dream radiation. That was why you had to use the robot arms, it was too dangerous for live people.

It was a secret project, and if the government found out, they would kill you.

They were floating over the Grand Canyon. They were paratroopers, come to free people from the corporations. The river was shining far below. Fleecy clouds were running underneath the gondola, and she could see the river shining way below.

The bears were keeping them up. There was a covey of other balloons ahead, and she could see the bears under them, sailing along. Your balloon wouldn't go if you didn't have a bear under it, the bears were like the engines.

They were the good guys, because they used bears instead of gasoline engines.

She looked over the edge of her gondola. There was her own bear. He was beautiful, his fur gleaming in the sunlight, rippling with the wind of their passage.

Ish had his arm around her at the rail of the back deck. Their bear was downstairs watching television, and the hard times were over, and they were a happy family. That was what marriage was all about, whether you cared enough to work things through. They cuddled on the sofa, watching the movie. The movie was in Technicolor.

I wonder why Technicolor is so much like the color in dreams, *she said.*

You just think it is because you're watching this movie in a dream, *her husband said.*

Oh yeah, *she said.* We'll have to watch it again when we're not dreaming.

She could tell he didn't want to do that, he was bored with the movie. He didn't like World War II movies. Not at the end of the day, when he was tired from working. But they didn't have to watch the whole *movie, just a few minutes of it to check for Technicolor.*

John Wayne was in the lead balloon. The squadron floated in over the snowy mountains. It was clever of them to come in over the Sangres, nobody would be expecting an attack from the middle of America, they would be expecting an attack from the sea.

The Germans had taken over America, but now the rebels were fighting back. They would drop the atom bomb, and the mountains would collapse and bury the time gate forever.

They floated in over the Sangres at sunset. The mountains were a radiant pink. She was amazed at the detail you could see from this distance. She could see the stitching on their white balloons. Like the stitching on a baseball. She could see the pink light on the white balloons. She could see the men's cruel faces. They all carried machine guns.

Why was she so frightened? There were no bears under the balloons!

She and her husband stood on the back deck rail, and watched the invaders float toward them. She put the binoculars on John Wayne's face. His grin was evil. A sick, twisted grin. He had come to corrupt America. Why had she ever made love to him?

He felt her watching him and he looked right into her eyes. He bared his fangs. He showed the claws on his hands. This had happened before.

I'm really getting tired of vampires, *she said.*

You're the one who fucked him, *Ish said.*

That made her furious. She wasn't the one who'd invented the damn vampires. It was the men who'd done that. No woman would ever build a vampire.

She was going to tell him that, she was going to blast him, but he was gone.

He'd gotten up during the commercial to take a leak, and then he'd gone out to a bar because she was so hard to live with, and he wasn't coming back. He wasn't ever coming back. He'd been killed in an accident on the street. The machine-gun bullets had hit the car, and he'd crashed into a light pole, and he was leaning over the steering wheel dead.

The horn was howling and wailing, the unending siren trumpet of hell.

third iteration:
the practice of the
natural light

This is the dream's navel, the spot where it reaches
down into the unknown.

—Sigmund Freud, *The Interpretation
of Dreams*

19: the first day of spring

Jody couldn't remember when she had slept so well. To have a good man's arm around you all night long, to come awake and have it still there, his slow breath on your back—

She lay quietly, not to wake Shade. To prolong the moment. Morning sun glowing against the drawn blinds. Neither cat was on the bed. She supposed it was a little too strange for them, this large new body where there had been, for so long, only their mother.

Since she couldn't rise and go to her computer, she rehearsed the dream mentally, memorizing its passages and details for later entry. As dark as the dream had been, it had not left her disturbed or depressed. It had been instead, somehow, purgative.

It probably meant the end of Ish, and that was a little sad. But not much. Not with this warm strong body snuggled up against hers. Love in the real world.

She closed her eyes and saw the running clouds again, the Colorado River far below. Of course it had been the Colorado. New America, where had that come from?

She saw her bear, his fur glistening in the high sunlight. This was the second time with the bears. What was that all about? She opened her eyes to the pristine light. The shadows of the aspen's branches, sprigged out with new buds, moved on the slats of the blinds.

It was perfect. Except she needed to pee. Really bad.

She could hold it a few more minutes, let the man snooze a little longer. They were such animals, the men. She gave a low, contented chuckle, deep in her throat.

"Penny for your thoughts," Shade said, and she nearly jumped out of her skin.

She pitched over and pounded on him with a pillow. He defended himself feebly against the downy onslaught, but was laughing too hard to keep his hands up. When she stopped to catch her breath, he pulled her down, and she snuggled in. He stroked her bare back with one hand.

"How long have you been spying on me?" she said.

"I just wanted to see how long you could be still if you had to. You've never quit moving since the day we met. The original perpetual-motion machine."

"And now," she said, "I'm moving again. I've got to go pee." She sat on the edge of the bed. "Don't you ever drain your lizard? It just now occurs to me, not once last night did you ever go to the bathroom. Unless you did it while you were upstairs prowling around."

"I wasn't prowling," he said. "Matter of fact, I need to piss right now. Wanta watch?"

"No," she said, "I get it first."

"Okay," he said. "Then I'll come watch *you.*"

"Don't you dare!" She jumped up and ran into the bathroom, closing the door behind her.

"Why not?" he called. "I was *there* last night, remember?" He rattled the knob.

"You stay out!" she said from the toilet, dabbing herself with tissue. "Besides, somebody's gotten me all messy, and I have to clean up."

"It's a good mess," he said. "I'm proud of it." She imagined him leaning against the wall. "Hurry up in there," he said. "Say, do you ever wonder how those phrases get started?"

"What phrases?" she said. A rinse would have to do for now.

"A moment ago, when you said, 'Drain your lizard.' Phrases like that, that you never hear and then all of a sudden everybody's saying them. Or like 'booking it,' meaning to move really fast. Twenty years ago, you never heard anybody say 'booking it.' "

"I never thought about it much," she said, preoccupied.

"Well, I happen to know how that one started," he said.

"What, 'booking it'?"

"No, 'drain your lizard.' That was started thirty years ago in Fayetteville, Arkansas, by a woman named Marianne Beasley."

"How could you possibly know something like that?" she said.

"I just do. Aren't you finished yet?"

She dried herself off, came demurely out the door. As demurely as you could come through a door when you weren't wearing a stitch. "Your turn," she said.

He made a thundering music in the bowl that went on so long she was convinced he had brought in a tanker truck. "You must have a ten-gallon bladder, cowboy," she said when he came back and slid under the covers to join her. "Hmm. Definitely a ten-foot hose."

"Look at the shadows on the blinds," he said. "The aspen buds. First day of spring."

"So it is," she said. "I think something else is budding out."

"Soon the smell of the lilac will be heard in the land."

"I thought it was the sound of the turtle will be heard. I never understood that. Do turtles make a noise? I've never heard a turtle."

"It doesn't mean *turtle* turtle. It means turtledove. It's from the Song of Solomon, and it refers to the sound they made. 'Turtledove' wouldn't have fit the meter."

He was in English teacher mode now, and she liked it. Big raw body she had just seen stalking in her chamber, all that male dangle and power, but now she imagined him in spectacles, a tweed jacket with elbow patches. Her very own cut-out dress-up doll. Men think women want a certain sort of man. They don't. They don't want any sort all the time. They want a man they can dress a thousand different ways, a man for all moods, a man for all seasons.

The saddest women are with the men who never change.

"I should have known that," she said. "You ever think how many things there are that we have all the information, but we just never get around to figuring them out? I mean, we know more than we know we know, but we just don't use it."

"No," he said.

"Why not?"

"Because I've figured it all out."

"I'm going to hit you with the pillow again."

"Not that. Anything but that."

She found it hard to imagine a better way to spend a morning. Blind Lemon announced himself at the door, butted it farther open with his wide flat head, leapt onto the covers, and began making biscuits, purring all the while like a prop-job taxiing to take off.

"I guess you're accepted," she said.

Now Blind Lemon marched over both of their bodies, sniffing their hands, their skins, wherever he could find a bare patch. He nuzzled in Jody's lap, still purring.

"He's figuring out what we've been doing," Shade said. "He smells me on you and you on me. And then all the smells we made together."

She had always thought herself matter-of-fact about the body, but now she blushed. "I wonder what the world is like for him," Jody said. "I think about it sometimes. Walking in darkness. Living on hearing and smell, and both of them so intense. They must be like explosions in his brain. They must just drive him on. How could you ever think?"

"I don't believe the boy feels the need for much thinking. I believe he exists in a state of perpetual Zen awareness."

"I envy the animals sometimes. They're more helpless than we are, but they're more alive than we are, too. We live so much in our heads."

"Yep. Plastic America. The only senses we find acceptable are the long-range ones—sight and sound. All the old, close ones—smell, taste, touch, inwardness—all *verboten*. That's why the big-boobed bimbo's our ideal. Eyes only, the shape of the body. A topological construct. Doesn't have a damn thing to do with real sexuality. It's just commercial misdirection, the channeling of sexual energy into consumerism. And it has all happened in the last century."

She heard a strange bitterness in his voice, almost as if he took the things he was describing personally, almost as if he had personally watched it all happen. She wanted to distract him, get him away from the mood, get back to the happiness.

"I thought you liked my topological construct," she said.

He grinned. "I do. I do."

"Anyway, it's not our fault," she said. "Evolution did it to us. It's just that those close sensations are so much more powerful for the animals than they are for us."

"Speak for yourself, *chica*."

"Oh, so the man's an animal now."

"I have a pretty good sense of smell."

"I'd better go shower, then."

"Don't you dare."

He rolled over, took her face in his hands. He buried his face in her red hair, snuffled and sniffled. "Piñon smoke, from the fire last night. Cumin, from the chili."

"That doesn't prove anything," she said. It felt amazingly good to have his face in her hair, her face in his big hands.

"Ginseng and chamomile," he said. "That must be from your shampoo yesterday."

"You could have seen the bottle in the bathroom," she said.

"Candlewax," he said. "That's the oil from your scalp. God, you have clean oil."

"I change it every week."

He slid down a little, trailed his lips along her brow, her temple, the masseter of her jaw, her underthroat. "Adolfo," he said.

"Pretty good," she murmured. "Twenty-four hours after the fact. But you're cheating. You probably really noticed it last night."

"It's only sixteen hours," he said. "And I did. Top note is fruity, citrusy. An aldehyde, probably. Middle note, ahmm, jasmine and—something. I don't know that one."

"Tuberose," she sighed. He continued to nuzzle her throat, snuffling, exploratory. *This is when the vampire bites you.* "You have an amazing fund of information." *Bite away, lover.*

"Bottom note is powdery—sandalwood, cedar. I'm guessing, ah, um—moss?"

"Show-off."

He trailed his lips now to the nape of her neck, kissed, sniffed. A tingle ran along the nerves in her arms and legs, flashed from the tips of her fingers and toes, vanished into the air. "Soap," he said. "That black Spanish stuff."

"Magno." The male was whuffling her fur, recording her. The male was a part of the sun. From the sun all life. "Caswell-Massey in San Francisco. You can't get it here anymore."

"Fur," he said. "Fur in sunlight. Static."

"She rides there," Jody murmured. "I carry her around."

Now the male snuffled her collarbone, pushed his nose into her armpit. He growled, a low rumbling sound, a sound of aggression or threat, but not quite. A sound of hunger, but not quite. It was that other sound. That urgent sound.

She giggled and twisted away. "Stop it, that tickles."

He seized her, snuffled along her ribs, under her breasts.

"Leather in sunlight," he said. "Vinegar. Formic acid. Milk."

Her nipples rose into the air. He kissed them each, then ran his nose along her belly, the hollows on either side. That almost tickled too, but this time she didn't flinch away. Her breath was coming in short sharp bursts, she couldn't seem to inhale fully.

"Blood," he said. "And sweat."

And tears, she thought.

"And," he said, and nuzzled between her thighs. She clamped them together, tried to hold his head away by grabbing his hair. The power in his neck was startling, like the horse the last time she had tried riding, twisting irresistibly against the reins.

"I'm not clean," she whispered.

"Clean is for weaklings," he said, and gently took her hands away, and burrowed again into her fur, and he put his mouth against her and said, in a muffled voice: "God."

It was the best sex Jody had ever had. By far the best. It was sex in another dimension, it was time travel and the origin of the universe and the beginning of life on Earth and she felt, in a way she could have sworn was literal, the lusts of the dinosaurs vanished lo these sixty million–odd years, alive and transmitted down the cat's-cradle of the genes into her spine.

She had no intention of saying any of that to Shade, though. As if it would give him power over her, control. Men were too fatuous as it was, too pleased with themselves.

But afterward she glowed and radiated and she could tell he knew anyway by the wide smile on his face as he watched her bustle about the kitchen making breakfast.

"That was pretty amazing," Victorio said. The light from the window spilled across his bed. He could see a cut of blue sky, the lilac branches tossing in a light breeze. Soon their buds would break open, and the scent of their blossoms would fill the town. "Were you there, too? Did you see the thunderlizards mating? Did you hear the squeals of the protomammals?"

Toni nestled against his chest. "I think it's time for you to meet my parents," she said.

"It's the first day of spring," Victorio said. "Maybe that explains it."

• • •

"You know what I wish?" Toynbee said. He had his head on his part-ner's chest, and he could feel more than hear the lub-*lub*, lub-*lub* of that powerful pump.

"What?" Leonard said.

"I wish they would just forget about us. Leave us out here and just forget ever to call us in. Give up on the whole operation, but some-how forget we were ever a part of it."

Leonard laughed. "Wouldn't that get awfully boring? I mean, how long can you stand this town? It's like Rip Van Winkle, it's like being buried alive. A pocket in time."

"But *I'm* here," Toynbee said.

"So you are," Leonard said, and kissed the top of his head. "And I'm going to make you a cup of coffee and fetch the paper."

He rolled out of bed and went to the French doors to look out on their small patio. "Pretty day," he said. "What are these bushes back here by the wall?"

"Lilac, I think."

"Well, they're about to bloom. Do you mind if I open us up?"

"I don't mind at all," Toynbee said. He was propped on his elbow, watching. What a beautiful lad the American was. Naked as Adam, the supple muscles flexing as he moved. Toynbee's heart did a lurch as the muscles in his lover's ass clenched and relaxed, shifting as he shifted his weight to throw the doors open and fasten them. So rare, that. One thing to have the appreciation of beauty born of sexual attraction. Quite another and deeper and better to also have the sheer aesthetic appreciation, heartbreaking beauty in its own right.

Leonard turned back toward the bed and saw Toynbee watching. Spring light lay across his body like a blessing, modeled its curves and hollows, glistening in the thicket between his legs. He laughed at his partner's expression. "What?" he said.

"Michelangelo's *David*," Toynbee said. "Except with a bigger—"

"What is this? What's gotten into you?"

"First day of spring," Toynbee said.

Colonel Wilbur Goodloe Hall sat up in bed in his silk pajamas, reading the papers. *Santa Fe New Mexican, The New York Times, The Wall Street*

Journal. A silver coffeepot was on the stand beside the bed. He scratched his chest. He felt good this morning, really good.

The door opened, and his wife came in, still in her dressing gown. He lifted an eyebrow. What now? "Greetings," he said. "Want some coffee?"

She sat on the edge of the bed. Something he remembered her doing from early in the marriage, forty years ago. "Where's your Indian girlfriend?" she said.

"Off in Arizona. Some kind of tribal gathering."

He didn't ask about her consort, the alternative-building-styles contractor. He knew she never brought the young man home. When they got together, it was in one of the cottages the Colonel kept available for visiting business partners.

"Do you have a busy day today?" his wife said.

The Colonel set his paper down on the covers. "Why? What's up?" If there was some kind of trouble, it was big. She never came to him for help anymore.

She leaned forward, unbuttoned his top two buttons. Put a hand in his shirt and stroked his chest. Her eyes were heavy-lidded, her voice husky.

"I was just thinking about old times," she said.

Well, well, well, the Colonel thought. This was so unusual it was actually pretty interesting. Betraying Tanya with his wife, what a hoot.

He felt himself stiffening, and, as if she knew, she slid a hand under the covers and took hold. He gasped at the shock. Then he caught her up and rolled her on her back. She was laughing silently, and the look on her face was the look she had worn the night they eloped, a look of happiness, yes, and affection, yes, but also of mischief and triumph. She had escaped, she had vanquished her father and mother, she had put herself beyond their control forever.

Well, well, well.

Bruno Sandoval rose from his knees. He folded the rug he had been praying on. He lifted his wife's picture from the mantel and, as he did every morning, kissed it. He set the photograph back and went into the kitchen to make breakfast.

Already the crocuses were poking their heads above the dark soil in the back garden. Soon the narcissus, the grape hyacinth, the irises. Already the forsythia was yellow against the back wall of the garden, and soon the lilacs would come.

"A beautiful morning, *mi esposa,*" he said. "You should see this day. I will look at it for you. I will put my fingers in the earth, and smell the smells for you."

From across the hills there came the rumble of a four-wheeler.

"The children on their machines again, *mi corazón.* And who can blame them? I wish they had better ways of enjoying the spring. But I suppose we must all celebrate in our own way."

While the bitter coffee was brewing, he warmed two flour tortillas in a buttered skillet. He took a crockery pot of *carne adobada* from the refrigerator, and a small dish of black beans. He heated the *carne adobada* in the microwave.

So he, too, was a slave to the machines. He laughed at the thought.

When the *carne* was steaming, he placed a couple of spoonfuls and a spoonful of the cold beans on each tortilla, them folded them rapidly. He carried his breakfast through the house in a paper towel, chewing and drinking from his coffee cup and talking with his wife.

"I'm lonesome, *corazón,*" he said. "If you were here, you would be surprised at this old man, the things he might ask of you."

He felt he needed company, needed to see friends. He needed a woman, if the truth be known. This he did not tell Carmelita. Probably she knew, and if she knew, she understood. But it would not have been a proper thing for a man to say to his wife.

He thought of Jody Nightwood, and laughed at himself. Silly old man. But surely no harm in asking her to dinner. Just to have the company, no? Just for the conversation, and the beauty of a woman sitting across the table, and the sound of a woman's voice.

But he could not deceive himself. He was imagining that it might happen again as it had the last time. He knew it would not. That had been an old man's last blessing. Still, he imagined it, and why not? "Your husband is an old goat, *amore.* A fool."

No harm in a telephone call, though. Soon.

20: settling into a stable orbit

Jody and Shade had a great weekend, one long picnic. Lunch at Geronimo's. Then they wandered around downtown. A man who would look in shops without complaining—wow. On the other hand, he was getting some pretty good sex out of the deal. Then back to Canyon Road to stop in at a few galleries. It had been a while since either of them had done any new art.

On Canyon, they got to talking about upper Canyon Road, what an ideal place it would be for your multimillion-dollar compound if you had a multimillion. Discovered they had both explored the trails up beyond the Audubon Center. Decided they wanted to go walking in the woods, see the creek running high with spring thaw. So Shade went back down to the municipal lot and picked up her car, the Pontiac. She would never forget his face when he'd first seen it, as if he had found a lost love after a lifetime of loss. She'd made up her mind that it would be their car for special occasions, and right now, every occasion was special.

That was one of the things love did, freshened your life. She hadn't had the Pontiac out since Bruno Sandoval, had forgotten the solid joy of riding high in the beautiful old machine.

She waited in the Leslie Flynt Gallery, struck by the huge light-filled landscapes of a painter she had never come across before. The scenes were so beautiful that they very nearly came off as sentimental—and yet the execution was so fine, the light so heart-stoppingly

228

well done, that you couldn't write the work off. It was a puzzle, of sorts.

Two men came in, the ones who had been wearing blazers at the poetry reading when she met Shade. It seemed a very long time ago now, but she thought every face at that reading must have been permanently printed on her mind. Although Santa Fe was a small enough place that you kept seeing the same faces over and over, and after a while you felt almost as if you knew people even if you'd never traded a single word with them. From the way the two men were standing together, she was sure now that they were lovers, and she smiled to herself, the indulgence of one satisfied lover for all others, anywhere met in whatever circumstance.

The men seemed uncomfortable, and in a moment left, and she hoped she hadn't offended them by too obviously watching. Maybe they had thought she was a gay-hater.

After stopping in at the Audubon headquarters to drop their fees in the box, she and Shade set off into the woods. They went a good two miles, steadily climbing. Could have gone farther, but it was getting late, and the mountain shadows got cool in a hurry this time of year. The creek was busy and musical, running in small rapids over its rocks, slowing and fanning in clear shallows. Patches of snow still clung to the northern banks and hollows. They found someone's impromptu shrine, put together of stones and incense and leaves and other small effects. It might have been a memorial to a vanished love, or simply a prayer to the wilderness.

They made love for a long time that evening, slowly and easily, with none of the furor and urgency the morning had brought. They fell into a deep sleep and woke early, tremendously refreshed. They made coffee and mimosas, working happily together in the kitchen, and then a massive frittata filled with potatoes and chiles and bacon and cheese. They went to a matinee of *No Cure for Love*, the new movie by Jonathan Wacks.

They came back to her house for cocktails and dinner. His place, by unspoken agreement, was too small and temporary and unsettled, and felt neither personal nor welcoming. By Sunday evening, zoned out on the sofa together before probably one of the last fires of the season, Jody was feeling secure and comfortable enough to broach a topic she had been worrying about all weekend. Well, maybe worry was too strong a word.

"You know, I took Friday night off from the dream sessions to be with you," she said.

"I know," he said.

"I don't want to—this, what we have, being together—" You can't just say *love*. Too shocking. "It's so wonderful, I don't want to do anything to mess it up."

"But?"

"But. Well. I'm kind of a workaholic, and— No, I'm discounting myself when I say that. Apologizing in advance. Shit. I'm not sure how to say it."

"When you start something, you see it through. If you neglected your research, you wouldn't be able to live with yourself. You'd feel guilty, and the guilt would get in the way of what we have together. So I won't be seeing you on weeknights for a while."

"That's it," she said. "Do you mind too much?"

"No. I've been seeing it coming."

"What do you mean, no?" She dug a sharp elbow into his ribs. "Just plain 'No'?"

"Oh, it was a *trick* question. I meant to say, I'm devastated, I've never met anybody remotely like you, I don't know how I'm going to get through a single hour away from your incredible presence, but I understand and respect the necessity for your decision, and I'll try to muddle through in spite of my own despair and depression."

"That's a lot better." She sighed, snuggled. "Seriously?"

"Seriously. I want you to keep doing what you're doing. Our relationship wouldn't be the same if you neglected your work. You have a life. I have a life."

Relationship. He'd said *relationship*. That was almost as good as *love*.

They spent the next forty-five minutes peeling potatoes, chopping carrots and tomatoes and celery, cubing flank steaks she thawed out in the microwave. They opened a bottle of Chilean red to put in the stock, and clinked glasses of it together.

A bedroom man, a shopping man, a hiking man, a kitchen man. She realized her uncertainty about combining work and love was an old message. She remembered how upset Mom had been every time Jody was late home from school, how the whole time she was growing up she had felt uneasy around her mother unless she was doing something "productive"—working in the store, cleaning the house,

doing homework. That had been one of the reasons, maybe *the* reason, that she had been so afraid to try for Williams College, to launch
out on her own—because it had been a goal *she* had chosen, it had
been a direction *she* had wanted to go.

She was so pensive that Shade gave her a bend-over-backwards
kiss to reassure her that in spite of his willingness to be apart from her
five nights a week, he did indeed desire her body very much, and in
fact right at that moment, and if she just happened to want to go
upstairs for a few minutes, he would prove it, and so they did, and he
did, and by the time they came back downstairs, *Mystery* was already
halfway over, and the stew had almost dried out. They dashed it with
water and more red wine just in time and saved it, and then they let it
simmer another half-hour while they played string with the cats and
then they ate, and then they were both sleepy even though it wasn't
even ten o'clock, so they went upstairs and went to bed and slept like
babies all night long and she dreamed again of bears, although she
would be unable, the next morning, to remember the details. Just
walking through the woods with a bunch of bears, having some sort of
earnest conversation as they went. Maybe about ecology. Maybe art.

Oh yeah. Their big claws clacking on the rocks as they walked.

"It was strange seeing that Nightwood woman today," Toynbee said,
yawning. *Mystery* had been a repeat, about the thirteenth showing of
the Jane Tennison piece where she solves the murder of a nightclub
manager, tracking the malfeasance back to her own superiors.

"Why?" Leonard said. "That's what we've been doing here.
Watching her."

"Yes, but that's just it. This time we *weren't* watching her. It was
so . . . out of context. It just felt really strange to have her wander in
like any other person. When we weren't on the job, so to speak. Gave
me a really peculiar feeling, as though I'd stumbled into a different
plane of reality. A world outside our own, you know. A universe of
different connections."

"This is such a small town, you keep seeing the same faces over
and over."

Leonard was being a little short, and Toynbee thought he knew
why. The lad hadn't wanted to watch *Mystery*, but had refused to say
so, instead venting himself in crossness. Poor fellow, he was getting

bored. He was a love, but he just wasn't domesticated. Not a lap kitten. Too bad. This sort of living, just taking it as it comes, was Toynbee's idea of heaven.

Toynbee was going to have to find something for Leonard to do, some way to keep his interest until the operation cranked up again. If it ever did. If Leonard got too restless—well, Toynbee would lose him, that was all. One way or the other.

"Today is the first day of the rest of your life"—on Monday Jody felt the truth of that cliché more forcefully than ever before. She was centered, secure, loved. She loved the power of her new ideas, like the Swivel, or the idea of dreamspace having a distinct geometry. I-space. She was newly confident of her correlations, her ability to synthesize.

It was instructive to find that even your analytical and rational abilities depended on the health of your emotions. They were not computerlike adjuncts of mere brainpower, but arose, with every other creative ability, from the very core of being itself. She would knit a sampler and frame it and put it on the wall: "A happy scientist is a better scientist."

The clinic was interesting again. She was getting plenty of sleep herself, at last, and so the sleeplessness of her patients seemed the cruelest of fates—not the inconvenience of a machine that needed a tune-up, but a genuine loss to the spirit—an injury, a sorrow, a grief.

Not only that, she was doing them a lot of good. She got two or three grateful calls a day. She put her patients at ease somehow, she could tell she did, and that was the beginning of healing. She'd always credited herself with a good bedside manner, but this was more. This proceeded from her own newfound easiness of spirit.

When it was like that, you could work hard all day and be energized rather than exhausted. Toni seemed to be feeling much the same way, happy and sparkling again. The old Toni. Did it have anything to do with Vic? "Oh yes, girl. It's better than ever. Too fine to be *legal*."

"Maybe we can double-date sometime," Jody said.

Toni gave her a blank look, then broke into a big smile. "Are you for real, *chica?* You know, I *thought* you was acting awful happy lately. Nothing like it, is there?"

"No there isn't," Jody said, feeling as though she were accepting a benison.

"I never thought I would find one I wanted to keep," Toni said.

They wanted to compare notes, but patients were waiting. The clinic was covered in patients all of a sudden. Not everyone was having a good summer, apparently. It was strange, treating the nightmare-haunted and somnambulists and tension-ridden, hearing people's deepest troubles. Made Jody a little spacy sometimes, giddy in a good way. As though Santa Fe had a soul only the privileged could see, and she walked that soul blessing its dreams.

They were getting a few vacationers who woke up in the middle of the night breathing hard and mistook it for apnea or a panic attack. As the summer went on the few would become many, all of whom would be relieved to discover that the only thing they were suffering from was altitude—their breathing habits during sleep hadn't adjusted to the thinner air.

After all the apparently random swings and swoops of her recent history, things were settling down. Like an attractor drawing the formula's successive iterations into a stable orbit—and the orbit wasn't around the Big Empty after all, but around love and friendship and learning and being productive. You could get used to living like this.

All week her dreams were vivid. Two of them, oddly enough, involved space travel. Flying saucers that came to Earth with a new sort of wine, which, if you drank it, allowed you to understand how to build flying saucers yourself. Though hers kept leaking air when she took it flying and then it changed into a bicycle with a low tire. Then a fishing expedition on a water planet in a galaxy her dream called Sinfonia. You had to fit yourself into a fish-shaped cybernetic diving suit, and swim among the fish and fight them on their own terms. When you killed them, it was like mating, it somehow completed their reproductive cycle.

The dreams felt hugely significant, though they had no obvious reference to her personal life. She found herself telling them to the other dreamers for a change. Everybody loved them, and she felt oddly pleased, as if she had made a good piece of art.

She did not dream of Ish.

Shade called her nearly every day at the office, usually at noon. They made an early dinner together before she went back to the sleep lab on three of the five nights. The weekend was as refreshing as the previous weekend, but this time more relaxed.

And the next week was the same, and the smell of the lilacs was indeed heard in the land, floating like guitar music down from the heights, rising from the valleys. For a brief while in the fragrant streets of that high desert town, you felt you were in Shangri-la. The most magically perfumed of all flowering trees graced your every breath, and yet snow still clung on the crests of the mountains. Her roses budded against the back wall, where she had set them out a lifetime ago, all during a cold and bitter January. The tulips broke the earth along the front walk.

Neither she nor Shade made any talk of moving in together, and for the first time she could remember, Jody felt contented enough to question whether she really would want such a cohabitation. Would she *want* to give up her space, her independence? She had lived half her life this way now, and she had gotten used to it, everything around her designed and fashioned according to her own wishes, her own needs. Was she really ready for a change?

Before she knew it, it was the first of May. Later she was to feel that the summer had passed in a dream, in a state of trance. That it had been a shining bubble in the river of time, and that within the walls of that bubble—so clear that you did not know there were walls, so gently curving that you did not know you were enclosed—all things had the timeless unhurried pace of eternity itself, in which all questions were answered, all needs fulfilled.

There were a couple of minor perturbations, which, however, immediately resolved themselves into what seemed an even more stable continuity, so that Jody felt that the newfound satisfaction of her life was not merely strong, but homeostatic—self-repairing, self-healing.

The first perturbation was Bianca, who made an appointment to see Jody one Wednesday, coming in at noon, a good hour before the early shift of dreamers was to start. "What did you need to see me about?" Jody said, feeling pleasantly superior. After all, this practitioner of the crystal arts had been forced to visit her, Jody, the scientist.

"I made the appointment for your sake, not mine," Bianca said, her voice a husky, piping whisper. She tossed her cloudy gray-blond hair. A forty-year-old girl-child.

"What do you mean?" Jody said.

"My internal self-healer came to me the other night, and—"

"Your what?"

"My internal self-healer. You know. The spirit who comes in your dreams to guide you and heal you. Sometimes the spirit transmits wisdom, sometime it performs actual healing activities, sometimes it just brings love and warmth. Everybody has one."

"Not me."

"Oh yes, you do. We all do. The self-healer is a manifestation of our positive energies—I mean, it *is* us, in a way, but it's our deeper selves. Anyway, I know you have one, because my self-healer, I was going to say, her name is Louise—"

Jody made a concerted effort not to laugh. Loren Wingo had said to consider all sources. The best way to break yourself out of dead-end thought patterns was to entertain completely atypical notions. Bianca was definitely atypical. Okay. Maybe Jody could learn something, could have her perspective usefully widened, however big a crock of shit all this stuff was.

"Louise," she said, finally.

"Yes. Louise told me that your internal self-healer told her—"

This was a little too much, though. "Wait a minute, wait a minute," Jody said. "I thought you said these things were just manifestations of ourselves. Now you have them on the telephone to each other, gossiping like a couple of old girlfriends—"

"No." The high, bright voice was surprisingly firm, and in Bianca's normally relaxed gaze there was now the stern glint of the teacher who does not accept your homework excuse. "*Your* self-healer is male. And I said they're manifestations of our *deeper* selves. If you go deep enough, we're all connected. I'm a part of you and you're a part of me."

And he is the egg man and we are the walrus.

"Real healing can't be confined to just one body. That's one of the problems with modern medicine. Healing has to be aware of its environment, of everyone and everything around it. So of course my healer is aware of your healer, and of what's going on with you."

"Let me get this straight," Jody said. "You're saying you can read my mind?"

"No," Bianca said, genuinely irritated. "I can't do any such thing. I'm just as much in the dark as anyone else. I said my *healer* was in touch with your healer. But Louise has to tell me these things, or I won't know them. That's what she's *for.*"

At Jody's expression, she hastened on. "Please just listen for a minute. I know you don't believe in self-healers, or the spirit world, or anything else."

"I believe in some things," Jody said.

"I'm not here to argue with you. I'm just here to deliver a message, and you can do whatever you want to with it. That's up to you." Bianca had been leaning forward earnestly. Now she sat back and favored Jody with a look Jody would have sworn was maternal.

"I really hope you'll pay attention, though. You have an awful lot vested in being tough-minded, and so sometimes you push people away. But you're really a nice person underneath. And you do care about others, even if you are awfully naïve about matters of the spirit—"

It was shocking to be called naïve by someone you thought of as a princess of naïveté.

"And your self-healer says that you're potentially an important being, maybe a boddhisattva, maybe a shaman. That you have a very great gift to offer the world, and we must all protect you and help you to find your true way."

This is how astrology works, Jody thought. *Offer the suckers sweet bait, offer us pretty descriptions of ourselves and our importance, and we will automatically believe it.* But a warmth went through her veins nevertheless, and she wanted to hear more.

"Anyway, your internal self-healer can't get through to you, and so the message has to come through another channel. It's a warning, and it's very important you hear it."

"Let's have it," Jody said.

"There is somebody in your life who is not what he seems."

The hairs lifted on the back of Jody's neck. *Shade,* she thought.

"This person does not have your best interests at heart. This person has been using you for his own interests, and he will be breaking away from you soon."

He, Jody thought. *A man.*

"I'm not sure, but it could have something to do with the burglary here at the office. That was in my mind in the dream, your self-healer was pointing at the glass on the floor, but I couldn't hear what he was saying then. It was like the sound was off, or like he and Louise were in one of the sleep chambers and I could see them but not hear them."

It was ridiculous to let this mumbo-jumbo get to her, Jody thought.

"Please, please be careful. Your healer says the situation could be very dangerous."

Be wary of the dark stranger. Tread carefully, or your life may be forfeit.

Jody's heart was beating way too fast. Her first instinct was to get rid of Bianca and curl up with an anxiety attack, but she resisted. Buck up, girl. Think it through. Look at how this nonsense plugs right into all your leftover childhood messages. You're unworthy of love, and if you do find a good man, something's bound to go wrong.

"I really thank you for your concern," she said. She managed a halfhearted laugh. "I imagine it took a bit of nerve to deliver that message to someone so unsympathetic."

"Not really," Bianca said, the wide-eyed child again. "I just do what needs to be done. I don't have to feel responsible for the state of your insight."

Jody felt a sudden irrational desire to confide in Bianca, talk about her sexual dreams. Perhaps it was the intimacy of Bianca's warning, breaking the ice between them. Perhaps also a sense that of all the people on earth, Bianca would be the least critical.

She also felt a little nervous, their roles at the moment strangely reversed. Bianca the instructor, Jody the pupil. That meant vulnerability. What the hell. Now was as good a time as any. "There's something I've been wanting to talk over with you," she said.

Bianca was delighted to hear about Ish. She clapped her hands together. "Of course! He's your healer! Oh, you're so lucky!" She put a hand on Jody's forearm. "He's so *cute!*"

This is getting way out of hand, Jody thought. "I don't think that's possible," she said. "Is it? I mean, all we do is—I mean, I don't think they would let—I mean, can a healer—"

What *do* you mean, Jody? What *they?*

"I don't see why not," Bianca said. "Louise and I don't, because we're both hetero, but I've always thought sex was very healing, don't you?"

A hetero healer? Did that mean there could be— "Well, yes, but—"

"Do you ever do it when you fly? You do have flying dreams, don't you?"

"Yes," Jody said. "I mean yes, I fly. But—" She was about to say no to Bianca's first question, when she remembered the floating episode with Ish, in what she thought of, without noticing that she was doing so, as their first dream together.

"Goody," Bianca said. "You might be a shaman after all."

"What are you talking about?"

Bianca explained that in dream life, sexual energy was the key to other realms of existence. She explained that in many cultures, shamans had sexual relations with their spirit guides, who might or might not be the same as self-healers, that in some African tribes the shamans actually traveled by flying along on giant erect penises, like witches on their broomsticks. Of course, most shamans had historically been males, but not all by any means—

"You must be a mighty shamaness, then," Jody said.

Bianca laughed, a sudden pealing as if someone had struck a triangle in the room. "Oh no," she said. "Not me, not by a long shot. I just really like to *fuck.*"

It was such an incongruous statement, coming in that child-woman voice, that Jody had to laugh, and then they were setting each other off, and even when they were able to stop, throughout the rest of the conversation, they were prone to sudden fits of giggles.

Jody asked about the lucidity that appeared to accompany all her sexual episodes. Bianca said matter-of-factly that *all* her dreams were lucid. A flash of envy went through Jody like a sudden neuralgia, and it occurred to her that all our darker emotions were pain signals.

Bianca said that Jody's lucidity probably *was* another sign of shamanism, though, even if her own wasn't. Especially considering Jody's inexperience, and since the sexual dreams were the first to become lucid. She produced a blizzard of suggestions for further reading, several of which were titles that Jody remembered from Loren Wingo's suggestions.

She wanted to know more. Jody was at first a little embarrassed, but Bianca's curiosity was so natural, and she was so frank about her own episodes, that it wasn't long before they were laughing again and trading details in a way that Jody found eerily reminiscent: two women talking over the romantic habits of their boyfriends. By the time Bianca left—she had to go dream, and there was a patient waiting—Jody was in a curious state indeed. With every assertion of Bianca's, she had felt her own skeptical resolve stiffen—and yet, having tasted such acknowledgment, she wanted more: she wanted, with all her heart, to be recognized as a shaman.

One of the good effects their conversation had was to settle Jody's nerves. She was no longer feeling the creepy panic that had been her immediate reaction to Bianca's "message." Another astrological effect, she thought: We believe the good stuff, ignore the bad. From time to time during the next week, though, the warning would come into Jody's mind, and she would have to stifle her response, put it in the closet with all the other irrational fears.

She tried to dream of Ish again. By damn, she was going to ask him personally who the hell he'd been talking about—and she was going to give him what-for for telling Louise about it before he said anything to Jody. Was that any way to carry on a love affair?

Of course she was unable to do so. She dreamed, instead, of a great bear who stubbornly refused to find Ish, and growled that if she kept insisting, he would eat the fellow.

When the second perturbation occurred, she felt immediately that it was the answer to the first one—that it had been what Bianca's dream was warning her of—and she was flooded with an immense relief. This in spite of the fact that she had persuaded herself she had never for a single second placed any credence whatsoever in what Bianca had to say.

Early on the first Saturday in May, after Jody had recorded her dream and gotten dressed, Lobo said he needed to talk. *Probably angling for a raise.* "So talk," she said.

"I'm leaving," he said.

"Well, you could have told me last night, so I could have gotten Blossom to cover for you. I was really planning on meeting someone for breakfast." He had at this point only another hour on duty, but that hour was most of the time she had available for breakfast. She had not mentioned to anyone that she and Shade were seeing each other, although she assumed most of the people who knew her had seen her by now in the frequent company of a tall, tigerish man.

"That's not what I mean." Lobo was abrupt, displeased. "I can finish out my shift. I mean I'm leaving the clinic. I've been accepted into the M.F.A. program at Iowa."

"Well, congratulations," she said. "That's good, isn't it? Didn't you say it was the most prestigious program in the country?"

He nodded curtly. "I got in on the strength of my novel," he said.

"*The Wolf and the Light*?" she said.

"No," he said. "That was a pile of sentimental claptrap. This is a new one."

Which he'd probably written most of while he was on duty. Which was all right, that had been part of the arrangement, so long as he covered his responsibilities. Made him more affordable. "Well, congratulations," she repeated. "When does the semester start? September?" Actually, this was convenient. The study ended in mid-July. She wouldn't have to feel bad about letting him go when it was over, he had something to go to.

"Well, that's the thing," he said.

"You *are* going to give me some notice, aren't you?" she said, in growing alarm.

He shook his head, flushing as he had flushed when she'd caught him out about staying overnight in the office with Lucia. "I've got a lot of things to take care of. A lot of business. I've got to find a place to stay, and I've got to get a job there, and—"

"How much time can you give me?"

"Well, that's it," he said. "This is my last day. It all came up really suddenly, and—"

"Goddammit, Lobo, that's just not fair!"

He wouldn't look at her. "It all came up suddenly," he said again. "I have an awful lot of business to take care of. It isn't just a matter of hopping in a car and driving to Iowa City."

She was furious, to no avail. After this morning, he was gone. Sorry, he knew it left her in the lurch, and he didn't expect any severance pay, and in fact if she didn't want to pay him for the last two weeks, he could live with that, but he was out of here.

She controlled herself. What was done was done. No use going off on him, it wouldn't do any good. She wished him well, said he'd been a good worker, said of course she'd pay him for the last two weeks, and got the hell out of there herself.

She still had plenty of time to have breakfast, which had been one of the reasons she had swallowed her temper. No point in losing a pleasure just because you were faced with an inconvenience. She met Shade in the bar and grill of the St. Francis. It had been planned as a celebratory breakfast, the beginning of their weekend, but now—

"Where the hell am I going to find somebody for the night shift?" she said. "This means *I'm* going to have to take it until I do, and that's going to play hell with the study. I mean, I could put myself on the early dream shift, but then I wouldn't have *any* time for myself—eight hours working, eight hours dreaming, and eight hours watching the other dreamers." She fumed. "Besides, that's not my natural sleep period. I don't know if I could make the adjustment, even if I tried. I guess I could shift Blossom to the night shift and take the afternoon shift myself—just not schedule any appointments after one o'clock. But she's still in classes, and I know she plans to go to summer school, and she might not even be *able* to take it."

"How about letting me do it?" Shade said.

Jody was stunned. It hadn't even occurred to her. "I wasn't hinting," she said.

"I know you weren't. But I'm serious. Look at the pros: I've got loads of free time. What do I like to do with my free time? Learn things. Try things I haven't done before. I think I'd enjoy being a part of your study. And you know I could handle the job."

"You *are* serious. But what about your sleeping time? Could you adjust your body clock? What about our time together?"

He grinned. "We vampires do tend to snooze during the day, you know. I could sleep during your office hours—no particular advantage being awake then, anyhow, as far as I'm concerned, since you're not available. Then I could take the night shift. Then we'd have the same time together we do now. On weekends, well, we'd have to make some kind of adjustment, we can figure that out. Really, can you think of a better solution?"

"How much would I have to pay you?"

"I'll take it out in trade," he said.

They agreed he'd come in Monday afternoon, sit through the one-to-nine session with Blossom, see how she handled things. Jody would clear her appointments, show him the ropes, get him started. What the hell, maybe she'd stay through the whole session. It had been a long time since she'd observed a session, and with Shade around, it might be fun again.

When she got back to the office, Lobo was gone. No note, no good-byes. Not that she would miss him that much, but it made another strange little death. Mortality.

She spent the rest of the morning checking the files, making sure Lobo hadn't dogged it in his last few days, or deleted anything important. Not that she was *expecting* any trouble.

Not how she'd planned to use her Saturday. Shade said he thought he'd spin out to Bandelier, he hadn't seen it yet. She felt mildly put out that he would go without her, but there would be time for that. They would hike down to the upper falls at least. Maybe all the way to the Rio Grande. She canceled her disappointment with generosity, telling him to use the NSX, it would be more fun than his car, and it hadn't had a good run in a long time.

She found Lobo's personal files—strange he hadn't erased them. But then again—the ego of the writer. Almost unbearable to eliminate a single one of your deathless sentences, however casual, private, random, or mind-numbingly ordinary.

She gave in to her curiosity, at most a venial sin. She found a good-bye note to Lucia, so flat and unemotional it might as well have been the termination clause of a contract. Maybe it was, as far as he had been concerned. I'm on to greener pastures, so long, have a nice life. Goddamn all goddamned men, anyway. Her irritation at Shade's jaunt to Bandelier returned.

Then she found the text of the novel, and began to skim.

It was called *American Dreamer*, though he had apparently, to judge from some of the file names, also considered *Santa Fe Dreaming* and *The Nightshade Document*.

A handsome young lab assistant, who was also a novelist, had a passionate affair with the dream researcher he worked for, one Judy Nightshade. Judy Nightshade was a complex woman, driven by the demons of ambition but repressing a sensual and passionate interior nature. There were details of a body Jody had often seen in the mirror, though Lobo had made her sexier and more glamorous. There were also descriptions of dreams by various subjects in the experiment, apparently intended as poetic interludes. She recognized most of the dreams.

The love affair became triangular when the researcher's partner, a beautiful Hispanic psychiatrist, could resist no longer. Many scenes of the writer/assistant in bed with both women, clinically graphic exercises interspersed with extended monologues on the meaning of love, sex, life, death, and writing, all delivered by the novelist-hero, to the apparent fascination of both women. Eventually, it seemed, it was the writer/assistant who had the insight that led to the Nobel Prize–winning Grand Unified Theory of Dreams, which he announced one night in yet another three-way love scene. The researcher, unable to bear failure, stole the idea, took credit herself, and, with the collusion of her partner, went on to fame and fortune.

In order to keep him from talking, and because the Theory of Dreams implied a formula for a Virtual Reality Pill (worth billions), the researcher hired a couple of goons to break into the lab and kill the young novelist. But he killed them instead, putting on a Jackie Chan–style display of martial arts. Then he confronted the researcher, throwing the formula for the Virtual Reality Pill onto her desk. "Keep it," he said contemptuously. "I don't need it. And you don't have anything to fear from me. The only person you have to be afraid of is yourself."

The researcher and the psychiatrist finished their lives bound together in a bitter lesbian affair, protecting their guilty secret. The novelist, his suitcase in one hand, his laptop in the other, set out on the open road, not a drop of bitterness in his heart. He didn't care a lick for money and success. He was a free man. He had books to write, and he still had his own dreams. Nobody could take those away. In the last chapter a drop-dead blonde in a red convertible pulled up beside him on I-40 west of Albuquerque. She was, as it happened, a movie star, going home to L.A. after a week visiting her folks. "Where you headed?" she asked the writer.

"Wherever you are," he said. "At least for now."

At first Jody was furious beyond all measure. She felt violated, not merely in her own person, but violated in her responsibility for the others in the study, in her responsibility for the integrity of the study itself. *This* was the treachery Bianca's dream had referred to.

The subjects had all signed a release for the use of their dream narratives and medical records, of course. But she had not thought to make the release specific to her research only, and she had not thought to make Lobo sign a confidentiality agreement. She could still sue, if the book was ever published, but she had a strong feeling the suit would be futile.

But then, as she read on, she began laughing. After the fifth sex scene, when the women got into an argument about whose turn it was to perform fellatio, and the winner began talking to the writer's cock, addressing it, between mighty slurpings, with the reverence due the totem of all authority and mystery, praying to it, she had to stop and find a box of tissues and dry her eyes and blow her nose. She tried to read the passage aloud, but couldn't get all the way through without breaking down again. If anybody ever took this farrago seriously enough to publish it—

Well, no, from what she'd seen of fiction lately, publication was entirely likely.

The hell with it. She'd track Lobo down at Iowa, throw the fear of

God into him with threats of legal action, and make him change the names. Then she'd forget it. Nobody in the real world would ever give a good goddamn, anyway.

It was two in the afternoon, and she was hungry again. She'd been reading for at least a couple of hours. She was going to *have* to show this stuff to Shade. They could take turns reading passages to each other. It would be their evening's entertainment.

When they went to bed, she would pray to his dick. Then, when he was helpless with laughter, she would climb on top of him and fuck his eyeballs out.

21: inclusions and exclusions

Jody hadn't thought about how it would feel to have Shade watching while she slept. All she had thought about was how to cover Lobo's absence for the rest of the study. But during the weekend, she began to be nervous. Saturday night and Sunday night she lay awake after Shade had gone to sleep beside her, thinking about it.

She wasn't certain she could handle the vulnerability, the exposure. An intimacy greater than marriage, in a way. In marriage, the partners didn't watch each other sleep. But she couldn't bring herself to say anything to Shade about how she felt, and anyway, what choice did she have? There were simply no other arrangements in place.

What if she dreamed of Ish? Oh no.

She couldn't let Shade see that happen. He mustn't see her in the throes of orgasm with another man, even a dream man. She had to make sure she didn't dream of Ish anymore.

So of course he showed up, on the very first night Shade took the shift. The dream was simple. Jody and Ish were in the sleep chamber, and they had no clothes on, and they made love. They were aware that someone was watching, beyond the glass. It was as though they were Adam and Eve in the garden of Eden, and God was watching his creatures go at it. Just the way he'd designed them to. It was also as if the devil were watching, on a large-screen closed-circuit TV. Jody was embarrassed at first, but Ish seemed unconcerned.

This is no secret, he said. Nothing wrong with letting them see this.

They made love in perfect innocence then, albeit an innocence spiced with the excitement of observation, just as a girl loves to have her mother watch her play dolls or a boy loves to have his father watch him play cars in the sandbox.

Actually, Jody had preferred playing cars in the sandbox herself.

She knew she was dreaming, but in the dream somehow, because it was set in the very sleep chamber in which she lay, Ish was real. Jody was convinced that her lucidity had somehow opened a barrier between the worlds. In the back of her mind, as she rode Ish, crying out in wild and wilder abandon, she hoped that Shade misunderstood, hoped that he was misled into thinking he was only watching a dream. It was very important not to let the word get out that dream lovers could be really there. That was the real secret, the one they had to hide.

She had several orgasms, and the orgasms went on a long time. Her last coincided precisely with her awakening, as if the waves washed her each one a little farther onto the beachhead of reality. She felt peculiar and ill at ease, but proceeded as if everything were normal. Made her recording, got up, dressed, and—it was strange leaving Shade there, but the other two dreamers were still sleeping, so his shift had not ended—went home for breakfast.

When she got back to work, before her first patient, Toni came into the office and gave her the Look. The one with the lifted eyebrow and the big I-know-a-secret grin. Toni didn't say anything, just sat there smiling brightly until Jody broke down laughing.

"He's the one, isn't he?" Toni said. "The big fellow working the night shift when I came in. You went out and got yourself a vampire!"

"He's the one," Jody said.

"Is this like a competition, Jo D.? Just had to go out and get a bigger one than mine?"

"You know it, girlfriend. Speaking of—how are things going with you guys?"

"Don't even ask. It would just make you jealous." Toni got up and came around the desk. She leaned over and planted a cool kiss on Jody's forehead, then patted her hair. "I'm so glad for you, love. Glad for us both." She gave a little 'bye-now wave at the door.

When Jody and Shade got together after work for an early dinner—at his place for a change, an arrangement that allowed him to sleep until she let herself in with a bag of hamburgers and woke him with a kiss—she asked what he thought about his shift. She wanted to know if it had been obvious what sort of thing she was dreaming, but couldn't bring herself to ask outright.

"It was fascinating," he said. He said he'd never watched people sleep before, not in that fashion. Had lain on an elbow once or twice to watch a sleeping lover, as we all have, but that was quite different. In those cases your attention was not on the act of dreaming, but on the dreamer, the person. Dreaming was only a sort of weather that crossed the beloved landscape. "Maybe I'll learn a little something about what you're up to," he said.

His attitude, in short, was blissfully professional. Too professional. He said not a word about her orgasm, till finally she could stand it no longer and broke down and asked him if he had noticed. "Yes," he said. "I was watching the readouts when you had the first one. I knew something was up because your alpha rhythms started going really crazy." He went on to say that Angela Epstein, in chamber number one, had apparently had a similar event.

"Angela?" Jody said. "I don't believe it. It must be catching."

Shade didn't grin slyly, he didn't crack dirty jokes. He seemed entirely matter-of-fact. All just clinical observation, ma'am. She was certain, later, that he had understood her sensitivities, and was being careful, because later, after she had relaxed, he finally began to kid her.

And so it was that John Shade came to be included in Jody Nightwood's dream life.

Late one Wednesday afternoon in mid-May, Toni came into Jody's office again and asked Jody to come to dinner a week from Saturday night at her parents' house. She was radiant, could hardly contain herself. "Vic and I are getting married," she said.

"Girl," Jody said, stunned. Then she got up, held her arms wide. "Girl, I can't believe it. Come here." They had a long big hug—well, a long intermittent hug, because they would draw back and look at each other and burst into tears again and hug some more.

Finally, after fifteen minutes or so of this and the destruction of half a box of tissues, they set into some serious talking. There were no more appointments, and Shade was already on duty handling the sleepers, taking a double shift because Blossom had final exams.

It was to be an October wedding, just when the aspen were turning, they hoped. Toni, who, for all her apparent rebelliousness, always came back to the classical, the traditional, would have preferred June, but June simply wasn't feasible. She and Vic would honeymoon in Hawaii for three weeks—she was going to have to make arrangements with Jody to cover the clinic while she was gone. Where would they live? Well, that had yet to be worked out for certain; Toni knew what she wanted to do if she could talk Vic into it, but she wasn't going to say anything about it right now, just keep it as a great big surprise for everybody later.

"Girl, are we going to have some *parties!*" Wedding parties, housewarming parties, party parties. The first party, if you could call it that, was going to be Saturday night at Vida and Allegra's house. Have you told them yet? No, girl, I haven't. You know they know about him, they always know about my men, but this is going to be a shock, making it permanent. I mean, I know they'll be great, they had to figure it might happen someday, but it'll still take some adjusting. That's really one of the reasons I want you to come over, help make it easier on them. They love you so much. And you like Vic—you do like Vic, don't you?—so if they see you think we're good for each other, it'll go that much easier.

Jody didn't ask whether she could bring Shade. It was pretty clear he wouldn't belong—Vida and Allegra were going to be feeling enough stress without the presence of yet another male, and a stranger at that—and if she asked, Toni might feel compelled to say yes.

"That's not the only reason I want you to come," Toni said. Jody waited, but Toni was looking at the floor, a very uncharacteristic gesture. Jody pulled a Toni-as-therapist move, and held silence until finally her friend spoke again.

"It's Vic. I—there's—well, something I haven't told him, and—"

"Toni, you're kidding me! He doesn't *know?*"

Toni shook her head, looking near tears. "I mean, when is a good time? Oh, lover, you were wonderful, and by the way, I just want you to know my parents are lesbians?"

"But you *have* to tell him, girl. It isn't fair not to! *You* aren't embarrassed, are you?" Ashamed of Vida and Allegra—Jody couldn't imagine it.

"Of course not. By the time I even understood how my guys were unusual, I was long past being able to be anything but proud of them. It's just—with me and Vic, it wasn't *about* my parents, it was about *us.* The subject just never came up, and I—but now—I'm sure it'll be all right. Vic is such a *good* man, and I know it won't matter a bit to him, but—"

"Well, you've got to tell him before you haul him over there. Good Lord, girl. *You're* the psychiatrist. *You're* the one who talks to *me* about being open and up front." Jody had a sudden suspicion: "You're not going to try one of those *Cage aux Folles* things, are you?"

"I'm going to tell him," Toni said. "I'm going to tell him tonight."

"I hope so," Jody said. "Because I'm not going over there if he doesn't already know."

"He *will,*" Toni insisted, a little irritated now. She softened. "I just figure that if he *does* have any adjusting to do, it'll be easier on him if he sees someone else there who loves Vida and Allegra almost as much as I do, and it's somebody he knows and respects."

Vic respects me, Jody thought, with an inexplicable flush of pride. "So I'm going to be the graphite rod in the nuclear family," she said.

"Girl, that's the worst pun you've ever made."

"You know, things aren't going to be the same between us," Jody said.

"We're still going to be best friends."

"Not really. You've seen it. You know how it goes. Vic is your best friend now."

"It's life, girl. It has to happen."

"Yeah, I know. I just—I just hate losing you."

That set off another tear fest, after which reassurances, hugs, then happy gossip, excited plans, have you picked out the dresses, what about the silver, who's doing the invitations—

When Jody left the office that evening, she went up to Shade, who was sitting at the observation desk working on the computer, and kissed him on the back of the neck with such tenderness that he swiveled around and gave her a quizzical look.

"Later," she said.

Thursday evening, the next time they were able to be together, she explained about not being able to take him to Vida and Allegra's on Saturday night. He didn't seem to mind.

"I'll just have to fuck you that afternoon," he said, which comment led to a wrestling match—he had to be punished for his presumption—which in its turn led to her getting fucked before heading back to the office for her dream shift.

"Don't be such a sexist," Shade said when Jody pointed out the feedback nature of that recent cause-and-effect sequence. "I got fucked, too."

Okay, Shade said. He was on the phone in his bedroom. I'm glad to hear it. I didn't think so, but you can't afford to overlook the obvious. Yeah, Wingo's a funny name.

He listened a moment. Then he said, No. As far as I can tell, I'm the only man in her life right now. Well, it's important, because there's been a development. I'm working with her in the lab. Full access to everything. It's a much better approach.

He listened again, then gave a short laugh. Right, Mom. Build it on trust. Then his tone darkened. I don't want her hurt, do you understand? She's a remarkable woman.

He listened. What if I am? When has it ever colored my judgment? You want your little boy to be happy, don't you? Fine.

He listened again. Yeah, he said. Yeah, she's cooking okay. But it might be good to stimulate her a little. Put her in contact with— No, somebody unrelated. I was thinking Christopher Langton up at the Institute. The artificial-life guy. Well, I figured you'd know the name, but he's not in the family, is he? Not even a distant relative, good. Me? Oh, perfectly innocent. I met him doing research for one of the novels.

He listened. He laughed again: So now you're a literary critic?

"So what is it?" Leonard said. "What's the big secret?" He was making a point of being restless and anxious to get out of the car. He hadn't had his exercise yet, and he wasn't in the mood to be carted to hell and gone. He'd had enough of that lately.

They'd been all over the state. They'd gone to Ruidoso and seen the Hurd's polo field out in San Patricio and gone by Fort Meigs, falling now in disrepair as Meigs himself was less and less able to keep it up and could find no satisfactory buyer. They had stayed overnight at the Lodge in Cloudcroft, and looked out the dining-room window and seen the Trinity site. They had descended from the mountains to visit the malpais outside Carrizozo, the Valley of Fires.

They had gone from there to Las Cruces and had had dinner at the Double Eagle in Old Mesilla, and then had gone to El Paso and gotten very drunk in Juarez and had stolen the money and clothing of four men who tried to rob them in a back alley, but had let the men live.

Leonard had been happy for a few days after that.

They had visited Chaco, but neither of them liked to camp, so it had been rather an exhausting day trip, and Leonard had hated the flea markets and Indian markets in the Four Corners area as much as Toynbee had loved them. They had come across the northern part of the state, through Dulce and into Chama, and had ridden the Cumbres and Toltec. They had come down into Taos, and stayed at La Fonda, where Toynbee had sworn he heard D. H. Lawrence's ghost in the night, howling at Frieda. Next day they had visited Lawrence's ranch.

They'd taken the high road back to Santa Fe, and gone to see the wildflowers along the Rio Santa Barbara, and then had come down through Las Trampas and taken photos of the church and bought turqoise-embedded silver in La Tiendita and tried some of the owner's new bottled water from a spring on his own land, and they'd visited the Cardona-Hine Gallery in Truchas, as Toynbee had been begging to do for weeks, and had even had tea with Barbara and Alvaro.

But now Leonard had had it with scenery, he had had it with tradition, he had had it up to here with art and glorious sunsets and geological marvels. He was ready to be in a real city again, Lisbon or Rio or New York or Tokyo or even back in D.C.

He wasn't made for sitting around doing nothing, and that's all traveling really was, basically. You sat in a car all day long. The car was moving, but you weren't. You were sitting on your keister. Leonard needed action, and he wasn't getting any. They hadn't heard from the control in weeks. If the operation didn't crank up again soon—

"Another minute or two," Toynbee said now. "You're going to love it."

Toynbee hoped he was right. Oh, how he hoped he was right.

He had brought them down through town on Palace, and now he cut over to San Francisco by the El Dorado Hotel. He took them across Guadalupe, and onto the winding narrow lane that was West San Francisco, where old adobes in all stages of remodeling crowded the street, and coyote fencing leaned to and fro. He pulled into the driveway of a two-story home, a brown, thick-walled establishment with a spanking new sun porch across the front.

There was a for-sale sign in the front yard.

A real-estate agent, male, met them on the front walk, and led them in through double doors on the sun porch to an ancient interior, chattering all the way. The floor was made of wide planking burnished with age, the windows were set into a two-foot thickness of walls, the ceilings were *viga* and *latilla,* there were patinaed tin sconces, the plumbing was medieval.

As soon as he had a chance, Leonard pulled Toynbee aside. "What the hell is this?" he snarled. "Are you wanting to play house?"

Toynbee shushed him as the agent found them again. "Later," he said. "I'll explain just as soon as we're alone." They finished the tour, and then Toynbee asked if they could stay to look at the yard while the agent rushed off to his next appointment.

"Look at this lot," he said to Leonard once they were alone. "It's nearly a half-acre. And the house! I mean, I know it needs work—the plumbing—but twenty or so would cover everything, and the price on this place! It's simply incredible. This lot, the house, all of it right downtown, and just three hundred thousand. You just don't find bargains like that around here anymore. Remember how you could see the mountains from windows in the loft?"

"Will you tell me what's going on?" Leonard said. "Because I am not planning to settle down and play patty-cake with you in this podunk town—"

Toynbee interrupted before Leonard became too negative: "No." He drew in a breath. This was the moment. Put it all on the line and see what happened.

"I want you to be a part of my life. From now on. Forever. You know that, and I'm sorry if it sounds sappy, but there's no use pretending otherwise. But that's not why I brought you here. What my idea here is—well—with our backgrounds—"

Suck it up, boy, spit it out.

"Don't you think we'd make a great pair of private detectives?"

"Private detectives?"

"Listen, love. I've made a decision. When this operation is over, I'm leaving the agency. I have a bit of funding set aside, enough for a few years. This is my kind of town." He rushed on, trying to ignore the skepticism on his friend's face.

"The house could be our office as well as our home. There's separate bedrooms, with baths, so we wouldn't have to be, we wouldn't have to be domestic partners if you didn't want. But we *know* we make a great working team, and there's tons of money in this town, and there would be an immediate need for our services, and we would be the best in the area, and—"

A species of tenderness came over Leonard's face, a sort of pity. *Well, all right,* Toynbee thought. *At least I'm not looking at outright rejection.*

"You've thought all this out, haven't you?" Leonard said.

"I have done that, yes."

"And you'll buy this place with or without me? And stay."

"Yes. I know you're tired of Santa Fe, but you could be the field agent, you see. The one who does all the traveling, flies off to Sierra Leone and Zanzibar—"

"Well, then. I don't suppose there's any harm in my thinking about it awhile. I mean there's no rush, is there? Let me think about it. When this operation is over, well—"

"Take all the time you want," Toynbee said gratefully.

Leonard took his friend's arm, began walking them back toward the car. "I've been a right bastard lately, haven't I?" he said.

"I wouldn't say that," Toynbee said.

Leonard laughed. "Yes, you would. And that's just how you'd say it. The thing that scares me the most is I'm beginning to sound like you." He got in on his side, Toynbee on the driver's side. They fastened their seat belts. Toynbee backed them out into the street.

"Only thing," Leonard said. "I wouldn't be able to kill people. Private detectives don't get to kill people, except in the movies."

"You're terrible," Toynbee said happily. "But there would probably be some dealers you could have at, don't you think? That sort of thing. Types nobody would weep for, the cops wouldn't be bothered with. Why, we could do some real good. Help clean up society."

Friday morning, Jody got a call from Bruno Sandoval. He invited her to have dinner with him that night. Her first reaction was embarrassment that she had not called him recently, he had had to call her. Her second reaction was a wave of pleasure and warmth.

"I'm seeing somebody now," she said, though she and Shade had not planned on getting together that night. Fridays, with the free weekend coming up, were easier to skip.

"Please invite the gentleman as well," he said valiantly.

"I'm not sure that would work," she said, imagining the scene. Shade, I want you to meet my seventy-year-old dear friend and one-night stand. Bruno, meet a man who's younger than you, handsomer than you, and better than twice your weight. I'm sure you two must have a lot in common. Please chat amongst yourselves while I powder my nose.

"Of course," Sandoval said. "Please accept my congratulations, and remain assured of my friendship." He and Shade *did* have a sort of old-world courtliness in common.

"Wait a minute," she said. "I wasn't saying no. I'd really like to have dinner with you. I'll have to make some arrangements, that's all. And I'll have to leave early, no later than ten-thirty, so I can be back here in time for my part of the dream sessions."

"*Bueno,*" Sandoval said, his voice almost lilting with happiness. "You understand—*quiero nada que*—I wish nothing more than to be your friend."

And if that's *true, you're not half the man I think. But I believe you would die before you would offend me.* They settled on Pasqual's at seven—close to the office, so she could go directly to her dream session afterward. She hung up the phone, glowing.

She had *three* men loving her. A dear wonderful courageous father-figure, a great big Superman-quality hunk, and the finest dream lover a gal could want. Okay, so most people wouldn't count the dream lover. But then again, most people didn't *have* anybody like Ish.

They sat at a back table. Jody ordered the filet, which was magnificent. "I'd never thought of Pasqual's as an evening place," she said, "but this is very nice."

Bruno was beaming over his own grilled tuna. "You like the filets, no? This is what you ordered the last time we dined together." She hadn't remembered, and now blushed, thinking what else had been on the menu, later that evening.

"Sorry," she said. "Not very feminine, but I like red meat."

"No, no. You cannot imagine. In this town, a woman who has appetite, who is not afraid of the blood. For me, it is a very beautiful thing. *Como mi esposa.*"

"Well, they're right, though. The vegetarians, I mean. I always feel guilty."

"Why are they right? Examine your teeth, my good doctor. Are they the teeth of an herbivore? We do not know why *el buen Dios* has made us as we are, but He has."

"The killing, though."

"But we have all brought death, and we all walk under sentence of death ourselves. It may sound foolish to a modern woman, but I am one of those who prays for the souls he has slain, who asks forgiveness. When my own time comes, I will have no complaint."

Jody assumed he was thinking of his war experience, of the fact that some of the souls he had prayed for were those of other men. And she felt a chill, the communication of shadowy experience: She sat in the presence of one who had taken human life. It was a barrier she could not imagine crossing. She could not imagine life on the other side of that barrier.

She saw how his ancient Christianity might be necessary, though for her it was a dark and forbidding faith, a brooding nightmare whose halls she refused to enter.

It hit her with a shock that Pop might have killed men. The one time she'd pressed him about the war, he had said that battle itself was mostly a great confusion, in which you did not know where you were or what you were doing. It was like a tornado. It made no sense and no sense could be made of it, and therefore there was no point whatsoever in talking about it.

She looked up and saw, at the door, just coming in, Toni and Vic. At almost the same moment, Toni saw her. The speculation on her face was apparent even from across the room. Jody smiled and waved, resolving that Bruno Sandoval's presence required no explanation at all, that in fact any attempt to explain would be insulting. Let Toni wonder.

"Ah, my two doctors," Bruno said, following Jody's eyes. What? Had he seen Toni after all? If so, he'd never mentioned it. Toni and Vic came their way, and Jody and Bruno both stood. "Toni, I'd like you to meet my dear friend Bruno Sandoval," Jody said, uncertain of her manners. Ladies first, or age before beauty? What a poorly trained generation we were.

"Charmed," Sandoval said, executing a small bow over Toni's hand.

"And this is—"

But Bruno Sandoval had already taken Vic's hand, and shaken it, and was looking up saying, "It is quite a pleasure to see you again, Mr. Vigil."

"A pleasure, Mr. Sandoval," Vic said. There was something in his face Jody had never seen there before. A species of respect, she thought. Vic looked at the little man the way he might have regarded a worthy opponent in the boxing ring, or a fellow cop he trusted.

She felt, as she had not for a while, the outsider's bafflement. Mostly she'd settled in, Santa Fe was unquestionably her home. But there were these connections, relationships a newcomer could never completely penetrate. History. Old dark history.

They invited Toni and Vic to sit with them, but Toni said, "Thanks, it looks like you're almost through, and anyway we have some plans we need to talk over."

Jody felt a bit on display for the rest of the meal. Whenever she glanced toward Toni and Vic, they were in deep conversation, not paying her any mind at all. Still. She was going to have to formally introduce Toni and Vic to Shade, and soon. Make the situation absolutely clear.

"How do you know Vic? Mr. Vigil," she amended.

"He helped me once through a very great grief," Bruno said. Had Vic been the cop who'd worked with Sandoval on the motorcycle shooting? She didn't ask, because she didn't feel she should refer to that painful time unless Bruno brought it up first.

No, she remembered now. That fellow hadn't been local, had been an Anglo from somewhere in the East, New Jersey or something.

Sandoval walked her back to her office in the warm and breezy night. Her loose skirt blew pleasurably about her thighs, and she felt her hair tossing in the wind. "You are a remarkably beautiful woman," he said at her door. "It pleases an old man just to see you."

She was left without her usual defensive self-deprecation. It would have shown too little respect. She bent, and kissed him goodnight.

The first week in June, Shade took Jody up to the Santa Fe Institute to meet one of the scientists there, Chris Langton, who had pioneered the field of artificial life. Which was not, Shade explained, the same as artificial intelligence. Though there were connections. Artificial life had begun as an attempt to model evolution on computers. Langton himself was a fascinating fellow, who had had, after a hang-glider crash, a number of life-changing out-of-the-body and dream experiences. Which was why Shade had picked him for Jody to talk to. That and the fact that he was the only one at the institute whom Shade knew really well.

Along the way, he told her what he knew of the Institute. It was supposed to be the center for a new way of doing science, a synergistic and cross-disciplinary place where the top thinkers in all sorts of fields could come together and be free to pursue knowledge for its own sake. It was also supposed to be oriented toward public service, science that included the public, that reached out to it, and was concerned with issues of the quality of human life.

It was housed in what had been the home and outbuildings of one of Eisenhower's generals. A mile and a quarter out Hyde Park Road, they took a left onto a winding muddy gravel lane climbing a hillside. They pulled up in front of an outwardly nondescript, relatively low-slung edifice, nothing at all resembling Jody's idea of a think tank. They walked first to a bench under a couple of trees on the edge of the hill, from which there was a spectacular view of the ski basin. The green mountains seemed to hang over them, disembodied, a separate sky.

"I really want to ski over the top of those," Jody said. "Would you go with me?"

"Sure. Tell you what, why don't we hike it first, say a couple of times this summer? Familiarize ourselves with the route?"

They went in through a couple of big blue doors to a blond desk in a wide, tile-floored, high-ceilinged corridor going off at right angles forward and to the left. The corridor's interior walls were of glass, and looked into a courtyard of trees and geometric concrete.

Shade told the receptionist they were there to see Chris Langton.

"Oh, you know what," she said. "He had a family emergency."

"Damn," Shade said. "He did? Nothing too serious, I hope."

"He did leave a message. He's sorry he can't be here, he'll call you when he gets back to town, and he's arranged for Dr. Mindanao to see you in his place."

"Dr. who?"

"Mindanao. Dr. Sunday Mindanao. He's here on an interim basis, helping Dr. Langton with the Bad Animals project. I'll just give him a buzz."

Shade looked at Jody, shrugged a question. She spread her hands, why not?

"I'll just take Dr. Nightwood around a little while we're waiting," Shade said. The receptionist might or might not have heard him, preoccupied with the phone, someone who didn't know where Dr. Mindanao was just at the moment but knew how to find him.

Jody had expected something a little more governmental. Guards, security cameras, ID cards, sealed corridors. But the atmosphere here was entirely casual, more like faculty offices in a prosperous but disorderly middle-class college. Satellite photos on the walls. Some sort of free-standing topographical model in a glass case. A long-haired fellow in blue jeans passed them going the other way as they strolled up the corridor, ambling along with papers in his hands. A harried-looking woman in a business suit came out of a side door and hurried click-clack across the tiles. People nodded, but no one paid them any especial mind.

Shade led Jody through what seemed a large conference room and out onto a tiled veranda running along the back of the house. It looked out over the edge of the hillside. Depending on where you stood, you could see Los Alamos, Chama, or Albuquerque. The whole state of New Mexico spread out below. They stayed a moment in the fresh air, then went back in.

The corridor made a rectangular hall around the central courtyard. Doors opened off it into suites that had once been bedrooms or guest quarters and were now offices and computer labs. Looking into the courtyard, you could see the enormous vanes of concrete that pillared the construction. The walls were thick, but the house, Shade said, was made of concrete block, not adobe. The effect of the whole was a curious fusion of fifties glass-and-steel starkness and warm Southwestern style. Shade thought the concrete slabs of the courtyard were an architect's mistake, that greenery would have been more rewarding.

When they'd made their circuit and come back to the desk, they found a gray-haired and portly fellow waiting for them. He wore an expensive gray suit, a muted maroon tie, and an air of regal annoyance. He introduced himself, in a soft Caribbean accent, as Dr. Sunday Mindanao. His specialty was artificial intelligence. He had in fact begun as a physicist, and didn't have much use for so-called scientists who didn't know their physics. Soft sciences, indeed.

He led them, not back to his office, but to a small, glassed-in conference room just to the right of the entryway, got them seated in comfortable, fabric-backed gray chairs at a sleek wooden table, asked if they wanted coffee or a drink.

When they had said no, Mindanao sat, and asked, "Now, how may I help you?"

Jody had had a professor in a genetics class who had managed to convey, whenever she had come for an office visit, and without saying a word, that she was a charming young girl, but really, what was all this nonsense about becoming an expert herself? Only extremely smart people like the professor ever got to sit in a rich office and pontificate.

She realized that she was waiting for Shade to take the lead, and that Shade was showing her the respect of not doing so.

"I was hoping," she began, "to compare notes on a few matters regarding chaos theory and complexity theory. I am currently conducting a study of dream activity in human consciousness—" *Listen to yourself, Jody.*

"I'm studying dreams," she said, "and I think there may be a connection."

"Dream activity?" Mindanao said. "If there's a connection, I fail to see it."

"Well, I read in the paper a few months back where Dr. Langton said we wouldn't have true artificial intelligence until we had an intelligence that could go insane. That seemed suggestive to me. Not that I think dreams and insanity are the same thing, but maybe—"

"Dr. Langton is not an expert on artificial intelligence."

And you are, Jody thought. But in for a dime, in for a dollar. She explained her model of dreaming as the perceptual equivalent of a feedback state, feeling more gauche and simpleminded as she went. "So anyway, that's one possibility," she finished.

Mindanao sat a long time without saying anything, looking through the glass to an interior office rather than at either of them. His attitude was that of a man thinking how to explain adult matters in comprehensible terms to a couple of children.

"How familiar are you with chaos theory?" he said at last. "Perhaps the best approach is to review the fundamentals." He proceeded with a lecture on the origins of chaos mathematics in the work of Lorenz and others. Then he went into the math itself: Iterated nonmonotonic functions—

"Anything with a hump," Jody said. *And thank you, Loren Wingo.*

Mindanao shifted smoothly to Feigenbaum's number, the Henon attractor, Poincaré maps. The fractal characteristics of strange attractors. He wanted fractals, did he?

She countered with Koch snowflakes, and sieves and sponges. She remembered a fragment from Asimov or Hofstadter or some other popularizer: "Isn't it silly," she laughed, "how they used to call them 'mathematical monsters'?" Monsters because, unlike other curves or areas or volumes, they were discontinuous at every single point.

Discontinuous at every point: She thought of her Swivel notion of dreams.

Mindanao said, "Do you know anything about catastrophe theory?" Chalk one up for him, and he knew it, too. She didn't follow the math, but catastrophe seemed to be about changes of state. How does ice suddenly and all at once become water, at the crossing of a certain threshold? How does the leaf decide to detach from the tree at one particular moment and not another?

How does the conscious mind suddenly cross over into dreaming?

The relation to chaos, Mindanao said, was the onset of turbulence. How did a smooth, linear flow suddenly become turbulent? One suspected it bore some relation to the way the multiplication of attractors became infinite at Feigenbaum's number.

"A tiny little seed," he said. "The crossing of an infinitesimal decimal point, triggers utter chaos. On one side of the border, smooth flow, stability, predictability. One point farther on, and suddenly there is a cascade to violence, chaos, madness."

He was, it seemed to Jody, for a moment, unusually poetic.

He switched now to complexity theory, and spoke of emergent properties of complex systems. Jody had heard a lot of language about emergent properties before, but had never been able to get anyone who knew anything about the subject to go beyond a simple definition of the term. Sometimes she suspected nobody knew anything else about it beyond the ability to point at something and say, "Lookit that there, that there's an emergent property. Yup. Emergent, all right. Damn straight. Emergent. Emergent as hell."

"I wonder if consciousness might not be described as an emergent property of sufficiently complex brains," Jody said, and Mindanao raised his eyebrows. "And I wonder if dreaming might not be either an emergent property of consciousness, or an inevitable corollary."

"There's no such thing as consciousness," Mindanao said, moving anxiously in his seat. "It's an illusion. Like rainbows. There are not actually any great arcs of color reaching across the sky. They only seem to exist because of the perceptions of the observer."

Jody had read the same metaphor in *Time* magazine a few years ago. "Yeah," she said. "In the case of the rainbow, I take your point. Illusion, existing only in the perceptions of an observer. But in fact, all illusions *require* an observer, do they not? So, in the case of consciousness—if it is an illusion, then who's observing it? Unless you want to maintain that the illusion is perceiving itself, in which case—"

"I'm afraid you miss the point. You're speaking of things you know nothing about. I remind you, this is my particular field of expertise—"

"Human consciousness?"

"The modeling of intelligence. I have written several books on the subject, you know. You might look into them if you'd like a better background. Of course the mathematics—"

"Just give me the straight dope, Doc," she said. Shade was doing his best to smother a smile. "What's your best take on this consciousness beeswax?"

"The brain is the hardware," Mindanao said, "and consciousness is merely the programming that runs on that hardware."

"Interesting metaphor," Jody said. "But it strikes me as being wired backwards. What I mean is, the human brain invented computers, not the other way round. Isn't it a bit misleading to then turn around and use the brain's invention as our best-guess model of the brain?"

"There's a reason we have designed these artificial intelligences," Mindanao said, huffily, "and it is quite correct to interpret the structures of our own intelligence according to—"

"Yes," Jody said. "But I can think of so many obvious differences that the metaphor seems to me to be almost totally worthless. For one thing, you can turn computers off and on. You can store the program separately when it isn't running."

"I anticipate the day when we will be able to do the same thing with the human brain."

"You *anticipate*. Here's another problem with the metaphor. Brains evolved, and if they have programming, the programming evolved simultaneously—but computers were built, and programs for computers have been written in a detached and separable manner."

"Miss Nightwood, what exactly is your point? I've done my best to offer you my expertise. But you appear more interested in refuting me on matters which I have studied for a lifetime and in which you are a novice. I really don't need all this *jerriso.*"

"My apologies," Jody said. "I appreciate your time."

Mindanao's remark had set off a string of firecrackers in her brain, and she wanted to get away and think: There's a *reason* we have designed these artificial intelligences—

What was that reason? Why *had* we invented computers? Not to model human awareness. That was a latter-day attempt, a recent development. We had invented them to store and manipulate data that our own brains didn't handle as efficiently. We had invented them not as *models* of our brains, but as supplements, as the expansion of certain capacities.

There were some things our brains did not remember well. We stored the flavor of a slice of Key lime pie magnificently well. The texture of a lover's face. The sight of a double rainbow against a wall of blue-black cloud. But numbers, digits, bits—data?

Only rare, freakish minds stored these well and handled them nimbly. Minds like Mindanao's, presumably. Such memory wasn't the main task of the human brain. Our memory did not work like the memory of computers. So what was our memory *for?*

And how did it relate to dream? How was it that the dead walked in our dreams, and walked not merely as they once had been, but in brand-new flesh and favor?

She thought she knew. And it was just what she needed.

Outside, walking to the car, Shade said, "Sorry about that. They're not all such turkeys. Langton is actually a pretty great fellow, really approachable."

"Hmm?" Jody said. "Oh, never mind. I've seen the type before. Because they have an out-of-sight facility with one little area of human accomplishment, they believe all understanding is theirs. I've seen poets and musicians and actors and businessmen with the same disease. Besides, he's probably entitled. I am an amateur in his arena. I'm sure I came off as brash and obnoxious. *You* sure didn't have much to say," she added.

"Figured it was your show," he said. She stood waiting at her door while he got in, unlocked it from the inside. "What's on your mind?" he said when she slid in.

"What do you mean?"

"I saw you back there. You got an idea. That's why you were so ready to leave."

"Maybe you're getting to know me too well."

"Not well enough, I'd say. When are you going to include me in your thought processes? I could be pretty useful, somebody to bounce ideas off of. It's not like I'm stupid." He started the engine, put them on the winding drive down the hill.

"Of course not. It's just—okay. The function of memory in humans. It isn't to preserve data. We aren't tape recorders, computers." She was excited now. "The primary function of intelligence—*any* intelligence—is to create models. We don't store raw experience, we store patterns of experience—simulations."

"I think that's pretty generally understood," he said.

"Yes, but— *Everything* is a simulation. I don't perceive you directly. I'm creating a simulation of you this very moment. You're creating a simulation of me."

He brought them onto Hyde Park. "I'll let you be in my simulation if I can be in yours."

The connections kept sparking, networks of implication lighting up like strands on a Christmas tree. "Even our so-called egos are simulations. We use them just as we do any other model, to predict the behavior of the system—only in that case, we *are* the system. Probably any sufficiently complex brain will begin to model itself along with the rest of the universe. That's why we wonder about cats and dogs, they're right on the border. The people we call egotists—they don't have *big* egos, they just have *faulty* ones—bad models of how they really work."

"I'll buy it for a dollar," he said. "But what's different about it, and what does that have to do with dreams? You do think it has something to do with dreams, don't you?" They came around the last big curve, all of Santa Fe waiting below.

"I do," she said. "But that's the part I haven't got clear yet. I mean, I can *see* it, I know it's all there, but I don't have any words for it. It's frustrating."

"Yeah," he said. "That's the way a book is when I'm writing it. I can feel the shape of the whole thing, but I can't explain it. The only way to explain it is to write it."

"Memory and dreams," she muttered. "Memory and dreams."

They were at the turn onto Washington Avenue. "I better create me a simulation of this here traffic," he said. "Or we're never gonna get home."

Colonel Wilbur Hall was on the phone in his office. "Well, you understand," he said, "we're proud to have you interested. It is a very exclusive development."

The woman on the line spoke for a moment. "Yes," Colonel Hall said. "One of the oldest in Santa Fe. I respect your family, and I'm honored you'd want to invite me. It's just that we don't quote actual prices until you're ready to make a serious—"

The woman spoke.

"No, honestly, not to anyone. What? I can do that much, sure. From the high sixes—I mean very high—to the mid-sevens. A couple in the mid-high-sevens, but. No problem? Good. *Good.* Glad to hear it. Fine. Well, you just fire off those bona fides, and—"

The woman spoke again.

"We can work with that time frame. No problem. I mean, it'll have to be after the Buckaroo Ball, of course. All I'm thinking about right now. But it sounds like that'll work for you. Just let me review your fax materials, and then we'll schedule a tour ASAP."

When the Colonel hung up, he clapped his hands together over his head. "Hot damn!" he said. Funny the way it was working out. This damn spy business was actually going to help him turn a buck. He'd been pissed when the Archuleta woman showed up at the Super Bowl party in Nightwood's place, but now—

Never heard of her damn family, of course. Have to check that out. If it was as old-line as she said, that could help with the county commissioners. Wouldn't think she'd have that kind of money, but you never knew. Around here, you just never knew.

Jody was finally able to get Shade and herself together with Toni and Vic, but it took some doing. Toni was thinking of almost nothing but the wedding, and seemed to have an activity scheduled every single night. When they finally convened, in one of the side rooms of the bar at La Posada, the meeting was irritatingly anticlimactic.

The men shook hands warily, two large and territorial creatures, and thereafter traded only the most cursory of remarks. Toni, of course, was familiar with Shade already, if not in his role as Jody's lover, and anyway her mind was not on Jody's romance, but her own. She was all over Vic, and Shade, for his part, was far less demonstrative than usual. Withdrawn.

Jody had hoped for a glad foursome, the association of two like-minded couples. A dual friendship to replace what she was losing with Toni. Based on the way things were going this evening, that would happen when hell froze over. She watched the way Vic looked at Toni, the way his face changed every time. She watched Shade's face and saw nothing.

She realized, after her second 101 on the rocks, that she was becoming angry and depressed, and made herself stop drinking. Vic and Toni had a dinner appointment, and Jody used that as an excuse to leave earlier than she had planned.

In the car on the way home, Shade was silent. No commiseration, no sympathy, no reassurance. Just a damned vacuum in the passenger's seat.

In the bar, Vic said, "How long has she been seeing him?"

"About three months, a little more. It started when we were— when you and I were—having our trouble. That's why I didn't say anything then. Why, don't you approve?"

Vic considered his drink. "I wouldn't say disapprove," he said.

"What is it, then? Because sometimes he makes me feel strange. But I think maybe she feels the same way about you. Maybe it's this female jealousy thing."

"Don't play the shrink on yourself. No, he's like—I keep thinking of wolves. Jaguars. It was obvious I spooked him, and I can't figure out why. He's a beautiful animal, and he's smart enough to know we aren't competing."

He took a swallow. "I think he loves her, all right. But I wonder if she's safe."

Toni put her head on Vic's shoulder. "Why not, animal? *I'm* safe with *you*."

"Good point," he said.

Jody had not been going to ask Shade in, but at her door, he said softly, "Try not to worry about it. Sometimes the chemistry's just wrong. Give it a little time."

That was all it took to get the tears started, and once they were started she needed to be held, and so it was that she let herself be carried in, and then up the stairs. He helped her undress and tucked her in, and rubbed her with warm oil, and when he finally came to bed himself they did not make love, but she burrowed into his back, her mind slipping sideways out of reality.

She dreamed she was flying high over the city, clinging to the shoulders of a giant bat. But the bat's fur was soft and she nuzzled into it, flying warm and high and safe.

22: family secrets

Shade didn't seem at all upset about not being invited to the announcement dinner at Vida and Allegra's. She'd wasted all that angst, and it turned out he didn't even *want* to go.

"Not my strong point," he said, "family gatherings. Besides, those people don't know me from Adam. Although it might be fun to watch the fireworks." Jody had told him the situation with Toni's parents, dressing it up as a comedy of manners.

"There aren't going to be any fireworks," she said.

"Pity," Shade said.

He had asked one unusual favor—unusual in that he didn't ask favors. He wanted to borrow the NSX and take it out for a moonlit run. "Been a while since I did that," he said. "Put a good car through its paces in the mountains at night."

The van was in the shop for a tune-up, which meant she'd be either using the Pontiac or hitching a ride, but she'd said yes: "You'll be careful, though, won't you?"

"Always," he had said.

When the day came, Jody decided she didn't want to take the Pontiac out. Vida and Allegra's neighborhood had once been a good one, and still was in some ways, but more and more the children of the traditional families were running wild—no discipline for the darling little scions—and tagging and vandalism were way up. Instead she got Toni and Vic to give her a ride.

Which made her feel as though she were back in high school, going along on a friend's date in a friend's car. Earlier, when Shade had picked up the NSX, he had been so eager to get going, he'd hardly slowed down to give her a hug and a kiss, and that didn't help.

Vic rang the doorbell, which Jody appreciated. The modern practice of honking the horn out front was rude and peremptory, she felt. Toni disagreed: ringing was inefficient and a waste of time. Jody gave Vic credit for having improved, already, his bride-to-be's manners.

She squeezed into the front seat of the tiny square-back Tercel, Vic insisting on sitting in the back. "It's really better for me," he said. "I can sit sideways and stretch out."

The little four-wheel-drives were ubiquitous in Santa Fe, far more common than the emblematic Range-Rovers. They were the lower middle class's equivalent, tough little bugs that lasted forever and could go almost anywhere a Rover could. Few people got into situations rugged enough to justify the fifty-thousand-dollar price differential, anyway.

In theory, Jody approved of Toni's practicality and thriftiness, but in practice the car was so underpowered that in hot weather you couldn't run the air conditioner and climb hills at the same time. Besides, it was damnably cramped. You risked dislocating your shoulder to fasten your seat belt, and forget wearing a hat if you were over five-two. Think what it must be like for somebody Vic's size. She realized she had never seen him in anything but an official car.

"Do you even own a car?" she asked, twisting to look into the backseat.

"No," he said. "I have a departmental ride, and I never saw the point of tying up another four hundred a month in steel and rubber." He seemed to understand the source of Jody's question: "I thought Toni's folks might prefer not to have a cruiser parked out in front of their house. Even an unmarked. I mean, they're going to have enough adjusting to do."

"Boy, that's the truth," Jody laughed. From the expression on her face, Toni didn't think it was a laughing matter. "Lighten up, girl," Jody said, punching her arm.

"What with me being Indian and all," Vic said. "I mean, I think I've told you I have some Spanish blood, but for these old patrician families, that just makes it worse."

"Toni," Jody said in a rising voice. The night was clear and beautiful, but Toni was concentrating on the road as though she were piloting them through a driving rain.

"She says they're not bigots, but even so," Vic said.

"Toni," Jody said. "You *promised* you'd *tell* him."

"I'm not offended," Vic said. "You have to allow for human nature. You have to assume it'll take them a while to adjust. Tell me what?"

"This is ridiculous," Leonard said. He was driving.

"I don't see why," Toynbee said. "It's a beautiful night—look at that moon—and we're out in it enjoying ourselves and doing what we do best." Leonard had been restless to the point of distraction lately. "I don't even feel like a *spy* anymore," he'd complained.

Toynbee had rationalized that unless Leonard saw some action soon, there was no telling what he might do, even to the point of blowing the mission. So he had pretended control had called one day when Leonard was out, and had said to resume observation of the subject. Toynbee had the feeling this operation was dying the slow death of neglect, anyway. It would be shut down when their superiors got around to it. And in that case, no harm done.

It had worked. Leonard might make fun of the exercise, but he was into it nevertheless, you could see that. He was like a cat with a piece of string. Make the string dandle, dawdle, jump. The cat knows you're responsible, but doesn't care. He can't help himself, he just *has* to go after that live bit of wiggling waggling cord.

"I can't follow too close," Leonard said. "That big cop—"

"—might be good enough to notice a tail. Sure, be careful." Toynbee loved it when they did that Huey, Dewey, and Louie thing, finishing each other's sentences.

"Wonder why the hell she's not driving herself," Leonard said. "That's really anomalous. It could be a meet, you know. I've never been convinced that partner of hers isn't in on it. And what about the cop, after all? He *could* be the agent for the other side. It'd be perfect, kind of a purloined-letter thing. Hide in plain sight."

Toynbee was only partly listening. "You ever wonder why she never sees any men?"

"What about that old coot? She spent the night at his place."

"I thought your theory was *he* was the agent."

"Naaaah. He's just an old soldier."

"Too old to be her lover," Toynbee said. "I don't know what was going on, but it didn't read like a romance to me."

"Maybe she's gay. That would be a hoot. All same as her nemeses."

"I don't think so. I've read her journals, remember."

"You haven't read the latest stuff," Leonard said. "Maybe she switched allegiances."

"You know better than that."

"Yeah. Occurs to me, though, long as we're back on the job, maybe you ought to dial up the old fax modem and see what she's been up to lately."

"I don't think that's a good idea." The Brit wished he did think it was a good idea. He had enjoyed reading her journals. Miss Jody Nightwood had an interesting mind. But the failed burglary had spooked him. This was as close as he wanted to get for the time being.

"Shit," Leonard said. "I think I know where they're headed."

Shade whipped the car right at Peñasco, then through town, then left where the road took off into the high country. He had gone relatively slowly, no screeching tires to bring somebody to a front door. But once out of town, he accelerated.

He was taking what they call the High Road to Taos, the back road through the mountains. The moon was full and brilliant, and he didn't need his lights, though he had them on. You would not have thought a human could have driven a car so fast in such terrain. He used the whole road and he never touched the brakes and the NSX went like a rocket on rails.

He would be to Taos and home again in less time than anyone could believe, just in case anyone were to wonder. Taking the back road like this, only a few people would see him, and none of those people would be the type who liked to talk to the police.

His head was killing him and the aura had already come over his vision. He was seeing colors in the trees and skies that the moonlight itself could not deliver.

The headaches were coming on more frequently now. They always did when he was in love, he had no idea why. It was a hell of a thing, though. He'd managed to hide this one from Jody for the last two days. She was way too inquisitive. If she ever got any idea just how serious the headaches were, she would start probing and would never let up.

Tonight was as far as he could have pushed it, though. He couldn't have gone to Toni's parents' place even if he'd been invited. No way he would put Jody at that kind of risk.

He knew what the headache was, and he knew what he had to do to get rid of it. It wasn't the sort of thing you told your girlfriend, though. It wasn't the sort of thing you told your mother, for that matter. Not that his condition interfered with his work. Sometimes it even helped.

But it was the sort of thing that would make people think less of you. He was a sick man, you might say. And the cure for his disease— a temporary cure, but he knew from long experience the only cure— was, well, it was not socially acceptable.

Somebody was going to die tonight, and it wasn't going to be John Shade. Some happy, innocent partygoer walking the streets of Taos right now. It would be a bloody death, if a quick one, and you could read all about it in tomorrow's paper.

A sign told him he had just entered the National Forest. The road rose steadily, black path in the moonlight. He put the pedal on the floor. The needle floated past 130.

Vida, as usual, answered the door. "So this is the enemy," she said, peering up at Vic. "Wow, he's a big one. But we'll cut him down to size."

"Cut away," Toni said. She was pissed. In the car, after stringing them along awhile, Vic had confessed he already knew about Toni's parents. "Hell, I'm a cop," he had said. "Besides, it isn't like they're strangers in town." He had just been waiting to see how Toni would handle it, he said. He figured if she didn't want to talk about it, it wasn't his place to bring it up.

Vida led them through the entry and through the arches into the great room, taking Vic's arm to show him the way. At the single step down into the great room, she squeezed his biceps ferociously. "You must do some lifting," she said.

"I do," he said. "One of my bad habits."

Vida laughed raucously. She insisted they all sit, bared her own biceps, made a muscle. "What do you think of that?" she said, challenging.

"Pretty impressive," Vic said.

"I got a book you *have* to read," Vida said. "It's not designed for you penis-bearing types, but. Shit, I better make drinks. Allegra will whip my butt if she comes in and there's nothing in your hands. What does everybody want?"

Vic asked for mineral water, but, when Vida mocked him and said he was going to need stronger medicine than that, he took chilled Tanqueray Sterling, on the rocks, with a twist. "I was planning to keep my wits about me," he said. "But I see now I may be in the wrong company for that strategy." Jody had Shade's invariable drink, 101 on the rocks, and Vida shook three Boodles martinis, very dry, for Toni and Allegra and herself.

Allegra made her entrance, appearing in the doorway from the kitchen, and coming through the wide arch of the dining room as Cinderella might have descended the stairs into the ballroom. "I thought I heard the chime of a cocktail shaker," she said. She was resplendent in high heels and a tight Italian suit worn over a black silk turtleneck, her hair pulled into a ponytail. Except for the heels, she looked like a male Italian street punk turned fashion model.

She waved an unlit Silk Cut in the inevitable ebony holder, and Vic was on his feet instantly, hovering at its tip with a lighter flame cupped between his hands. Jody had never seen him smoke, so where had the lighter come from? What a boy scout.

"He's certainly *trying* hard," Allegra announced to the rest of them grandly, as one might praise the behavior of a child while managing not to acknowledge the child himself. "I'll give him that." Then, turning to Vic: "Tell me, young man, what makes you think we'd allow a brute like you to do the nasty with our little baby the rest of her life?"

"Hell, it's just a family gathering," Leonard said, disgusted. "The partner broad and the cop are getting married." He took his earphones off.

"Me father was a motorman," Toynbee said, parody Cockney. He was humming under his breath. He didn't remove his earphones.

"He was, actually," Toynbee continued. "He loved it. Then, when we had to move to San Francisco, he got a job as a trolleyman. 'I'm a very lucky man,' he used to say. 'All the way across a sea and a continent, and I got me same job again.' "

"Fascinating," Leonard said.

"You never speak of your family. Don't you miss them? Do you ever go back for visits?"

"My father beat my mother and me, okay? When I was eighteen, my first year in college, I came home unannounced one weekend, and shot him in the back of the head. Now do you want more of the Walton Family reunion, or can we get the hell out of here?"

They settled on Maria's for dinner, because they could probably get in without reservations. When Leonard hung a right onto St. Francis, Toynbee said, "I don't believe that about your father, you know. I think you just *wish* you had shot him."

During dinner, Vida asked Vic about growing up on the rez.

"You know how it is," he said. "Like anybody's childhood. It was wonderful, because it was all there was. And it was boring as hell, but I didn't know that because I didn't have anything else to compare it to."

"Nuclear zombies," Vida said. "Doesn't sound all that boring to me."

What the hell? Jody thought. She had that feeling again, the feeling that everyone in Santa Fe *knew* things—in all of New Mexico, for that matter. Things she was left out of, could never learn no matter how long she stayed. Ancient history, family secrets.

"That old story," Vic said dismissively. "Anyway, nothing's more boring than zombies. That's what *makes* them, the boredom. I loved the light, the rocks," he added. "I was a loner, didn't fit in. But I loved the desert and the mountains and the animals."

"Well, you'll fit in just fine with us," Vida said, patting his forearm in a gesture that was so surprising and so tender it almost brought tears to Jody's eyes.

Allegra was watching Jody's face. "And what about your childhood, dear? As long as we've known you, you've never talked about it. And do you know, Little Rock seems even stranger and more curious to me than the Mescalero reservation."

"I had a very boring childhood, too," Jody said.

"Oh no," Vida said. "There are always skeletons in the closet. I remember once, when I was nine, our dog disappeared. And Daddy said he'd just wandered off, and would probably come back, but he never did, and we all cried, and we made signs, and we went around to all the neighbors' houses, have you seen Blinky, he has a ring around his right eye."

Vida had known all along Blinky wasn't coming back, because she had seen her father burying the broken and bloody body in a patch of trees. He'd probably been hit by a car, and the father had felt it kinder not to tell anyone else, and the really curious thing was that Vida, even as a child, and not quite understanding why, had never said anything either, had never even let her father know that she had seen him.

"In fact, I forgot all about it until *his* funeral," she said. "My father's, I mean. Then it all came rushing back, so you see what I'm talking about."

"Everyone always sees *what* you're talking about, dear," Allegra said. "We just don't always know *why* you're talking about it."

"Oh, you," Vida said.

By the time dinner was over, they were laughing and joking together as if Vic had been in the family all his life. He showed a species of wry humor that Jody had never seen in his behavior before, one that matched Allegra's sensibilities perfectly. After dinner and before drinks, he went back with Vida to the exercise room to check out the equipment, and all of them went to watch.

He showed Vida a couple of isolations she hadn't tried, and then the two of them got into it a little. "Come on, ladies," Allegra said. "It's getting numbingly macho in here." She led Toni and Jody back to the great room. Jody was irritated at being included among the "ladies." She felt a shameful little flash of envy—wanted, irrationally, to get Vic and Vida into a long run or a skiing competition, and whip their butts.

Vic and Vida joined them a few minutes later, flushed and happy.

Over drinks, Vic relented and told stories from the rez (though none included zombies). Vida and Allegra helped each other narrate the early days of their marriage—never legalized, but that was what it was nonetheless. Jody even got into the act, she and Toni relating the travails of odd-couple roommates, one a poor Southern white and the other a western Hispanic, at good old ivy-league Williams. All of the stories were of bigotry and trouble, and yet somehow, now, in this company, all of them were funny rather than tragic, heartening rather than bitter.

At one point Allegra produced a couple of Cuban cigars, offered one to Vic. He asked if he hadn't better go outside to smoke it. "Don't be silly," Allegra said. The room was plenty big enough, she said, and well ventilated. But they did go apart to a far corner where the draft was stronger. When Jody looked their way, they were talking seriously, and she realized it was the ritual examination of the bridegroom by the father of the bride.

Though Allegra was the mother of the bride, technically. Roles were so confusing.

Finally, it was time to go. Vic and Toni and Jody stood, accepted their jackets. In Santa Fe, even in the middle of summer, the nights were often in the fifties or low sixties, and could feel a bit nippy, so you always went prepared. Vida and Allegra threw wraps around themselves as well, saying they would follow the group out to say good-bye.

"Who's here?" Toni said when they went out. "Where's my car?"

A silver-gray Range-Rover stood in the driveway, and the Toyota was nowhere to be seen. "What do you mean?" Vida said. "Your car's right where you left it." She was laughing, and now Allegra was smiling, and Toni caught on.

"Mother!" she screamed. "You *didn't!*"

Then Jody caught on.

"You wouldn't let us get you one for graduation," Vida said.

Toni said she couldn't let them do this either, it was too much, and Allegra said don't be silly and Vic said wait just a minute, I believe there's *two* of us involved in this decision now, and we love it and we'll take it and thank you very much indeed. And hugs all around several times more and more laughter until they were afraid they would wake the neighbors.

So Jody rode home in a Range-Rover, the first time she'd ever been in one. She didn't think it was a whit better than the NSX, though that wasn't a fair comparison. Her mood had turned darker the happier Toni and Vic had gotten. She had a fine set of cars.

But nobody had ever *given* her one.

"Well, it's a good thing I went," she said. "I sure helped smooth the troubled waters."

"Oh, girl," Toni said. "Your time will come."

Vic and Toni waited while Jody let herself in, then waved and drove off. Jody could have sworn she heard them still laughing, even when they were out of sight. She went through the kitchen, into the garage, to check. The NSX was back. The engine was cool.

dreamer

. . .

Someone kept ringing, but she couldn't find the telephone. So it had to be the doorbell. Ish was at the door. He was wearing a hat and a trench coat, and he pulled the coat aside to show her the gun in the shoulder holster. There was a badge on the holster. He was warning her to be careful, not to talk. If she told him anything, he would have to use it against her.

They were married, but he was a cop. Jody was afraid to make love to him, but it would be suspicious if she didn't. She dangled her arm out of the window while he lay on top of her and slid it in. She was holding the note out where her father could take it.

There was a tug at her fingers, and the note was gone. But she didn't know who had gotten it, Pop or a wild animal. She saw Br'er Fox, dressed in a hat and a trench coat, sitting at a campfire in the woods. He and Br'er Bear were reading a sheet of paper. But that was only if they were the ones who had taken the note.

There was a picture of the gun on the paper. That gave it all away.

Pop was sitting at the foot of the bed. He had been watching while she made love to Ish, but now Ish was gone, and she was sitting up bare-breasted. She knew she should pull the covers over herself, but she didn't. She wanted Pop to see her breasts.

He was very sad. He was crying. It was because he was going to jail.

She gathered him up against her breasts, a little baby, suckling. It was stupid of the cops to think that a little baby could have committed the murder. But then she realized they were right. That's why he was being a baby, he was trying to get away. It wouldn't do any good, they would just wait for him to grow up, and then they would put him in jail. It was her fault for drawing the picture of the gun. She hadn't meant to cause all the trouble. She had seen the gun on the shelf under the cash register, and she had turned it into a picture so it wouldn't be a real gun.

She had hired Alvaro to come to the store and do the painting.

It was a spooky painting, with a great big gun in the light in the foreground, and a dark pool of blood just behind it, fading off into blackness. Around the edges of the painting, Alvaro had drawn a cartoon strip that showed how the murder happened.

Nobody had seen the cartoon yet, but it would be in the Sunday paper, and everybody would know. That was the trouble with art. You couldn't use it to hide things.

Jody had to buy the painting, so nobody would see it, but her mother wouldn't give Jody her allowance. Her mother wanted to make them suffer. You're both going to jail, she said. The two of you are going to pay for what you did to me.

All Jody had done was pick the gun up off the floor. If she had left it there, then Pop wouldn't have been guilty. Nobody could prove a thing, it was just a gun on the floor. But now she stood in the middle of the room holding the gun, and it was bleeding all over her hand.

Ish was sitting at the kitchen table in his undershirt. I saw that, *he said.*

23: murder mystery

Shade called Jody on Sunday while she was brewing the first pot of coffee, and they spent the rest of the morning together, reading three newspapers. Two of them reported a grisly murder in Taos the night before, a woman's throat ripped open by an unknown assailant.

She shuddered. "Isn't that awful?" she said.

His eyes seemed exceedingly wide and dark. "Yes," he said. "Terrible."

He looked down at his paper again, and she noticed something—or rather, noticed the absence of something that might have been expected. He didn't wear reading glasses.

"How old are you?" she said.

"In cat years or human years?" he said.

"Seriously."

"Two hundred and fifty-three."

"I said seriously."

"Sorry, gave you my IQ by mistake. Ahm, ah. Forty-three?"

"And you don't have presbyopia yet?"

"I have Presleyopia. As I get older, everybody looks more and more like Elvis."

"I didn't think you were the vain type. That could be what causes your headaches, you know, if you need reading glasses and won't get them."

278

He put down his paper. "I'm vain enough," he said. "But not about that sort of thing. My eyes are just fine, and I don't need glasses. Call it a genetic quirk."

"I worry about you."

"I find that frequently, when people start worrying about their lovers, what they're really worrying about is themselves. Something bugging you?"

"Aren't you the cynic all of a sudden?"

They made love that evening, but her mind wasn't on what she was doing, and she couldn't find her orgasm. Finally she rolled him over and made the moves that she knew would finish him off, and immediately fell into a deep sleep, one that she would have called dreamless, except that she was a researcher and she knew better.

All the next day at work she felt a low-level unadmitted dread. Monday night she dreamed twice that she had killed her mother, Tuesday night that Pop had, and Thursday night again that she had. "Something's eating you," Shade said at lunch on Friday, muffalettas on the patio of The Burrito Company. "You frown all the time and you don't talk. It's like dating the Sphinx. You've even been snapping at your patients, and that's not like you."

"Is that what we're doing?" she said. "Dating? Listen, I've had some things on my mind. Sorry I'm not cheery Pollyanna all the time. If it bugs you too much, bail."

"Mind if I finish my sandwich first?" he said, raising one eyebrow.

"It isn't the relationship. It isn't us." She wondered if he would be that way in a marriage, impossible to offend, to get a rise out of. Something not desirable about that. Unfair.

She came back from lunch to find a message on her machine. A lawyer with the Little Rock firm that had handled her father's estate, such as it was. Would she please return his call at her convenience? Fear struck through her like a cold wind through a flimsy blouse.

The lawyer sounded young. He was brusque and uninterested. A lockbox had come to light, a lockbox belonging to her father. There had been nothing in his papers referring to it, which is why it hadn't been discovered earlier. The bank, noticing during a routine updating that the box hadn't been visited in better than fifteen years, had begun inquiries.

No, they couldn't open it and tell her what was in it. Only she could open it, and she would have to come to the bank personally to do so. Great, just what she needed in the middle of June, a trip to Little Rock, where she no longer had any friends and where the temperature would be ninety-six and the humidity ninety-three, or vice versa.

The lockbox frightened her badly. That night she dreamed again of murder and being chased by the police, but now there was a lockbox that was also a coffin. She was racing the police to get to it first. If they opened it, it would blow up, killing everybody in the office. Glass scattered across the floor. Then she would be on the run again, guilty again.

The worst scene was when she opened the box and her white-faced mother sat up, laughing like a hysterical vampire. She was holding a grenade, which was also a bloody fetus, an aborted little lump she had clawed out of her own belly.

Jody woke up on that one and couldn't get back to sleep. She found a memory in her mind, one she hadn't allowed herself in many years. Her mother and father, upstairs, in a bitter shouting quarrel—stomping around, slamming doors.

Herself down in the store, minding it till closing. Streetlights already on outside, a light rain misting the streets. Gloomy in the store, but she had to wait till complete dark to turn on the store's lights. Saving those pennies. The smell of fresh lettuce, potatoes.

Staring at the gun on the shelf under the register. Pop's service .45.

They were arguing about her. She heard her name flung out like a curse.

Something was going on here, something she had to deal with. As soon as it was late enough in the morning, she called Toni, and arranged a consultation for Monday.

Over the weekend, she remembered other arguments. *Frequent* arguments. Herself crouching in despair, below, in the store. Pop had *not* been kind and quiet and forbearing, not with his wife. Only with Jody. She could see his red face now, swollen with residual anger when he came down to take over the register. He would give her a couple of quarters and tell her to go get a root beer float at the soda fountain, her favorite.

She was afraid of what might be in the lockbox. Repressed fears were surfacing. Thoughts that had run through her mind after her mother's death, and then after her father's. Cockroach thoughts, scuttling back to darkness while she pretended not to notice.

Her mother had not really died of an overdose. Her mother had been shot, and it had been covered up somehow. Her father's death not really a robbery, but retribution from the cops.

Or Pop, injecting the heroin while her mother slept. The heroin he had bought on the street. His shooting another sort of payback, maybe he was in debt to the dealer.

The gun had disappeared one day, perhaps after that first argument Jody had remembered. She had never seen it again. Had never had the courage to ask what had happened to it. Had been relieved not to have to look at it when she minded the store, think its cruel thoughts.

What was in the lockbox? The gun? A packet of heroin and a needle? A confession?

She kept her distance from Shade. He knew about the dreams, because she had faithfully reported them all, galling as the task had been. One dream, she might have rationalized skipping it. But a pattern of dreams, no way. The research had to be basically honest.

But she wasn't about to let him any further into her secrets than she had to.

"I see a pretty clear pattern," Toni said on Monday. "How about you?"

"I don't see a damn thing," Jody said. "I'm just having these panic attacks while I'm awake and nightmares when I'm asleep. They feel like they're coming from nowhere."

"Which is why you can't defend yourself from them, because they're from nowhere. Doesn't that sound like a setup to you? A program for helplessness."

Jody was irritated. "I can see *that* much."

Toni was not a stickler for the view that the patient must figure everything out for herself. She thought it was the information that was important, however you got there. If you waited for the patient to do all the work, how much more damage might she suffer?

Besides, Jody was strong-minded enough to know the truth when she heard it, and strong-willed enough to act on the truth when she knew it.

"Look at it, girl. This has to be about three people: you, your mother, and your Pop. Your mother keeps winding up dead, and either you or your Pop keep winding up guilty. Also, what about that nursing scene, where you showed him your breasts?"

"Shit," Jody said. "Plain as the nose on your face, isn't it?"

"You expected to be spared because it was a cliché?"

Jody laughed ruefully. "I guess so. I guess I thought maybe smart people didn't have to do it all. If you can prove you've read the chapter, you get to skip the pop quiz."

"The Pop quiz."

"Oh no. I'm not accepting that one. Now you're pushing it too far."

Jody expected her panic to vanish after this revelation, but it didn't. The newly remembered conspiracy theories of her mother's death obsessed her, and she brooded on the lockbox. She had another dream: In this one her father did not appear, at least not obviously. Jody shot her mother with a toy gun, the long-since-unfashionable sort that fired a cork on a string. She was a young girl, and she unwrapped her present at Christmas, and it was the gun. When she pulled the trigger, the cork made holes in her mother like the holes Dick Tracy's bullets made in gangsters. Then she was a grown woman, and she hung a paper-doll cutout of her mother, punched full of holes, on her Christmas tree every year. Her children asked why, but she wouldn't say. Couldn't tell them the bitter satisfaction she felt, the dark triumph.

When she woke she thought, *Oh. Popgun. Pop gun. Damn you, Toni.*

But she went back for another consult. She was afraid if she didn't get out of this spiral soon, she was going to lose Shade. Not that he was acting as though he wanted out. Just that she was so preoccupied they were hardly spending any time together, and when they did she felt sealed off and unreal, and so she was afraid he would just, somehow, vanish.

Besides which, he was dead right. It was interfering with her handling of patients, and that was unacceptable. You owed your patients the best you could give.

Toni said she was still convinced Jody was suffering from a female version of the Oedipus complex. Jody had loved her father—a love that included the usual unacknowledged sexual yearnings—and had wanted to steal him away from her mother. Had wanted her mother dead, so she could have her father all to herself. But why hadn't Jody's worries gone away when she accepted all that? Toni was pretty sure there was a core issue involved that Jody hadn't dealt with yet. But what other core issue could there be? Toni had no way of knowing. It probably involved Jody's mother, though, since she was the one who kept getting bumped off.

"So how do I find out what the issue is?"

"Try asking your mother," Toni said.

"She's dead, goddammit!" Jody burst out. But Toni just smiled, and then Jody saw what her friend meant. Exactly what Angela Epstein had been talking about for the last month, how she'd learned, as a result of the study, to rid herself of nightmares.

Dream, dreamer. Turn and face the beast.

"One other thing you need to do," Toni said. "Go to Little Rock and find out what's in that goddamned box."

Jody made the reservation as soon as she left Toni's office. An overnight trip, that's all it would be. She would stay in the Capitol Hotel, that fine remodeled old luxury inn. She would ask Shade if he wanted to go along. Now that she'd made up her mind, she found herself ready for his company again. If only he was ready for hers.

He was. He wanted to go. He thought it was a great idea. It had been a long time since he'd been back to Arkansas. It had been since his college years.

"So you went to school there?" Jody said. "Now that I think of it, you've never said."

"For a while," he said. "Got my degree somewhere else."

"Do you realize you *never* talk about your past or your family or any of those normal things? What's the big terrible secret? I trust you, and I know how you behave, and I know your body really well, but for example I don't even know where you're *from*."

"Transylvania," he said.

"Oh, come on," she laughed.

"No, it's true. My father was a planter in Virginia. As soon as I was grown, I struck out for Kentucky." He grinned. "Back in the Revolutionary era, when everything past the Appalachians was still wilderness, that whole area, Daniel Boone territory, parts of what would later be Tennessee and Kentucky and West Virginia, all that was known as Transylvania."

" 'Across the trees,' " she said, and he nodded.

All the rest of the week, she concentrated as she fell asleep, telling herself she would see her mother in her dreams and would confront

her and would not be afraid. But each night her brain slipped away
into the onset imagery, a river gnawing gradually at its margins until
suddenly the whole bank caved and slid under, and irrational car-
toons—gleams and flashes of lucidity—flickered and wiggled across a
dark and moving surface.

Finally, on the Friday before her flight, it happened.

*She was a spy chasing someone down a rain-soaked street, wearing a trench
coat, holding a gun upraised in her right hand. The street was supposedly
Cantrell Road in Little Rock, but it was flat and straight and shining in the
rain, not uphill or downhill, and there were no cars.*

This can't be Cantrell Road, *she said, and immediately became lucid.
Which was great, because it meant she could change the story. She didn't have
to shoot the woman running down the street. That woman could be her mother
if Jody wanted.*

But that woman wouldn't come out as long as Jody held the gun.

Here, *Jody said.* You're safe. Look, I'm giving it to you.

*She leaned down, and slid the gun along the street. When the bowling ball
scattered the pins, her mother looked out from the end of the alley.* You left
one, *she said.*

True, the tenpin was standing.

*A wave of love and pity swept over Jody. Her poor mother, all her life with
not enough pins. People kept knocking her down and taking them away.*

That's okay, *Jody said.* You can keep that one. It's yours.

*But it wouldn't be enough. You had to knock down the critical number of
pins, or the machine wouldn't reset. You had to knock down 89.2 percent of
them.*

*They were in a formal living room—dark wooden floors, a grand piano,
antimacassars on the overstuffed furniture. Her mother was a trim grayheaded woman in a gray suit, wearing a lace shawl. Her mother was with MI5.
Jody was about to hear something that would topple governments. The grayheaded woman unscrewed the top of a bowling pin. No, it was a decanter disguised as a bowling pin. How clever. She brought Jody a snifter of brandy, then
sat and crossed her legs.* It's more than time we had this little talk, *she said.*

I'm sorry it's just a dream, *Jody said. This was the sort of room her
mother should have had when she was alive. This was the sort of woman she
should have been, a woman who did things, a woman who counted.* I'm sorry
you're not really alive.

That hardly matters now, *the woman said.* You know why I brought you here?

Jody nodded. Tears ran down her face. But you were supposed to! *Jody cried. She was a little unlovely baby, wailing and soiling her chair.* You were *supposed* to.

Things don't always happen the way they're supposed to, *her mother said.* It's time you grew up and dealt with the knowledge. Are you ready for your assignment?

They both knew the answer was yes. Jody had graduated now. She was ready to work for her country. She felt an airy swelling in her chest, an elation born not of joy but of knowing what your duty was and knowing that you would do it, regardless of personal cost.

They lay on the rug together, going through the dossier like two schoolgirls going through a photo album. It was all in there: how her mother had never been able to love her, not from the moment of her birth. Whatever biological system motherhood usually triggers had simply misfired. Not her mother's fault, but she blamed herself horribly. But no use, impossible to feel anything for this red stranger who had torn her life apart. How her father had loved her, and tried to protect her from the knowledge that her mother didn't, which of course had been impossible. How he had blamed his wife, too, and how the strain of the cruel situation had driven the couple apart, deepened her mother's depression, and eventually of course killed her.

There was a dream in the dossier, and they spread out the photos and looked at it. Of course. There was Jody making love to her father. It was her mother's dream. It was a dream her mother had had when Jody was a girl, and that was why the screaming fit that time.

Jody's father was old and potbellied and his penis was a shriveled little nub. He wasn't sexy at all. That little girl needed to put her clothes on and get out of there.

It was good to be able to look at the pictures without shame.

There were other photos. Photos of the mother, the father, the girl. The store when the long light of sunset came in the front windows and lit up the counters. There was a photo of the boy who had shot her father, which was good, because he had never been caught.

The others are all dead, *the grayheaded woman said. She was back in her chair, and Jody felt a little embarrassed to be caught sprawled out on the floor. She got up and straightened her skirt. She picked up the papers, but they kept sliding out of the folder. The gun slid out of the folder and thumped on the area rug. She picked the gun up and put it in her holster.*

We can't do anything for them, *the woman said.* It's the girl we have to save.

The agent looked at the photo of Jody Nightwood. Jody was a grown woman now. They didn't know where she was, but they had used computers to age her face. It was a strong face, set in a cloud of red hair. A good mouth. High cheekbones, a prominent and wonderfully sculptured nose dusted with freckles across its high bridge. Wide clear eyes, bright green.

This is a beautiful woman, *the agent said, amazed.*

Yes, *the grayheaded woman said.* She's well worth saving.

Jody woke with an unparalleled sense of liberation. She practically sang her dream into the recorder. She felt as though a thousand perceptions a minute were flooding her mind, and yet as though she could hold and entertain each one in perfect clarity.

This was like clean nuclear power, this sort of healing. It was like being able to tap directly into the genius of the sun. She felt as humbled as she was elated. Other people knew this about dreams. The other dreamers in the study knew. It was what Rafael and Bert and Angela and Bianca and George kept trying to tell her when they took her aside in the hall.

She had been so fixated on proving her intelligence that she had neglected the real importance of dreams. Forget theory and forget abstraction—this was *life*.

She wanted to talk to Toni. She wanted badly to get home and work on the dream in her journal. But their flight left at ten. They'd packed the night before—Shade took only one light hanging bag and his laptop, naturally—and brought the luggage to the lab with them.

It seemed a little silly to be rushing off to Little Rock now. No hurry about the lockbox, now that she had had her transfiguring dream. But a good agent always follows through on the plan. As soon as she had cleaned up and dressed, they hit the road.

He'd heard the dream when she recorded it, of course, but she waited in vain for him to comment or ask questions. It was his code not to talk about the dreams he heard, most especially hers, and it was a good code, but just now his reticence was maddening. Couldn't he tell how *big* this was? So she told it to him all over again, explaining.

"Some people have things happen to them that dreams can't fix," he said. "And I think you would be making a big mistake to back off your theory at this point."

"Boy, are *you* a bundle of laughs this morning. What you say is true, but your timing sucks. If I didn't know better, I'd think you resented my happiness."

"You're right," he said. "I've got no business stepping on your mood."

"This is more than a mood. But don't worry, I feel too good to let you or anyone else bring me down. And for your information, I don't intend to 'back off' my theory. My work is my work. It's just that now I have a much healthier perspective."

They came to the Escarpment, that black jagged edge of volcanic stone where the high world fell away to Albuquerque, and far beyond it in the haze, the vast and stunning tedium of Texas. "God, that's a beautiful sight," Jody said.

They stowed the van in long-term, and Shade horsed her two huge bags and his light one easily through the concourse while she carried his laptop and her overnight kit. For once in her life, she was relaxed, strolling to their terminal rather than hustling.

She didn't even tense up during takeoff, and bouncing through the rough air over the mountains, she realized that if the plane crashed, she would meet her death calmly and without fear. The important thing wasn't how long you lived, she saw, but whether you closed the circle, whether you found the peace of completion.

They got to the hotel too late to see the lockbox that day, so they went up the stairs past the faux-marble pillars—she wanted to walk—and found their room and stowed their luggage. It was odd to look out the window at the city she knew so well, and yet was now a stranger in.

Homeless in the universe.

It was too early for dinner, still good daylight, and she wanted exercise and air, so she talked Shade into walking over to look at the old family store.

They crossed the Wilbur Mills Freeway, which had not been a part of her childhood, on the Main Street Bridge, which had, then found her old street. "This neighborhood looks a little rough," he said, and there was something incongruous about his timidity, like Christopher Reeve playing Superman playing Clark Kent.

"It is," she said. "It is now."

In fact it was a lot rougher-looking than she had remembered, a lot worse than it had been even at the time of Pop's death. But she felt no fear, felt instead an unexpected aggressive recklessness: The assholes weren't going to take her past away, by God.

She had been hoping, without realizing it, to find the building in ruins, uninhabitable forever, no memories overwritten. What happened was that she didn't find it at all.

"I know this is the block," she said. They had been back and forth three times. "This has to be it. This has to be where it was. They've torn the damn thing down."

She shivered in the hot fetid air. She stood looking into a parking lot between a ratty laundromat and a liquor store that seemed to double as a pool hall. Inside the pool hall, dark men leaned on their sticks, looked their way. A block away, the lamps were coming on.

"I think we ought to get out of here," Shade said.

"Damn them, they've torn the damn thing down," she said. She was afraid she was about to cry. There was a sagging screen door on the liquor store/pool hall. It opened now, and a trio of young men stumbled out, carrying their cues. Two of the men wore X caps backwards, and muscle shirts. One had a red bandanna tied around his head and wore no shirt at all.

An older man stood in the open doorway. "Ya'll come on back in now," he said.

"We help you, bro?" Bandanna said.

"Yay, blood," one of the black caps laughed. "Don't reckon you lost, do you?"

"We're leaving," Shade said.

"Naw, don't be in no hurry," Bandanna said. "Come on in and have a drink."

"Yay, and bring yo bitch witchou," the one black cap said. "We friendly people."

"Why don't you murdering motherfuckers mind your own business," Jody said.

The silent black cap flipped his cue, caught the small end, and whipped it at her face. Shade had somehow moved between them, and now he had the pool cue in his hands and broke it and then he had spun the boy and run him stumbling down the street till he tripped and fell.

Bandanna showed a glittering blade.

"Don't," Shade said.

The other black cap, the talkative one, had slid back against the wall of the store. Bandanna was trying to make up his mind.

"Come on in here, you damn fool," the old man said. "Can't you see what you dealing with? He stick that thing up yo ass and break it off."

"We're sorry," Shade said.

"Get out of here, man," Bandanna said. "Take yo bitch and head north."

"You got it," Shade said. He grabbed Jody's arm and hustled her along the street, into the distant light, toward the bridge and safety and the rest of their lives.

"Fucking white-bread sonofabitch," Bandanna called after them.

They sat at the Capitol bar, not so crowded now that Kenneth Starr's minions had finally given up and gone home, now that there were no more rumors to spread, no more false witnesses to intimidate with threats of their own pitiful prosecutions.

"That was incredibly stupid," Shade said. He didn't seem angry, just factual.

Jody didn't answer. She was feeling a sort of guilty exhilaration that she couldn't explain but didn't want to apologize for either. The maître d' came into the bar to tell them their table was ready, and they went in to dinner at Ashley's, across the marble lobby.

She wanted the focus off herself, and she asked him, over the shared Chateaubriand, where he had learned to fight like that. "I've always thought you must have been in the military," she said. "Were you in Vietnam? I could see you as a Ranger."

The topic didn't interest him. "I was an irregular, once," he said. "I guess you would call it. I thought I was fighting for something. Revenge." She was startled to see tears in his eyes.

"I found out you can't *get* revenge," he said. "No matter how many people you kill, you can never kill the right ones. Something you still need to learn," he added harshly.

She wanted to ask if he'd really ever killed anybody, but she didn't dare. Instead she explained about her father, his death. Shade might have deciphered some of the circumstances from overhearing her dreams, but she'd never told him the whole story.

How could such things happen? Such stupid and senseless things.

Somebody just walks up and shoots a good man, and that's it, no jus-tice, no punishment.

Shade said he thought there was a window for moral develop-ment, just like the one for acquisition of language. Either it happens in the window, you imprint on a good moral model, or it never happens, and nothing can fix you. You're morally dead, a dead man walking.

"That's not very comforting," she said.

"I didn't mean it to be," he said.

For dessert, he had a slice of Mississippi mud pie with two scoops of toffee ice cream. She talked the chef into making her a root beer float. Which *was* very comforting.

The next day she went to the bank and opened the lockbox. The gun was in it—her dream had been that true. For the rest, a packet of Pop's love letters to Mom from his days in the service. Her costume jewelry. Envelopes of photos taken through the years. And an album contain-ing nothing but pictures of Jody, all ages, her father's notes written under them.

"That was his real treasure," Shade said, and she wound up in his arms, crying in a bank vault. Oh bankerman, do save these silver tears, someday they will appreciate.

Back at the hotel, she wanted to go shopping, and he said he wanted a nap. She freshened up and headed out. But as soon as she went through the glass front doors of the hotel and onto the street, she realized she had left her traveler's checks in the bedside drawer.

She rode back up in the mirrored and paneled elevator, which was almost large enough and luxurious enough to be rented out as a suite itself.

When she let herself back in, Shade was hanging up a telephone. It wasn't the motel phone, though, it was some sort of peripheral to his computer.

"I forgot my traveler's checks," she said. "That's a cool telephone."

"It lets me dial from my address book," he said. "Anywhere in the world."

"What kind of computer *is* that? I don't think you've ever had it open around me."

"When I'm around you I'm not thinking computers," he said. He winked, but the tone of his voice was curiously flat. "It's a prototype," he said. "I got it from a manufacturer I was researching for one of my novels."

"I'd love to play with it sometime. I mean, that is, if you don't mind."

"Sure," he said. "Sometime."

"Is something bothering you? You're acting funny."

"You're not gonna like it," he said. "That was my agent. He's finally nailed down an appointment with an FBI scientist I've been trying to interview."

"Shit," she said. "Where to this time?"

"Washington. D.C. I'm really sorry. I know this puts you out of joint, you need me to cover the lab. But I've been trying to get with this guy for a year, and—"

She took a deep breath, straightened her shoulders. "I'm disappointed," she said, "but damned if I'm gonna let it come between us. You've been patient about my work. As for the lab, I can probably get Blossom to handle the night sessions while I double up on the day."

"I hate to put you in that bind," he said.

Her voice trembled only a little: "How long will you be away?"

He came to her, folded her against him. "Probably three days or so. There's other business I should take care of as long as I'm there."

"Shade," she murmured against him, "tell me honestly—you aren't getting bored, are you? These trips of yours aren't to get away, are they? Because you don't have to play that game."

"No," he said, his voice rumbling in his chest. "Boring is the last way I'd describe you. I don't have to leave till tomorrow, by the way. I can go to the airport with you in the morning."

"That's good. Because if I'm going to be doing without you the next few days—"

She felt between his legs. "I thought you were going shopping," he said.

"Shopping? What shopping? Let's check your fluids here. Oo, nice dipstick. Nope, not low at all. Tell you what. Let's check *my* fluids."

The next day, driving back from Albuquerque alone, she realized she had gotten over her fear of being separated from him, of being alone. She had gotten over all her fears, she was a free woman. What was interesting was that her first impulse was to share her newfound well-being. She wanted to learn more about this side of dreaming, the human side—not how to describe them or formulate them, but how to inhabit them more fully, summon them more easily, tap more deeply into the powers they had to offer.

How to teach others to use them. When the study was over, when she had published her theory—she knew what to do with her life. She was ready to be a real doctor at last.

24: dead men walking

Shade called on Monday, to say that he was really sorry, he knew it would jam her up, but he was going to have to be away for a couple of weeks. As long as he was on the East Coast, he really needed to go up to Manhattan, talk to his editor, his agent. His broker.

"Hey," she said. "Maybe I'll pass the time reading your novels."

"You don't have to do that," he said. "You probably won't like them."

"It isn't that," she said. "They're keeping you away so much, I figure I better scope out the competition." His laugh was tentative. She thought maybe he was having a little trouble adjusting to this new unworried Jody. This new grown-up Jody.

"Ah, but you're going to have to give me your pen name again," she said. "I know you told me, but I've gone and forgotten."

"Ooo, that hurts," he said. "That really hurts."

She realized with a shock that the summer would be half over by the time he got back. But it didn't hurt that she dreamed of Ish almost every night in the meantime. In the one she liked best, they were Superman and Supergirl, flying over New Mexico, then mating in midair. She'd had a flicker of conscience at first, remembering that Supergirl was supposedly some sort of Kandorian bottle-city relative of Kal-El's and feeling vaguely incestuous. But then she had reminded herself that it was a dream and she could redefine their relationship.

The fun part had been streaking around picking up their super-

293

clothes where they had scattered all over the mountains, moving so fast the hikers couldn't see their nudity.

She dreamed of Pop, too, perfectly ordinary dreams in which he was contentedly minding the store, and her mother came in smiling to help, or she stocked groceries and then they went up to dinner. Dreams and memory. She had been working on an idea before all the business with her mother and her father and the lockbox had come up.

"They come from the spirit world," Bianca said, speaking of how the dead appeared in dreams. Jody had begun talking to Bianca fairly regularly. She still found the woman's mysticism a little silly. Okay, unscientific. But she had developed a new respect for the shrewdness of her insight. Plus which it was great to have somebody to talk to Ish about.

"The physical realm is only one manifestation of existence," Bianca said. "It's just a sort of projection of the spirit world, which is the actual real world. When we're awake, we forget. But in our dreams, we can actually fly around freely in the spirit world."

Jody stayed skeptical, but she listened. Something was coming together in her mind. That night, she and Ish met in a laboratory. They were assembling androids. The androids were all the dead people. This is where they came back to life. It was heaven's lab, where the new flesh was put on, incorruptible. You had to copy a file from your own brain, the one that had the person in it, and download it into the body on the table. Every time a new android sat up, naked and blinking, the lab had a party. They made Jody's father and Jody's brother. Jody and Ish sat in Jody's office afterward, wearing paper hats and drinking champagne. They were exhausted but happy. How wonderful it was that the dead came back to life.

His face was flushed and his tie was loosened and she loved him dearly.

All the next week, she worked on the idea that Mindanao had inadvertently triggered: Our brains were modelmaking devices. That was the main thing brains did, create models. All brains. They were ceaseless fountains of invention. What was different about that notion, Shade had asked. And what did any of it have to do with dreams?

Try this on for size, Mr. Shade. Instead of processing data in order to create their simulations, the way a computer does, our brains automatically produce simulations from the moment they become functional. Without regard to "reality" or data. And then they try the already existing simulations against the incoming data, and some of them match up. And we put all those that match up into a general structure and make rules about that structure and call it reality.

Dreams were freewheeling generation, loosed from the constraints of consensual reality. The health of the machine, doing what it did best, sailing along in its natural joy. The simulations of dreams didn't match up, they related only to themselves. It *was* a feedback process.

She was not just mapping dreams when she was mapping I-space. She was mapping the core architecture of the brain itself. Her theory, her simulation—it was a model of the modelmaker. No wonder the shape was so complex, so recursive.

A strange attractor of strange attractors.

Shade wasn't around and she had to talk to someone and this wasn't the kind of thinking that Bianca was good at. "Oh yeah?" Toni said, teasing. "Well how do you feel about old dead Papa Freud now? You've got to admit you've just gone through a classic bit of analysis."

"I think dreams *can* do that," Jody said, surprising herself. "I don't think that's what they're *for*, though. It's like, it's like the immune system. The point of the immune system isn't recuperation from sickness. The point of it is staying healthy. I think, in a healthy mind, dreams wouldn't operate in a Freudian way. But none of us is really healthy. The world is too crazy, and even if we're not seriously dysfunctional, we're all under too much stress.

"Healing and health are two different things," she insisted. "They come from the same source, but they're different. In sickness, health manifests itself as healing. In health, health manifests itself as radiance, as transcendence. We tend only to recognize it in the former guise, because in this sick world that's mostly how it goes. Christ in rags."

"Lord, girl," Toni said. There was a sort of baffled admiration in her eyes, a look Jody had never seen there before. "Where did *that* come from?"

"I think I got it from Ish, actually."

"Ish?" Toni said.

Saturday, on her way home after the Friday-night dream session, she went by Garcia Street Books. Sure enough, they had a couple of Shade's—Marcus Gandy's—paperback titles on the shelves. Probably she could have picked them up at the big Furr's on Pacheco just as easily, but she had wanted to buy them in a real bookstore. Besides, this way she could stop in at Downtown Subscriptions and have a cappuccino while she looked them over.

When she got home, the light on her machine was blinking. She hoped it was from Shade, but it wasn't, it was from Loren Wingo. He was going to be in town next week to take care of his shopping, and wondered if there was any chance he could stay at her place.

Don't try to call him back, because he was calling from a pay phone at the ski lodge. He would give her another call when he came into town, and if it wasn't going to work out, don't worry, no problem, he had some other alternatives. It's just that he'd really enjoyed the other night and it might be pleasant to get together with her and Shade again—

It was frustrating not to be able to call Wingo and let him know Shade was out of town. What had he done, hiked up to the ski basin just to make the call? From where he'd said his cabin was, that would have been a minimum fifteen-mile round trip. She wanted also to let him know that it would be fine for him to stay at her place, but remind him that since she had patients during the day and the study ran during the week, she wouldn't be home that much.

She caught up on her chores, went for a short run, just a couple of miles, just enough to get her blood moving, came back and horsed around with the babies awhile. Then she showered, ate lunch, and spent the rest of the day reading Shade's novels.

They just weren't her sort of thing, it turned out. One violent scene after another. The vampire spy was always chewing open some bad guy's throat, just when it looked as if the bad guy was going to win—crash a nuclear missile into the Empire State Building in the modern one.

The other one was historical, set during the Civil War. The Civil War bored her silly. She hated Civil War stories. The immortal vampire spy uncovered the conspiracy against Lincoln, too late to save him. John Wilkes Booth had just been a pawn. You would be shocked to discover who the real villains were, the cover promised, but she wasn't shocked at all.

She had the impression, without being an expert, that the period details, the dialects, were exactly on key. Some of the dialogue was good, but a lot of it was hokey. She didn't think the plots held together all that well, either. This was boys-with-their-toys stuff. Move the action figures around and watch them die. Blow them up, run them through, throw them off rooftops.

It was sad to find someone you loved so lacking. Nobody said you had to be a good writer to be a worthwhile person. None of us were good at everything. There was no doubt of Shade's intelligence or live-liness. Why, then, was it so deflating to discover that, in this one small arena, he was a hack? Was it because it was his chosen arena?

His ineptitude, if it had never been demonstrated, would never have mattered.

What could she say to him? Maybe she'd better toss the books and never admit to having read them. But then she would be carrying a guilty secret, the secret of her own low opinion.

She dreamed of Shade hiking the trails over the mountains. He was looking for a telephone booth. He was trying to call her to let her know that he wasn't coming back because he was dead. He had killed himself because the books were no good.

If she had been able to call him back, she would have forgiven him, but it still wouldn't have worked. You couldn't fuck a zombie. Because of the smell, the dead smell.

He just kept walking away into the mountains, farther and farther. Then he was skiing, and he went off a cliff. She saw it from a long way away, with her binoculars.

Then it had all happened a long time ago, and Jody was living alone in a cabin in the woods. There were two graves out back. One of them had a statue of her favorite cat, Yellow Bear, and the other one had a big old-fashioned standing radio for a tombstone.

Wingo called her again on Monday, this time at the office, and she said fine, come on over and she would give him a key, but she wouldn't be seeing him in the evenings, or would be seeing him only briefly and intermittently, because because because, and explained Shade's absence. He came by in midafternoon for the key, and when she got home after office hours, she found his small knapsack of gear in the guest bedroom, but no sign of the man himself. He was appar-ently out taking care of business, whatever his business was. If he came in, he came in after she'd gone back to the lab, and then she didn't get home the next morning before work.

Finally, Tuesday evening, having made arrangements by telephone, they had dinner together, a couple of pizzas at her place, and drinks.

The conversation was pleasant, but no sparks flew. She told him what had been happening with her dream life and her idea of the brain as primarily a modelmaker, and he seemed interested but not overwhelmed. He said he was glad she was branching out into what he called the qualitative side of dreaming. Then he said that we could read about it all we wanted to, and we could study our own experience all we wanted, but there was no substitute for the experience of someone who had Been There. He mentioned his friend again, Dead Men Walking.

She said she was interested but dubious about hooking up with a guru. Actually, a good part of her resistance came from low-level annoyance, the fact that Wingo hadn't seemed all that impressed with her latest thinking. She was shrewd enough to see her own motives, and Wingo assured her she could retain her independence and her skepticism and that at the very least she would get an informative close-up of the shaman's mind and belief structure that would tell her, surely, something, and that Dead Men Walking was a freethinker who would be at least as interested in her perceptions as she was in his.

The last proved to be enough of a sop to her vanity. She was curious, she told herself. On another level, she was having a fantasy that the shaman would recognize her intuitively as a fellow adept. You're the one we've been waiting for, he would say: You're the one all our legends foretell.

She told him to go ahead and set it up, but not to use her real name. She didn't want this hurting her credibility as a researcher. Wingo thought that was silly, but agreed.

He was in town till Thursday afternoon, so they would try to have dinner again tomorrow night. But then, Wednesday afternoon, he called her and begged off, said there was someone he really needed to see and that was going to be his only chance.

Then again Thursday morning, she didn't make it home for breakfast, and when she got to the house after work, Wingo was already gone. He had left a packet of literature for her, a couple of the books he had recommended on his first visit, and what turned out to be chapters from his life's work, *A Theoretical Model of Heaven*.

She had a couple of hours before she had to leave, fixed herself a martini and relaxed with Wingo's manuscript. A little mental stimulation, that was just what she was in the mood for. "One of the most catastrophic effects of the dogmatic phenomenon," she read, "is that a very great number of people have been driven away from religion entirely. I say catastrophic because I believe that we earnestly need religion. As devoted to the scientific methodology as I am . . ."

Well, maybe I don't want that much intellectual stimulation, she thought. Funny, Wingo had seemed a lot more interesting in conversation. She put the manuscript aside. Maybe later, when she was feeling like studying. But she still wanted something to read, something casual and beguiling to go with her martini. She wandered the house, looking.

Not Shade's books. She'd struggled on through *Vampire Go Boom,* but hadn't been able to make herself finish the Civil War novel, and wasn't interested in trying again. Something she hadn't read before. She scanned the bookshelves in the study, as if she could, by dint of sheer desire, come up with a new Elmore Leonard or Patricia Cornwell.

In the drawer of her bedside table she found the issue of *Vanity Fair* she had picked up, what, two months ago now? and had never gotten around to. It would have to do. She carried it back down to her chair in the living room, topped off her martini, settled in.

She despised and enjoyed the magazine, its snottiness and attitude, its fixation with money, objects, and possessions, its pathetic obsession with movie stars. On the other hand, she had as great a fascination as anyone else with the gossipy trashy lives of the useless rich.

And sometimes the writing was good.

She waded through the hundred or so glossy redolent pages before you got to any actual content, perfume ads bursting with odor like an insanity of crushed flowers. How long before they put the scent of new leather into the luxury car ads?

And then she found Chipper. There he was, modeling one of the tight Italian suits that had been in for the last few seasons, his full lips rouged and pouting, his cheeks ineffably hollowed, his lank blond hair given a middle part and a schoolboy flip. Talk about Peter Pans. He hadn't aged a day. He had to be thirty-seven, but he was playing twenty-five.

The ad featured four such apparently young men, walking barefoot on the beach though dressed to the nines in every other regard. They looked sullen, pampered, and dissolute but somehow radiantly healthy nonetheless. They looked kept.

And she felt nothing. None of the bitterness, and no least rush of the physical attraction that had remained so powerful even after she had learned to hate him.

Poor Chipper. Dwindled to nothing more than a picture on a page. Banished to the Phantom Zone at last. She laughed till she hurt. Then she got up and went to work.

Shade was due back on Monday. Wingo had made Jody an appointment Saturday morning at ten to meet Dead Men Walking. That way she would be coming fresh from a dream session, and might have material for him to work with.

The address Wingo had given her was on one of the short little streets back in between Guadalupe and St. Francis on the east and west, and Water and the river on the south and north. Boys were washing their trucks and lowriders in the warm sunshine. She went up to the gate in a wall around what proved to be an older duplex and, seeing no buzzer, opened the gate and walked through. She heard a bell ring faintly somewhere inside. The courtyard was surprisingly lovely, leaflight shifting over a flagstone walk. A reflecting pool was set in an area of raked gravel, and odd volcanic stones projected in arrangements that would have seemed random if they had not been, somehow, so harmonious. A vine-covered portale ran across the front of the duplex.

Her number was the door on the right, and just as she stepped up, a deep voice came from a speaker she had not seen, over her head: "Come on in. All the way back, through the kitchen, last door on the left." She entered a darkened living room, so spare that it did not seem as small as it was. It held a futon in sitting position, a tatame table that probably doubled as a coffee table, a bentwood rocker, a lamp, a crowded bookcase, and, notably, no television.

An efficiency kitchen was beyond the living room: glass-fronted cabinets, a white stove and sink and refrigerator that looked to be original issue—rounded and domestic rather than sleek and sharp-cornered. The floor was laid not with linoleum, but an excellent Italian tile.

The back door of the kitchen looked onto a screened porch, and the door on her left opened onto what had obviously once been a narrow hall but had now been expanded, by means of a double opening in its far wall, into the anteroom of an office.

A big man in a beaded white T-shirt sat behind a desk in the office. His gray-black hair was pulled back under a white silk scarf, and he wore, depending from a turquoise and bear-claw necklace, what seemed to be the life-sized golden skull of a rattlesnake.

He had the face of the man on the 1938 nickel.

"What are you doing here?" Jody said.

"I might ask you the same question," Victorio said.

"It's you? This is you? You're Dead—" She couldn't bring herself to say the name, it felt too silly. "*You're* Loren Wingo's big shaman?"

"And you, I presume, are Wanda Weedwacker."

"Wanda *who?*"

"Loren's idea of a joke. Said you were too embarrassed to let him use your real name. I might have known." He indicated a chair: "Have a seat if you like."

"But this changes everything."

"Yes. That doesn't mean you have to keep standing up, though."

She sat, feeling as though she had walked through a door into another dimension, into one of her dreams. The windows of the office opened onto yet another small and subtle courtyard, and she followed the movement of light and shadow out there rather than look into his eyes.

"Well," she said.

"Well," he said.

"*You're* the one with the zombies," she said. In her mind, things were falling into place with a rapidity that made her dizzy. *This* was the problem Toni had been having—not the shrink and the cop, but the shrink and the medicine man.

"Everybody wants to talk about the zombies," he said. "Forget the zombies."

"But are you a real shaman?"

He leaned back, crossed his feet on the desk and his hands behind his head. God, his arms were big. He was wearing faded jeans and a glistening pair of black Air Jordans. "*Shaman* isn't the right word," he said. "I keep telling Loren not to use it. Shamans are culturally specific. I'm pretty much an outsider, even in the culture I grew up in. Are you a real seeker?"

"Well, if you aren't a shaman, what are you? A medicine man? A witch doctor?"

"Cultural clichés," he said. "I never gave it a name. Sometimes names are misleading. I don't exactly print up business cards, you know."

"Well, we can't go on with this," she said. "Not now, when we know who we are."

"It's your call," he said. "Whether you can separate the roles adequately. No problem for me. What you have to understand—here, in this room, in this role, I'm not Victorio." The yellow eyes were probing her. She felt as though she were under the scanner of a CIA computer, or being sized up across the veldt by the alpha male of the pride.

"You don't know *me*," he explained. "You know somebody who's going to marry your best friend. A good-old-boy half-Indian cop. This is a different world. Different rules. But I can tell you this: I wouldn't shrug it off, our meeting. This is no coincidence."

"What kind of shaman or whatever are you?" she said.

"Freelance," he said. He sighed, gave her a rundown. Part of it was the sort of thing Wingo had told her—true shamans didn't choose their callings, in fact often fled them. She noticed he was using the word himself, even though it wasn't the right one.

He had resisted his own calling for years, but things had kept happening. What sort of things? Things. Being of mixed heritage, and having always been an outsider, even on the rez, he didn't practice as a Navajo or as an Apache—or for that matter, as a *curandero*. He could have trained in the Blessing Way and the Healing Way and many others, but had felt it would not be proper. He was not pure. He was of both, and neither, and only half believed any of it.

But the powers that made shamans did not care what culture you belonged to, and they did not care what you thought or what you believed. You came into your gift not from adherence, but from paying attention, and from learning, and from understanding what was necessary.

So that after a while, though he was neither Navajo nor Apache nor Hispanic, the *diné* came to him, and their cousins the Apache came, and the descendants of the conquistadores came, and he gave them all and each whatever he was able to give. And then, because he was of many worlds, but not completely at home in any one, he was able to work with white people, too, those ultimate dispossessed, the ghostlike wanderers of the world.

"Sometimes I think," he concluded, "that white people have been brought to us on purpose, to bring us all together, to create one Way for all the tribes. My friends laugh, but that is the gift of the white people, is it not? And their curse: abstraction and synthesis."

"Are you asking me? I don't know anything about white people."

"Maybe I've just spent too much time talking to Loren." He smiled. "He tells me you think you might be receiving the calling."

She was irritated. "I never said any such thing."

"He didn't say you said it. He said it was what you thought."

"I have no intention of giving up my research," she blustered. "Of becoming some sort of, of New Age female Timothy Leary crystal-gazing channeler—"

"Nobody says you have to," he said. "Follow your science to its end. But that is studying a thing from the outside in. You formulate the questions and the questions formulate the answers. You put a quarter in the slot, and the machine plays a record. There is another way, in which you cease putting your dreams in boxes, and instead put yourself in your dreams. Give yourself over, learn to live *in* them and let them shape you. I *can* teach you to do that, and the way I understand it, that's as valuable for your research as it is for your psyche."

"I don't think I even believe in this stuff," she said.

"What have I been telling you?" he said. "The method stays the same. Belief doesn't matter. Now. Let's get serious. We've already wasted a lot of time, and I have better things to do. Do you wish to pursue your education or not?"

"Pursue," she said.

"You understand that you're an apprentice, not a master?"

She bridled, but said, "I understand."

"You understand that you can make no presumption on the master-pupil relationship because of anything you know of me as Victorio? That, yes, I am that person, but this is a separate realm?" She nodded. *What the hell am I getting into?* "And you understand that even though you have to follow me, I don't know everything? I'm still learning, too."

"Actually, that one's the easiest," she said.

He grinned. "Any questions?"

"Yeah. What are your rates?"

"You'll find out," he said. "When it's too late. No, I'm kidding. I don't have rates, exactly. That's part of the process, finding out what's fair. I mean, it isn't exactly *me* doing all the work, you know. People usually pay me what I'm worth. Sometimes in money. Sometimes in favors. Sometimes just by passing the good on to others. That's how it is with Loren. I think he's a very valuable man, and I don't charge him."

He asked her if she was ready to get to work, and she said what work, and he said he had to examine her, and she said what examination. He asked if her dreams had given her a totem animal, a familiar, and she almost said no, but then she remembered the bears, could that be her totem, and he said *Mmm*, just like a damned psychiatrist, just like Toni. She told him about Ish, her internal self-healer (though not about the sex, not yet), but he didn't seem as impressed as Bianca had been. He said that was a New-Agey notion, the internal self-healer, and he didn't traffic in it much. Although maybe it matched up with the shaman's spirit guide.

He asked her what her most powerful recent dreams had been, and he listened. He asked her what the most powerful dreams in her life had been, and he listened. He asked her why she thought they were so powerful, and she tried to explain.

She told him about the Center for Dream Control, and, as she was doing so, suddenly remembered the closing image of Vic, of Dead Men Walking, standing high in a white robe with a rattlesnake around his throat. Voice shaking, she told him about that image.

"What do you think it means?" she said.

"Don't be in too much of a hurry for meaning," he said.

"But it has to be significant. I mean, I might have subconsciously picked up on the fact that you were a—a—" She pointed a trembling finger at the golden skull: "But how could I have known about *that?* It is a rattlesnake's head, isn't it? How did you get it?"

"Never mind," he said.

"But what are my dreams telling you? Do you think I might be for real?"

"It's always the beginners who want to be reassured of their talent," he said. "Ever notice that? And you *stay* a beginner until you give up that need. The great talents don't need reassurance. It isn't because they finally got enough of it. It's because they grew up and quit asking for it and concentrated on the work instead."

"*I* need information as much as I need reassurance. And I really don't thrive under this Zen tell-you-nothing-but-whack-you-with-a-stick-when-you-get-it-wrong approach."

"Your dreams might be telling me that there's a great spiritual battle shaping up and that it has chosen this part of the Earth to play itself out, and that you are central to the conflict. Or they might be telling me that you had a conflicted youth and have an extremely vivid imagination. It isn't important what I think about them. And I'm not trying to mystify you. What I'm trying to get across *is* information—information on how to pay attention to your dreams. You've already learned a lot—from sheer intuition, I'd guess. That mother dream was a true healing dream, for example. But you more or less stumbled into it. You have to learn to do that sort of thing immediately, and on purpose. You may have to learn to travel out of your body—"

"Do you really think that's possible?"

"I said *may.* In any case, beginner, I'd say you have promise but a lot to learn. And if you don't lose the smartass attitude, I'm going to have to whack you with a stick."

"That sounds more like Victorio than Dead Men Walking."

"Yeah, well, it's lunchtime, and I'm hungry."

She realized she was, too. She invited him to join her, but he thought it would help her keep his roles separate in her mind if he didn't. She asked about telling Toni, and he said it was up to her. Toni didn't tell him about her patients, and he didn't tell her about his clients. It was a matter of professional confidence, after all.

He set her a dream exercise, a mutual dream on Sunday night. Mutual dream? she said. We both dream the same dream, he said. It's the only way I can really check out your dream territory. Do you think that's really possible? she said. That question is really getting old, he said. Why Sunday night and not tonight? she said. Because I want you to have a little time to absorb all this first, he said. Besides, I have another appointment tonight.

She asked about their next meeting.

I'll get in touch with you, he said. Dream first.

25: rainbow weather

She would see Shade again in less than forty-eight hours, but all Jody could think about was her dream assignment. She didn't believe for a second that it would happen, and yet she was anxious for Sunday night to arrive. Anxious to run upstairs and force herself to sleep.

Let's see, how would that work exactly?

She realized she was feeling the same anxiety she had once felt before a prom date, though there were no sexual overtones in her relationship with Dead Men Walking. She thought of him by that name and not as Victorio. Interesting. How had the transition occurred? She wondered if, when she next saw him with Toni, he would seem like Victorio to her, or like Dead Men Walking. She was afraid she would jump the gun and dream the dream, whatever it was, on Saturday. But she didn't. At least she didn't think she did. When she woke Sunday morning, her dreams vanished before she could think them through. That almost never happened anymore.

Oh no, another worry. What if *that* happened tonight?

Maybe Dead Men Walking had planted a suggestion somehow, but she grew calmer as the day wore on. She let the cats out, did some gardening while they prowled and explored.

The ground was awfully dry, and she was worried. This place was always on the edge of drought. Snows had been good, and the reservoir was full, so the city wasn't into water rationing, but the monsoons were late again. It had rained twice at the end of June, and not a day since. The temperature, which in a wetter summer would not have gone over eighty-five, was now touching the low nineties for a high. At seven thousand feet it still felt balmy, even at noon, in the shade of the aspen, but without rain, that mildness wouldn't last.

She wore a hat and long sleeves as she worked. The air might be cool, but the sun was brutal; for one thing, there was less of that cool air for it to pass through. At these altitudes you could get sunstroke without ever getting heatstroke.

She put her tools away at six, went for a short walk to work out the kinks and cramps, came back and showered, called Pizza Hut and ordered a meat-lover's special and a supreme, both with hand-tossed crust. Deciding it was another martini night, she got the Boodles out of the freezer, sliced off a twist, rubbed the glass, and then discovered she was out of vermouth. Oh, well, call it a very dry one. She shook the gin over ice, poured herself a tall flute. She hated the traditional flat "cocktail" glasses—they didn't hold enough, their surface-area-to-volume ratio was too high, so that they warmed up too quickly, and they spilled too easily.

She ate pizza and watched *The X-Files,* a bad habit, but not one she cared enough to break. It was about dreams, naturally. Precognitive dreams. She thought about having a second martini, but this close to bedtime, it might interfere with her dreams. Made you drowsy now, but then you woke up at three in the morning when the metabolites kicked in, and couldn't get back to slumberland. Besides, she needed to cut down. Getting that little first adipose layer on the tummy, not so bad, but if you didn't check it, it got out of hand in a hurry. After Fox and Scully, she put on a record and tackled Wingo's manifesto again. She wasn't hardcore enough for *The Outer Limits,* and besides, the science on the show was usually pretty bad.

In forty-five minutes or so, she was yawning.

There was no way she was really going to have a mutual dream. Those things didn't happen. Especially not if you wanted them to. She went up, brushed her teeth, washed her face, put her head on her pillow, and disappeared immediately from the planet Earth.

So here she was, standing naked in the woods on a path covered in pine needles.

These people were going to have to get her some clothes one of these days. But she was warm enough. Sunlight filtered down through the tall trees. Okay, where was he?

When she turned around, he was there, sitting on an elephant. A big one, gray, with a legend stenciled onto its side: DEPARTMENT OF MOTOR WEHICLES.

You were trying not to think of an elephant, *he said.*

She was trying to figure out what a wehicle was—maybe a two-seater?— when he threw a leg over and dismounted, floating to the ground You're naked, *he said.* Not bad.

He wasn't wearing much himself, a cliché breechclout. Moccasins. The bearclaw-and-rattlesnake necklace. Hey, *she said.*

I didn't mean it that way, *he said.* I meant it was a good sign.

Where did the elephant go? *she said. There was no elephant. There was only an empty path, a wide empty path climbing the mountainside like a power-line cut.*

Forget the elephant, *he said.* We have work to do. You need to show me around.

How? Where?

Your choice, *he said.* You're naked, we could probably fly.

Ish was beside her, holding her hand. She felt her loins loosen, her lips grow moist.

Who's the twerp? *said Dead Men Walking.*

He's the one I was telling you about, *she said.*

Hmm. *Dead Men Walking went all the way around them, studying. Ish seemed to become transparent, a statue of clouded crystalline, though he breathed and moved.* Interesting, *said Dead Men Walking.* I've never seen one like this before. But he doesn't belong here right now, and he knows it. Beat it, bud. No ectoplasmic pussy tonight.

Ish was gone.

Okay, *said Dead Men Walking.* You're holding it pretty good. What do I need to see next?

They were in the Center for Dream Control. Ish was there, of course, but he was in uniform, and he pretended not to notice them. He was under orders.

This is wild, *said Dead Men Walking. He leaned over the console, his bare hips flexing under the loincloth.* The Savage at the Computer. I heard that, *the shaman said. But he didn't turn around. His fingers flew across the keys. He punched up a dream on the big monitor. It was them, standing in the woods with Ish.*

Look, *the shaman said.* It's us. Unbelievable.

There's a time delay, sir. *Ish stood at attention in the corner.* Speed of light, you know.

So I see. *Even as they watched, the screen showed them appearing in the lab, Dead Men Walking leaning over the keys.* Better take your eyes away, *he said now, the real one said.* I don't think you want to see the screen-in-screen. Too much feedback.

Very wise, sir, *Ish said.*

Hey, they don't call me a shaman for nothing, *Dead Men Walking said.* This is absolutely crazy, *he said, walking around, checking the electronics.* Machines in dreams. Who does machines in dreams?

Why not? *Jody said.*

Well, *said Dead Men Walking,* you don't *need* 'em in dreams. Dreams are biology. Machines are to do things biology can't. But dreams can do anything.

Maybe machines are biology, too, *she said.* You don't need bodies in dreams, either, but there they are. *Dead Men Walking didn't respond. He had picked up the red phone, punched in a number. She could hear it ringing over the line. A voice answered.*

Shit, *said the shaman, almost dropping the receiver.* The damn thing *works. He spoke into the mouthpiece:* Honey, it's me. I'm sorry. Go back to sleep.

Of course it does, *Ish said proudly.* I invented it.

Well, un-invent it, *said Dead Men Walking.* It ain't natural. Besides, I thought I told you to quit following us around.

Ish was gone. Jody looked up at the big monitor. Ish was riding the elephant. He was in a safari of elephants, trooping through the jungles of Rangoon. Mickey and Goofy and Uncle Scrooge were riding elephants, too. The Beagle Boys were creeping through the underbrush. Black Bart waited at the temple, hidden in the ruins.

Can we get out of here? *said Dead Men Walking.* This place gives me the creeps.

They were on a mountaintop, still naked, ankle-deep in snow. They were also in the malpais, standing under a thousand-year juniper on a flat outcrop of black volcanic rock, the warm wind moving shadows across them, the ancient wind, which never rested.

Looking off to the left, you could see the Upper Falls of the Frijoles at Bandelier. Looking right, Chaco opened in the distance, huge mesas in the ancient sun. But it was green, and water ran in its channel, and tiny people moved in the paths between the gleaming dwellings.

That's better, *said Dead Men Walking.* I was beginning to think you weren't hooked up right. *A hawk sailed in the wind, crying.* Much better. What next?

She called up a flurry of images from her childhood: mopping the boards of the grocery floor; sitting on the toilet bleeding with her first period; walking the beach with Pop in Florida that one time before it all went bad; her mother scolding her for coming in late, the very night she had lost her virginity to Trey; his gun under the register. But the images weren't important, they were ego toys, a pack of picture cards she was dealing across the table. The table was the black rock of the malpais. She threw her hand down in a scatter. I fold, *she said.*

Good, *he said.* Because that isn't the real game. It's good you know that. *He had one card in front of him, facedown. He turned it over. It was the bear.*

It wasn't clear what happened next, because she was with the bear. She was the bear, *perhaps. But there had been a long rambling gallop amid the rocks and trees, there had been hunger and ferocity and then blood in the mouth and then sleep in a cave on a bed of needles. And after many seasons, it seemed that something had killed her.*

They had torn her apart and left her body in the woods, her bones in the cave of the bear. She was a green and radiant skeleton, she was death come alive. She was Osiris, Lord of the Underworld, and she glowed in the caves of darkness, a terrible beauty.

I see, *said Dead Men Walking.*

He was sitting across the cave from the skeleton. You're getting ready for something. I don't know what it is, but we don't have long to bring you up to speed.

She was radioactive, and that was why the drought. Why Chaco had become so dry. She had walked it, blazing angel of death, and the crops had withered and scorched.

She was standing in the snow again, and her flesh had returned, but she could feel the skeleton Osiris burning in her like a thousand hooks, like a thousand question marks. Dead Men Walking stood beside her, except that now he was Ish.

I didn't know you could do that, *she said.*

One of us can, *said the shaman.* I can't tell which.

You know I love you, *she said.*

I know, *he said. He didn't take her hand because he still looked like Dead Men Walking and it might have been confusing.*

The trouble is the real world. It all makes sense when we're here.

But I can't take you into the real world with me. They would think I was crazy.

Rules of the game, *he said.*

You're the one I can talk to, *she said.* You're the one I've shared everything with. But I feel like I'm betraying that other man.

As she said it, she saw Shade, sitting in his cave.

You can't trust him, *said the shaman.*

No, *she said. Now Shade was reading her diary. He had no right to do that. All the shameful things, the secret things. He was reading it aloud to his dead wife. She lay in her coffin. She had been dead a long time. Shade sat and read to her. As he read, he changed. He became a monster. He was a dragon in his cave, wearing glasses, reading to a dead woman.*

His tail grew longer and longer.

Poor beast, *said Dead Men Walking.* Poor sad bastard.

If we're shamans, *she said.*

You aren't a shaman, *he said.* Not yet. Maybe never.

Why can't we make it rain? *she said.* Isn't that the sort of thing a shaman is for?

There's only so much to go around, *he said.* If you use your power for one thing, you may lose it for another. Before you shift the bad luck to another tribe, you have to ask what the interest on the loan might be. And rain is big. Rain is very very big.

As they watched, a storm began, dark thunderheads cascading over the crown of the Truchas range and rolling down the valley. Hard gray rain slanting in, roaring against the rocks. It raged toward them like a silver-tipped grizzly, and then, just at their feet, fell back and shattered into a stunning double rainbow. Every color was distinct, and both arcs were complete, and she knew that the bitterness was gone from her bones, that Osiris had broken in light in the sky.

A branch of lightning stroked into the rainbow's center.

What's the matter? *he said. It was true, she hurt with sadness, the loss of Osiris.*

The rainbow, *she said.* It's so beautiful. I want it to be real. But it isn't. It's just an illusion. It's all in my head. It's just a dream.

What would you do if it was real? *he said.*

Well—just look at it, I guess.

The magnificent bow stretched across the sky, shedding its glory to all the air. Under it the trees were grateful, under it the birds flew, the people lived and sang and danced and died.

So keep looking, *he said.*

She woke with every detail of the dream sharp in her mind, but too late to record it in her journal. In spite of that, she didn't lose it. All through breakfast and into her day at the office, whenever she closed her eyes, she was back in it. It wasn't like other dreams. It was no vanishing phantasm, no mist blown away by the morning sun.

It was inhabitable.

She was tremendously excited. Had Dead Men Walking really had the same dream? This was too much. She couldn't wait for him to call her. The hell with it, she was going to call him. But then she realized she had no idea what his phone number was, or if he even had one. Check the directory under Dead Men Walking? Sure.

Then she looked, just in case. Nothing. She could call Vic at work, of course—and at the thought, she saw she had been thinking of them as two different people, as though one could put on the badge and go in to work and all the while the other could stay there in that curious duplex, wearing a golden rattlesnake around his throat.

She didn't think Dead Men Walking would like it if she tried to get to him through Vic, and there was no way she was going to go through Toni. So she stewed and fumed, and met with her patients. At least she didn't have to watch the afternoon dreamers. Shade had said he'd be back in plenty of time to take the night session, and please let him do it, and so she had been able to move Blossom back into her usual shift.

Shade was coming in on the shuttle, and they had agreed there was really no point in their trying to get together before the night shift. All of which was just fine with Jody. She felt different about him somehow. Maybe the bloom was off the rose.

She had no intention of telling him about the scene in the dream, or indeed any of the dream, or any of her work with Dead Men Walking. What was happening to her was much too private, this double life, this difficult balance. Walking in both worlds.

She sensed an equal distance in Shade, that he was keeping secrets as well. Perhaps merely his writing, the fact that he knew it wasn't what he wanted it to be. Perhaps simply the not-uncommon inability to share himself on the deepest levels.

But when he showed at the lab, big and rumpled and familiar, she was happy to see him, and went into his arms gladly and got a good long hug. She had wondered how she would handle it if she had another spirit-dream, if she would go so far as to actively conceal it from Shade, but that night everything that happened in her mind was ordinary.

And things were ordinary but wonderful the rest of the week, and all the rest of the dwindling summer. When she wasn't practicing her spirit-lessons, she was a scientist working on her theory. The two activities were somehow one, fed each other. When she had first come out of the spirit dream, she had been afraid that it would blow her theory apart—that in order to accept its apparent reality, she would have to give up her logic.

But instead she studied her math and read more on brain chemistry and everything she learned swiveled into dream, into mystery. She walked into a continual ongoing revelation. She felt new and vulnerable and supernally alert. The leaves shaking in wind possessed a tremulous light, the shadow of an ant on the sidewalk brought her joy. She saw so much, so clearly, so fast, that there was nowhere to put it. You could become so wise your brain exploded.

She had the dizzying sensation that she was approaching her own personal Feigenbaum number, that her happiness and awareness were undergoing a more and more rapid period-doubling. And what would happen when she hit the Zone of Turbulence?

Dead Men Walking had finally called, and set up another conference. By that time she had become skeptical again, alternating AC/DC between visions. She still remembered the dream perfectly, still felt its power. But it was one thing to have, under suggestion from someone else, a mythical evocation, and it was quite another to actually share a dream.

The conference went more like a lawyer's deposition than a séance. She was cagey, probing. Told him the general story, but withheld the details. Waiting for corroboration. Which didn't come. His comments were vague, all-embracing. Fortune-teller stuff, suitable for all occasions, grist for the gullible. This time he made no suggestions, gave her no exercises. By the time she was ready to leave, she had become convinced he was faking it. She could learn a lot from him, no doubt, would stay with the program awhile. But.

He followed her to the front door. As she fumbled for her keys, he said, "What happened to the elephant?" and grinned and went back into the darkness of the house, leaving her with her brain in ruins again and bright exultation leaping and sparking up from her spine.

After that the rains came. The dry weather broke, and they had a real rainy season at last. She went out with Shade into the street after a five-o'clock shower in late August, and they watched as the rainbow came out. "Isn't it beautiful?" she said.

People drove slowly along the street, or walked dogs on the opposite sidewalk, and the people gawked, not at the rainbow, but at Shade and Jody watching the rainbow. No one looked up, no one seemed to notice the incredible show in the eastern sky.

"Where do you think we're headed?" Jody said, eyes on the ring of color. "You and me."

"I don't have any idea," Shade said. "Where do you want to head?"

"I don't see marriage, do you?" He didn't say anything. "What I see is you, in a couple of months or a couple of years, moving on. You're not a Santa Fe type, not really, and let's face it, I belong here. I may be a newcomer, but this is it. This is home."

"It doesn't have anything to do with Santa Fe one way or the other," Shade said.

She leaned her head against his shoulder. "Shade, I love you. And it's none of my business. But I think you lost somebody once, and you've never gotten over it. It took me a long time to see, but I think your secret is grief. You live in grief."

"Where did you learn to do that?" he said, staring where the colors were now vanishing.

"In dreams," she said. "I think I learned it in a dream."

"Well, don't dream those dreams anymore," he said. "There's things I don't want you to know." The rainbow was gone, and a flurry of cool drops blew over them and chased them back inside to their drinks, and dinner, and reading quietly together under the lamp.

Across town, on the patio, Toynbee said, "Wasn't that incredible?"

"Yeah, incredible," Leonard said.

"Well, I'm sorry," the Brit said. "I'm just sorry as hell I enjoy the sight of a rainbow."

"I'm like a bug in a jar," Leonard said. "I'm like a bug in a glass jar, and the jar has a fucking rainbow on the label, and I'm supposed to say, 'Wow, what a beautiful rainbow.' "

"Well, I'm just sorry as hell," Toynbee said.

26: anasazi heights

The end of August came, and the end of the DormaVu study. Jody threw a party in the lab for all the participants. George, Angela, Bert, Bianca, and Rafael—one and all, they told her how wonderful it had been and how much they had learned. For herself, she had learned enough not to discount them. If they saw her as a leader, a teacher, who was she to protest?

It was going to be wonderful to have her evenings free, but on the other hand, what would she do with herself? She felt lost after the party, wandering the empty lab alone. Maybe it was a good thing she had taken up her studies with Dead Men Walking. Maybe her willingness to work with him had been partly because, somewhere inside, she had seen this coming.

In mid-September, Toni announced that she and Vic had found a house. "We aren't going to move in till after the honeymoon," she said. "But you *have* to come see it!"

Jody decided to drive the Pontiac, she wasn't sure why. Maybe because Shade hadn't been interested, and maybe that was a sign that their time together was almost over, that he didn't want to share in her friends' future because he wouldn't be there for it.

And even though she was more contented than she ever had been, and told herself she would do fine if and when he left, it was still a lonely feeling.

Or maybe she was driving it because she fully expected Toni and

Vic's place to put her little shack in the shade, as she sometimes felt their impending marriage and apparent perfect happiness put her own love affair just a little in the shade. Friends weren't supposed to compare such things, of course, but friends did compare such things, of course. Jody never thought of herself as lacking for money, but she sometimes envied the four-hundred-year-old baronial resources of Toni's family, and Santa Fe was *the* town for house pride—more people spent more time talking about, planning, building, and showing off their local intimations of Pickfair than in any other place except perhaps L.A. And no matter how nice a place you had, there was always somebody around the corner ready to make you feel like the poorest relative on the block.

So maybe she drove the Pontiac because it grounded her, gave her a history, and in its antique and massive elegance spoke of solidity and resource.

Or maybe because in her last dream she and Ish had made love in its backseat.

So anyway she piloted the large smooth beast across town, and went down Washington, and out along Hyde Park Road and past the Institute, waving the fig in Mindanao's general direction as she went by, and up past Ten Thousand Waves. She came to a road she would have missed except for Toni's very precise directions. It crossed the creek on a very new and elegant wooden bridge, went around an outcrop of stone, and began rising. The Pontiac slowed immediately, but ran smoothly and without laboring, and she was proud of it.

It was a good road, freshly blacktopped and precisely lined. "I would have sworn this was National Forest land," she said aloud. She wondered who had bribed whom, and for how much.

It was only a mile to the gate. Two huge cairns of old masonry bracketed the boulevard entryway. A bronze plate set into the cairn on the right bore the legend ANASAZI HEIGHTS. Now, where had she seen that before? She drove through. No guardhouse? But there it was, a quarter-mile in, hidden around a turn. A cheerful young man in a uniform that seemed a cross between the dress blues of the air force and an 1890 London gentleman's evening wear took her name, checked his list, made a phone call, and waved her on.

The drive wandered, divided, rejoined. Where were the houses?

She came into an open area, the drive wandering along the edge of a ridge. Stunning views of Santa Fe spread out below, the Jemez

Range forty miles west. It was a clean and beautiful morning, but wait until later in the day—talk about sunsets. Right on schedule, her inferiority kicked in, and she patted the Pontiac's seat. "I got you, babe," she sang.

On the slopes to her left she saw tumbles of stone, glimpses of ruined walls and foundations. What was this, some sort of newly discovered archaeological site? She hadn't read about it. There was no way they could build on such a site, there was no bribe big enough. But glass glinted here and there in the trees or from angles and corners of rock.

She came around another bend, through a grove of aspen, and onto a higher level of the ridge, and there were Toni and Vic, in a graveled parking area, leaning against Toni's Range-Rover. She pulled up beside the Rover, got out, exchanged hugs.

A bordered path of combed gravel led from the parking area through a meadow of wildflowers, and Toni hurried Jody along it, almost skipping in her excitement. They went by the ruins of a full-sized ceremonial kiva, beautiful concentric circles, chambered compartments. Then the path met and followed an old stone wall.

"It's beautiful," Jody said. "But surely they won't let you build on a site like this."

Toni's laughter echoed in the walls of stone all around. "Wait'll you see, girl." Vic was striding along behind them more deliberately. Jody couldn't tell how he felt about all this. The Anasazi would not have been his forebears, they were supposed to be the ancestors of the pueblo tribes, the Hopi and Zuni, not of the later incursions of Navajo and Apache. Still—wouldn't he see it as a desecration of the heritage of the Old Ones?

Or was that just Dead Men Walking?

She had seen him twice more, and he had given her exercises, which to her mind had been almost as much fun as algebra homework, but which she had faithfully followed. He was trying to teach her to roll out of her body at night and travel the spirit world. She didn't really believe it was possible, thought it was just a species of dreaming.

"What is it with white people and this believing crap?" he had said. "I'm not asking you to *believe* anything. I'm asking you to *do* something." He had warned her not to be casual about her practice. There were soul-eaters out there, hungry ghosts who would come after you when they saw you free of your body. Especially if you let your lack of belief make you unwary, if you wandered around going gee whiz like a gawking tourist in a London ghetto.

Why was that? she had asked. Why should there be evil spirits?

Not evil exactly, he had said. Just hungry. And it was just the way things were. Every good thing drew the hungry spirits, as light draws insects. Those who had any experience of goodness knew it in their bones: They must walk carefully, and in respect, for fear that virtue itself, that great imbalance, might trigger the worst of catastrophes.

Jody thought she could hear the wings whirring around her this very minute.

They went around an outcropping of gray stone, and there, below them, set into a half-dozen copses of aspen, and with a hundred-mile view of the valley below and the mountains beyond, was another set of ruins, this one on two levels. The same familiar mortared walls, the circles and chambers. And the clean wind shook the flowers in the green grass all around, and the aspen shivered with excitement, and the warm sun dazzled on a a pool of water—

But these walls stood higher. And Jody saw, again, here and there in the tumble and maze of the stones, the glint of glass. And the outside gate to the whole compound—it was the familiar Anasazi post-and-lintel, centuries-old wood set in hand-split stone, with the familiar heartlifting vista, whatever magic it was that looking through a portal delivered—

But something was wrong. Something was wrong with the doorway. It was too big. The Anasazi had been small people, and their windows and doorways accordingly miniature. This thing was big. Big enough for Vic, big enough for a pro basketball player—

And she got it finally, and Toni laughed again to see the look on her face, and even Vic, catching up to them where they had stopped, had an amused smile on his craggy face.

Toni led them down to the gate.

"There's almost five acres in all, and there's another parking area right over there, close to the house, you can't see it because it's screened off, but I wanted to bring you down this way to surprise you." Inside the large gate and its tumbledown walls was another gate and another wall, both cleverly hidden from above by the topology of the hill and the outer wall. The inside wall was a good six feet high, and its gate was set with steel bars and operated electronically.

"As you can see, it looks open, but it's really secure," Toni said. "This wall is monitored by cameras and electric eyes hidden in the outer wall, and there's a state-of-the-art system for the whole house and grounds. Red Rover, Red Rover, send Wilbur right over."

At her last words, the steel gate opened smoothly and quietly. "It hasn't been programmed for our voices yet," Toni apologized. "So we have to use a preset code."

Jody was, for once in her life, speechless. Toni took them down a flagstone path past beds of wildflowers, over a footbridge crossing a tumble of water that might have come from a spring in the side of the mountain or might have been entirely artificial, through a double set of doors (also voice-operated) that would have put the Inn of the Anasazi to shame, and into the house. It was incredible, and incredibly huge. The floors were flagstone, or—Jody could glimpse on other levels, in other areas—planks of pegged and polished wood. The ceilings were *viga* and *latilla,* of a bright clean wood, probably pine, that had been washed with a light white rinse to take out the yellow and impart a clean rosiness, and then sealed. The heights of the ceilings varied, but ran from ten to twelve feet. Where they were—a complex of spaces that appeared to function as den and entertainment area and great room—a wall of glass looked out over the view.

The spaces of the dwelling opened into each other and rose and fell from level to level with the contours of the hill. What was a floor became a walk past the indoor garden of an impromptu sunroom. What seemed walls became wide square columns when you went around a corner. There seemed to be a stone fireplace in every wall, every column.

"Are all the houses like this?" Jody asked in a small voice.

"Not like this," Toni said. "Oh, I see what you mean. Yes, they have the same architecture. Everybody gets his own set of ruins. But the houses are completely different. This one is called Cascade, the Cascade House. That's because of the way it follows the shape of the hill, or maybe it's because it has that spring on the property. A lot of people might not like having so many different elevations, but Vic and I both love it." Her voice went into tour-guide mode: "There are three main levels, but as you can see, all the levels have levels, too. The spring actually feeds the pool through an underground viaduct, or it will when we move in. You went by the pool, but you probably didn't know that was what it was—"

"You don't mean—" Jody began.

"Yes, the kiva. It fills up. The water's ozone-purified, which is environmentally friendly, and it's solar-heated, so you can use it all year round. One of the side chambers is a hot tub with an underground sauna beside it. There are hidden tracks for a set of Plexiglas panels, so in the winter the whole area becomes a spa and solarium. The panels are computerized."

She stopped at a cabinet built into a stone column, placed a finger on a flat black plate. The doors retracted, and a monitor and keyboard slid out. Toni punched up a map of the lower level and then the two other levels. "The whole house is computerized," she said, punching buttons. "Right now I'm laying in lights and music," she said, "for where we're going next. Everything's on the system—lights, sound, alarm, doors and windows, heating, cooling—the house is passive solar, and a lot of it's bermed into the hillside, but all of the sun surfaces have louvers you can adjust for the time of year. You not only get built-in access to the Web with the purchase price of the home, you get your own lifetime paid-up home page. There."

Gentle lights came on above them, the sound of flute music sifted down. Toni took them up a curving set of steps to the second level. "This is kitchen, pantry, dining area, party room," she said, pointing from spot to spot. Countertops of pink granite stretched along the near wall, inset with sinks, appliances: A Subzero recessed into a stone compartment of the same granite, a bright blue AGA, part of a central island that had its own sink and wet bar. "Individual cooler compartments," Toni said, sliding open drawers on either side of the mammoth range. "Also, this level has a mud room and a complete bath, for when you need to wash up coming in from outside. Away over there, that door, that's an underground walkway to the pool."

And so it went. They toured the dining area, which had two stone fireplaces at either end and two crystal chandeliers. Again, from both kitchen and dining area, there were staggering views out across the valley below. Jody was numb, in shock, lost and dazzled. If Vic and Toni had suddenly disappeared, she couldn't have found her way out alone, and that was somehow, in spite of the vast space of the house, a very claustrophobic feeling. A bitter envy spurted suddenly in her veins, boiling together with an equally bitter contempt. How much did something like this *cost?* The vanity of it, the sheer, self-aggrandizing human *folly*—

"Look at her face!" Toni crowed. "Vic, I told you. She thinks we're a couple of money-mad, house-proud fools." She laid an understanding hand on Jody's arm, her pleasure in the house too great to mind her friend's doubts. Jody wondered how Vic really felt about the place. She simply couldn't imagine him in this, this overblown materialistic insanity. A mark of her envy, because she never thought in those terms. She liked *things* herself.

"No I don't," she protested. "It's *wonderful.* I'm just—overwhelmed." She had to respond, pretend an interest at least. Toni might be laughing now, but she was capable of hurt feelings. "What about the next level?" Jody said. "What's in it?"

Toni took them up another set of stone steps, these narrower and with a carved bannister, into an area that seemed more private and zoned off. A half-height stone wall ran along a landing looking down on the areas below. Behind her on the risers, Vic said quietly, "I like it, you know. I like it a lot. That was the hard part, coming to terms with that. That I could want something like this, that I could enjoy it." They came to the top of the stairs. Toni had vanished ahead. "Once I admitted the truth—" he shrugged, grinned helplessly—"I didn't see any point fighting my natural inclinations."

Toni poked her head out of a door down the way. "Come on, you've got to see the guest room. This is where you'll stay when you come out to visit. You and Shade," she amended.

Guest room with full private bath and view. Two more smaller guest rooms, with a connecting bath. Master suite with full view of the valley, built-in entertainment wall, sunken tub, Jacuzzi, skylights, hillside views. Reading room and library. Down a short flight of steps, an office/study with glass on two walls, looking up into the hillside trees one way, out onto the cascading stream the other. Built-in computer console. "All the computers come with the house," Toni said, "and are fully integrated and online. We're going to get a lot of work done here."

Jody thought of her own computer, how badly she wanted to get back to it, get out of this high-priced madness and into her own small comfortable life, get back to work on her dreams, her diary, her own forever-dwindled love. She had been oohing and aahing, forcing out delighted compliments at every turn, and she was running out of things to say.

She had a vision of someone at her computer, a stranger. A funny fellow, in a tricorn hat and stockings and a powdered wig. But menacing somehow. Dangerous.

"Oh," she said. "Vic, that reminds me. I don't suppose you ever heard anything about that fingerprint you sent through, did you?"

Vic was suddenly and obviously embarrassed. His face darkened, his version of a blush, and he looked frighteningly angry, but it was clear the anger was at himself.

"Damn," he said. "Damn me, I'm sorry as hell."

"Hey," Jody said. "No big deal. I'm sure it's not on record anywhere, anyway. I just happened to think of it, looking at the computer here."

"No, it's unforgivable of me," he said. "I said I would do it and I didn't. I got all wrapped up in my love life and I kept putting it off, and—"

"He gets worked up about responsibility," Toni said, patting his arm. "It's sort of a code-of-honor thing. It's my fault, I distracted the poor guy, tricking him into marriage."

"Really, it doesn't matter," Jody said. "I forgot all that crap a long time ago."

"I'll do it today," Vic said. "Just as soon as I get back. I'm really sorry."

"Really," Jody said. "Forget it."

She tried to be cheery for the rest of the tour, but the day had come totally apart. She was losing her friend to this high castle, and summer was over, her wonderful summer of freedom, and blackness moved in her spirit, and when they stepped back outside she saw that clouds had come up and there would be no sunset after all, and she could have sworn she saw, out of the corner of her eye, quick little creatures slithering into the shadows of rocks.

The control had finally called back, a week after Toynbee had put a query through channels. As requested, the control had called in the evening, when Leonard was usually out and away: he had taken to bar-hopping, and Toynbee was afraid he was scouting the local talent, though Leonard swore he wasn't, was just going stir-crazy and had to get out.

"Okay, what is it?" the voice said. An American Southerner. You forgot how heavily dominated Washington was by those types, for all its influx of internationals.

"I'm worried about the operation," Toynbee said. "I think we have a personnel situation developing." His heart was thumping. He was playing a double game.

"What sort of personnel situation? Can't it keep? Frankly, I don't think this operation is gonna be viable much longer anyhow."

Toynbee laid it out. It was a question of morale. He was afraid that if his partner didn't get an assignment soon, he would lose it, blow the whole thing off. Even if they were about to cancel the operation, that wouldn't be desirable, would it? Was there anything they could find for Leonard to do, no matter how inessential? Some little bit of activity, orders from on high?

"This will have to go in his jacket," the control said.

"Really, don't you think we might avoid that? He's a good man. Much better than I am, if it comes to that. And this is such an unusual situation. Don't you think, all things considered, that an unofficial solution might be best? Quietest?"

The control agreed, finally, to see what he could do. Toynbee hung up, drenched in a fine sweat. He had pulled it off. He *thought* he had. He had bought them a little more time together. Without Leonard knowing, and without getting him in trouble, either.

He was under no illusion that Leonard would stay, finally. There was no chance that he would give up his life to settle down in Santa Fe with Toynbee. That private-detective idea—laughable, really. Sheer desperation.

As was this. Amazing what you might do for love. Everything was coming apart. He and Leonard were heading, unavoidably, for some sort of trigger-point in time, he saw that quite clearly. And yet he would try anything, anything, to postpone that moment.

A few more days. A few more hours. A few more minutes.

God, it was getting black out there.

Colonel Hall shook his head. Silly bastards. As if he didn't know exactly what was going on with those two queers. But it might be amusing to trifle with them a little.

Let's see, what sort of preposterous and inane busywork could he assign them? Preferably something that would let him watch their antics. His personal clowns.

Thunder rumbled with sudden authority, shaking the walls. Big thunder, if he could hear it all the way in here. When had that come up? Hell, it had been clear three hours ago.

His eye fell on a formal wedding invitation, just opened, on his desk.

Leonard swiveled on his bar stool. Look at it come down.

He had been about to head home, feeling guilty. He hadn't been the best person to live with lately. Toynbee had put up with a lot. Wouldn't hurt to give him a decent evening for once. A spot of cuddle, as the Brit might put it. Leonard wished he had a valid reason to use a British accent himself. He was good at it. He would have been a good actor.

No way he was going out in that mess, though. Have another. Wait a few minutes. Around here they sometimes came big, but they hardly ever lasted long.

A slender blonde stood at his elbow. Pretty fellow. "It's really coming down," he said in a soft and youthful tenor. "I find it exciting. Do you? Buy you a drink?"

"I'm taken," Leonard said.

The street was a dark river shattered with rain. The river was rising.

The downpour caught Jody on Hyde Park just before the turn onto Washington. You could hardly see a foot in front of you. Headlights appeared suddenly, a dazzle of spears in the darkness. The rain made a drumming roar on the roof of the Pontiac, and under it you could hear the guttural rip of the tires in the sheeting water.

She decided to take Paseo to Don Gaspar to Cordova, then Pacheco to Siringo and home. Stay off the main thoroughfares. There would be idiots trying to drive sixty and seventy, full of the false confidence of hurtling metal. There would be trucks hydroplaning, pileups.

The low spot at Marcy wouldn't be running yet. The dip on Don Gaspar might be a problem, and crossing St. Michaels on Pacheco the other one. But the old Pontiac rode high, and she would take it slow and careful while all the little buzzbombs foundered and drowned.

She felt alone, depressed, comfortable, and safe.

. . .

The rain lasted three solid hours, an unheard-of deluge. She knocked around the house in her bathrobe after a long hot soak in the tub, bubble bath and oil and the works. She carried a big tumbler of icy gin with her. Something silver for the darkness. She left the lights off, enjoying the unaccustomed gloom, the shadows blasted away by intermittent lightning.

The way they came back, so sudden and perfect.

She went from window to window, watching the show. Her world gone savage and unfamiliar. The cats were hiding. She spoke reassuringly to them when they peeked out, but they were taking no chances. They knew she couldn't help if this stuff got inside.

When the rain slowed to a drizzle, Shade called. "Sure, come on over," she said. They might as well share the loneliness. They made love on the sofa while the thunder grumbled and receded, and she cried after she came.

Just before dark, they put on boots and rain gear and went carefully down the slick path to the arroyo. It was still drizzling, slightly, a fine chill spray that blew here and there and into their faces and was more nearly a mist than a rainfall.

The arroyo was running, full flood, a tormented river. Boards and bottles went by, dived under, surfaced in the distance. Bushes, boxes, branches snagged with plastic. Once a whole tree. A section of the bank caved in across the water, then one a hundred feet away on their left. You could hear the water, a constant urgent groaning that was also a growl of power.

Vortices, upwelling shapes, and chaos.

"It's beautiful," she said. "Isn't it beautiful?"

"You wouldn't last a second out there," he said. "Did you know the carrying power of water increases with the square of the velocity?" She knew that, or at least could have figured it from the formula for kinetic energy. It seemed a singularly unromantic observation. "At twice the speed, it'll wash away four times as big a rock."

"I wish it would rise and rise and wash the whole world away," she said.

"Be careful what you wish for," he said.

fourth iteration:
the death bardo

You know nothing of yourself here and in this state.
You are like the wax in the honeycomb: What does it
know of fire or of guttering? When it gets to the
stage of the waxen candle, and when light is emitted,
then it knows.

In a similar way, you will know that when you
were alive, you were dead, and only thought yourself
alive.

—Attar of Nishapur

Dreams are mostly empty space.

—The Holy Ghost

27: a wedding at holy ghost

When it finally happened, it happened fast. It seemed to start with the wedding.

Toni and Vic had both wanted a quiet and private ceremony, but there were all the friends of the family, some three generations' worth. You couldn't hurt their feelings by leaving them out, especially not the old traditional folks, who would think that an understated service meant something was wrong with the marriage. Then there were Toni's own friends, dating from high school and before. Then there were Vic's friends, not so many, at least not so many who would care whether or not they got invited to a wedding, but still a few. And there were others, invited for political reasons, because yes, even marrying you must take politics into account. Colonel Hall, for example, to smooth the way to buying their house. And then Hall had, rather rudely, asked if he could bring a couple of friends and the easiest course had been to say yes.

Then, as long as it was going to be a big wedding anyway, why not make it a double? That was Vic's idea. They'd all been sitting around the big house getting drunk after an exhausting day of showers and fittings—well, Vic was exhausted from being on duty—when Vida and Allegra fell to reminiscing about their own courtship. They considered themselves well and truly married in every sense but the official, but there had never been a ceremony. In those days you didn't have ceremonies for gay couples. Thanks to the panic-stricken lobbying of a few moral dwarfs in the state legislature, gay marriages were still not recognized in New Mexico, as indeed they were not in most of the rest of the country, for similar reasons.

But that didn't mean you couldn't have your own observance, couldn't enjoy, like any other citizen, the solemnity of sanctifying ritual.

A wistfulness was on Allegra's face as she spoke, a longing as vivid and plangent as a sustained minor on a guitar. "Why don't you guys get married with us?" Vic said. Toni's jaw dropped in amazement. Then she laughed. It was a wonderful idea.

From that point, it appeared that roughly half the population of Santa Fe might be involved, and besides Vida had always dreamed of an outdoor wedding, and Toni didn't mind, and the idea seemed a natural to Vic, and so they ditched the plans for the Cathedral and brainstormed until Vida came up with the idea of renting the pavilion at Holy Ghost, and that settled it. With any luck at all, the weather would be warm and bright and the aspen would be at their peak, and no stained glass in the world could be more glorious.

The only drawback was that it would be a long car trip for some of the more elderly friends of the family, but they could arrange chauffeured limousines, for those that is who didn't have their own, and they could rent padded chairs instead of simple metal folding chairs, and a big tent, which together with the pavilion would offer shade or shelter from the rain, whichever proved to be necessary when the great day came.

They had a power of work to do, and less than a month to do it in. Invitations had already gone out, and new invitations would have to be printed and sent immediately. Caterers must be found who were willing to set up so far away from the city. Arrangements had to be canceled, new arrangements made. It was all very exciting and fun and adventurous, at least to Toni and Vida and Allegra.

Vic was smart enough to stay out of the way and complain about nothing.

Jody was out of the loop. Toni hardly came to the office at all, and Jody had to carry some of her load with the patients, though they did cut back the number of appointments. Jody called Toni a couple of times at home, but the conversations were unsatisfying: Either Jody was lamely talking about her day and Toni was absentmindedly saying, "Hm. Mm-hm. Sure," or Jody was subject to a blizzard of boring details, the ongoing argument over the train of Vida's gown perhaps.

Allegra was the mother, but she wanted to wear a tux, and Vida, for all her muscle, wanted to wear a bridal dress, so that was all right, but Vida wanted a long train and Allegra—

Shade wasn't much better company, and the truth of the matter was, Jody found herself resisting getting together with him. She thought of going out of town by herself until the day of the wedding, maybe taking the van camping in the mountains. Just shut the clinic down and get away. Work on her theory deep in the woods. She saw herself sitting in the passenger seat on a bright crisp morning, door swung open to the swaying wind, typing away, coffee at hand, running her onboard computer on generator power.

But she was afraid Shade would be gone for good when she got back. As much as she didn't particularly want him and his damned moodiness around right now, not at any one given moment, she wasn't quite ready to let go of what had proved to be the major relationship of her life so far and please God not the last and please God not the best either.

If he was going to leave her, she wanted to watch it happen. Mom and Pop had both vanished into thin air, no good-byes, damn their eyes. She was never going to let that happen again. Probably Shade wasn't the leave-in-the-middle-of-the-night type.

But still. So she stayed, and resented staying. Resented Shade and couldn't let go. Resented the daily drudgery that was all she had left to fill her time, and yet wanted to fill her time. She geared her willpower up, pitched into her theory. *That* was going well, at least. She had designed a family of strange attractors that seemed to her to reproduce the patterning of dream imagery. They required eleven dimensions, a fact she thought had to be related to the supposed eleven dimensions of string theory in physics, but she didn't know enough string theory to do anything with the idea. The shape of I-space allowed for local manifestations of "normal" physical law in some of the dimensions—if you included time in your definition of "local."

Shade seemed plenty interested in her theory, at least, if not in her.

She had decided she was going to publish in book form. The hell with the tight-ass little psychological or medical journals, where they would crucify her, and let no whimper escape to pique the interest of the wider world. She would write a book, a popular book—but one containing a genuine theory with hard edges. Dreams were hot and were getting hotter. Of course they were, poor empty America, nothing in it to feed the soul, and in fact the whole point and purpose and financial scheme of the place seemingly aimed at locking every last human into place, mere cells in the corporate organism. So maybe a popular book would sell like hell to the dream-starved masses, and they would tolerate the math and the science for the sake of dreams and then let the envious and the jealous and the weaker-minded froth in their futile criticism.

She had developed in the last few weeks, as you may have noticed, a somewhat adversarial stance. Her dreams were full of war and battle again. Ish had left her. Why, why did he show when she was happy with Shade, and disappear when she was not? It wasn't *fair.*

She persisted with Vic's—sorry, Dead Men Walking's—exercises, but had nothing remotely resembling an out-of-the-body experience. OBEs, she was calling them now, nonexistent as they were. Obies. She had one dream in which she *dreamed* she had an obie, in fact couldn't get back *in* her body because her body was busy dreaming and she couldn't get its attention, and she was adjusting to the idea that she was going to have to walk around in the nude, a naked spirit, an unclothed and living ghost, when she woke up. But she was lucid all the way through the dream and was perfectly well aware, in spite of her concern, that it was not a real obie.

The day of the wedding dawned as beautifully as ever a day had dawned in New Mexico. The wedding party made a great long progress, like Loren Wingo's time-worm, very like it in reverse because the older friends of the family were at its head, and, whether by design or intuition, the caravan got younger the nearer it approached its termination. Drivers along the way pulled over, assuming a funeral, helped in their assumption by the vanguard troopers in their black gear and astride their motorcycles. One of whom was Vic, wearing white tie and tails under his leathers, because he had thought it would be funny and wonderful to lead the way to his own bondage, throttle, throttle, vroom, and Toni, getting looser and wilder the closer she got to the perfection of her contentment, had thought it funny and wonderful too.

Jody drove the NSX. Bright red for the gaiety. She thought she was twenty or so back in the line. Shade was beside her after all, and it was impossible, despite the gloom of the preceding month, not to feel happy and free, surpassingly happy and free.

They made good time to Glorieta, and then they slowed to a crawl for the six miles to Pecos, and then they wound slowly through that sleepily puzzled town and crept up the crooked and climbing road past the monastery and along the Pecos River, traveling in roughly the direction they had come, but on the other side of the mountains now. And the Pecos glittered and bucked and descended along the way like a hallucination of continuous transparent bells, now on one side and now the other, and astonished fly fishermen, a few of whom probably were not (despite all her experience to the contrary) anal-retentive, back-stabbing cowards, paused standing in shine between fruitless casts and wondered what was happening, how all this pageantry had come so noisily to divide the careful tedium of their pretentious and sanitized communion.

And they came to a bridge, and a sign pointing across the bridge that said IRON GATE and pointing along a little road to the left that said HOLY GHOST, and because of the sign apparently Shade said the lines of what was evidently a poem:

> "Let us roll all our strength, and all
> Our sweetness up into one ball,
> And tear our pleasures with rough strife
> Thorough the iron gates of life."

And she smiled at him, and he said:

> "Thus, though we cannot make our sun
> stand still, yet we will make him run."

And that seemed a good enough motto with which to seize the day. And now the caravan crept even more slowly over one-lane wooden bridges under which ran the thready, superluminous clarity of the Holy Ghost broken on the world's dark rocks and between summer homes set back in pockets of the year's last green, sweet private prospects that somehow wore the look of coming abandon, as if they knew they were soon to be shut down and soon to lose the spirits that had given them habitation and soon to be forgotten in drifting snow.

And they climbed a tall narrow trail, limos longer than the curves they nevertheless managed to negotiate and Cadillacs and Beemers and Range-Rovers and Ultimas and Integras and Porsches and six-tired pickups with roll bars and fog lamps and five kinds of antenna waving over their glossy muscularity, and rusty old Galaxies and Buicks and every sort of vehicle almost save bicycles and horse-drawn sulkies. A boy and a girl in a dilapidated truck going the other way pulled into one of the few wide spots, and watched, and after a few moments realized this was not a parade that would end soon, and cracked themselves two new beers and laughed and pointed.

They passed over a high ridge with a view of the whole wilderness and at last down into the campground, and began filing into the parking spaces, the limos nearer the pavilion, and the boy and girl, still watching from their high vantage though the road was clear in front of them now and they could have gone on, saw a brilliant confetti of people spill from their automobiles like tasseled seeds from tight pods, and swirl through the valley on currents of merriment.

They had not been there fifteen minutes when the ceremony commenced, and Vic and Toni and Vida and Allegra stood beside each other, radiant on a bridge over Holy Ghost Creek, and said their vows and, more swiftly than Jody could have believed, were man and wife and lover and lover, and then it was on to the reception, which was not over swiftly. For the good things that last as long as our lives are confirmed in an instant, and the instant passes, and we must therefore celebrate at length. Too small to perceive, almost, those instants, too small for our emotions to inhabit, and so we must arrange for their memory to live in us.

And the wind shook the aspens to glory on the vaulting slopes of the mountains, and the blue of the sky was so deep and clear as to be almost intolerable, and the bright water ran and the music of the bright water went on and on as it would for thousands of years yet.

There were a great many people at the reception whom Jody did not know, but a surprising number that she did. Shade kept at her side loyally all the afternoon, and she was the first person Toni ran to for a kiss and a hug, after of course her parents, and so Jody was accompanied and established and truly a part of it all and not alone.

Colonel Wilbur Goodloe Hall was there, and came up and greeted her. Perhaps he hoped to sell her also a home in Anasazi Heights, but there was no chance of that. He spoke of deteriorating neighborhoods and the necessity for people of good quality, people who actually made contributions to society, to associate with other people of good quality, and to be secure in their environs. There was, she thought, something cruel in his tone, something mocking, the edge that one senses under the veneer of a cultured sociopath, and he made her uncomfortable.

He spoke of how his old neighborhood in Jackson had run down, how it and really the whole state had become tribal, had gone over to the blacks, and that was why he had left. He laughed and said the same thing was happening here, but in reverse: The Anglos were moving in and improving the neighborhood. She had run into his attitude before. It was true that bigotry was general in the United States and for that matter general across the races, and that it was not localized to the South, and it was true that there were very many good-souled Mississippians who were not infected with it. But there were some Mississippians who carried their evil with them with a naughty gladness, a defining perversion, there was an occasional Mississippian who, like an overly manicured pedophile with photos of nude little boys, could not wait to sidle up to you and show you a little flash of his corruption to see if you shared the taste.

The whole time he spoke, he did not look at her. His eyes were up and down on Shade, cold and rude and finally dismissive as Shade played the dumb bored jock who just wants to get his old lady home and get her in the sack and is hoping he won't have to propose to her to do it because she's all emotional because of this damned wedding.

When Hall finally moved on, Shade said, "Who the hell is that?"

"Sorry about that. He was a patient once. He sold Toni and Vic the house, which is the only reason I didn't just walk away. I think the deal is final, but I didn't want to take a chance on doing anything that might cause trouble for her."

Bruno Sandoval proved a good antidote for the Colonel. He was there as Vic's guest, and Jody thought she understood now the remark he had made a few months back about his "two doctors." He hadn't meant Jody and Toni. He had meant Jody and Dead Men Walking.

Toni had stolen Shade away for a dance, and perhaps Sandoval had waited for that moment to have Jody to himself. Tears ran down his face when he spoke of how beautiful the ceremony had been, and she assumed he was thinking of his own marriage and missing his wife. But later she saw him dancing with a vivacious, blue-eyed, gray-haired woman, and then escorting the woman laughing to the drinks table, and she was glad for him but oddly jealous.

She and Shade danced together, and he was a marvelous dancer, swift and light on his feet, and she thought how strange it was that they had never danced before and wondered if perhaps they should make a point of it, if it would help keep them together.

Then Vic and Toni and Vida and Allegra danced all in a ring, and Toni waved Jody and Shade in, and it was warm and happy and full of laughter and her old hope revived itself like flames from a fanned coal, that they might make a friendship of couples.

Afterwards, she spotted the gay couple from the reading and the gallery, the one sitting on a wall of the pavilion looking up at the light-struck aspen and the other standing behind him with a hand on his companion's back. Feeling a remnant regret, that she had perhaps somehow offended them at the gallery, she went over determined on comfortable sociability.

When she came up to them, though, she saw that the sitting man was crying. The standing man handed him a handkerchief, and he wiped his eyes, blew his nose.

"Oh, I'm sorry," she said.

The one who looked like Tom Cruise smiled, a brilliant white smile like Cruise's. "Not at all," he said. "He always cries at weddings and funerals."

"Which is this?" the sitting man said. His accent was British.

Jody felt an impulse to put her hand out and pat him on the shoulder, but resisted. He stood, and delivered a smile himself, if a rueful one. "My apologies," he said. "Really. I've always been an emotional chap." He looked at his companion, and had to dab his eyes again.

"Are you friends of the family?" Jody said, at a loss for words.

The Brit seemed unable to speak, seemed almost to be choking.

"Friends of a friend," Tom Cruise said, still smiling.

"Wasn't it a beautiful ceremony?" she said.

"It was, it was," Tom Cruise said. "Beautiful." The Brit had teared up again, and now he had to turn away and look up at the mountains.

"Well," Jody said. "Well—it was a real pleasure meeting you." She shook Tom's hand firmly, and walked away for a glass of champagne. Some things you just couldn't put right.

Shade wanted to walk the trail a bit, and they headed back for her car, where they had stowed more serviceable shoes.

"It's a steep access from here," she said, pointing up the hill from the trailhead. "But you get a good three-quarter-mile hike through the aspen. It comes down to the creek at the far end of the camp-ground, and then runs along the creek for a couple of miles, very level, meadow walking. We can go up here, or go down to the end and walk the meadows."

"We're here," he said. "Let's do this one."

She ran her finger over the map graven into the wood of the trail-head sign. "See how it runs up the mountain and hooks up with the Windsor Trail," she said wistfully. "I've always wanted to ski over the top. You could leave a car here, put in at the ski basin, maybe camp one night up around the lakes somewhere, then come on down here."

"Let's do it," he said.

She was thrilled. "Really?" she said. "You'd really go with me?"

"It sounds wonderful," he said.

He went up the switchbacked access like a goat, waited on the trail for her. She was breathing hard when she caught up, but he didn't seem winded at all. "You damned animal," she said, and he laughed. "Why would anybody buy a stair-climber?" she said.

They walked the trail in silence, except for exclamations at a clump of wood mist or the fat-coned firewheels that she called rocket daisies, or long sighs standing in the shifting impossible shadow and luminescence of the aspen.

After an hour's slow wandering, they came down to the creek, and he bent and scooped up handfuls of the water and drank. "Aren't you worried about Giardia?" she said.

"How could I be hurt by something called Holy Ghost?" he said.

When they got back to the pavilion, the dancing seemed to have ebbed a bit, though Vida and Allegra and a few other couples were slow-waltzing, and the serious drinking had begun. The light was get-ting longer, and the older couples were leaving, so that Toni was busy with almost continual good-byes. Vic and Bruno met them, arms around each other, weaving a bit, and put snifters of a pale amber liq-uid in their hands. "Bellinis," Sandoval said. "He is corrupting me. It is a peach liqueur and champagne. He said you would like it."

Jody hated Southern Comfort, but this was no time to be picky. "Guess what," she said. She thumped Shade on the arm. "He's declared himself."

"You're getting married?" Vic said, incredulous.

Jody laughed. "No. But we're doing something almost as dangerous. We're skiing over the mountains together. Just as soon as we can after enough snow falls."

So then they had to explain. Vic was concerned. Extreme cold was tricky, tricky stuff, especially at high altitude. They had better practice the route first, and take plenty of the right gear, and plenty of food, and let the rangers know, and—

Sandoval thought it was a wonderful idea. "This is a woman, eh? Listen, if this hulking gentleman defaults, you give me a call. I have taken this trail many times myself in my younger days. Let me tell you where you must be most careful of your trail—"

So all was merry for a while longer, but then the light went behind the mountains and cold shadows flooded the valley, though in the flat world it would be day for hours yet, and most of the people had gone, and finally Vida and Allegra and Vic and Toni kissed the lingerers good-bye and left it for the caterers to clean up and headed off, Vida and Allegra to the home they had never slept in as a married couple, and Vic and Toni to their hotel in Albuquerque, whence to the airport in the morning, whence to San Francisco and then to Hawaii for three weeks. Three!

They had agreed it would be all right to cut back the office schedule for the duration of the honeymoon so that Jody wouldn't be overloaded: "And then you need to take a trip, girl. You been working way too hard, way too long."

With the advent of evening and the litter of the party and the new emptiness of the campground, Jody felt her depression returning. "Let's get out of here," she said to Shade. She felt, suddenly, that she wanted nothing more than to curl up with a cup of hot chocolate under a blanket in her chair, and be alone, except for her warm purring babies. Her friendship with Toni was over, and winter was on the way, and not even the promise of high clean adventure could forestall the chill knifing into her bones. "You drive," she said.

Shade piloted the NSX down to Pecos at speeds she could not believe, but he seemed in total control, and she felt anyway too fatalistic to protest.

Zooming up the highway toward home, she had a worrisome thought. "What did they do about Vic's motorcycle?" she said.

"One of his cop friends rode up in the limo with Toni and her parents. He took it back."

"Well, that takes care of that," she said.

28: the plot thickens

Jody was deciding whether to put graphs and how many and quantified data and how much in her book and whether or not to include them in the main text or exile them to an appendix, which seemed by far the more intelligent move, at least for a book that aspired to popularity.

Among her professional readers, the psychologists would no doubt disdain her psychological expertise, the physicians her medicine, and the mathematicians her math. She felt the familiar frustration of any well-trained generalist in the age of the limited, anyone who was able to make connections across usually disparate realms: Nobody to talk to.

Except Shade. He had gotten fired up about her book. They sat hours in the evenings, hammering out points. He made her explain the workings of her attractors over and over until he got them completely, and then he became more excited. He asked her to let him take disk copies of her work home, to study on his own time. She acceded, somewhat reluctantly. Surely he wasn't planning to steal her theory and bring out a book himself—

Come on, Jody. Lose the paranoia. This isn't Lobo's novel.

But the book, working on the book—it had replaced their sex life, she sometimes thought. Not good. She would worry about it later. When she got through with the book.

"It'll take a year, maybe more," he said once. "To bring the book out, you know. Probably more, because it's so dense and technical."

"You think it's too dense?" she said. "I'm writing as plainly as I know how."

"That's not what I mean," he said. "I'm just warning you what to expect. Publishers move slowly. And with something like this, they'll be even slower."

"Hell, I've got to sell the damn thing first," she said.

Another evening he came in grave and somber, lacking his recent enthusiasm. And for once he didn't want to talk ideas. "Have you ever thought of the danger?" he said.

"Danger?" she said. "What danger?"

"To you. If you try to publish."

"What are you talking about?"

"There could be people out there who consider your work too valuable for general release. Who'll want a monopoly on it. And the only way to get that is to get rid of you."

She giggled. "Have you been reading your own books? I thought *I* was paranoid. It isn't like you can patent a theory. If you could, think how much money Newton could have made. A nickel for the gravity, folks. Just a nickel, one low rate all the time, anywhere on Earth."

He frowned. "It's not that far-fetched. Theories have applications. Maybe there are people who want to get to those applications first and control them."

"No way," she said. "I think my theory might be important for *understanding* dreams. But I can't imagine any conceivable commercial application—or any application at all, really, except maybe the well-being of individual humans."

"I can," he said. "Not commercial, maybe, but—"

"What?"

"I missed it at first," he said. "One of the things you're working on is the architecture of intelligence. Not the brain, I understand that. But the patterns produced by the brain. You *have* to be touching on that subject. It's too deeply linked to dreaming for you to avoid."

"So?"

"So suppose your ideas could be used to help develop true artificial intelligence. Machines that didn't have the same biomechanical substratum, but that generated similar operations. That would have tremendous commercial implications. Not to mention the military—"

She was incredulous. "You don't really think that's likely, do you?"

"Listen, I'm just saying sometimes what we're doing has a wider impact than we realize it does. I'm just saying it pays to be careful. Tell me this. If you knew your life was in danger, if you knew it could get you killed, would you be willing not to publish?"

"Shade, you're scaring me. Do you know something I don't?" She thought of his fascination with science, his mysterious connections to the Institute. His mysterious arrival on the local scene, how little she really knew of his background.

"Not at all. It just occurred to me, that's all, and so I'm asking. Maybe I do spend too much time thinking up spy plots."

"What would I do with myself?" she said. "Wouldn't they shoot me anyway? How could they know I wouldn't double-cross them and publish after all?"

"You could go into top-secret research," he said. "You'd be protected. You'd be amazed how many scientists it happens to."

"And disappear from the real world? Thank you, no. I have a life and I like it." Then the obvious struck her, like a fall of sunlight past a broken cloud, and she laughed in relief. "Shade, listen. This is not only silly, it's completely moot."

"What do you mean?"

"Even if you assumed there was some deep dark master spy out there who would want what I've got—which I don't grant for a minute. If the book's already published, they're not gonna kill me, right? I mean, what would be the point? The information would already be public knowledge. And," she summed up triumphantly, "how the hell are they going to know I'm working on it until it gets published? Huh? Tell me that."

"Okay," he said. "Okay. I just wanted to bring the subject up."

"Well, you brought it up. You did your duty."

"Yes I did," he said. "Yes I did."

That night she dreamed that spies were after her, but it seemed to be a comedy, very British, almost Gilbert and Sullivan. One of the songs was a corker, and she was sure she would remember it when she woke—there had been a delightful rhyme on "intelligence" and "Pass me over that jar of jelly, gents," which then segued into something terribly clever about Jelly Roll Morton and Horton the Who—but it vanished as soon as she opened her eyes.

She had the feeling she was forgetting something else, some little nittering fact the dream had brought up, a neglible bit of history that was nevertheless of tremendous importance. But she had to go to work and it was one of those dreams that crumbled faster the harder you tried.

She and Shade did get away once while Vic and Toni were gone, hiking the trail over the mountains. It was late October, and if they were going to reconnoiter before the snows came, they had to get right after it. Actually, there had been a dusting of snow three days after the wedding, and it was already cold up there after sunset, and more might come at any moment. They convoyed to Holy Ghost in the van and the NSX the day before their trek, and tracked down the ranger and let her know what they were up to, and left the van and drove back together in the NSX. They would use a similar arrangement when they skied over the top.

Shade convinced her they could make the hike in a single day if they started early, so they packed for emergency camping only, and drove up to the ski basin before sunrise, and set out shortly after dawn. When they reached Spirit Lake, around noon, she was sorry they hadn't decided to make an overnight—not because she was too tired, but because the mountains and valleys and forests were so stunning she wanted to take her time, absorb as much as possible. They did eat a long lunch, and then napped half an hour in a sunny spot out of the wind. There were ghosts in the mountains, Jody was certain. Old presences, one with the wind and the sun and the stones. Old time still there, still haunting the high places, its last refuge.

They came on down, and she did begin to get tired then, jolting and sliding on the crooked trail, though Shade seemed unaffected. How could such a big man move so easily and so lightly? In the late afternoon they struck the Holy Ghost trail, and not long afterward came into the part of it she recognized, and so she knew they were safe, and let go a tension she hadn't known she was holding. By sunfall, they were crossing the footbridge over the creek into the campground, and they walked slowly along the road and there was the van glimmering in the dusk.

It was ten o'clock by the time they had collected his Mustang from the ski basin and gotten back home, and although she had eaten along the way probably two pounds of M&Ms and peanuts—trail mix for lazy people—besides breakfast and lunch, she was possessed of a ferocious hunger, and they collected a twelve-piece box of KFC's finest and finished it all, throwing fragments of skin to the babies, and fell asleep on the sofa and woke up at two and went to bed.

Monday she was so sore she could hardly move, and sore but elated all week, and bragged about the hike to Consuela and her patients and anybody else who would listen. Toni and Vic were due back that weekend, and she couldn't wait to tell Toni all about it, though she was hoping Toni wouldn't one-up her with wonder stories of The Greatest Honeymoon in Recorded History.

Toni didn't call, and Sunday evening Jody called her but only got the machine. Monday there was a message on the machine at the office, Toni wouldn't be in today, but would be in full-time starting tomorrow. Tuesday, middle of the morning, Toni came into Jody's office. She didn't look happy. Wedded unbliss already? Or maybe she was just suffering the letdown blues. Back in the real world, back at work.

Jody had a taste of those blues herself. She was between patients, and was busy updating the dreamer logs and binding them for delivery to DormaVu, a tedious job she had postponed as long as possible. "Could you have dinner with us tonight?" Toni said.

"Sure," Jody said happily. "I've been trying to get in touch with you. I've really missed you guys. How was Hawaii?"

"Seven o'clock," Toni said. "My place. Just you. Hawaii was fine."

She turned and left the room. Jody wanted to call after her, "What's wrong with Shade?" She felt insulted somehow, but she'd already said yes, and she didn't want a quarrel with her friend over her lover. Best go along with it, see what the objection was.

"My place" meant the apartment still. The message on Toni's machine had given the new number, but explained that the house wasn't ready and this number would be the active one for a few days yet. More weirdness. Toni didn't usually like to entertain at the apartment, seeming to prefer going out or using her parents' place. Before the house, she'd never taken much interest in where she lived, and the apartment was tiny and plain.

Maybe it wasn't Shade at all. Maybe she and Vic really were having newlywed troubles, and were planning to seek Jody's advice. It didn't seem likely—Toni preferred giving advice to taking it—but who knew? Jody put the matter out of her mind and got back to work.

That evening, Jody was happy. She'd made love to Shade just before leaving, showering and dashing madly out to the garage afterwards. From work in the afternoon, she'd had a long talk with him—he had been the one who called, and had seemed happy just to yak for a while, none of that male impatience to get off the line, which was just that they hated talking on the telephone but which always felt like they didn't want to talk to *you*.

He hadn't been upset about not being included, said he had plenty to keep him busy, and said he'd be waiting with his clothes off when she got home.

"When?" she had said. "Home from work, or home from Toni's?"

"Both," he had said.

One down, one to go.

The apartment was ground-floor, one of five, the building and the small common lot screened by a dilapidated coyote fence. Entry was off a dirt alleyway. It was still just barely light, the sun having just set. A deep ruddiness was on everything, banking off the fading clouds. The shadows were that much deeper and stranger. Jody let herself through the gate of the postage-stamp-sized terrace to Toni's place. Double sliding glass doors led in through a small living room, directly back to a kitchen/dining area on the other side of a two-seater bar.

Through the glass, Jody could see Vic and Toni in the kitchen, kissing. It was a long kiss, and looked pretty intense. For some reason Jody found the sight disturbing, as though it meant they were in league against her. She supposed it was because she was jealous, and reminded herself sternly to update her emotions, she didn't have any need to be jealous anymore, what had she just gotten through doing, let them top that.

She stepped back into the shadow of the wall, waited until they broke the clinch, gave it another thirty seconds, and rapped on the glass. Toni had gone to the stove. Now she turned, saw Jody, and came to let her in. Something was wrong with the way she moved.

She didn't have her usual bounce. There had been a motion Jody had been expecting, that motion of delight when you first realize your friend has come, and it hadn't occurred.

Vic hung back, leaning against the kitchen wall. He was watching Jody with a look that she imagined he gave to suspects in the cases he was working. Toni was at the stove again, her back to Jody. "Do you want a drink?" she said. "It's just pasta and red sauce tonight."

"Bourbon, I guess," Jody said. No one had offered to take her coat, her purse.

Vic got a glass from the cabinets. He pulled a tray of ice from the freezer, cracked it, splashed it half-full from a bottle standing on the counter, handed the drink to Jody.

"Look," Jody said. "What's going on here? I'm really getting a creepy feeling from you guys. Have I done something to piss you off? If I have, why the hell did you invite me over? Why don't you just say what's bothering you, and I can apologize or leave?"

Toni sighed, straightened her shoulders. She turned to look at Vic. "I can't do it this way," she said. "Let's just out with it, okay?"

"Okay," Vic said. "Probably better that way anyhow."

He turned to Jody. "Can I take your coat? You want to sit down?"

"Why don't I just find out what the hell is going on first, and then I can decide whether or not I'm going to stay for that drink," Jody said. Her legs were trembling. They hadn't been this weak coming down the Holy Ghost trail. "Right now I'm thinking I'm out of here."

"Jody," Vic said, startling her. She couldn't remember that he had ever used her name before. "Why don't you tell us what that study of yours really was?"

"What are you talking about?" Jody said. "You know everything I do. I told Toni exactly what it was." Toni was staring at her now, and Jody stared back. "Listen, Toni, you agreed it would be okay for me to use the office. If it turned out that it bugged you after all, I'm sorry, okay? I mean, I'll pay rent for the time, or—or whatever you—"

She was afraid she was going to break into tears.

"That's not it," Toni said.

"What is it, then? Do you think I'm skimming somehow? Do you want rent *and* a cut of the proceeds? I've spent most of it already, but you're welcome to what's left. You're not acting much like a friend right now, you know."

"Read this," Vic said, handing her a sheet of paper.

The paper was crisp, heavy bond. It bore the seal of the Justice Department of the United States of America. There was only a single short message:

You have submitted a request for information to our files. You are hereby advised that the material in question is classified information vital to the security of the United States. You must return any documents which may have inadvertently come into your possession immediately herewith, and you must be advised that further requests for this information will be denied. If you retain any improperly obtained material, or fail to heed any of the requirements of this directive, you are subject to penalty for treason against the United States of America.

"I don't get it," Jody said, handing the paper back.

"I never told you about the prints," Vic said.

"The prints?" Jody said stupidly.

"The prints from your computer. The ones I forgot to run till you reminded me."

"I still don't get it."

"I sent a request through to the FBI, Jody. To see if they had those prints on file. At first I thought I was getting somewhere. They were the prints of an interesting sort of fellow, a small-time con artist consulting for various government agencies. A British national who became an American citizen when he was fifteen. But when I tried to follow up, find out what he was up to now, all of a sudden the curtain came down. I got this letter the next day."

"I'm trying real hard here, but I still don't see the connection. Why would somebody like that be interested in what's on my computer? Are you sure you haven't made a mistake?"

"Somebody's made a mistake. I don't think it's me."

"Listen, Vic, so you've got some sort of spooky criminal running around doing weird things. So you don't like getting warnings from the Justice Department. I'm sorry. But why take it out on me? *I* didn't do anything to you. And as for you—" She turned back to Toni.

"What does any of it have to do with *you?* Why are you giving me the cold shoulder?"

"Jody," Vic said again. "Look at it a moment. There's an inexplicable burglary at your home, involving your files. Somehow or other, somebody representing one of the clandestine agencies is involved. Not long afterward, there's *another* inexplicable burglary, this one at your office. We look around, we wonder why. What could it possibly be about? And the only thing that comes to mind, the only possible connection, is that you are running some sort of big study for a company with connections to the CIA."

"For God's sake, Langley? My God, Vic, get *real.* Maybe they are connected, but why do you think I left them? Other than that I hated the work," she added. "And for that matter, what about Toni? She worked for them, too. Does that make her some sort of spy?"

"I was a long way from anything relating to production, Jody. I patched up people's emotional troubles so they could keep reporting to work, I advised on aftereffects."

"This is so ridiculous. I can't believe you two are doing this to me."

"We're not *doing* anything," Vic said. "We're trying to understand something."

"Well, understand this. I'm not a goddamned spy. I never did any kind of clandestine work for Langley. Hell, the study wasn't even Langley, it was DormaVu."

"A wholly-owned subsidiary."

"Yes, but a *subsidiary*. Toni knows all this. She saw the entire proposal when I was trying to get the study, and I gave her a copy of their protocols. She also knows, or she ought to know, that there is absolutely nothing secret about any of the data. I told her at the outset that she was welcome to review any and all of the information the study generated. She has a key to the files. At the time, I was thinking maybe we'd come across something of interest to her in her work. She hasn't been interested, but the offer still stands."

Jody shook her head, as if to free her anger, like static electricity from her hair. "Dammit, Toni. I really hate this. *Read* the damn files. There's *nothing* going on. I wish there had been. I was just a damn pill-pusher. I didn't even know whether the pills I was handing out were the real things or the fakes. I took records of physiological and neurological changes—none of which, I might add, showed anything outside the norms. I recorded the dreams of the subjects, and what can I tell you? They were just *dreams*. You can check all this out for yourself. Hell, you can read my private journal, if you want to. You can read my goddamned *book,* as soon as I get it written. If you can find *anything* in *any* of that that could conceivably interest the CIA or the FBI or ATF or the KGB or the KKK or the fucking *Gestapo,* go to it."

"She's really mad," Toni said to Vic.

"Damn right," Jody said. She could feel herself radiating in the infrared, she felt as though her hair were standing straight out, fully charged. "*I* get burglarized at home. *I* get burglarized at the office. *I'm* the victim. And my friends treat me like I was the fucking criminal."

"It's my office, too," Toni said mildly.

"Is she that good an actress?" Vic asked Toni.

"No," Toni said. "She's intelligent enough, but she's no good at hiding her emotions. Repressing them, yes, but not hiding them. Look at how flushed she is."

"Some people call it honesty," Jody snapped. "Some people would say that if you had a friend and she was having thoughts like this, the *honest* thing for her to do would be to come to you about it, not sneak around behind your back laying traps."

"It wasn't like that," Vic said.

"How was it, then? And what business is it of yours, anyway?"

"We may have handled this wrong," Vic said. "That's my fault, not Toni's. She didn't come to me with any suspicions. I went to her. She wanted to do just what you said, approach you directly. I talked her out of it. If I've done you wrong, I hope you'll forgive me."

Jody looked at Toni, who gave her the same gaze back—flat, considering, neither friendly nor judgmental. "Why couldn't you come to me directly?" she said to Vic. "What's so all-fired threatening and dangerous about me?"

"Jody, I'm a cop. I see shit all the time. I see incredible shit. I see what people can do to each other. I'm as good a judge of character as you will ever meet, and I get surprised all the time by what people are capable of, what parts of themselves they keep hidden.

"When I sent the fingerprint through and hit this sealed record, I got a really bad feeling. A hunch, okay? Maybe it was connected to the perp, and had nothing to do with you. The truth is, I had the feeling when I walked onto the burglary scene at your office, before I ever ran the print. Then I put it out of my mind, I ignored it out of existence. Now this has kicked it back in.

"I hope you can understand," he continued. "I've seen the way these people work. I know more about it than I want to. If it had been just you, I would have dropped the whole investigation then and there, and left you to your fate. I'm not in the business of keeping people from playing with the Devil, and I don't walk into the fire to save them when they get what's coming. But this was different. Toni was involved. Toni was your partner. Whatever you were doing was your business—"

"I wasn't *doing* anything, dammit!"

"Maybe, but I had no way of knowing that."

"You were my fucking *guru*." Jody was crying now, tears of helpless rage. She despised them, felt them as weakness. "You were inside my *dreams*."

Vic shrugged. Toni didn't react. So she had known. Maybe Dead Men Walking came home to bed and told her funny stories about the little Anglo chick who wanted to be a shaman. "How could you?" Jody whispered. "How could you?"

"Jody, I learned a long time ago that unusual knowledge doesn't mean *all* knowledge, and unusual power doesn't mean *all* power. The stupidest thing a shaman can do is assume he's in control. All I knew for certain was that if you *were* into some dirty business, you weren't just putting yourself in danger. You were putting Toni in danger. And I had to do something about that, because I'm in love with Toni for-ever."

Jody was somehow shocked to hear Vic state his affection so plainly.

"You're right," she said. "You could have handled this a whole lot better. Both of you. Maybe you meant well, but it's going to take me a while to forgive you. If I ever do."

"Fair enough," Vic said.

"So where does this leave me?" Jody said. "Twisting in the wind? No idea what's happening to me, or why? Some sort of spy-versus-spy nonsense that I don't know a damn thing about that I've somehow stumbled into, and no friends I can count on to stand behind me." She picked up her drink from the counter, hoping the movement would forestall more tears. The ice was almost totally melted.

"It's probably nothing," Vic said. "It's probably just the way I feel about Toni that's making me overreact. Overprotective to the point of paranoia. I don't have any physical evidence to connect the scene at your office with the break-in at your house. And as far as the print from your house, well, the guy's got a history. Just because he's con-nected to this or that set of spooks, that doesn't mean he's working for them when he does the job at your place."

"So what the hell was he *doing* at my place? What does some lat-ter-day cross between James Bond and a petty thief think he can pull off my computer that is of any earthly use to anybody?" But she was thinking of Shade, and his odd warning.

Don't publish. Your life may be in danger.

"Who knows?" Vic said. "One thing you learn in my job is that a whole lot of stuff just never adds up. Things happen that don't make any sense and never will."

"Yeah," Jody said bitterly. "That's what you told me before, and I believed you. I believed you, and I put it all out of my mind."

She tried to raise the glass to her lips, but her hands were trem-bling too badly. She felt a sudden overwhelming urge to throw the drink in their faces. Before she knew she was going to, she gave a great cry of rage and hurled the glass with all her force across the living room. It struck the plate glass of the sliding doors into a radiating star. The liquid dripped.

"You two," she said, her voice husky. "You two can go straight to hell."

She strode to the doors, yanked them open, went out. A shard of glass fell to the floor.

"Is she going to be all right?" Vic said to Toni.

"I think so," Toni said. "Her anger's a good sign, means she's in good working order. And anyway, there's not much help she would let us give her right now."

Outside, Jody sprinted for the car. She pounded on the steering wheel, then put her forehead against its rim and sobbed. When she had recovered sufficiently, she found a Kleenex, dried her face. She cranked the engine.

It was a good thing for the general public that traffic was light on the way home. And a good thing for Jody there were no cops patrolling Cerrillos. As it was, she left a family of five in a battered old Nash white-faced on the side of the road, and a young lowrider in gang colors straddling the median and jabbing his index finger into the air behind her.

Shade was sitting downstairs, in her chair, reading under the lamp. Her manuscript. "I lied," he said, as she crashed through the door from the garage. "I still have my clothes on." Then, seeing her agitation: "What's the matter?" He set the pages aside, came to her. She flung her purse across the room. She wanted to howl, but she couldn't talk.

"Jody, what's the matter?" He took her arms in his grip. "Are you hurt? Can you breathe?" She shook her head violently, stared in his face, the tears boiling over.

"Not hurt," she managed, her voice a croak. "I can breathe."

"What in the hell is going on?" Comprehension dawned. "Did you fight with Toni?"

She nodded. What was his part in all this? Why was he so interested in her work? It had all started with him, when she had seen him in the arroyo. Who *was* he?

"Baby, baby," he said. "That's awful. Come here." He folded her roughly against his chest. She resisted, stiffened herself. He didn't force her, patted her hair. "Listen, it happens. It happens with the best of friends. What did you fight about?"

Blind Lemon was bumping her ankles. No way. No way she was telling him.

But he soothed her and murmured encouraging things, how it would get better, how when you fought with somebody you loved, it hurt the worst of all, but whatever the problem was, they would work it out, she and Toni would work it out, because they were true friends.

And she was able to resist no longer, and wilted into his arms. She didn't care if he was a master spy from Altair, sent here to kill her before she could develop instantaneous transportation as a result of her research into out-of-the-body experiences. She needed someone to cry to, someone to hold her, a warm body in the night.

He lifted her in his arms and carried her as lightly as a baby up to bed, and gently undressed her, and washed her face with a warm rag, and tucked her in, and got in beside her and drew her against his chest, and she wept for an hour. Blind Lemon and Static joined them, lying heavily against their legs, purring. And she fell asleep at last.

And Ish came to see her again.

29: the shit hits the bloody fucking fan

She was driving the bus backwards, stuck in reverse. Down the dark narrow streets near the plaza, except that it was also the Windsor Trail at night. She was barely missing parked cars, rocks, trees. The bus was out of control, careening downhill.

If it hit anything it would blow up. No, that was that movie. This was a dream. Ish sat on the front passenger seat. His life, the lives of all the passengers depended on her.

She walked down the aisle of the bus. It was a church now. Fay Jones had turned it into a church a long time ago, after the crash. Right there on the rocks, where it had landed. You came and you sat in the Church Bus, and you thought about all the innocent victims. Flight 800. Six people dead in the Arkadelphia tornado. Vic and Toni, murdered in their sleep.

It was a beautiful idea, a church of mourning. It was a beautiful idea to use the wrecked bus as the memorial. Like the sunken Titanic, *except you could go in.*

Ish was sitting in the very back seat. He was an old man, and he didn't look very good. The cords of his neck sagged, his hair was white and thin, and he leaned forward on a walking stick. He pretended not to see her, because she was a ghost. She had died in the crash. He had mourned her a long time. He had come here on their anniversary every year since.

Ish, *she said.* Will we ever make love again?

I don't see how, *he said, waggling his lowered head no.* After all, you're dead.

He lifted his head, and the blue eyes were clear and startling. They weren't yellow at all, they weren't rheumy and old. They were the eyes that could see right through you and love everything they saw. Joy leaped in her veins. He was still here. He was still Ish.

He smiled, a young man's smile in the hollowed and drooping face. The shit has really hit the bloody fucking fan, now, he said. His accent was British now, and she realized that he had been undercover with MI5 for years now. The war has finally started, he said.

She could hear it now, outside their wrecked airliner, the sound of gunfire, the whistle of incoming shells, the whump of distant bombardment. This was their last stand. They had gotten behind the enemy lines after all, had crash-landed in the mountains of Tierra Nueva.

She held out her arm, and he rose, shakily, and took it. They went out through the jagged hole in the fuselage, stepping carefully. Out into the cold and the blowing whiteness and the hip-deep drifts. America's last hope, mom and pop, two guerrillas at the end of the world.

They went out, the old man and the ghost, to do battle.

Several miles away, high in the hills off Hyde Park Road, a man sat in the private office of his 7,500-square-foot villa. On the television in the far wall, a Howard Stern rerun was playing. Every so often, a message scrolled from right to left across the screen, like the local station's thunderstorm warnings: *Line check completed. Line secure. Commencing line check.* In the upper-right-hand corner of the screen, the time blinked: 3:13. 3:13. 3:14.

"We've got a problem," said the voice on the phone.

"You damn well better have a problem, Freddy," said Colonel Wilbur Goodloe Hall. "And a big one, to get me out of bed this time of night."

"The shit has hit the fan," said the voice. "You've got to get on the stick."

"Are you going to tell me what you're talking about, or are you just going to sit there spouting clichés? Because I was having me an A-1 dream, and I believe I could get back to it. There was this nigger girl with a pussy where her mouth was supposed to be—"

"Will you can it, you overblown asshole? This is big enough to bring us both down."

Colonel Hall sighed. "What is it now?"

"It's those two clowns you're controlling. They've screwed up big-time."

"Who sent me those clowns? Did I pick 'em myself? Or did you, in your infinite fucking wisdom, decide they were the very best men for the job?"

"It doesn't matter. You're going to have to handle it."

"Handle what? What have they done?"

"They've left tracks, that's what they've done. I don't know how, I don't know where. Probably during that phase-two intromission."

"The burglary, you mean. Which *you* ordered, may I remind you. Maybe if you had given me credit for a little decision-making. Maybe if you hadn't insisted on sending in every damn play from the side-lines—"

"Shut up, Hall. What's done is done. The point is, they're made."

One of these days you and me are going on a hunting trip in Mississippi, Colonel Hall thought to himself. *Long time from now, when all this is behind us and forgotten. Yeah, we'll get out there in our hip boots, waving our shotguns and drinking bourbon in the blind. Watching them ducks fly in. You'll be eating it up, doing it just like the good old boys do. Thinking how you're really a good old boy yourself, even if you do hail from Hoboken. And right about then, good buddy, you are going to pay for that "Shut up." Yessir, you are going to pay dearly.*

"We flag their files," Freddy said. "Right? The computer gets a request from the feebs. Can you identify this fingerprint, any and all information available on one Toynbee Tarkington. It looks legit, but we don't give the feebs just any old thing they ask for. My man tracks it back, guess what? It comes up a favor for a friend, and guess who the friend is?"

"How the hell would I know?" Colonel Hall said. "Half a the time I don't even know what goddamn language you're talking."

"The friend is a Santa Fe cop. Who just happens to be a very close friend of the subject."

"Okay, so you're talking about Vigil."

"Wake up, Hall. Yes. Light finally begins to dawn. That's right, Vigil. Now how long do you think it'll be before Benjamin's bunch are all over this? We might as well stick a big red flag in the ground and yell, 'Over here! Hey, Look over here!' As soon as he catches on, they're gonna know we've got men on the ground, and as soon as they know *that*, they're going to be all over us with hobnailed boots. We have to terminate the operation immediately."

"But you said you hadn't gotten the stuff yet."

"I don't. We don't have dick. We got dick minus squat equals less than zero. We got one redheaded looneytoons medical chick with a wacko theory. But may I remind you, this is an option operation? Option A: Find out what Benjamin is after and get there first. Option B: If Option A don't fly, don't leave anything for anybody else. Do you read me, Hall?"

When I was in the service, Colonel Hall thought, *I would have been on your ass like a rooster on a doodlebug. You goddamned little peckerwood.*

"The subject has to be canceled," Freddy continued. "I want you personally to see to it, and I want it done ASAP. Today. This afternoon."

"That ain't gonna fly, good buddy. I close a sale this afternoon."

"Don't you understand me yet? *Forget* your damn sale, this is important."

"You don't know what you're saying. We're not talking ordinary sales here. I clear an average two hundred K on every one of these units personally, and that's not including seller's percentage or builder's fees and contractor's fees. Those babies can bump it up another hundred, hundred and fifty, by the time you're done talking."

"You mean kickbacks."

"Call it what you want. So I've got twenty-six sites, already sold four, five if I close today. That's three months from opening. Figure I sell the rest over the next two years, which I will, there's no question about that. You can add it up yourself."

"Big deal, Hall. Michael Jordan makes more in a month. Uncle Sam spends more in an hour and a half. You were glad enough to sign on for this project."

"Freddy, *you* came to *me,* I seem to remember. Something about I had done good work for my country in the past, and you really needed somebody on the scene, somebody with a built-in, ready-made cover. Seems to me the conversation went Please Please Please Pretty Please. Now you're telling me you don't care about the cover anymore? Now you're telling me, 'Fine, Colonel Hall, you put yourself in danger, you took on a job you didn't have to and that didn't make you any money at all and could maybe blow up in your face, and all for loyalty to your country, but now that push comes to shove, hey, thanks a lot, *hasta la vista,* good luck, nice to see ya, hope you enjoy twisting slowly in the wind.' Well, it ain't gonna be that way, Bubba."

"Maybe you didn't read the fine print, Hall. It ain't about you getting your rocks off playing secret agent mastermind, and you quit when you want to. It's about you sign on, you finish the damn job. You may be a big noise in Beanfart City, but it's levels and levels to this game. You're junior in this league, and that means you follow orders."

We'll see about that, Colonel Hall thought. *Michael Coonass Jordan notwithstanding, three mil per annum puts me in touch with people you never even heard of. See you in a duck blind, boy, couple years down the road.*

To his interlocutor he said, "You and me have some understandings to come to. But for right now, let's just concentrate on the situation at hand. So the operation needs to be terminated. I assume you want all the files removed, too. And I assume it would be smart if everything looked accidental. That's a complicated set of circumstances to pull off."

"Accidental, schmaccidental. It's not gonna fool Benjamin."

"No, but the less attention from outside agencies, the better."

"Speed is the thing here, Hall, not finesse."

"I can do all this," Colonel Hall said, "But not on your schedule. It's going to take two or three days, but it'll be done right. That should be plenty of time."

"Dammit, Hall—"

"What are you gonna do? What choice do you have? Do you think you can have another team on the ground here, and cover your tracks, and do it any quicker than I'm going to do it?"

Freddy sputtered with anger. "This goes in your jacket, Hall."

"Fine. Put it in my jacket. Put any fucking thing you want to in my jacket. Right now, I'm the man on the ground and I'm calling the play."

"Do you have the guts to do a woman?" Freddy was trying contempt now.

"I brought down a couple of does last big hunting season," the Colonel said. "They was off limits, but I got to tell you, they went down just like the bucks."

"What the fuck, Hall? You think bagging a couple deer makes you James fucking Bond?"

"'Nam, you moron. I spent a whole year backcountry."

"That ain't in your file. I don't believe it. You're too damn old."

"Right. Right on both counts. I was old. And I was invisible. You might want to think about that before you go writing any shit for my jacket. You might want to think how there might be some people reading it that know *me* better than they do *you.* Anyhow, bucko, I've got a plan for the girl. It'll take a couple of days, but it'll be slick. There won't be anything to tie it back to you. Actually, I'm glad of the work. She's one judgmental cunt, I can tell you that."

"Hall, this better work. It really better work. What's your plan?"

"This time, my little gaspergoo," the Colonel said, "it's your turn to be kept in the dark. You'll find out when it happens, mudsucker." He hung up the phone. He got slowly out of his chair. He grabbed his crotch. Damn, still had a big one. Time to see if he could get the dream back. Wonder what Miss Jody Nightwood would have to say about it?

As he left the office, the phone began insisting. He let it ring.

Jody was up in the middle of the night with cramps and nausea. Leaning over the bowl, heaving, saliva dripping from her teeth. But nothing came. She realized she hadn't eaten since lunch the day before. Squatting ingloriously on the toilet, hunched over, moaning. Again nothing, nothing but miserable undignified noise.

She couldn't deliver, and yet her guts kept roiling and clamping.

It was poison, somehow. She knew that. The venom of friendship gone bad. She was trying to heave Toni and Vic and Shade and all of it out of her system. She drank water till she was distended, and threw that up. She tried to be quiet, but that was impossible and she assumed she had awakened Shade and she was grateful he chose not to come in and comfort her and she hoped he had gone downstairs and even gone home.

It was over, finally, after an hour or so, leaving her weak and trembling, filmed with greasy toxins. She showered then, hot as she could stand it, scrubbed her skin till it hurt. She shampooed her hair twice, brushed her teeth three times.

She put on her robe and went downstairs for a glass of milk.

Shade was sitting at the kitchen table in the darkness, with his head in his hands. He didn't look up till she flicked on the lights, and then he winced in pain. "How are you doing?" he said. "I didn't know whether to help or let you be."

"You chose right," she said. She swung open the refrigerator door, got out the milk. Got a glass from the cabinet. Poured. "What's the matter with you?"

"Same old same old," he said, lowering his head to his hands again.

"Headache?"

He nodded without lifting his head. She felt a stab of anger. She was tired of his goddamned headaches. The way they upstaged her own troubles. But she went over to him, put her hand on his back. "We make a great pair tonight, don't we?" she said.

She sat beside him. "Want some milk?" she said.

"Maybe some blood," he said. "I'm too far gone for milk."

She realized she wasn't afraid of him anymore. Maybe it was the way he was suffering, how it made him smaller and more human. In her league. But more likely it was just common sense coming back. Bleak early-morning light filtered grayly into the room. She saw that the episode with Toni and Vic had all been a misunderstanding, confusion piled on confusion. Just one of those terrible things that happen without a reason. There were accidents in people's emotional lives too. In traffic, a sweet grandmother took her eye off the road a second, crossed the centerline, killed a happy family of four on vacation to New Mexico.

The same thing happened with emotions. Good people destroyed each other, and the causes were just as senseless, just as random.

She and Toni weren't destroyed, but they had been hurt bad. There was a lot of rebuilding to do. They would get back together, but just now, just at this flat predawn empty moment, Jody didn't give a good goddamn. Let it ride. Let the bitterness wear itself out.

She and Shade sat till the sun came up, and then longer. As soon as she knew Consuela would be there, Jody called in sick, claiming a stomach virus. Toni would think it was their quarrel, but let her. Hell, it *was* the quarrel. The quarrel *was* a stomach virus.

She talked Shade into coming up to bed with her and trying to get some rest. They needed to be like the animals, she said, like Static and Blind Lemon. Not think about love and not think about pain, just huddle together and keep warm.

The bedside telephone woke them about noon.

It was Colonel Hall's office, calling with an invitation. Jody listened to the explanation, a lengthy one, but listening was quicker than trying to get off the line. "Thank you," she said at last. "That sounds wonderful. I'll certainly try to make it."

"What was that?" Shade mumbled, his head under a pillow.

"Oh, the damn real-estate company is throwing a housewarming for Toni and Vic. Tomorrow night. They do it for all their customers, show them what a warmhearted agency they are. Toni and Vic think they're going out to make a final check before moving in, and to change all the voice codes on the doors and so on, and we all jump out and say, 'Surprise!' "

"Are you going?"

"Are you kidding? Besides, I couldn't take you. Individuals only. It's far too exclusive for dates, don't you know. Puffed-up pricks." Shade could not tell and she could not have said herself whether her concluding imprecation referred to the real-estate company or to Toni and Vic.

She left him to wallow in drowsiness awhile longer, and went down to make herself a late breakfast, hungry at last. But he was downstairs not fifteen minutes later, and she could tell by his eyes that the pain was worse. She felt she should do something to try to help, at least show some affection, but she had no emotional resources left, and they said good-bye at the door like a couple locked in a fifty-year loveless marriage, like two doctors changing shifts.

30: rosen what and guilden *who?*

After Shade left, Jody decided she wasn't going in to the office the rest of the week. If Toni could take three weeks off, Jody could take three days off, even on short notice. Let Toni cover for *her* awhile. She went upstairs and pounded her bus-crash war dream into the computer. It was like pushing a Buick up a hill, but it had to be done.

But then she figured she'd had it. She couldn't stand drooping around the house any longer. It wasn't enough to bail out on the office. She was going to get away, completely away. Today, this very afternoon. Take her manuscript with her, maybe finish it up. It was basically done, but she kept finding things she had to go back and plug into her scheme. There was that weird backwards cause-and-effect thing, for example. How did her theory explain that? Was it related to the driving-the-bus-backwards dream? Then there was the mutual dream with Dead Men Walking. What was she going to do about that? It had happened, she had no doubt of it, but if she admitted it in her book, how the literalists and reductionists would howl. But if she left it out, then her theory wasn't honest, wasn't true to her own experience.

That was the thing to do. Put Toni and Vic and the rest of it out of her mind, get busy with her own work, her main purpose in living. She called the Lodge in Cloudcroft, and they had a room. Fine. She could be packed in an hour, and she could be there not too long after dark. She would take her skis, maybe it would snow in the Sacramentos.

What about the babies? She called Shade, and he was there, and he agreed to cat-sit. He thought it was a *very* good idea for her to get away for a while. He wasn't going to be worth being around for the next couple of days anyhow. Until his head quit hurting.

Oh, how *was* his head, was he sure he was capable? Let him worry about that, he would be fine. She wasn't imposing? No, he was happy to help out. On one condition.

And what was that?

That when she got back, they would follow through on their plan to ski Windsor Trail down to Holy Ghost. Just as soon as it snowed enough. He did think it was good for her to get away, do some private thinking. But he also thought it was really important that she not let the trauma of her quarrel with her friends keep her from getting on with her life, fulfilling her dreams. He thought going over the mountains would be a very important message to herself.

You *are* leaving me, she thought, hanging up. That's going to be your big good-bye scene. One last romp in the snow, go out the same way we got together. Something to get me solid again, standing on my own two feet so you won't have to feel so guilty when you split.

Jody was between Oscuro and Three Rivers when Shade got the first call. It was sunset, glorious with a broken rack in the west. The front moving in. He had cleaned the cat box, drawn fresh water, filled the food bowls. He had even gotten the brush and curried Blind Lemon, who loved it, who rolled and offered his chin and then his belly.

Then he had gone upstairs and logged on Jody's computer. He was reading the last dream with Ish, shaking his head, when the desk phone rang. He picked it up, said hello.

It was Toni. She sounded taken aback to hear his voice. "Ah, I was just calling," she said. "I, ah, wanted to see how she was feeling. Consuela said she was sick—"

"She's not here," Shade said. "I'm house-sitting."

"House-sitting? Where did she go?"

"I'm not sure she would want me to tell you," Shade said.

"So she told you about it?"

"She told me you had had a fight."

"Well, listen. I guess she's still angry. I don't blame her, but I don't blame myself, either. But I'm still worried how she's doing, okay? She's my friend. We've had fights before."

"I think she's going to be all right. She *is* pretty mad."

"Can you give her a message? Can you tell her that Vic said not to worry about the burglaries and the fingerprints, it's probably all just a big confusion. He's worried she'll fixate on it, and he wants her to know there's just no reason to."

"What burglaries?" Shade said. His voice crackled.

"She didn't tell you? About the fingerprints on her computer? The break-in at the office?"

"Break-in at the office," Shade said.

"Yeah, and somebody stole her files on the computer. She gets really freaky sometimes, things like that, violations, and we were afraid we'd kicked her fears back to life. But if she didn't say anything to you, maybe she's not so worried after all."

Shade tried to pin Toni down on the details, the timings of the burglaries, but her voice grew more reserved, suspicious. If Jody hadn't told him, maybe he wasn't supposed to know, for whatever reason. "Just tell her I called, okay? Just tell her I called, and I love her, and to call me whenever she gets back and she feels like talking it over."

When Shade got the second call, Jody was pulling the NSX into the portico of the Lodge. A wall of black cloud on the western horizon marked off the last rimfire, and overhead the stars were already out in the blueblack sky.

Shade was pacing the upstairs of her home, thinking. Jody was in trouble. A lot more trouble than he had thought. He had been lazy, made too many assumptions.

The kitchen phone rang, and he picked it up and barked, "Shade." Forgetting where he was, too deep into business mode already. His office greeting.

"*¿Qué?*" said the voice. "Oh. This is Miss Nightwood's companion, is it not? From the wedding, we met. I am Bruno Sandoval."

Sandoval was surprised to hear that Jody was out of town. How long? Oh, then she would not be able to attend Friday night's housewarming. The man's voice was full of disappointment. Oh, well. He had just been calling to compare notes. He had thought he might buy the couple a present of fine liquor, and he was calling Jody to find out their preference.

"The housewarming's tomorrow night," Shade said.

No, no, it was most definitely Friday evening. Sandoval had just received a call from the real-estate office, Colonel Hall himself on the line, and the gentleman had definitely said Friday, the ninth of November. One might mistake Sunday for Monday, but never Friday for Thursday.

"I'll give her the message," Shade said.

It was a setup. It had to be a setup, get Jody out there on the mountainside alone. That man, Colonel Hall. He had to be one of Freddy's people. His two little buddies at the wedding, the Brit and the cutie-pie. Flaunting it, and Shade hadn't caught on.

At least they hadn't made him yet. If they had, they would have already tried to kill him.

"No matter," Sandoval said. "Since she won't be able to attend. But you might let her know that I called. You don't happen to know what they like to drink, do you? The Vigils?"

"No," Shade said. "Apparently I don't know anything about anything."

Jody slept most of the day Thursday. She woke up at eight, groaned and covered her head and rolled over into sleep again. She woke up the next time at ten. This time she made herself get up, wash her face, brush her teeth. She dressed, went downstairs. Breakfast was over, Rebecca's was closed until eleven, when the lunch hour started. But they brought her a cup of coffee in the lobby and she waited. Then she saw nothing she wanted on the menu, had a tuna sandwich. She climbed wearily back up the stairs. Forced herself to keep climbing, explore the peculiar little closed-in bell tower, from which you could see half of creation. A newlywed couple had gotten there first, were spooning on one of the benches. The quarters were narrow, and Jody looked once out of each window and went back down to bed.

She told herself it was just fine to sleep her life away. The room was expensive, and there were things to see and do all around, and if she didn't want to sightsee, or visit Fort Meigs, or hit the Ruidoso flea markets, she could at least work on her book.

But she told herself it was okay not to. It was her money, her time, her room, her life, and if she wanted to retreat into her cave and sleep till the seasons changed, that was just fine.

She woke at six, and went down for supper. She wished momentarily that Shade was there, so that they could have the Chateaubriand, but she thought better of it immediately. She had a filet instead, her perpetual filet, Jody the meat-eater.

She met nobody's eyes, not even the good-looking fellow who sat alone at the bar and kept glancing her way, hoping to be invited over. She felt as though this were the trance, and not her sleep. As though reality were waiting for her back in her bed, and she was staying up simply to bank enough waking hours to allow her to go back under. Ballast for the deeps.

Back in her room, she made herself watch a little TV. CNN, but the talking heads seemed to be speaking in unknown tongues, she could follow none of it. There came a knock at the door. A hostess with a large snifter of port. Her discrimination had apparently impressed the chef, and this was his compliment. She could not now remember what she had eaten.

By nine, she was back under the covers, and falling like a stone in a well to darkness.

Beyond which, light.

Ish sat on a stone wall bordering a green meadow. He was crying. Sobbing his heart out.

What is it? *she said.*

This is the night of your death, *he said.*

Oh, *she said.*

It's all right. I've arranged a sacrifice. A couple of stooges to take your place.

You take such good care of me.

I can't help you much longer. That's why I was crying.

After the first death there is no other, *she said.*

I don't know what that means, *he said.*

Me either. But it's beautiful.

They were walking in the long hall. It was the hall of the ancestors. Here were all the memories, disappointments, murders, disasters. Crazy ghosts writhed behind smoked glass like wind-maddened flames, exhibits in a zoo. The snake cages.

We're going to have to do something about the vampire, *he said.*

The brass plaque under the plate glass said DRACO. Behind the dark glass, the vampire wasn't moving, was frozen in his black immortality like a milky swirl in a block of obsidian.

Fierceness and anguish, a twist of black paint on a canvas.

There was a coin slot beside the plaque. Put your money in, and the vam-

*pire would step forward out of his gloom, would roar and grimace, mechanical
monster.*

Thirty guilders for the show, *Ish said.* Rosin up your stern and bow.

"God, it's a beautiful night," Toynbee whispered into the mike of his
headset.

"Mind on the job," Leonard's voice came in his ears.

"Yes, but have you ever *seen* so many stars?"

"They'll be there when we're gone."

Toynbee shivered, though the night was warm for November. It
was adrenaline, he knew. He couldn't believe he was really doing this.
He was badly frightened, but not because he thought he was in physical danger. Because something new was about to happen. Whatever
happened, after this his life would be forever changed. *He* would be
forever changed.

He would be a killer.

How existential. There could not be a more existential act, the taking of another human life. Whatever the cause, whatever the justification, you were placing yourself in a different realm. You were
presuming on fate itself, and there, in that dark but asterisked realm,
that realm of the spirit that must be so much like this black and restless and star-maddened night, you were forever stripped of your own
humanity, your own defenses.

It was the commitment that was frightening. The willingness to
die to everything that you had been before. To stare over the moral
precipice into the Big Empty.

As their victim would call it.

And all for the sake of love.

"And some must live, and some must die," he whispered. The
wind moved on the hillside, and the scent of juniper moved across
him. An owl called, somewhere in the arroyos.

"For God's sake, pipe down," came Leonard's voice.

Toynbee was hunkered behind the low wall of the kiva. Just
around the hill, but blocked off by it, so that his view of the sky was
not obstructed, the lights of the Cascade House blazed. Leonard was
sitting on a boulder closer to the home. He was situated so that he
could see the lights of her car coming up the long drive.

She would have to stop in the parking area, get out, walk the flagstoned path to the entrance. As soon as Leonard saw her lights, he would radio his companion. Leonard would be waiting in the parking area, pretending to be Hall's host, welcoming her to the housewarming, explaining there had been a delay, putting her at ease. Toynbee would make his way down the path. Just as he emerged into view behind her, the lights would go down. Leonard would hold her while the Brit applied the ether. They were going to make it look like an animal attack, a bear, and that was why Leonard had asked him to help.

Ostensibly why. It couldn't be done long distance, and it would take two because they had to be certain of controlling her with a minimum of struggle.

All well and good. Meantime, Toynbee was shivering in this magnificent night. He hadn't been outside at night, in what amounted to wild country, in a very long time. He had forgotten how *big* the night could be, how all fences and barriers and categories disappeared into a single unending infinite savage onrolling continuity. It wasn't just the stars. It wasn't just the urgent wind, a restless spirit forever prowling, that existed only in and by means of its restlessness, a ghost that did not exist unless it was itself being haunted. It was—

There was life all around him. He could hear it, some of it. A rustling in that thicket. Something scrabbling on stones in an unidentifiable draw, the slowing cascade of the stones themselves after the scrabbling stopped. A muted thunder of sudden wings right at his ear, a predator mistaking him, swerving off at the last moment. Or a panicked nightbird?

He thought he could *smell* it, too, the bigness. The strangeness. Under the juniper, musky occasional whiffs of this and that. A skunk, from far off.

And most important, he could *feel* it. The whole wide night crawling with uncountable alien life. Definitely alien. Nothing from another galaxy could be farther from his usual life, his usual world, than the creatures going about their invisible business all around.

There would be many deaths on this hillside tonight. Jody Nightwood not the only innocent uttering a small sharp protest and relaxing thereafter to nothingness. He told himself that. And what of her innocence? Innocence, guilt, innocence guilt innocence. Words, nothing but words. Creatures lived, and creatures died, and it was all the old immutable inevitable sacrifice to nothing larger than the god Chance, the only god, the one that had made the universe and all its planets and stars. Here, on this hillside, tonight, he was just one of the creatures, participating in, caught in a rhythm older and larger than he could possibly control.

This is what he was thinking when he saw the shadow move. It was a big shadow.

His vision had long since adjusted, and he had no doubt that he had actually seen it, that it was no trick of the eyes. Something had crossed from one juniper to another, just up the hill. Had crossed very rapidly. He radioed Leonard: "Get up here."

"Now what?" came the voice.

"I don't know, but there's something moving around up here."

"Come on, buddy. Don't get the night shakes now. She could be here any minute."

"You don't understand. This is something *major.*"

How ironic it would be: clawed to death by a bear himself, while he lay in wait to be a bear to another. Now he heard something, a brushing of branches. There, was that a *shape?* Something dark on the lighter soil of the hill, not a tree.

"Get up here *now.*"

"Seriously, compadre. Get a grip."

"I've *got* a goddamned *grip,*" he whispered urgently. "There's a large animal prowling here. By the size, a bear. I seriously do not wish to wind up as bear meat tonight. Do you copy? Do you *copy?* You're the shooter, and you've got the cannon."

Toynbee was carrying a .32, but he had no confidence of its utility against something the size of a bear, even supposing he could steady on and hit the creature in the first place. His partner had a .45 automatic in a holster on the back of his belt.

"He's probably not interested in you. Just checking you out. He'll go away if you hold still. Look, it'll add authenticity. There'll be tracks, maybe. Hey, he might even come in and gnaw her a little after we've done our business and got the hell out."

Toynbee shuddered at the thought. "I come up there," Leonard continued, "we could jeopardize the whole operation. Especially if I have to shoot."

"Then *jeopardize* the damn thing. Listen, ducks, I'm sorry, not cool under fire and all that. But I'm worried here. This thing is not going away, it's heading *toward* me. Even if he doesn't charge, I'm going to be worthless. How can I concentrate on the operation?"

There was a muttered curse in his ears. Then silence. It seemed a very long silence, though it must have been less than thirty seconds. Then Leonard was beside him. He had not made a sound, he was really very good at this sort of thing. Immediately, Toynbee's confidence returned, and he let out a breath he hadn't realized he'd been holding.

Now that he'd made the decision, Leonard seemed cheery enough, not at all put out. He patted his companion's leg. "Not really your line of work, is it?" he said, sympathetic. "Don't worry, you're doing fine. Now show me your big old bogeyman."

"I last saw something—" Toynbee began. He didn't finish.

A large shape dropped onto the path where it wound around the hill into darkness. Between them and the lights of the house.

"What the fuck," Leonard said. Toynbee could feel him reaching under his jacket for the automatic, rising to his feet. Toynbee stood, too, though his legs were shaking, and his own arms felt nerveless. He should be reaching for *his* gun, but the action seemed pointless.

The shape straightened, walked in their direction. It was a man. A large man.

"What the *fuck*," Leonard said.

Toynbee couldn't get over how *big* the night felt. The lonesome wind, that in a few minutes would prowl their bodies. The rope of stars overhead, set in such a clarity of blackness that he felt up and down reversed, felt he was about to fall into the sky.

"Stop right there, buddy," Leonard said. He had the automatic fully extended. The man stopped. It was too dark to see his features. "What the hell do you think you're doing? Don't you know this is private property?"

He spoke over his shoulder to Toynbee. "Radio headquarters. Tell them we've got a prowler at Cascade." Then, to the dark shape on the path: "Unless you see fit to hightail it out of here right now, friend. Probably an honest mistake on your part. Hiked in over the hill, didn't know where you were. I won't take you in if you don't make me."

The shape neither moved nor spoke.

Toynbee found himself curiously unafraid. This was like a great trance, or a great dream. The infinite night. The wheeling stars. The wind. This creature sent by the fates, from the plane of the fates. This creature who though he appeared in the shape of a man was no man.

"Forget it," he said to his companion. "He knows better."

"What are you talking—oh. You think he's a player. Maybe so. I don't see how he could have tailed us, but you're right. Make the safe assumption. Good call, buddy."

He gestured with the automatic, just a little wave of the barrel. He said to the shape, "That so, friend? Is what he's saying true? Are you something more than a happy wanderer here?"

Toynbee was thinking that if it had to happen, this really wasn't a bad way. A lot of people, they had to meet it alone. In a hospital, a nursing home. At sea, clinging to a board.

"Do you love me?" he said.

"What the hell?" Leonard said. "Don't flake on me now."

"He's going to kill us, ducks. We're dead men."

"He's not going to kill anybody," Leonard hissed. "Not unless he can walk with nine rounds in his chest and three in his head. Get it *together*, man. You're freaking me."

"You're going to kill us, aren't you?" Toynbee said to the shadow.

"Yes," the shadow said. The voice was a low rumble that came from everywhere, like the near-subsonics of a jet, or a meteor's thunder broken in the hills and gullies. Toynbee recognized the voice. He had heard it at the Archuleta woman's wedding. That man, of course.

"It speaks," Leonard said. "Tell you what, bud. You can help me out here. You can lie down, facedown, right where you are, right now. That'll simplify matters a whole hell of a lot. That way, I won't have to pull this trigger."

"Do you love me?" Toynbee said.

"*Yes*, I bloody well love you, you bloody fucking cretin. If you *must* fucking know. If I *must* say it right this fucking minute."

Toynbee smiled in the darkness. It would be all right now. It would all be all right.

"You understand, I *have* to kill this fellow now?" Leonard said. "Can't let the word get out we're queers, can I? You understand this means the operation is well and truly fucked?" To the shadow in the path: "Sorry, pal. I won't make it hurt."

"She's not coming, love," Toynbee said. "*We're* the targets."

The shadow laughed at that, a great wild call full of an innocent joy and an innocent savagery. It was a beautiful sound. It was like being forgiven. Everything was fine.

"Do you know our names?" the Brit said. "It's such an anonymous trade. I would like to think that someone might say our names at last."

"Sure," John Shade said. "You're Rosencrantz and Guildenstern."

"What do you know?" Leonard said. "The fucking bear knows Shakespeare."

Toynbee laughed. That was pretty funny. "Lovers to the end," he said.

"Lenny Michaels and Nigel Toynbee Tarkington," Shade said. "Lovers to the end."

"Nigel?" Leonard said.

31: clouds for brains

Jody spent Friday doing typical things, ordinary things. Went for a long run along the road. Drove out to the Valley of Fires and took a walk in that strange wild landscape, a black and frozen violence now seeded with secret life, whole individual ecosystems breeding in pockets where, a millennium ago, huge bubbles had formed in molten stone, now broken open.

She went into Alamogordo, but found no good flea markets. She visited a shop that described itself as an outdoorsmen's and sporting goods store, but had the presence more nearly of a worn-out dry-goods. Yellowed diatribes were pinned to all the available walls, cursing abortion, describing Bill Clinton as the Antichrist, raving against gun control. A young man in combat boots and a full set of fatigues came in, a wild gladness in his face, and struck up a passionate conversation with the manager about the most deadly knife for a hand-to-hand fight.

She got the hell out, feeling as though she had fallen into a pit of snakes at the zoo. She thought of her dream, the monster under glass, wondered if it had been precognitive.

All the day long, she felt she was idling, in neutral. Processing something. Coming to terms with something internally, wordlessly. She didn't think about her home or her babies or Shade or Toni and Vic or her patients or her book. She just went and did and was.

. . .

"Red Rover, Red Rover, send Wilbur right over," Colonel Hall said, and the door opened. He didn't like this part, ceding control of the house. It would be better if you could figure out a way to make people give you money, and then you owned them instead of them owning something of yours. Drugs, for example. He had always stayed away from that line, not so much because of the danger as because of the contempt he had developed for the regular troops in-country, weaklings who couldn't face death unless they were totally jazzed.

Who couldn't face death like a white man.

He went down the walk, and over the running water, and through the front door, and into the main house, the living area. He opened the computer terminal Toni had opened, and keyed up the access menu. He pulled down "Set Code" and then "New" off that and, then toggled "Macro." He wrote a brief command that instructed the house to open the next time anyone said "Freudian Sleep" to it, and to institute voice-recognition thereafter. He said the words "Freudian Sleep" aloud when he came to that part of the command.

Now Mr. and Mrs. Vigil could set the entry system to recognize their voices and their voices only. It would be a little ceremony they would have when they came out for the surprise party this evening. He smiled to himself.

They were going to get a bigger surprise than anyone knew, weren't they?

Time to check the scene, make sure the body was out of sight, but discoverable if you cleverly steered a drunk partygoer in the right direction. He looked around the house one last time. Shit, the Vigils were getting a bargain. He needed to rethink his pricing.

It was gray and windy outside, the sky rolling with heavy clouds. Major snowfall on the way, no doubt about it. That could be a problem, if it broke loose before tonight.

Something glinted on the gravel walk by the kiva, a familiar bit of metal, but in these circumstances, bad news, very bad news: a cartridge casing, .45 automatic. He stooped and picked it up, drew in his breath. Those clowns. Even one bullet hole in the body—

He hurried up the walk. More casings, four of them, and he gathered them as he went, feeling absurdly like Hansel following a trail of crumbs. He was going to have to detail the terrain, goddammit—some would be in the bushes—then erase his own tracks.

He knew the body was wrong as soon as he saw it, even from a distance, even before he saw the other one. Male by its size, by the way it had fallen.

They were off the trail, thank God, but the whole area was drenched with blood. Bushes, the earth itself, a huge rock they'd obviously tried to use for cover. Jesus Christ, it was like those dye-dumps they made to target a hillside for a bomb run.

Both their throats were torn open, the Brit's head almost totally severed from his body. The pretty boy had pretty obviously gone first, blazing away. Putting himself between the animal and his faggot lover. Well, aren't you special. No sign Tarkington had resisted at all. The Colonel had seen that before, the pacific fearlessness of the doomed.

Had to be a bear. Colonel Hall almost giggled at the irony of it, but there was too much work to do. How the hell to handle it? Discover them himself, right now? No, no, no, no. No direct links. Probably wouldn't matter, but you never took the chance.

Besides, it wasn't the cops he had to worry about, it was Benjamin's people. He had to keep them away from his own operation as long as possible. Not to mention, this hit the papers it would queer the sales for a few months. His cash flow wouldn't like that.

Queer the sales, hah. How's that for word choice?

Well, then. He couldn't move the bodies, too fucking obvious. Any decent cop, let alone forensics, could tell they'd been handled by more than a bear.

Police the scene, then. The guns, holsters. Count the rounds, see how many more shells he had to find. Remove any agency ID, if they had been stupid enough to carry, but leave the personal stuff. Red flag if you took that. Find the garden hooks and the bear jaw.

Colonel Hall took off his shoes, his socks, rolled up his cuffs. Probably no need to worry about leaving fibers, but he had to be careful not to step in the blood. This was going to be like that party game, getting to the bodies without touching the blood. Twister.

He wished he thought he could get away with moving some dirt, cover up some of the signs, but there was no way. He threw a look at the sagging sky. Now he *wanted* it to snow. It would be better if a lot of time passed before the bodies were found. If the scavengers got at them, if months of weather blurred the scene. Gay tryst, couple of strangers from out of town, nobody misses them for months. He could make sure the gay angle got in the news.

Somewhere there was a bear full of bullets, but with any luck he was well back in the woods, dead or dying in privacy, undiscoverable. A possibility the bear was still around, and in a pretty bad mood, but Colonel Hall was in the zone now, he was invulnerable. He had been here before. It felt good, it felt damn good. A hell of a lot better than jungle-bunny skag.

Now of course he was going to have to make sure nobody did go outside, nobody wandered up the trail. In the meantime, hope like hell it snowed like hell. If it snowed soon enough, heavy enough, he could cancel the housewarming entirely. That would be the best thing, all the way round. Make sure some time passed.

And there was the Nightwood factor. He was going to have to see to that himself, and right away. No more tricky accidents. Bullet in the head, just another drive-by.

He was leaning over the pretty boy, trying to slide the holster off the belt and then redo the loops and the buckle without disturbing the body's position. He stopped and stood up, so suddenly that he almost lost his balance and fell on his hands and knees in the blood.

The fucking woman!

If she'd been here, seen this happen—hell, the cops could be all over him any minute.

Now wait a minute, Hall, get a grip. Think it through.

Never rush. Always think it through. If she'd seen it, the cops and medics would have been here a long time ago. Ergo, she didn't see it. Her body wasn't here, so either she hadn't come at all, or she'd come after it happened. Hung around waiting for everybody else to show up. Gotten cold, gotten angry, and given up and gone home.

Unless they'd done her, and *then* the bear had gotten them. He was in real trouble if that had happened. But it wasn't likely. Timeline on that just wasn't likely. Besides, the body was nowhere to be seen, and they hadn't been supposed to hide it.

So she didn't come, or she got here after it happened. If she got here after it happened, then she was out there stewing around, mad as hell. She would have called his office, not the home office but the real-estate office, that was the number he'd left, and his secretary would have taken the message, and when the Nightwood cunt kept after her, the secretary would have gone to check her calendar, just to calm the woman down, and then the secretary would have discovered, to her horror, that she *had* given out the wrong date, oh, I'm so sorry, I was so certain it *was* the eighth, please don't blame Colonel Hall, it's really all my fault, how can I make it up to you?

If that was the case, why wasn't his beeper going off? Why wasn't his secretary on the line, oh, Colonel Hall, I'm so sorry but I've made a terrible mistake?

He had an impulse to go to his cell phone right now, but no.

And if the Nightwood slut hadn't showed at all? Could she possibly have made him? Definitely hostile at her sister-bitch's hitching.

No way, no way. He'd read her fucking journals, all the way till they'd stopped tracking her for a while in the middle of the summer. The woman was a goose. She had clouds for brains. He'd read the journals, and laughed all the way through. Words words words ideas ideas ideas feelings feelings feelings. What fools these mortals be. The woman never had a clue.

She didn't know she was going to die, and when she died, she wouldn't know why.

Okay. Take a deep breath. Finish up here.

After all, you're giving a party tonight. Unless it snows. Come on, snow.

Jody woke on Saturday morning to find that the snow was general over all of New Mexico. Cloudcroft itself had had more than a foot, drifting a lot deeper in places. Another front was on the way, due in three or four days, depending on which channel you believed.

The sun was out now, though, and the skies as flawless as a curved glass, and the world a clear and shining and beautiful place entirely. Her mind felt as clean and clear and shining. She was, she understood now, a very sane woman. A very healthy spirit. That was what her dreams had done for her, that was the gift that Ish had given. She knew what she thought of Shade, and she knew what she thought the burglaries were, and she knew how she felt about Toni and Vic. What they had done, how they had handled it, had been callous and stupid. But she saw the whole situation dispassionately now, could understand how they had made their decision.

There was no hate left in her, no fear. Just a readiness, almost an eagerness. Joined, in that rarest and happiest combination, with a very great patience.

Which was a good thing. Because although she would have forgone the last night at the Lodge and driven straight home that morning, the roads, even down on the desert floor, wouldn't be clear till a good deal later in the day. So. Might as well take advantage of the situation. Might as well put on the old skis and go for a glide. Be good practice for the mountain run, too.

She found a trail that wound three miles out and eventually went along the rim of the mountains, so that she could pause and catch her breath and stare into the vast whiteness of the what seemed the entire world stretching out below, and she stayed out till midafternoon, and then she thought she would stay over the last night after all, see if she couldn't perform in the dining room once more as epicure enough to score another glass of port from the chef, who had come out to her table the night before and chatted a moment, and was really, when you got down to it, pretty cute and might even bring the good stuff up himself this time.

32: clearing the decks

Benjamin George was on the telephone. Sitting in darkness in his office. *That's fine*, he said. *You did what you had to. No, there shouldn't be any more threat to Miss Nightwood. Once we have what we want, there'll be no reason for them to go after her. You set up the meeting. I'll neutralize Davenport. Oh, and John—you can stop calling me Mother now.*

When he had hung up, he said, *Mandrake?*

A green light flickered in the darkness. A gentle voice said, *Yes, Benjamin?*

More treachery. I'm going to betray one of my own agents now. I'm probably going to get a fine young woman killed, an innocent woman. But I don't have what I need on Freddy Davenport yet. And I have to stop Freddy. So what do you think of me now?

I think whatever you need me to think, Benjamin.

I know. That's the problem. Benjamin sighed. *Get me Hendrix on the line.*

Speakerphone, Benjamin?

Yes. I can't bear to touch the receiver his voice is coming through.

There was a pause while Mandrake dialed the number. Then a voice came over the speakers: *Hendrix here. Is that you, Benjamin?*

Yes, Colin. I need you to handle something for me. You remember Operation Dreamer, I told you about it something over a year ago?

You could hear the excitement in the voice from the speaker: *Sure I remember.*

It's come to a head in Santa Fe. My man is going to call you with the time and place for a meeting. He's going to turn over the information we want. I want you to send a couple of our top men. No slipups, do you understand? This is my most important project ever.

You can trust me, Benjamin, the voice on the speaker said.

It didn't make sense, John Shade thought. Why bother with hard copy, when he was going to send the whole package over the wire as soon as Jody was finished? Coded, of course. As the hard copy would be. Benjamin was a literate man. Maybe that was it.

Maybe for all his traveling in virtual realms, he still somehow preferred an actual piece of print to hold in his actual hand. It didn't matter. If Benjamin George wanted an old-fashioned meet with an old-fashioned hand-over, he would get it.

Shade shut his computer down, got up, went into his living room. He looked out at the sunny arroyo. It was going to be over soon. It was all going to be over.

He didn't know whether he was glad or sad. He hated love, sometimes.

Jody pulled into her garage in the middle of the afternoon on Sunday. The day had been almost as bright as Saturday, just a few clouds drifting over, and it had been a gorgeous drive back, if a slow one—some of the roads still dicey—and she was feeling good.

When she opened the door to the house, there were Static and Blind Lemon, waiting anxiously. Static jumped immediately to her shoulder, quacking like a duck, and almost knocking her back down the concrete step. Blind Lemon gave a long caterwauling explanation of just exactly what it had been like while she was so thoughtlessly out of reach, then uttered a few satisfied beeps and marched her to the food bowl. Nothing wrong with it, full to the brim, and looking starred and pristine rather than mumbled to small pebbles, but not edible in his opinion until she put her fingers in it and made that rattling sound and made the smell come out.

She thought that perhaps Shade would have taken the chance to vanish while she was away, but he called before she had been in the house an hour. "Did you finish your book?" he said, affecting a disinterested tone.

"Didn't even come close," she said. "Never even tried."

"Um," he said. "Well, I hope you had a good time."

"How about I cook for you tonight?"

He seemed a little surprised, but agreed readily enough.

She logged on, checked the dates on her files. No changes she could tell. Maybe the hour-line on the most recent one. She was pretty sure she'd left the house by then.

She called Toni and Vic at the new number, but got a machine that said they hadn't moved in yet. She punched up the number at the apartment, and Toni answered. "How was the housewarming?" she said. "I'm sorry I missed it."

"Yeah, I heard about that," Toni said. "It got snowed out. Guess we'll have to have one of our own when we get moved in. Won't be a surprise, but."

"The snow must have hit a lot earlier here," Jody said. "Good thing I left when I did. Geez, it must have moved in *fast*, though. It was totally clear when I cut out."

"What?" Toni said. "Oh yeah, I guess so. Listen, girl, you sound good. Sound like we're all right again, and I'm really happy about that. But I been packing all day, and I'm *still* packing, and now Vic's hollering at me to come help him find the scissors and the tape."

"I gotcha," Jody said. "Crazy days. Don't worry about a thing. Give me a holler when you're clear, girl. We need to talk."

"Love you," Toni said, and hung up.

"Love you too," Jody said.

When he came over, Shade seemed amiable enough, but distant. She asked after his headache, and he said it had gone away, he felt fine. All during the meal, she watched him, with the dispassionate eyes she had gotten in her dreams, the eyes that could see clearly because they did not presuppose, because there was nothing they *needed* to see, *had* to see.

She saw how veiled he was, how many secrets he carried. And under that, stirring whenever he looked her way, she saw a true affection. It would never do her any lasting good, it would never free itself of all the layers and layers of grief, but it was there.

"You've changed," he said.

"Yes," she said.

"Good," he said. "This is a better you."

After dinner she broke open a bottle of Martell XO. she had been holding back, and they each took a warmed snifter down to the living room. Shade had laid in some of last year's wood while she was away, and they built a fire, and sat comfortably in its light only.

"I'm not in a hurry to finish my book," she said.

"Mmm," he said.

"I want it to be just right. I want to take my time, think it through. You should never never rush the important things. Especially when it seems you most need to."

"Mmm," he said.

"It may take me a year or more to finish," she said. "I'm not worried about anybody stealing it," she said pointedly, looking straight at him. "Let them steal if they want to. If anyone tries to publish before me, I'll step in and sue. I have plenty of evidence of prior discovery."

"I think that's a very intelligent approach," he said.

She couldn't quite tell in the firelight, but she thought a smile flickered on his carven face.

They watched the flames a long time.

"I do want to go over the mountains with you," she said at last.

"Hmm," he said.

"The next time it snows."

She poured them another sip of cognac each, and they made their plans. The coming weekend looked likely, according to the forecast.

When the cognac was gone, Shade rose to go. It seemed perfectly clear, though neither of them had said a word, that they would not be spending the night together. Perhaps they would never spend another night together, it was too soon to tell.

He was walking the arroyo home, the arroyo where she had first seen him. At the back door, she rose on tiptoe to kiss him good night. He held her close, and desire flamed all along her body, and she pressed into him hungrily. God, he felt good. She thought of taking him up to bed after all, using him frankly and unabashedly. But that was the wrong sort of dispassion.

The next week went by peacefully, appropriately. Jody actively enjoyed her patients. She and Shade had dinner together every night, once at SantaCafe, otherwise at her house, always concluding with cognac in front of the fire. They didn't sleep together. Bruno Sandoval called Monday evening, welcoming her back to town, and she had a great time telling him their plans for the ski trip while Shade sat watching the fire and listening. She could tell Bruno would have given anything to come along, and she felt a faint remorse for stirring his discontent.

On the other hand, he was truly glad for her, and if you couldn't wax eloquent to your friends about the things that made you happy, who *could* you tell?

On Wednesday afternoon she had her last appointment at three, and she and Shade spent the rest of the afternoon helping Vic and Toni with the moving. Just like Toni to buy a million-dollar house, and then save five thousand by doing all the packing and lifting herself. There wouldn't have been that much—neither Toni nor Vic had maintained a lot of inventory—except that Vida and Allegra had storerooms full of art and furniture and gizmos and goodies, heirlooms they had just been *waiting* to pass on down the line, to see safely ensconced with the next generation.

Getting the decks cleared. That's what Jody was doing. Clearing the decks for action.

She noticed again, while they were loading and unloading the moving van, the formality between Shade and Vic, the distance. Not open hostility, but they hardly spoke to each other the whole time, coordinating their efforts by means of that silent male communion that told each of them just when to grab what corner of which heavyweight, and where to set it down.

The forecast was perfect. Heavy snows in the mountains, starting Friday afternoon to evening, and lasting at least till early morning. They called the rangers at Holy Ghost to give them the word, and then Friday, after work, convoyed the van to the campground. The plan was to get it there before the snow hit, just in case it came on down the mountain and shut the roads.

They drove back to her place in the NSX, ordered pizza. Cognac, as it turned out, went really well after a few slices of the meat-lover's special. They finished the bottle.

That night it snowed.

33: shootout at the sun horse café

The plan was, the roads permitting, that they would drive up to Truchas in the early morning, go see Barbara and Alvaro. Then they would come back down to Cordova for a late breakfast at the Sun Horse Café. From there, they would head for the ski basin, get into their gear, load on their packs, and start out on the trail, somewhere around noon.

With any luck, they'd be at Spirit Lake by nightfall, and would set up camp.

It seemed a lot of driving around, a lot of preliminary business for a day that would conclude with hours and hours of supreme physical effort, but Jody had her reasons, and Shade apparently saw no point in arguing. It was her show, after all.

The roads did permit. The snow had been heavy above nine thousand feet, but only an inch or so had fallen lower down, and it was melting rapidly. Shade rapped on her back door just before dawn, as she was in the kitchen filling a thermos with fresh coffee. He was carrying a black alligator-hide briefcase. She let him in. "You're not taking that on the trail, are you?"

"Of course not. I thought I might want to jot a few notes at the café. Possible scenes for my next book, etcetera."

"Lock it in the trunk when we leave, then. You leave that out where people can see it, we're bound to get broken into."

"They'll be looking to steal the car, not the briefcase."

"Probably. But it's the ride I want. Are you ready to go?"

"Ready, Eddy. You look wonderful."

She did and she knew it, tall in her boots, her red hair pulled back, the black turtleneck showing under the silver-and-black ski suit. He was impressive himself, a huge handsome man in gray gear, perennially youthful, supernally fit, somehow tanned in the middle of winter. If he had wanted, he could have been the darling of any resort on the planet.

Alvaro greeted them at the gate, courtly in his mustache and goatee, his slouch hat. Inside, he took the hat off his bald head, and she thought again how he resembled Sean Connery, the Costa Rican version. He had just prepared a pot of steaming tea, and they sipped it gratefully. Barbara was on the treadmill upstairs, getting her exercise early. A committed vegetarian, she had discovered *The Zone* by Barry Sears and *Protein Power* by Michael and Mary Dan Eades, and now Alvaro protested that she made him eat too much meat, and had even pressured him into using the treadmill on occasion and walking once a day.

But Jody thought his color was better, and he had not complained of his back in a long while, and he seemed less tired, his dark brown eyes quick and flashing.

"Some breakfast?" he said. "But no, you're eating down below."

"You know what I want," Jody said.

He insisted on pouring them out good glasses of El Patrón, early though it was—"You'll need it, you adventurers, you"—and then led them up the stone path to his studio. He pulled out recent pieces, and pieces in progress, and held them against the wall for her admiration.

Tears came to her eyes. "These are dreams," she said.

"Yes," he said. "You might say so. Ah, I have a surprise. You wait."

He got Shade to help him with a canvas from the tallest rack of all. Jody caught glimpses of rose and pink. When finally they leaned it against the wall for her inspection, she caught her breath. It was a companion piece to Osiris, but this one was in dawn colors, and the skeleton was clearly female, breaking out of a black earth that might have been the grave or night itself. The eyes were blank but shining, were somehow made of pure white light.

"*Ceres Waking,*" Alvaro said.

"It's mine," Jody said. "As soon as I get back. Name your price."

"Make sure you do come back," Alvaro said. "I'm worried for you. Wouldn't a mushroom be easier?"

She didn't want to leave the painting, or the studio, but it was time to go. Barbara was downstairs when they went back by the house, fresh from her shower, and came out to hug them when they wouldn't come in for more tea.

"See, Alvaro," she said. "If you would work out, you could do things like Jody's doing. You're never too old." Indicating Shade and laughing: "You could look like him."

"*Ai*," Alvaro said. "I don't *want* to do such things. I'm happy in my indolence."

In the car, heading down to Cordova, Shade said, "He's really good, isn't he?"

"Yes," Jody said.

"Excellence is a strange thing," Shade said.

Sun Horse was a little building that had once been a house, tucked away in a pocket off one of the higher streets in low Cordova. It now had plate glass in the front wall, and a counter running the length of the main room. The owner served breakfast four days a week, and dinner only by appointment for special parties. She was a great cook.

Shade left his briefcase on the front seat when they got out, and Jody noticed that he didn't lock his door, waiting till she walked ahead to close it.

She said nothing.

It was nine-thirty, and there were two other couples sitting at tables, a lone farmer at the bar lingering over his coffee and sweet roll. When Jody and Shade were seated, and the owner's incredibly beautiful daughter had brought them coffee, and they could hear their bacon sizzling in the skillet on the other side of the counter, Jody said, "Why?"

"Why what?"

"I don't know. Why me, I guess. Or maybe the question is *how*. How did you decide on me, what made you come to Santa Fe just to check me out? I'm hardly a household name in research circles. I can't imagine how you would have heard about me in the first place."

"What are you talking about?" he said. But there was no conviction in his voice.

"What hurts is that you lied to me," she said. "That you kept on lying when you didn't have to anymore. You could have told me the truth. I was so crazy for you, it wouldn't have mattered. You could have admitted you broke into my house, stole my files. You could have said, 'But that was before I knew you, before I fell in love with you,' and I would have forgiven you. You *did* fall in love with me, didn't you? I know you did."

"Yes I did," he said. "And it wasn't like that," he said.

"It was exactly like that. After we met, after we made love, you broke into my office. Just what did you think you were doing? Nothing I have is so valuable, and by then you must have known I would have given you anything you wanted, free for the asking."

"You don't know what you're talking about," he said. "Let it go. This is not a line of inquiry it's safe for you to persist in."

"I have to go to the bathroom," she said. "Alvaro's tea. When I get back, we're going to talk about that briefcase of yours." She rose, and headed for the back of the room. Halfway there, she turned. "And don't go sneaking off," she said. "You've only ever made me one promise, and you're going to keep that one. You're still going over the mountain with me."

His astonished laughter followed her to the rest-room door.

When she came out, it was to seem to her later, she came out into fractured time. Local unrealities. There were two men in suits at the front windows, holding long black guns.

There was a fragment when Shade was rising from the table, throwing it forward in a scatter of chairs. GET DOWN, he cried, but since there can be no sound in a stilled quantum of time, the words must have appeared silently, in large print.

The glass fell apart.

Shade catapulted in her direction.

She felt very weak, as if somebody had asked her a question and simultaneously struck her behind the knees. She was on the floor, in a wreckage of broken wood. The floor was warm and slippery, and she thought for a moment the cooks had spilled their bacon grease.

Shade knelt at her feet, firing toward the window. People were on the floor. She was on the floor, but she felt as though she were in the forest, a standing skeleton, and the wind was blowing cold between her bones.

Then she knew it was time, blowing through the holes in her body.

Shade was carrying her, and it felt very good. It felt like Pop, carrying her upstairs to bed, when she was a young girl, and had fallen asleep in the store.

They were walking on broken glass. Her head dangled, and she could see a man in a black suit, lying on the glass. The man was dead, a hole in his head. Poor man.

Shade dumped her in the seat of the car. He went away. He came back with white cloth in his hands, ripping it apart. *And then the veil was torn asunder.*

He bound her chest tightly. "I can't breathe," she complained. He pulled her leg straight out, and there was a terrible pain, like a black flash of lightning. Then she was better, and he was wrapping her leg, even more tightly than her chest. "Don't cut off the circulation," she said.

He went away again. He returned, threw something into the backseat. Black.

They were zooming up the road out of Cordova. They were going fast, impossibly fast. She couldn't seem to hold her head up straight, and she couldn't focus, but if she let her neck wobble just right, she could catch the speedometer rocking in the corner of her eye.

It said 75. She laughed. There was no way you could go 75 in Cordova. You would fly off the road and burst into flames. Shade topped the ridge at the Highway 76 junction, sliding sideways. There was a stop sign, she saw it as her car sailed past into the open air.

It landed hard, and the black lightning came back, but only a moment. She laughed again. She had seen that on TV, but she had never believed you could really do it.

They were falling down the road to Chimayo, the world a shifting blur. The speedometer floated in the corner of her vision. It said 100. 105. No way.

Shade was playing the radio with one hand. No, the scanner. Police voices, bored. He slid them sideways again, a long howling slide this time, and then they were rocketing past the Sanctuario, and cars went blip-blip-blip running into the ditches on either side.

Slew jerk slew at the cattle-guard curve, and then a roaring rocket uphill, pressing her into her seat, dragging her head back.

A voice came on the scanner. A familiar voice, but angry. The voice was cursing, the curses breaking into static. She couldn't understand what he was saying, but he wanted somebody to follow somebody, he wanted somebody to kill somebody.

It was Colonel Hall. Did he have to do every RAKBRAKBRAK thing himself?

"You idiot," Shade said. "Why didn't you see it coming?" She had never heard him so full of disgust. "You godcursed clotpoll, you blithering paltry tail-wagging moron."

"You shouldn't call people names," she said.

"Hey, buddy," Vic said into the phone. "So when you coming out to see us?"

"You didn't call me because you just can't wait to have three extra houseguests," his friend said. "What do you want now, Red Man?"

"I've been doing some thinking," Vic said. "It might or might not be related to that other thing, the fingerprint thing."

"Like that wasn't trouble enough. They know I put the request through, you know. I'm going to hear about it, down the road." Vic didn't say anything. The man on the other end of the line sighed. "So fill me in," he said. He sounded tired.

"I wonder what you could dig up on a citizen named John Shade."

"You're kidding," the man said.

"No, I'm not kidding. What, you know something? He has a record?"

"Listen, friend. You back off this one real quick. You've got a situation there. You don't mean to tell me you haven't ever heard of John Shade?"

"Of *course* I've heard of him, Carl. He's the one I'm *asking* about."

"Vic. Vic. There's no such person. I don't know who your guy is, but I know *what* he is. I just can't believe he's brassy enough to use the actual name."

"Make some sense here, Carl."

"John Shade is the code name for a special ops branch. Way outside the usual channels. Way *way* outside. It goes back. Predates World War II, because I've seen the memos, there was a huge stink when that Russian novelist, you know the one I mean, that porno guy, the pedophile, anyway, he used the name in some book or other, and everybody went apeshit. I mean internally only, it never hit the papers, but you wouldn't believe the flap it caused. This one's poison, Vic. Whatever it is, you need to back off it right now. Vic? Vic? You there?"

Vic cut the line. He punched Jody's number. The phone rang three times, and the message came on. He punched the number for the clinic. The phone rang three times, and the message came on. Now what? Who the hell did he call now?

Toni? Toni wouldn't know a damn thing, and she would worry.

Maybe there would be something at Jody's house. He jumped from his chair, grabbed his gun, his jacket, pulling them on as he went. He broke through the front doors of the station at a dead run, just missing the right door as the slow electronics slid them open. He sprinted across the parking lot, vaulted into his cruiser. Got the damn beast started, screeched into the streets.

What was the hurry? The situation had kept this long, what difference would a few minutes make now? But he had a bad feeling about this.

Dead Men Walking had a *very* bad feeling.

"Hold on, honey," Shade said. "I'm getting you to a hospital right now."

The car jolted and shuddered. They were standing still, and the world was whipping by them in a wild rush, like a battering wind, trying to shake them to pieces.

A red light loomed, and they were sideways again, sliding.

Oh yes. The highway, 285. "I want to go home now," she said.

Shade didn't answer. He made the engine loud, and then louder. The scanner was crackling with nonsense. Her head wobbled. She saw the speedometer. It said 115. 125. 135.

"All points alert," the scanner said. The voice was loud, urgent. "Gunfire reported at Sun Horse Café, Cordova. Three down. All units report. Suspect believed headed for Española or Santa Fe. Red late-model sports car. Armed and dangerous. All units report."

That's us, Jody thought. We made the news.

"Spawn of hell," Shade said. "Puppets. Boobies."

They sailed over a hill, into the air again. Black lightning. 140.

"That's Camel Rock," Jody said. "I love Camel Rock. It's gotten kind of hokey, you know. All the families in station wagons taking pictures. But I still love it."

Shade slid them sideways again.

"I love when you do that," she said.

• • •

Vic heard the squeal as he was booming down Carlos Rey. He felt a moment of guilt, then let it go. By the time he could get back to the other side of town, there would be twenty cars in the vicinity. If he was going to make a difference today, it would have to be for Jody Nightwood.

He slewed onto Zia, lights going, right full rudder.

Straightened out. Floored it.

"That's the Tesuque Village Market," Jody said. "You're going too fast. There's homes here. Children on bicycles."

"Maybe they haven't blocked Bishop's Lodge Road," Shade said. "I can take Paseo to Old Santa Fe, get you out St. Michaels to the hospital."

There was a black-and-white car on the road ahead. Sideways.

"Look out," Jody said.

Shade sent them into a slide. They went off the road onto the dirt, knocking down mailboxes like tin ducks in a shooting gallery.

"Wheeee," Jody said.

Nobody in the house. The cats howling for attention. One car in the garage, the Pontiac. What the hell was going on? Was there any way to leave a note? Something he could say that would alert her, but that Shade wouldn't catch on to?

The phone in the kitchen rang. For a moment, Vic stood frozen. Then he sprinted, banging through the door. He grabbed the receiver off the wall hook just as the third ring sounded. "Hello," he said, his voice rough.

"Mr. Shade," the voice said. "I'm a little surprised you're still there. But I thought, just in case. Listen, there is one turn, she is very deceptive. It is about a mile before you come onto the Holy Ghost Trail. You must watch for the big red rock—"

"Who is this?" Vic said.

Silence. Then: "I'm sorry. Do I have the wrong number? I was calling for Miss Jody Nightwood, and I thought you must be—my apologies."

"This is the police," Vic barked. *"Don't hang up.* Identify yourself."

"Dead," the voice said. "Is that you? Is that Dead Men Walking? This is Bruno Sandoval. Is something wrong?"

"Bruno," Vic said. "Maybe something's wrong and maybe it isn't. You've got to get off the line. No, wait, wait a minute. You don't know where she is, do you?"

"They were going to go over the mountains today," Sandoval said. "You remember. How we talked about it, at the wedding. First up to Truchas, and then to the Sun Horse Café for breakfast, and then on into the mountains."

"Sun Horse?" Vic said.

"The Sun Horse Café, yes. In Cordova. What's wrong?"

"Everything," Vic said. "I've got to get out of here."

"Don't hang up," Sandoval said. "I can help. You know I can help. Take a moment. Tell me what the matter is."

"John Shade is some kind of agent," Vic said. "He has Jody with him. I just caught a squeal on my radio, a shootout at the Sun Horse Café. We have to help her."

"The war has never ended," Sandoval said. He was silent a moment, just a moment. "Listen, my friend," he said. "By now there will be roadblocks everywhere, no? There is nothing we can contribute to that strategy. But suppose he avoids the roadblocks? There is only one route he can take. It is obvious, but we are the only ones who can see it, and we have no time. Here is what we will do. I will get in my car, run by the store, pick up the equipment we need. You must meet me at the ski basin. *Do not engage till I arrive.* Agreed?"

"That was cool how you did that," Jody said.

"Please don't talk," Shade said.

He had brought them to a halt on the other side of the cruiser, had come out firing. Not at the officers, though they ducked for cover. At the radiator, the engine block.

Then he was back in the car, and the engine was winding higher and higher.

"I'm sorry," he said now. "I can't get you to the hospital now, baby. They'll be waiting, and you could catch it when they go after me. There's only one chance left."

"What's that?"

"We're going skiing," he said.

"Oh goody," she said.

34: over the top

Colonel Wilbur Goodloe Hall fastened his skis to the rack on top of the Gelaendewagen. He was wearing a white ski outfit, head to toe.

Stupid, this whole operation stupid.

And he didn't exclude himself. It had been the boyfriend all along. So fucking obvious, but those clowns of his had missed it. *He* had missed it, had never even known about the boyfriend until the wedding, and then *still* hadn't put two and two together. Hadn't put it together when Michaels and Tarkington turned up dead.

A bear. Golly gosh gee duh, Colonel—ah reckon a bar musta kilt 'em.

Then Freddy Davenport's last telephone call. Sitting there while Freddy laughed and explained it all to him, how stupid he had been. Gave the new orders.

And then they couldn't even shoot the man. How hard was it to shoot somebody, for God's sake? Colonel Hall might have missed a few tricks on this one, nobody was perfect, and besides, those damned idiots they had stuck him with for eyes and ears—

But for crying out loud, how fucking hard was it to shoot somebody? You wait till he sets up a meet, so you know he has the package. You intercept his contacts, they'll find the car at the bottom of Cochiti Lake in a couple years maybe. Walk in the café like it's a robbery, everybody dies. Get the package, walk out. Simple, goddammit. Basic.

But they had fucked it up. They had fucked it up again. Almost thirty years, and things hadn't changed a bit. The people at the top were still idiots. Just new idiots, young idiots. Well, he would take care of it now. He would save all their asses one more time.

Up in those mountains, he would be a ghost. White on white, and the spook and the woman would never see him coming.

He went back into his garage, came out carrying an empty pack and a gun in a belt holster. Stowed the pack on the front floor, passenger side. Put the gun on, shrugged into his ski jacket, tugged the jacket down in back, covering the gun.

The Shade operative had to be going over the mountains. He was smart. Had to be, to have fooled Colonel Hall, to have stayed so fucking invisible. He was smart, and he was creative, and he had made sure he had a back door. But why the woman? Why was he taking the woman? Why not leave her on the floor of the café with a hole in her head?

Because she was part of it, you moron. She had been part of it all along. Their scientist, bought and paid for, farmed out to this backwater town so she wouldn't be an obvious target. Benjamin always thought ahead, years ahead of everybody else. How did he do it?

The problem was, when you tried to think like Benjamin, you couldn't tell whether you were making it up or not. You thought you had him, and he vanished in a cloud of smoke.

The woman had fooled him too. Playing the goose, the silly little bubble-head crackpot scientist. Obviously a whole set of fake files. Her "private" journal strictly for their benefit. It was going to feel good shooting the woman. Like putting a round in Benjamin's brain.

Now here came the missus, down the walk in her house robe. Middle of the day, no shame at all. More delay. Never mind. Keep it smooth. Never never rush.

How to Slow Down at Full Speed, by Colonel Wilbur G. Hall (retired).

"Business trip?" she said.

"Thought I needed a little exercise," he said. "Been putting on a few pounds."

She reached up, touched his cheek. That was the gesture that had got her married to him in the first place. "Just like old times," she said. "Be careful."

"You might be right," he said. "Don't wait up."

"I won't," she said. "But you know where to find me when you get back."

Just like old times, for sure.

• • •

Shade was idling up Hyde Park Road. No point in speed now, it would just draw attention. The police would have all the main arteries blocked, but probably no one would figure he'd take a dead-end road into the mountains. They wouldn't know he had a back door.

"We're going to Toni's house," Jody said.

"No we aren't."

They passed the Institute. "Fucker," she said.

"I'm sorry," he said. "It's the only chance we have."

"Not you," she said. "Him."

"Oh," he said. Two or three cars had pulled in behind him from various side roads. He steered to the side, let them go by. He waited. No Gelaendewagen.

Of all the damn luck. Colonel Hall would have laughed aloud, but he'd been trained to silent combat. Coming down the hill from his house, he'd seen the red car, that overstuffed bomb the Nightwood woman drove, creeping up Hyde Park. He'd pulled over immediately. Wait till they got out of sight to turn onto the road himself.

No need to follow close. He knew where they were headed. He let a minute go by. Two. Three. Four. Hell, let them get on the trail, get a mile or so out. Then take them down, where nobody will see. Might not even find the bodies till spring.

Wonder who they would find first, the two clowns he'd been running, or these two? Make a nice bet, if he'd had anybody to bet with on it.

He started forward.

Dead Men Walking horsed his cruiser around the turn off Washington, onto Hyde Park. He wasn't calling in. Get a dozen black-and-whites up there, twenty or thirty overwrought blue boys, SWAT team, helicopters, no telling what might happen.

The odds that Jody would make it out alive went way down.

Not to mention the odds for innocent bystanders. Too many bullets, too many dead people. Sandoval was right. Tracking was best. Stealth was best. Take the man down when he thought he was home free. Speaking of Sandoval.

There was the Allante in the rearview, bucketing up behind. Good man.

"Okay," Shade said. "This is the tough part. I'm going to splint your leg, suit you up. Then you're going to have to make it across the parking lot standing. I'll support your weight, but you have to make it look okay, make it look like love. Two minutes, max. Can you do it?"

"It *is* love," Jody said. She understood what was going on now. It was a fascinating exercise in abstract logic. "Why can't you just leave me here?" she said. "They'll find me. If you take me up there, I'll freeze. I promise I won't tell on you."

"Won't work," Shade said, gritting his teeth. He'd undone the bandage on her leg, and he didn't like what he saw. He tore a fresh bandage. He retrieved her ski poles from the rack, broke the claws off with his bare hands, and then broke the rods to halves. Lashed the halves around her upper thigh, where the bullet had gone in. "You've lost a lot of blood," he said.

"Why won't it work?" she said. "I don't care how strong you are, you can't carry me over the top. You'll sink into the snow. We'll both freeze to death."

"That asshole Hall is on our tail," Shade said. "He doesn't think I've spotted him, but I have. He'll be here any minute. If he finds you, you're dead."

"But I'm going to die anyway."

"You're not dying," Shade said. "Not today. I am."

"But I don't want you to die either," she said.

"It's about time," he said. "I've been getting bored and careless the last few years. Besides," he added, "I've done it before. It's not so bad."

It took Colonel Hall only a minute to locate the red car. No briefcase. One pair of skis still in the rack, the short pair. Blood all over the passenger seat. Good. All the more reason not to hurry. Hell, he probably didn't even need to go after them. No way they were going to make it through the night alive, not if the Shade op tried to bring her through.

He wouldn't, though. He would dump her when she died.

In spite of his training, in spite of his deliberately slow breathing,

Colonel Hall found himself anxious. He was actually feeling the pressure, for the first time since—well, the first time. It wasn't fear, though. It was desire.

He didn't want the Nightwood woman to die before he got there. He wanted the satisfaction himself. He wanted to look down his scope, savor the moment, and pull the trigger and see her head explode. She owed him that, all the trouble she'd caused.

Besides, there was the briefcase. It would be handy to have the briefcase.

He went back to his own car. Took the skis down off the rack, the poles. Got the silver suitcase from the back. Not the one with the camera. The other one.

Jody was riding piggyback. Piggyback in the snow. It was fun.

She knew she was in shock, but she didn't care. She knew she was dying, but she didn't care. It was like a lucid dream. You knew it was a dream, but you went on dreaming.

Maybe it *was* a lucid dream. What was the difference? We are always dead.

No, not a dream, it stayed the same too much. Shush, shush. Shade's wide back heaving against her belly. He had lashed her arms over his shoulders, hitched her onto his waist somehow. He was driving them down the trail fast, faster than anybody could go.

She couldn't imagine how he was doing it. She couldn't imagine why their combined weight didn't make the skis sink, big as they were. She had lost a lot of blood. Bled a lot of loss. Maybe that was why nothing hurt. They were climbing now. Piggyback was fun.

Bruno and Dead Men Walking had found the car. "Jesus," the big man said. "That has to be her, all the blood. They left her skis." His voice was deadened, full of woe.

"Our friend may not live," Bruno Sandoval said. "But we try anyway."

"You're right," said Dead Men Walking. "But there's something else."

"What?"

"That black car over there. The Gelaendewagen, three slots down.

I know who it belongs to. Coincidence is coincidence, but I don't like this one."

"Maybe he's on the slopes," Sandoval said. "He seems the type."

"Maybe," said Dead Men Walking.

"Anyway, it doesn't matter," Sandoval said. "The situation is what it is. We deal with it however we have to. Right now, we have to get moving."

This high, over ten thousand feet, fitful clouds shrouded the mountains, no matter how clear it was at lower altitudes. You skied into and out of fog, miniblizzards. The world jerked to white whirling nothingness, and then, presto, here we are, all bright and shining and open!

Colonel Hall was skiing steadily, taking his time. There was no way they could be going very fast, two on the one pair of skis. He expected to find the woman's body any minute, abandoned baggage. Expecting to, and hoping not to.

Drops of blood here and there, crimson poppies on the white snow.

The tiger was on the spoor.

Half an hour in, he stopped, took his pack off. Incredible he hadn't caught them yet. Must be running on sheer adrenaline. Any minute now.

He took the silver suitcase out of the pack. Time for assembly, now that he was out of sight of the rest of humanity, now that he was almost on them. Sling the rifle on his back, fling the case into a canyon, and go big-game hunting one last time.

He had bent to unsnap the catches when he heard the shush of approaching skiers. Of all the goddamned luck. Bad timing. He stood up, backed off the trail to let them by.

The skiers came into view sixty yards away, a big man and a very little man, maybe a boy. Slung rifle on the boy's back. Not a boy. He knew that silver-gray hair. He knew the Indian.

Colonel Hall put his hands on the small of his back, the right hand under his jacket, on the gun. Arched his shoulders, as if stretching, as if giving his spine a rest. Let them get by, shoot them in the back. Or if they'd made him, no problem. Ski mitts, poles in their hands, no way they could get to a weapon in time. He had them dead.

The skiers came swooping down the path, pulled up in front of the

Colonel. They pushed up their goggles. "Hey, boys," the Colonel said. "Fancy meeting you here."

The little man lashed his ski pole across the Colonel's throat, shattering the hyoid bone. The Indian grabbed his wrists when the Colonel's hands flew forward in reflex. The yellow eyes stared into his. His throat hurt like hell. He couldn't pull his arms away. It was like they were locked into place, like a tree had grown over them. He couldn't get his breath.

Wait a fucking minute. Wait a fucking minute. This wasn't happening.

His lungs were burning. He tried to kick the Indian, but his legs weren't working right, he felt them scrambling in the snow, running, trying to get away on their own. There was a knife in the silver case, serrated blade. He had to get to it, saw his own throat open, emergency tracheotomy. He had to explain to them that he needed the knife.

Hands at his back, the gun slipping loose. Wait a fucking minute.

Then he realized that was going to be his last thought.

No, it wasn't.

"He might've been innocent," said Dead Men Walking.

"What do you think that case is?" the little man said. He held up the pistol he had just fired. "What do you think this is?"

Dead Men Walking looked down at the collapsed body, a pile of white fabric. Except for the little round hole in the temple, you might think heart attack. The wreckage on the other side hidden, buried in the drift. Any blood running away under the snow, a secret spring. "What do we do about the body?" he said. "The evidence?"

"Nothing. It was his own gun, no prints. Whatever he was up to was bad. Whatever they find out about him does damage to whatever he was up to."

"What about his rifle? Do you want it?"

"Dead weight," Sandoval said. "Modern junk."

"Another mile," Shade said.

"What?" Jody said. "I was asleep." Somebody had tied her to a bumping packhorse, face down. Carrying the body out of the desert. She was the body.

"Don't sleep," Shade said. "Try not. To sleep."

That was funny. She laughed. "I'm a sleep *doctor*," she said.

"In another mile, we'll be close enough." The surging of his back and shoulders was continuous, was the rhythm of the world itself. They weren't moving at all. She was a small baby, lying warm and naked across the beating of her mother's breast.

"Close enough," she said. She was going back to sleep, she didn't care what he said. She needed her sleep. It was dangerous to try to get by on too little sleep.

She was going to grow up to be a dream scientist, and she needed her sleep.

"It'll be a little over. Two miles to the. Campground," Shade said. His breathing was deep and loud, as regular as a clock. Timed to the beating of the heart.

"They couldn't have. Gotten you. This far," he said. "But they can. Carry you in."

"They who?" she said. The doctors. The doctors would come and pick her up out of the crib and take her in to her mother, and she would be warm and naked and safe.

"Don't sleep. Please. Don't sleep."

"I don't understand it," Bruno Sandoval said. "We should have caught them by now. He couldn't have started more than forty minutes ahead of us." He was looking through the binoculars, far down the hill, where the path came into view for a good half-mile stretch. Parts of it were clear. On others, the clouds whipped and whirled, streamers of vapor flowing through crevices and over ledges like rivers on rocks.

They had topped the mountain an hour ago, making incredible time. Dead Men Walking was fast, powerful, young, enormously fit, and Bruno Sandoval was old. But there was something to be said for being a small man, a light man, a nimble man. He had learned it many years ago in the mountains of Italy, and he was glad to remember it now.

But the big man, the spy—even with a woman on his back, he was pulling away. "I don't understand how he's doing it," Sandoval repeated.

"I think I do," said Dead Men Walking. "Do you see them?"

"Not yet," said Bruno Sandoval. "Ten minutes, maybe. I know they haven't been through already, because there are no tracks. No one has cut trail. They should come out there, below that stand of juniper. But I don't have a good angle, and there's too much cover, too many trees. I need a good long opening, to lead him. I could climb higher."

"Forget it," said Dead Men Walking. "No point standing around waiting. He just gets farther ahead. Let's get after them."

Sandoval lowered the glasses. "No," he said. "This is it, I think."

"What do you mean?"

"Alone, you may be able to catch him. I doubt it, but maybe. But I'm an old man. I've done very well, but I can't keep up the pace much longer. We have to separate."

"What about you? Are you going to be all right?"

"There's twenty minutes of daylight, at most. From here, it is just possible I will have a shot. If I can get higher, if the clouds don't impede. A difficult shot, but if I wait any longer, he'll be completely out of range, and the light will be impossible. You go ahead. This is my stand."

"Can you make it out on your own? I have to save her. I can't come back for you."

"I'm not *that* old," Bruno Sandoval said. "If I get him, and you pack her out, I'll probably be able to catch back up with you. And anyway it doesn't matter. I've had a life, I've served my purpose. She's a healer. There are too few healers these days."

"I think maybe she *is* a healer," said Dead Men Walking. "A weird one, and I'm not sure she knows it yet. But—never mind. All right. I'm off. Good luck."

"I won't freeze. I can make it out," Bruno Sandoval said. But Dead Men Walking was already gone. No more argument, no more hesitation. Gone like a ghost in the spinning snow. Bruno Sandoval was alone in the mountains again. As he had always been.

Why would I want to make it out? he thought. *This is my home. I went to sleep one fine evening in the mountains of Italy, and I had a dream of a wife and children, and when I woke I was fifty years older. But I am still Bruno Sandoval, and the war is still going on. I knew that it would never end. In my dream, we pretended it had, but I knew better.*

He stepped out of his skis, dropped his pack in the snow, his rifle on top of that. He kept a loop of rawhide thong on the outside of the pack, and now he loosened the thong, used it to lash his skis, poles, and pack to the trunk of a pine. If he left them on the ground and a gust of snow blew in and covered them—it could happen at any moment—he was as good as a dead man. He would do as well to throw them all over a cliff and walk out barefoot.

Please, God, let the snow fall. In their chance and chaos, let the clouds open.

He reslung the rifle. This was the way it had always been, just him and the rifle. He scanned the rock face beside him for a route up, then began climbing. No way to know, in this scrambled wilderness, whether the top of the outcropping gave sufficient prospect, or if it put him behind other and higher promontories. All a gamble anyway. Handhold foothold. Pretty agile for an old man, but he didn't feel old anymore. He felt as lightfooted as a mountain goat.

Being small, he thought again. They thought it was a handicap. It was such an advantage. You didn't have the usual problems with gravity.

He came out on a fairly level slope, a sheer cliff looking in the right direction. So far, so good. A huge old ponderosa leaning outward from the edge, clinging by its roots.

In a hundred years, it would fall.

Still there were trees interfering with the view, breaking the line of the trail below. He needed elevation, he needed another ten or twelve degrees.

He hitched the climbing belt around the trunk of the ponderosa. Hunched himself into the air. When he came to the branches, he let himself out of the belt. He clambered from branch to branch. His breath was very short. He had to rest on each branch.

"Two minutes," he said. He would give himself two minutes more of climbing. Arbitrary. But there had to be decision points. If he couldn't do it in two minutes, he couldn't do it. At one minute and thirteen seconds, he was maybe thirty feet over the ridge. He could see a twist of the trail, maybe two hundred and fifty feet, clear between the trees where it skirted the bluffs of Holy Ghost creek. Below it, the dark artery of the tumbling water.

The air between was clear, may it please remain so. He was on a good strong limb, so he could brace his back against the trunk. This would have to be it. It wasn't going to get any better. Now. If the man wasn't covering, if he got a clear shot. If he could make a shot like that.

He wasn't surprised to notice how happy he was. Bruno the miniature bear.

He unslung the rifle. Checked the barrel to make certain it was unobstructed. Attached the scope. Wiped it with a cloth from a plastic bag in his pocket. Not one speck of lint.

He took off his gloves, clipped them to his waistband. Settled his back against the trunk. Rested the barrel on one drawn-up knee. Sighted down the scope.

Nothing to do now but wait.

"Oh but I. Do love you," Shade said. "Whatever else. Happens, be. Leave that."

Jody was jostling on his back, irritable and cold. He had stopped once, reached his arm over, pulled the hood from her head. He had pulled her hair, too, and she had complained. Now the cold air was getting in all down her back, and he was bumping around too much.

Are we there yet, Daddy? She couldn't sleep, she needed to go to the bathroom. No, you already went, back at the café. I don't care, I need to go again.

"You're on the wrong side," she said, her breath bouncing in her lungs, hurting her, coming out in fragments. Your-ur. On the. Wrong-ong. Side.

"There are no. Wrong sides," he said. "No right. Sides either. Forces. Just forces. Some gotta. Win, some. Gotta lose."

He was tricking her. He knew she was an idealist, knew she hated that argument. He was trying to make her mad, keep her awake.

He came to a stop. He loosened her from his waist, and she felt her arms and shoulders stretching, a fire of black lightning in her chest, blanking out her brain. He loosened her hands from his neck and let her down into the bedcovers gently and the pain receded.

All of this happening in darkness, as to a sleepy child, because she could not open her eyes. A hand under her head, lifting. Pulling something over. Ouch, the hair.

Oh, good. Warm. Ears warm again. Settling her head on the pillow. And now her hands came back. They had been gone for hours. Now they came back from nowhere, tingling. She saw them in her mind, crawling with electrical fire.

"There *is* a wrong side," she mumbled.

She wanted to get this settled before she went to sleep. Pop was always right. He was always out-arguing her. Not this time. She was a big girl now.

"The side that misuses things," she whispered. "You have to let things be what they are. They have to fulfill themselves. That's the only side that makes sense."

He had turned the lights out. But he was still in the bedroom, she knew that. He stood and looked at her in the darkness sometimes. When he thought she was asleep and didn't know. But she could always feel him. She always wanted him to come get under the covers with her and hold her. But he never did that anymore. She was a big girl now.

She opened her eyes. She was dying, and she wanted to say good-bye to him.

But it wasn't dark and it wasn't her room and it wasn't Pop. Oh yes. That's right. It was that other life, the one in her dream. The one with the vampire.

The vampire was looking down on her now. "That's the pretty side," he said.

The snow whispered and danced in the air between them, a billion billion individual flakes, not the handmade crystalline perfections of an infinitely attentive god, but the paratroopers of zero, drifting in to cover everything. Everything was lost, she saw. All motives, all jealousies, hopes, loves. Irrecoverably forgotten, gone forever. What did it mean to speak for love in a universe that forgot love as soon as it was made, that made it as carelessly and with as splendid and multifarious a precision as it tossed off these flakes?—The dandruff of chaos.

"But if everything fulfilled itself, where would we put it? There's not enough room in time. Death is the hydrogen the stars come from."

"See," she said. "You are a good writer."

And then the snow was gone, her bridal veil whipped away, and the cold leapt in with the long light, taking her throat, shaking her like a cougar rattling a rabbit. *This isn't fear,* she thought. *This is just the cold. I'm not afraid.*

Shade towered over her, but he wasn't looking at her anymore. He was holding the alligator briefcase, and he was gazing at something in the distance, something satisfying. "I envy you," he said. "I envy your life, and I envy you the death you will someday have."

He had a long black gun in his hand. He pointed it between her eyes.

"You have to click the safety off," she said.

"I hope you can believe that I loved you," he said.

Bruno Sandoval settled the crosshairs on John Shade's head.

He wasn't trying for a head shot, not at this distance. That would be insane. He was trying for a body shot. At this muzzle velocity, figure a drop of two to two and a half feet over the distance. Aiming for the head put you somewhere in the high middle of the torso—on a man that size, about five square feet of target. If you'd underestimated the distance, you still might clip a leg. With a .50 caliber, any hit was a death wound.

No point allowing for windage, not in these hills, not with these crazy random chaotic broken-up bursts of air. Hope it all evened out, that was the best you could do.

The man was not much more than a shadow, a black shape in the gust of snow. Standing sideways to Sandoval. Turn around, damn you. Face me square. What the hell was he doing, stopping like this? The snow went away. Light.

The man's mouth was moving. He was *talking.*

Sandoval found himself irrationally wanting to shift the scope, check on Jody. That wouldn't be smart. He probably had only the one chance.

The man pulled a long black gun out of his ski jacket. Sandoval would have to take the side shot, bad as it was. The man raised the gun, pointed it downward.

Just as Bruno Sandoval squeezed the trigger, John Shade turned, squaring himself to the bullet. He looked up, cross pasted on his forehead, directly into Bruno Sandoval's eyes.

Shade was gone suddenly. Jody didn't understand what had happened. She had wanted to see his eyes when she died, but his face had lifted away, as if he couldn't bear to watch what he was doing. So she had looked into the barrel of the gun instead. If she couldn't see her lover's eyes, she wanted to see death itself. Stare into its one unblinking eye.

Then Shade had vanished.

There was a clap of thunder, a single long roll echoing in the canyons. Another storm on the way. She understood. He hadn't been able to shoot her. It didn't matter, she would die anyway. She knew where she was, she had walked this far out before. This was where the cliffs were, and the meadow below, and the tumbling falls.

The parking lot at Holy Ghost was only a little over two miles away, but it might as well have been a thousand. She was sad for Shade's cowardice. Letting her slowly freeze. Shooting her would have been a good deal kinder.

On the other hand, she wasn't feeling all that cold anymore. She wasn't hurting, either. She was floating, really. Toasty warm and floating. Oh. This was what she had read about, when you gave up to the cold. The end isn't bad. The end is easy.

Well, so what? So the warmth was just an illusion, so she was really freezing to death. It was still real, even if it was an illusion. It was just as real as dreams were, in exactly the same way that dreams were. This was experience. If it was her last experience, it was a decent one.

This was exactly like floating off to sleep thinking good thoughts.

35: coda

There was a jolt. She grumbled. Pop picking her up roughly. They were leaving for Florida. Early in the morning, while it was still dark. Her leg hurt. Her leg had gone to sleep. It hurt when he jostled her. It hurt like black lightning in her chest.

Now he heaved her onto his back, grunting with effort. She didn't like it this way. It stretched her arms too much. It made her ribs hurt. She was too big.

Pop was getting old. He couldn't carry her anymore. Her feet hanging awkwardly, bumping. Pop was breathing hard. That girl is too big for you to carry around like that. What are the customers going to think if they see you? Where will I be if your heart gives out?

The van was going backwards. She needed to be driving if the van was going backwards. Mom and Pop were arguing. She was on the bed. Somebody was changing her diapers.

No. Not Mom and Pop.

The van jerked, stopped. Now it was going frontwards. They were delivering groceries. They were on their way to Florida, but they had to deliver the groceries first.

The big Indian was leaning over her. Yellow eyes. The light was too bright.

How's she doing?

405

Her eyes are open. Jody. Do you know me? Can you talk?

I know you. You aren't supposed to be in this part of the dream. You come later.

Jody, don't close your eyes.

Light's too bright.

The van was banging her around. Driving too fast. They went over a hump, that whee! moment of weightlessness. She loved it when Pop did that.

She's gone again.

No I'm not. I'm just making you talk in the dark. Watch over me in the dark.

How do they look?

They're clean. He did what he could. The leg's broken bad. Couple of ribs, but it missed the lung. I don't know how much blood she's lost, that's the key.

It always looks *like a lot. Is she bleeding now?*

No, but that could be bad news.

You go away. Both of you. You're not in this part. You come later, in the part when I die. This is the part where we go to Florida. Go to Florida, but don't come back. We won't come back this time. We'll stay by the sea, and nothing will ever go wrong.

She keeps camping gear in the bins under the bed, she told me all about it. There'll be blankets, insulating foil. Tape, gauze, antiseptics.

Got it. I'll clean her up, keep her warm. How long?

Forty. Maybe thirty-five, the roads are empty.

Jesus.

She's strong, she'll make it. Get on the phone. Get an ambulance, EMTs headed toward us. Cut the time in half. I can't do it and drive.

Shit, yes, that's smart. Let me tie this bandage off. She's got some kind of internal healer. Jody. Jody. If you can hear me. Jody, get in touch with. Dammit, what does she call him?

Ish.

Get in touch with your healer, Jody. Ichabod, Itchy, Itzak, Easy. Call him.

That's a damn good idea.

He was sitting at his computer in his bathrobe in the dark. He was older now, in late middle age, and having trouble with his weight, and his shoulders were hunched forward to his work, and she saw that he was not a warrior nor an athlete nor a demon lover, but a sort of a weary clerk whose only heroism was steadiness, fidelity.

The room was dark except for the flickering bluish light of the computer,
which washed over him and made arcs of shine on his glasses and washed all
the vitality from his worn and stubbled face. He knew she was there, but he
didn't look up.

Am I a ghost? *she said.*

Sort of, *he said.* Or I am.

He showed her what was on the computer. A nighttime roadside scene, a
jam of vehicles and strobing red and blue lights: cruisers, her van, an ambu-
lance. Two policemen had set out barriers, and were waving traffic around
with their coned flashlights. Three other policemen were talking to Bruno San-
doval and Dead Men Walking, who were leaning exhaustedly against the wall
of the van. The side doors of the van were open. Now a crew of med techs lifted
a broken body onto a gurney and were wheeling it rapidly toward the ambu-
lance.

Far down the road, other cruisers were coming, wailing and blinking in
the distance.

Am I going to make it? *she said.*

Oh yes, *he said.* I'll see to that.

He had turned to face her now, looking up from his swivel chair. With the
light on the side of his face, the shadows were kinder, and his face seemed
strong again, carved out of darkness.

They said I was a healer. In the other chapter.

You are. You began as a doctor, but now you're a healer. You've
always been one, but you were getting in the way of your own gift.

I don't know how to be a healer. I don't know what to do.

You don't have to. Healing will teach you. Learning is healing.

This is the last time I'll see you, isn't it?

I think so. I've put in for visiting privileges, but.

You've done so much for me. What can I do for you?

You've already done it. You are to me as I am to you.

I don't understand.

We all need models, we all need images. We have to be able to
imagine health, or it won't happen. You created me, and your life has
kept me alive.

The light from the computer was filtering through his body now. He was
transparent, he was thinning out, becoming a ghost, and less than a ghost.

Don't go.

Give us a kiss, lass.

He was gone, and the computer screen had fallen dark, but she put her face
where his face had been, and she felt the stubble of his cheek against hers in the

darkness and heard his breathing. There's one more person you need to see, *he whispered.*

Bruno and Vic were back in the van, leaning back in the seats. In a moment, Sandoval would crank the vehicle and take them home, under escort. The med techs had wanted to take them to the hospital, too, seeing how completely spent they were, but neither man had been willing to tolerate that. Only the fact that Vic was himself a policeman had prevented the cops from driving the van themselves and making the big man and the little man ride home in a squad car.

One of the cops had just brought a sack of sandwiches from Schlotzky's, and he'd offered them up, but the two men had been able to eat only a bite or two. They had drained two thermoses of coffee provided by the sandwich cop and his partner.

Toni was waiting, at Jody's house. They would all sleep there tonight. Vic had gotten her on the cell phone, and with great difficulty had persuaded her not to come flying down the road to meet them. But she had to do *something.* So she was going to stay at Jody's house and look after the cats until Jody was well enough to come home.

"You didn't tell them where to find his body," Sandoval said. "Are you planning to go back after the briefcase? Is that it? What's in the briefcase that's so important?"

"There won't be any body," Vic said. "There won't be any brief-case, either."

"Oh," Sandoval said. "You think he's a skinwalker?"

Vigil didn't answer. Outside the window, a cop waved them on. A cruiser pulled out in front of them, leading the way, its lights flashing. Sandoval cranked up, put it in gear. The van bumped back up on the pavement, a giant turtle clambering out on a log.

"Did you feel that?" said Dead Men Walking.

"What?"

"She's been in here, watching us."

"She's not dead, is she?"

"No. I think—I think she's just walking around. Now she's leaving."

"Well, tell her good-bye. Tell her we'll see her soon."

• • •

Jody was out of her body. She understood why.

Her body was battered and broken, lying in a bed in Santa Fe. It was not a good body to be in, just at the moment. It might or might not live, that body. No, Ish had said it would.

Not terribly important, in the long scheme. She sent a healing thought in its direction. A thought of pity, and a thought of love. The poor dumb suffering body, loyal servant.

As she had the thought, she saw her other companions, the cats. Who was keeping her babies? What would happen to them if her body went?

And she saw Blind Lemon, asleep on the computer though it was not running. And she saw Static, asleep on the bed. Downstairs, their bowls were filled with fresh food, the water was clean and full of oxygen. The cat box had been seined only an hour ago.

Toni was taking care, blessed Toni.

Blind Lemon blinked awake, sort of. He saw her, stretched out a paw. Purred.

Static rolled onto her back, arched her belly. Purred.

She had to be somewhere else now, Jody did. There was something to take care of still. Something to get settled. One more person she had to talk to. Very well. To go there, you had to see it. But how could she see it when she had never been there?

All right now. An office. It had to be an office. In Washington, D.C. Or nearby.

There would be book-lined shelves, old paneling. But very modern electronics. It would be like a lawyer's office, but instead of law books along the walls there would be novels, and poetry, and books on neurology and mathematics and philosophy and military strategy. A great many books on military strategy. Histories and biographies and psychologies.

And one whole wall would be computers.

The man in the chair behind the desk looked up, and blinked in surprise. He had just hung up the telephone. He was in his late thirties, but youngish, slender, with thinning blond hair, steel-rimmed glasses, pale blue eyes, handsome in an ascetic way.

There was a sort of ghost behind him. A big strange ghost, with three arms and three legs and eyes set all the way around a huge smooth head.

She saw that it was the ghost of a machine, and was a ghost not because it had died, but because it had not yet been born. The ghost loved the man in the chair.

I don't believe this, *said the man in the chair.*

Your choice, *she said.*

I think I'm going to decide this is a dream, *he said.*

Maybe it is, *she said.* Why did you try to kill me? *she said.*

It wasn't me, *he said.* You were never in any danger from us.

You put me in danger from the others. And then Shade was going to shoot me.

The man bowed his head a moment. I don't know what that was about, him shooting you. Not my orders. And there's nobody named John Shade. For that matter, I don't exist either.

Then how do you know his whole name?

There's nobody named John Shade.

Is what he said true?

What did he say?

He said you wanted to use my work to create artificial brains.

The man leaned back, steepled his fingers.

Why would you want to do that? I understand computers to help us do our own thinking. But why do we want to create new minds? Aren't there enough minds already?

The man leaned forward again. He was suddenly passionate. A flush rose in his face. No, he said. That's what the universe does. It creates souls. It creates them any way it can. It creates them from flesh and blood, and now it's going to create them from electronic circuits. Humans were a failure, just a step on the road. An interim solution. There's a whole race coming after us that will be truer and cleaner and more intelligent. We have a chance to do it right.

I see, *she said.* I'm sorry about what your father did to you.

In her mind there was an image of a young boy crying. The boy was huddled naked on a cot underneath a window. Now a door opened, and a naked man stepped in. He was carrying a long black belt, folded over, and he had an erection.

The ghost behind the chair wept. There were no tears, but it wept.

Now I *know* this is a dream, *said the man in the chair.*

So you have to work for the military, *she said.* Because they're the only ones who'll let you build minds. You do what they tell you to, but all along you have a purpose of your own. I understand that. But I think you're on the wrong side.

I'm on the side I have to be on. *He found a linen handkerchief, mopped his face, replaced his glasses.* This is an awfully consistent narrative, *he said.* Would I sweat in a dream?

Work it out, *she said.*

No one's going to hurt you now, *he said.* We just needed to have the information first. If the wrong people had gotten hold of it—well, a year's lead time is enough to change all the rest of history. You may think me evil, but I assure you, I'm better than the alternative.

The funny thing is, *she said,* all I wanted was to figure out the theory. And now I've figured it out, and it doesn't even seem important anymore. And what you do, all your intrigues and plans and strategies—they aren't important either. They're just like making money and setting records in sports and getting your name on a building or in the history books. It's all just busywork. It doesn't change anything, it just makes things more complicated. The only real work is health and peace and creativity and understanding.

It would be pretty to think so, *he said.* But the world is a murderous place, and it will remain so. Human nature won't improve, because it can't improve.

But your mechanical minds will do better?

They won't be mechanical. They'll be alive.

If they are, *she said,* they'll come to people like me for healing.

When Jody came out of her coma, Bruno Sandoval was there. She found out from him, later getting more details from Vic, that the shootout at the café had been declared a robbery attempt. The story was that one of the robbers had tried to take Jody hostage and escape over the mountains with her, but had been killed and they had not recovered the body.

Colonel Hall, who was not only an honorary colonel but also, as it turned out, an honorary deputy sheriff, and had had extensive military service in World War II, and then in Korea, and later in Vietnam as an adviser, had heard the situation developing on his own police scanner and, seeing the fleeing car, had heroically given his life in an attempt to save Jody's.

Jody was worried that they hadn't found Shade's body. She would be going back to Holy Ghost many times in her life, and she would no doubt be going over the Windsor Trail, and she didn't want to stumble across his bones herself. Nor did she want the trail to be haunted.

Not to worry, Bruno said. The same team of experts who had flown in to advise the local police on the most probable scenario for these strange events had discovered the bodies of two men near Vic and Toni's house. They had proven conclusively that the two had been mauled by a bear. It was a sad and ironic footnote to the main story, for these were the two charming young men who had been at the wedding. Their bodies had been taken care of in a private and decorous fashion, and Bruno Sandoval was of the opinion that something similar had happened with John Shade, and that Jody no longer had to concern herself in that regard.

When he visited one day alone, she told Dead Men Walking about her out-of-body dream—the man in the chair and the strange mechanical ghost who hovered near.

"That's a very powerful dream," he said. "Are you ready for that kind of power?"

"I don't know," she said. It was funny to talk about power when she lay here battered and nearly helpless, lounging in her nightgown all day long. "It was real. I don't have any question about that anymore. And if you can do that sort of thing, then you're not chained by normal reality. You're free to do anything you want, have anything you want."

He nodded.

"But it sort of changes the game, doesn't it? I mean, it makes you irrelevant on this scale of existence. I don't want to change the game. I don't want to be irrelevant."

"You're ready," said Dead Men Walking.

On the first day of winter, Jody Nightwood walked out of St. Vincent's Hospital under her own power, although she was leaning on Bruno Sandoval's arm. Sandoval was beaming, his silver hair scrubbed and brushed back, and he wore a suit and a tie and his newest boots. Vic and Toni were waiting in the parking lot with their Range-Rover.

Toni was staying the night with her, and maybe the next one too, and so on until Jody was strong again. And no argument. Well, all right, maybe some argument. Or at least negotiation. Jody explained what she wanted in return for allowing all this mothering.

So it was that on Christmas Eve, just at sunset, the six of them, Bruno Sandoval and Toni and Victorio and Vida and Allegra and Jody, walked up Canyon Road together, jostling with hundreds or maybe thousands of other celebrants, locals and tourists alike, and laughed and sang carols about things that some of them believed in and some of them didn't. They marveled at the thousands and thousands of *farolitos* lining the parapets of the buildings, those candles in sand-filled paper bags that are called luminarias back in Arkansas and are used to line driveways and walkways and not the edges of buildings, and they marveled at how those lanterns glowed and made a magic architecture of the night and climbed toward their kindred stars.

They jostled with others in the smoke-laden air on the fabled street free once each year of the noise and hurry of motors and given over to children and dogs and women and men, and they warmed themselves at the bonfires that are called *luminarias* in Santa Fe and are called bonfires back in Arkansas, and they stopped in at the homes of friends and had hot cider, and at one home their Jewish friends made fun but walked out with them to see the lights also.

Once a handsome young man bumped her and almost sent her stumbling, and then apologized so profusely she started laughing, and then she had to promise to have a drink with him before he would forgive himself, and Bruno Sandoval gave her a wink.

She thought to herself, *There's no reason on earth a healer can't fall in love and get married.* And the rest of her time on Canyon Road that evening, Jody Nightwood was an atom, a particle, no one remarkable anymore, no one hunted or praised or condemned or pursued, and she felt herself vanishing into humanity at last.

And she *really* looked forward to her dreams.

Acknowledgments

*I wish to thank my daughter, Lynnika Grace Butler, a splen-
did stylist in her own right, who corrected my Spanish and
Italian and would have corrected my Japanese if I had used
any; Frederick Turner, the genius of natural classicism, and
a man whose MacArthur grant is unforgivably long overdue,
for our many and deeply stimulating conversations about
creativity, science, beauty, hope, and the self-dreaming universe; Paul Lake, Michael McFee, and Johnny Wink, poets
all, who walked awhile in my dreams and in so doing gave
me the courage to continue; and Christopher Langton, a
most extraordinary scientist, for generously opening his
thoughts to me one sunny afternoon in the foothills of the
Sangre de Cristos.*

*Finally I wish to thank all those spirits, living and dead and
imaginary, who came to me in the night and blessed me with
the flavors and urgencies of their lives. Most especially I
wish to thank the lady who held my hand in a faraway and
hilly town and sang these words, which are not from Richard
Wilbur: "And steal some happiness along the way."*

Dear heart, you started this.

A Note on the Type

This book is set in a typeface called Méridien, a classic roman designed by Adrian Frutiger for the French type foundry Deberny et Peignot in 1957. Adrian Frutiger was born in Interlaken, Switzerland, in 1928 and studied type design there and at the Kunstgewerbeschule in Zurich. In 1953 he moved to Paris, where he joined Deberny et Peignot as a member of the design staff. Méridien, as well as his other typeface of world renown, Univers, was created for the Lumitype photo-set machine.

Composed by North Market Street Graphics,
Lancaster, Pennsylvania

Printed and bound by Berryville Graphics,
Berryville, Virginia

Designed by Iris Weinstein